FIRST KILL

First Kill

WILLIAM J. KENNEDY

ISBN-13: 9780692067727
ISBN-10: 0692067728
Library of Congress Control Number: 2016908025
CreateSpace Independent Publishing Platform
North Charleston, South Carolina

DEDICATION

To my grandchildren: Taylor, Ashley and Brennan

ACKNOWLEDGEMENT

I would like to extend my thanks and appreciation to all of the talented people in the Rehoboth Beach Writers Guild, especially those in the classes I took who had to suffer through my learning process. A very sincere thank you to Maribeth Fischer, the Founder and Director of the RBWG for her patience and encouragement.

To my writing buddies in the 'Gray Guys Group', Walt Curran, Frank Hopkins and Jackson Coppley. I had a good story and you helped me make it a good book.

Thanks to my new friends at CreateSpace for a great editing job and very smooth process for this first time author.

Crystal Heidel of Byzantine Sky Press created the great cover artwork.

Chapter 1

My name is Jonathan West, MD—collegiate hockey all-American, Ivy League–educated physician, adjunct professor of medicine, pharmaceutical industry executive, US government assassin (retired). If you Google me, you'll find several pages of material written either about me or by me. It's all relatively benign, the chronicle of a successful physician in the pharmaceutical industry, interesting to only a few. You'll not find any mention of my government work. If you review the newspaper headlines of the seventies, eighties, and nineties, you'll read accounts of death and mayhem, large and small, that altered the course of this country's policy or history. Some of it was my doing, but the accounts are without reference to me; many of these incidents are presumed to have been accidents.

I wasn't always an assassin; I grew into the job. My father and grandfather introduced me to guns at an early age. And cowboys—I loved cowboys. On Sunday nights, I'd put on my white cowboy hat, strap on my cap gun, and sit on the hassock as if it were a horse, watching *Hopalong Cassidy* on the family black-and-white television. When he shot the bad guys, I shot the bad guys. My grandfather would cheer. "You got 'em good," he'd say. Was that the seed? In college, I was a good student with the goal of becoming a physician but was distracted for a brief time with the dream of playing professional hockey. Still, I had a dream, a dream I had longer than that of being a physician. These two dreams collided after college and led me down a path that resulted in my becoming an assassin.

When I was a kid in upstate New York, across the Hudson River from Troy, the long, cold winters favored winter sports. Skating was the most popular outdoor activity from mid-November through March. Troy was the home of Rensselaer Polytechnic Institute (RPI), a hockey powerhouse in the fifties and sixties. A neighbor and good friend of my family was a devoted hockey fan, and he fed my love of the game.

The "golden years" for my hockey dream began in 1958, when I started playing high school hockey. We practiced on the RPI Fieldhouse ice at 5:30 a.m., and some of the RPI players would practice with our squad. The highlight came when Bobby Brinkworth joined their team in 1961. He would become a two-time all-American. I felt like part of their team and was definitely living a dream, a dream in which I was a better hockey player than I really was—or at least one with bigger aspirations than were realistic.

I filled out nicely, a solid 185 pounds on a five-foot eleven-inch frame, perfect for hockey at the time. When it came to choosing a college, my choices were limited. There were only a dozen colleges with first-class hockey teams. Harvard and I chose each other. They gave me a partial ride for hockey disguised as an academic scholarship.

This period was important in shaping me and pushing me in the direction that eventually led to my career as a US government assassin. I'm not saying Harvard or hockey made me do it. There were no classes on how to be an assassin, but the circumstances that hockey presented clouded my vision such that I made poor decisions that led me in that direction. I earned second team all-American honors in my junior year. The local Boston papers started talking about me as a consensus all-American in my senior year, and with that, there would be the possibility of an NHL invitation. The press seemed to like me, one reporter even calling me a golden boy—blond hair, piercing green eyes, and a nice smile. The notoriety went to my head. It shouldn't have. Brinkworth had been a much better player than I was, a two-time all-American, and he only got a minor league chance.

The last year in college was the time for sending out the applications for medical school. Instead, I decided to pass and wait for the chance to play in the NHL. I played as well in my senior year as I had the year before, but the talent pool I was playing against was better and the caliber of players in the Canadian junior leagues was outstanding. Earning second-team all-American got me no invitation from the NHL. To keep my dream alive, I played for a minor league team in Columbus, Ohio, the Checkers. Columbus could hardly support a team; the crowds were small, and the salaries were minimal—nothing like the NHL.

With all of my attention focused on hockey, I had failed to be aware of my vulnerability to the war in Vietnam and the draft. Selective Service got me! A Harvard undergraduate degree didn't keep me from being drafted, nor had any of my Boston friends or their well-connected families stepped forward to get me a deferment or a coveted spot in the National Guard. My degree from Harvard only identified me as someone who might better serve the army in the Pentagon rather than the jungles of Southeast Asia. Hockey got me nothing.

After basic and advanced individual training, I was assigned to the 902nd Military Intelligence Group (902nd MI), which was responsible for the internal security of the Pentagon as well as certain other government facilities in the Military District of Washington (MDW). When invited to join the group, I was excited and had visions of James Bond–like exploits. After all, it was Military Intelligence and the Pentagon. But once again, my expectations were much higher than reality. It was a good job, but no M, or Q, or Moneypenny, and no Dr. No. The job exposed me to the military spooks in the area as well as a lot of the alphabet agencies in Washington. There was a lot of intrigue, but intrigue is what you make of it and I had a tendency to make a lot more of it than there was.

Chapter 2

✳ ✳ ✳

I didn't wake up one morning and decide to be an assassin. It wasn't a career choice! It was a series of small steps. Well, there was one big step. Could other decisions have been made? Probably, but my options were limited if I wanted to be a physician.

In January 1971 I was in my last months of service in the army. The job in the 902nd MI Group wasn't nearly as exciting as it had initially sounded. Our mission was to ensure the offices in the Pentagon complied with security procedures, primarily the offices of the Department of Defense, the army, the air force, and parts of the Joints Chiefs of Staff. The marine corps and the navy were housed at other buildings in the Washington area. We roamed the hallways and offices during office hours, checking that documents were kept in a SECRET or TOP SECRET manner. At first we were in uniform and had to announce our presence when we entered an area. Of course, this alerted everyone in the area, and appropriate precautions were taken.

A new branch chief, Major Brenton Cunningham, didn't like the way we were forced to operate. The Pentagon was fairly open at the time, and anyone could walk in any of the three entrances. The major felt the 902nd should be ensuring the security of the building from those who intended to do us harm, not just making sure lazy or incompetent employees complied with the rules. He felt intruders would not follow any rules, and neither should we. The Cold War was still hot in 1971.

The major changed our method of operation. He took us out of uniform and put us in civilian clothes with civilian haircuts, even allowing us to grow facial hair, which was popular at the time. He set us free to roam the halls and offices, not only observing security breaches but probing for security breaches and, with time, causing security breaches. We could now wander in and out of offices unannounced, learn how to distract the staff, and, while they were distracted, remove sensitive documents.

Sensitive documents weren't hard to identify. They were stamped, with large red letters at both the top and bottom of each page, SECRET or TOP SECRET. If that wasn't obvious enough, they were always placed in distinctive folders. The major called these STEAL ME and YOU BETTER STEAL ME folders, and we were encouraged to do so. Once stolen, the documents would be redacted and taped to the door of the office where they had been obtained.

I was concerned we were targeting the low end of the pay scale. "Won't these secretaries lose their jobs? That hardly seems fair if the boss is running a loose office."

The major said, "No. When we redact the documents, there's no way for anyone to know how or where we got them. They could have come from the boss's desk or even his safe. He'll be the one responsible. The staff is safe."

The consequences of having a stolen classified document taped to an office door were severe. Field-grade officers and at least one general were forced to resign. The major was severely criticized after the general resigned, but he argued that the 902nd was taking security seriously. Such logic was tough to argue against.

The guys of the 902nd were a tight group. We had to be. Others knew who we were and what we did and avoided us. We were spooks, and everyone was afraid of spooks.

All in all, it wasn't a bad job. But by the beginning of 1971, it was routine. I was bored and counting the days until I got out in April.

The air force and the Federal Aviation Administration (FAA) didn't have a cordial relationship. Each felt the air belonged to them and felt the other was an interloper. They had to work together, if only to find out what the other was doing. The 902nd was assigned to monitor and participate in their joint meetings. They had a number of exercises the military would have called "war games" if it were just the military. Being a joint operation of the military and civilian agencies, they became "contingency planning" exercises. One of the exercises was evaluating the potential for an air hijacking.

Since 1966, the FAA had been concerned about the threat of airplane hijacking. Rod Serling had written a television movie, *The Doomsday Flight*, in which an airplane was hijacked for ransom with an altitude-sensitive bomb onboard. If the ransom wasn't paid, when the plane eventually descended, it would go boom. The FAA wanted the air force engineers and war strategists to help them with the problem. The air force really had only one solution: shoot it down. FAA was looking for more science and engineering input.

The subject was always on the agenda. While it was of little interest to the air force, it was always a hotly debated issue. Some felt the threat and risk were minimal. To them, it didn't make sense. If someone was going to hijack a plane for ransom, the feeling was that that person would want to be around to collect the money and spend it. The FAA team disagreed, reasoning that if someone was desperate enough to hijack a plane for money, he might be willing to die if he didn't get it.

One evening after one of the joint meetings, some of us went out for pizza and beer. We started playing what-if, and the game turned to the hijacking problem. Of course, we couldn't say "hijacking" in a public space, so we just said "the problem." Mike Allen, one of the FAA guys, was with us. For the sake of argument, I postulated that it could be done, that we had been too narrow in our thinking. I proposed a new plan, one that involved a passenger carrying a bomb, or a perceived bomb, and two takeoffs and two landings. The first landing would be to pick up the ransom after a reasonable amount of time had been given to round up the money, and the second takeoff would be the getaway. The second landing part was challenged because all the king's horses and all the king's men would be waiting for the hijacker. My response was, wait they could, but when the plane landed, the hijacker wouldn't be onboard, having parachuted out with the money.

"Right. And where's he going to get the parachute?"

"All the planes carry parachutes…at least for the flight crew…don't they?" As I responded, I became less sure of my answer. Didn't all commercial planes carry parachutes? I couldn't recall reading about anyone parachuting from a commercial aircraft. There had been a number of accidents and certainly the opportunity for exiting by parachute, but none had. Rather than argue this point, I conceded. "Parachutes could be delivered with the ransom money."

"Right. A hijacker would place his life in the hands of someone giving him a parachute to jump out of a plane that he was hijacking. Sounds like the perfect way to stop a hijacking: give him a parachute that doesn't work."

"All right, try this. The hijacker requests three parachutes, making them think he's going to make one or more of the passengers jump with him as a hostage. Then they'd have to give him parachutes that checked out. They couldn't afford to kill a passenger."

"But then he'd have to worry about the hostage when he got on the ground."

"No, the critical point would be making them think he was going to have a hostage jump with him. He would jump alone."

"Hmm. Okay, that might work. What about the jump site? How will the guy get away? Will he need a crew on the ground?"

I liked this; they were engaged now. In the meetings, they had been mostly silent, lulled by the lack of movement on this agenda item for months. "Yeah, he'd have to have help on the ground. But I like the way you're thinking. Ten minutes ago, you didn't think it could be pulled off, and now you're worrying about the details."

They all looked at me in silence for a few seconds and then at each other. It was a stare down. Mike Allen, the FAA guy, leaned forward, screwed up his face, and said, "Nah, can't be done. Not with the dummies sitting around this table." Everyone agreed, and we went back to talking about girls.

Chapter 3

*　＊　＊*

A week went by, and then my life changed in a flash. The telephone rang, and I was asked to go to the FAA liaison office on the fourth floor of the Pentagon. The room was in the A Ring, overlooking the courtyard within the Pentagon. It was the middle of February, but the leafless limbs had buds and the promise of flowers and leaves. In six weeks, the trees would start to fill the senses with their blossoms. If I had been blindfolded, taken here, and presented with this view, I would never have guessed I was in the Pentagon.

Inside the building was another story. The ceilings were high in the hallway, typical of 1940-era construction, with a drop ceiling in the office attempting to modernize the look. The large wooden desk was clean, with only an unmarked blotter—no pens, papers, or dust. No ashtray, even though the room smelled of tobacco smoke. Mike Allen was present. He introduced me to the other person in the room, presumably the guy whose office this was, a Mr. Anderson.

Anderson was probably in his midforties, about my height and weight. He could only be described as severe, with skin pulled tight across his face. His chin was a chisel leading his face and the rest of his body. Anderson had a military-style haircut, not the longish style of the day. Bushy eyebrows sat above steely gray eyes behind bookish eyeglasses. He held himself in a military manner, but when I said, "I'm pleased to meet you, sir," he told me not to call him sir. He was fit, although he hid this under cheap but elegantly worn clothes from the bargain rack at Korvettes. His real character was something else, something he was trying to hide. Manicured nails and Florsheim shell cordovan loafers suggested a moneyed status. Anderson made no attempt to be friendly.

After the briefest of introductions and no attempt at handshakes, I was invited to sit in the only seat available, in front of the desk. Anderson remained behind the desk with Allen to his left, the position of deference in the rank-conscious military. Anderson reached across to his phone and pushed a button. Three buttons flashed yellow and then went blank, holding all incoming calls.

Allen started the meeting with a formal tone. "I told him about our discussion last week and about your two-landing, two-takeoff proposal. He'd like more detail." This was a complete surprise. Our "discussion" last week had been part of a drinking game, and now I was in front of a suit being asked to justify what I had said.

"What I said last week was hardly a proposal. It was part of a drinking game, and it came up after we had downed a few—in fact, quite a few. The guys, led by you, thought it was so far out that I had to buy a round of drinks."

Anderson said, "Nonetheless, Mr. West, I found some merit in what you said and would like you to repeat it. Then, perhaps, we can have a discussion."

I repeated as much as I could remember. When I finished, Anderson told me his analysts had concluded that the scenario that had a hijacker armed with a bomb on an airplane was not viable. The reason being simply that a hijacker would want to live to spend the ransom. The analysts were being driven by the standard psychological profile that dictated that if a hijacker demanded money, then the hijacker had plans, and anyone with plans would not be suicidal. These profilers' analysis went a step further. Because a hijacker would want to live, airline staff, and perhaps even his fellow passengers, might see through his bravado and overwhelm him. They additionally feared that in the attempt to overtake him, the bomb would accidently go off.

"What do you think?" My hesitation to respond prompted Anderson to add, "This really isn't being totally fair or honest with you. I can sense your confusion."

I nodded agreement and started to reply. "I really…"

He interrupted me, his arm up off the desk, in motion as if he were batting my words out of the air as if they were buzzing bugs. He leaned forward in his chair, covering more of the big desk that represented his authority. His face became focused and serious. I had seen serious and focused before on a girl I once dated. Well, it wasn't the dating part that I remembered just then; it was the few seconds before her orgasm. She had had that same serious and focused look.

"Let me explain a few things you might find even more amusing," he said, apparently reacting to the smile on my face. "There was almost unanimous agreement that the hijacking you proposed was not feasible. There was one dissenting vote: mine, and my vote counts more than the rest. That's why I wanted to talk to you."

I felt bad now that I had smiled when his look reminded me of a girlfriend's orgasm, but, you know, memories are what they are. You can't control memories. They just get triggered and pop up. Forcing her face out of my mind, I tried to be as serious and focused as he was. "That makes me feel a little better, but I still don't see where this is going. The item has been on the agenda for the air force/FAA contingency task force for over a year and has gotten nowhere."

"You seem to think I might be finished. May I continue?"

"Okay." Being polite and paying attention seemed to be the way to get this meeting over.

Chapter 4

Anderson leaned back, elbows resting on the arms of his chair, palms facing each other with the index fingers of both hands touching his chiseled chin. "There are three different hijacking scenarios we've been working with. The first is the one that everyone is familiar with, the hijackings to Cuba. There are dozens of these. Most have been political statements or attempts by disillusioned Cuban nationals to return home. The number of these Cuban hijackings increased dramatically in 1969. That was when hijacking became an agenda item for the joint FAA/air force meeting."

Wondering where this history lesson was going, I shifted in my seat, nodded my head in agreement, and tried to remain patient and interested.

"The increased number of hijackings to Cuba has resulted in a sense of complacency that we find alarming. Most airlines, even those that don't service the southeast United States, accept the fact they may be hijacked to Cuba. They even plan for the possibility, carrying information such as radio frequency, flight patterns, and approach conditions for a landing in Havana. The second thing is the attitude of the Cuban government. Turnaround time in Havana is now less than three hours. Passengers and crew are often offered refreshments on the ground. This complacency has many of us nervous. It sets an atmosphere that invites something more serious and dangerous.

"There have also been hijackings with political overtones, primarily in the Middle East. We're watching these closely, but now they don't pose a problem to the US or to US interests abroad."

I shifted in my chair.

"There is much less information about the second type of hijacking. It hasn't happened yet, but the blueprint has been shown on television in England and here in the United States. In 1965, a new television series, *Thunderbirds*, premiered in the UK with an episode entitled 'Trapped in the Sky.' The plot involved an airliner hijacked for ransom. The unique twist on this is the hijacker isn't onboard but has placed an altitude-sensitive bomb aboard. Shortly after, in 1966, a plane hijacking was the subject of Rod Serling's *Twilight Zone* episode 'The Doomsday Flight.' While it has not happened, our analysts are confident there are groups of individuals with the capability to make such an altitude-sensitive bomb and conduct such a hijacking."

He paused, allowing time for this to sink in, a dramatic moment for him. The best I could manage was a look I hoped would not betray my boredom. He continued. "It requires a certain degree of sophistication—building the bomb, getting it onboard a commercial flight, and picking up the money. Timing is the only thing that's keeping us from giving this a high degree of credibility. Airplanes can stay in the air for a maximum of about eight hours unless equipped with extra fuel tanks. Anyone who looks into a hijacking like this will soon conclude there's insufficient time for authorities to collect any significant amount of money, put it in a designated drop area, and have the hijackers retrieve it. When planes can fly farther on a load of fuel, this may become a problem."

Not knowing if I was expected to respond at this point, I did nothing. Anderson had said three scenarios, and this was the second. I remained silent and continued to give him my full attention.

"While we don't consider the second scenario viable now, steps are being taken to neutralize such a threat. Currently, we are exploring ways to jettison everything in the cargo hold during a flight. Government agencies from several countries are working with the airline industry to develop screening devices— x-ray and the lot—to detect bombs in carry-on luggage. Some airlines, notably El Al, do preflight hand searches of all luggage."

He leaned forward in his chair, forearms resting on the edge of the desk, and his eyes became more intense. "So, we have two basic categories of hijacking up to now. The first, a crazy with a gun is on the plane and wants to go someplace. The second, a crazy with a bomb who wants money is not on the plane."

"Got it. But neither of them is a crazy on the plane with a bomb."

"Right. With that, we have a combination of the other two—a crazy on the plane with a bomb who wants money and expects, rightly or wrongly, that he will get off the plane with the money."

Feeling I had him, I decided to challenge him. "Why does the guy in scenario three have to be crazy?"

"Because a hijacker on the plane with the bomb has to be crazy, or, at the very least, he has to be desperate. Otherwise, why would he do it? The chances of success are minimal. He has to collect the money, get off the plane, and get away with the money. If he thinks he can do that in 1971, he has to be crazy. Law enforcement's too sophisticated now."

Thinking for a minute, I asked what the airline staff would do if they thought the hijacker was crazy. He responded that a crazy person probably couldn't get on the plane. Continuing my challenge, I asked, "What if he was sane when he got on and then went crazy?" He found that unlikely. Anderson was as guilty as the analysts of being narrow minded. He felt the hijacker was either crazy or not crazy, no in between.

Someone had told me that I bore a resemblance to the actor, Jack Nicholson. When I wet my hair, it became darker, and when I slicked it back, I could see a resemblance. Intrigued, I had made it a point to see one of his movies. He had a crazy demeanor, but more important, crazy eyes. While shaving one morning, I found myself trying the crazy eye thing in the mirror. It was eerie! My green eyes caught the light in a way that amplified the maniacal look I was trying to mimic.

"I don't agree. Your reasoning is wrong." This I said as I leaned forward in my chair, hands coming up with my wrists resting on the front of his clean wooden desk. His desk was facing into the room, the window behind him and the sun in my eyes—or, for this situation, on my eyes. "You must consider me a reasonable man—sane, certainly not crazy—to invite me here for a talk." It was a question to him, but he didn't respond.

My hair was longer than standard military, parted on the right. I liked the wet look, not the dry look popular with the longer styles. The wet look could be maintained throughout the day with Vaseline hair tonic, a product greasier than Vitalis hair tonic, which was used for the dry look. I lifted both hands from his desk and ran them through my hair, front to back, eliminating the part and giving my hair a straight-back retro look. As I did this, I opened my eyes, flared my nostrils, and turned my head to the side in my practiced Jack manner. My hands came back down on his desk, and I leaned in farther, violating his personal space. Moving my head to make sure the sunlight coming in the window was on my face, amplifying the green of my eyes, I came up off the chair, not standing, putting more weight on my legs, leaning forward, taking more of his space.

"In fact, I think this is a joke, more government bureaucratic bullshit, justifying your jobs inside the beltway of misfits, counting your days to retirement or to a big job in the airline industry where you can sell your contacts." I was rambling, not caring if I made any sense. My hands were moving now, not waving around frantically, just up off his desk, moving through his air, taking charge of his office. My voice had started off soft and low. You get people's attention better if you make them work at listening. Now I elevated my voice a notch as well as the speed at which I spoke. I was waiting for the moment when he would lean back, yielding his personal space to me. Waiting for the moment when the look on his face changed from serious and focused to something less—something less confident, less sure of what was going on. I had done everything I could with my face and eyes. And then it happened. He leaned back and yielded his space to me. Good. I was at my limit.

Reverting to a normal me, I sat back in my chair and relaxed my face and eyes. "That just proved my point. The hijacker doesn't have to be crazy. There just has to be some reason to believe he's not all there. I could see you with that doubt, and if I can fool you, I think I could fool most people. And if you fool some people, the rest of the people will be drawn in. Just the possibility that someone who might be a little unbalanced has a bomb in an airplane that's thirty thousand feet in the air would do the trick. Hell, you might not even need a bomb. It might be enough if they just think there's a bomb."

He reclaimed his space with a lean forward. I watched his eyes before he spoke. He was looking at two greasy palm prints on his desk where I had placed my hands after running them through my hair. "You made your point." He reached behind his desk to the credenza and grabbed a handful of tissues from a flat box. He handed them to me. I guess he expected me to clean up my mess. Thanking him, I wiped the grease off my hands and handed the soiled tissue back to him. He chose not to accept them, ignoring me, still looking at the grease spots on his desk. He asked me to leave so they could speak privately.

Chapter 5

* * *

I found a men's room, washed my hands, and combed my hair. I returned to the small waiting area outside of Anderson's office. The only sign on or near the door was an office number, no name. His secretary started a smiling contest with me. As I sat waiting, I got a "You're going to have to sit and wait until I tell you to go back in" smile. As time passed, she changed into a more aggressive "Don't even think about asking me how much longer" smile. The door opened after twenty minutes, and I was motioned in with a wave of Allen's hand.

Returning to my chair, I noticed my two greasy palm prints had been cleaned up. Evidence of a shiny smudge remained, indicating Allen, rather than the meticulous Anderson, had done the cleaning. Anderson told me they agreed scenario three was possible, especially if the hijacker appeared to be crazy and appeared to have a bomb. The crazy aspect of it had hit home. If someone was crazy enough to want to hijack a plane to Cuba, there were probably people crazy enough to hijack a plane for money, but they had doubts it could be carried off. Cuba was easy. Hijacking for money, escaping capture, and going someplace where you could spend the money was infinitely more difficult and took a lot more creativity. With scenario three much more of a reality now, they wanted to test it.

Anderson was still in charge. "I'm going to move the scenario-three hijacking to a higher priority and give it to a different group to study. See if we can put a fresh set of eyes on this without the built-in prejudices the current team has. We won't take it away from the air force/FAA team. That would raise too many eyebrows. We'd like it to stay with them and languish a little more with the low priority it's enjoyed in the past. It would suit our needs better if the status quo is maintained."

"Who's the 'we,' sir? If possible, I'd like to stay with the exercise."

"That's what we were talking about. We want you to stay on the air force/FAA team, and we also want you to be part of the new group. At first, we want you to be a silent participant. Let them work it out without your encouragement. I'll set the tone for them. We'll adjust your role as time goes by. Of course, nothing you learn can be passed to the old team. In fact, we would like you to be less vocal on that team too. To help you accomplish that, you will be dressed down at the next meeting, being told you are not a team player. Pushing the bomber-on-a-plane scenario is wasting time and resources. It should be all that's needed to account for your reduced level of participation at future meetings. We want to draw as little attention to you as possible."

"I'll be glad to do anything I can, sir. If I may ask a question?"

"Shoot."

"I'm having a tough time connecting the dots. It doesn't make sense that you invited me here based on something I said after a few beers."

Looking at each other, they shared a nod of agreement. Mike Allen, silent to this point, spoke. Leaning forward while Anderson leaned back, he said, "As you are well aware, this problem has been on the air force/FAA agenda for some time now, without much traction. It worries us that there is less interest than we think it warrants."

"You said 'we' several times. Who is the 'we' you keep referencing? Sounds like the FAA, you, and Mr. Anderson." Mike was easier to talk to. Might have been the beer history we shared.

Again, they looked at each other and nodded. This nodding was a signal. When Allen nodded, he was asking Anderson if he should say more. When Anderson nodded, it was agreement to continue. Allen continued. "As Mr. Anderson stated earlier, for the last several years, there has been an increased awareness of the potential threat to the security of the US in the form of hijacked airplanes, whether for ransom or political purposes. Because of the potential threat to national security, the concern is shared by a lot of government agencies, not just the FAA. The CIA, the DIA, and the NSA have all been studying the problem."

Looking across the desk, first to Anderson and then to Allen, I said, "But now it's only being championed by the FAA and resisted by the air force? Or am I missing something?"

Anderson spoke. "Neither Allen nor I are who we appear to be. Neither of us is FAA."

"I assume neither of you is air force either, so that leaves one of the alphabet agencies—CIA, DIA, or NSA." When they didn't disagree, I continued. "NSA?" Anderson blinked. "DIA?" Neither acknowledged. With surprise evident in my voice, I said, "CIA?"

Allen nodded with a two-finger salute, and Anderson nodded. I guess his NSA blink was a blink.

NSA I could understand. They had some pretty broad powers and had been flexing their muscle as Vietnam had escalated. There weren't any limitations on where they could roam in conducting their missions. The CIA had expanded their role with Vietnam, providing advisors to the Vietnamese since the early 1960s. There was even talk they were running operations all over Southeast Asia. All of that was within their charter because it was occurring outside of territorial United States. "But I thought the FBI was responsible for internal threats to the security of the country and the CIA was limited to offshore."

"You're on the new team. You're 902nd and know the implications of security. The team is bound by all the security restrictions you could possibly imagine. The top-secret clearance you have was validated as being sufficient to bring you in on this operation."

"Yeah, I get it. Break security and I go to jail." I said this with a cavalier tone, but I was struck by his reference to my top-secret clearance as merely being "sufficient," implying something really big.

"If you're lucky," Anderson said while looking down and picking at an invisible speck of dust on his sleeve, but I knew he was dead serious. I was being brought into something that had CIA involvement. If I fucked around with them, they'd send me to Vietnam, probably North Vietnam, with a target on my back that said "CIA—shoot me."

"You're absolutely right. The CIA has limited authority or responsibility within the continental United States. Up to now, hijacking has been a problem with planes diverted to Cuba. This is where the CIA, DIA, and NSA started to have an interest. At first, it was just a jurisdictional pissing match. The CIA felt the FBI shouldn't have authority for a flight that was diverted offshore to Cuba. FBI countered that CIA shouldn't have authority for a flight that originated in the continental United States and landed in the continental US, regardless of where it had been. If that was the case, the FBI would have to relinquish authority for every flight on the East Coast to and from Florida. These all had flight paths out over the Atlantic. Same thing with flights from Houston to Florida over the Gulf of Mexico. It was a mess and is still being debated above my pay scale."

"I can see where there could be some issues," I said. Bureaucracies were always more concerned about protecting their sandboxes than getting the job done.

"So we have a gray area on jurisdiction that is currently being studied. In the meantime, we have a threat that needs to be addressed. We're stepping into the gray area in the name of national security. The CIA isn't really concerned about hijackings to Cuba. What we are concerned about are a few hijackings in Europe that seem to have been conducted by small anti-Israeli radical terrorist groups. They've been relatively unsophisticated, but we feel in time, hijackings will attract the attention of the larger terrorist groups. The target could shift from Israel to the US and our European allies. The Israelis and El Al Airlines are very engaged in this. All luggage is searched by hand before every flight. When I say all luggage, I mean all—both checked and carry-on. The same thing could be done here, but the public outcry would be intense. Political pressure would be applied, and votes, rather than safety, would dictate the way forward. Safety, and ultimately security, would suffer."

Anderson paused, giving me a chance to raise questions. I had none, so he continued. "We have a long-range plan to reduce this threat. The plan includes x-ray screening of passengers before they board a plane, the same with luggage before it goes into a cargo hold, and bomb-sniffing dogs. But these things take time and money. There's also the issue of convincing the American flying public there's a threat that justifies the cost as well as the slight inconvenience of the screening procedure. In the absence of a real threat, it's merely an academic exercise that would rapidly become political. The debate would become public, with two nasty outcomes. First, our enemies would be alerted and perhaps speed up any plans they might have to do us harm. The second would be that any political debate would delay the implementation of the plans we feel are necessary for our security. These two things would have the chilling effect of amplifying the problem—an accelerated timetable by our enemies and a delayed timetable by our politicians. The results would be devastating. In the absence of a real threat to convince our politicians, we need a fabricated threat. To convince them, we need a test with a successful bomb-on-the-plane hijacking."

"Is the new group working on this?"

Allen was given the nod to address my question. "Last winter we increased our level of concern for this threat. Before you ask, the 'we' is the CIA. I had already been assigned to the FAA by the CIA to find out where the obstacles were and to get the thing moving. It was nearly impossible to work the threat to a higher priority without being obvious and therefore opening the potential for the political debate. The jurisdictional debate between the air force and the FAA over who owned the air convinced us of the need for a more covert approach. If we were to become too obvious, the politicians would take over, and that includes the political appointees who are the heads of these government agencies. The FAA seemed the best way to move this thing. If supported by the CIA, they had the visibility, the charter, and the manpower to pull it off. Mr. Anderson was assigned to be the liaison for the FAA," he said, nodding across the desk they were sharing.

"Major Cunningham was brought in to head the 902nd. As you well know, he revamped the responsibility of the 902nd to a more covert operation. You were already on the joint team, so it fit with the expanded role we saw for you as we went forward with this exercise. We had our eyes on you from the beginning. We were going to approach you after we had some plans in place. With your what-if drinking-game proposal, we decided to move up our invitation to you to join our team."

"So, my plan was the clincher?"

"Yes, but not for the reason you think. You were identified long ago as someone we wanted. On the joint team, you were not one of those stuck on the idea that it wasn't a problem. More important, when everyone else was giving reasons why it wasn't necessary, or why a hijacking couldn't work, or why it wouldn't happen, you were looking for a way to solve the problem. When you talked about that scheme during the drinking game, you were making the solution more visible, and that would have been contrary to the covert way forward we saw. You were too close to the plan we were developing. Bringing you on our team means you keep your mouth shut on the joint team. If you aren't pushing it there, no one else will and it stays on the bottom of the agenda."

"So, what's my role on the team?"

Without even a pause in the conversation, Allen said, "You're our hijacker."

Chapter 6

* * *

"You must be joking! I'm not a hijacker!" There was panic in my voice.

"When we get through with you, you will be." Anderson seemed to be enjoying himself for the first time.

I was stunned. This couldn't be happening. The excitement of being on the new team had gotten my juices flowing. Now I found myself in the center of something that was well beyond anything I could imagine or that I felt I was capable of doing. Another dose of adrenaline surged into an already overcharged body. "But I don't know anything about jumping out of airplanes."

"When we get through with you, you will." No doubt about it, Anderson was enjoying himself now.

"Perhaps I said that wrong, or maybe I'm not making myself clear. I don't want to do this. I don't want to know how to jump out of airplanes. I want to go back to walking the hallways looking for people who leave classified documents on their desks." There was a little less panic in my voice now. It had been replaced with pleading.

"Too late! As the Brits say, in for a penny, in for a pound."

"I don't want to be in for a penny," I said as I pounded on the desk, leaving telltale smudges on the newly cleaned surface. My protests were falling on deaf ears.

"Let me clarify something for you." Seemed that he was doing a lot of smiling and not enough explaining. He exuded confidence and preparation.

"The current plan is very similar to the plan you proposed." He looked and nodded toward Allen. "When Allen heard it, he called me and said he thought you had stumbled onto our plan. Hearing that, we had to start moving quickly."

"We only recently decided you would be the hijacker." Anderson looked to me for something—acknowledgment, agreement; I don't know. All he got was a continued look of bewilderment and confusion. "There are hundreds of men available to us, all trained, all government agents—CIA, Special Forces, active, retired. We're confident they'd all be able to do the job. The problem is they're government agents, all with information on record. When this event happens, the FBI will look for suspects with certain skills. They'll look for anyone who is jump qualified, particularly Special Forces, and those with survival skills and escape and evasion training. Anyone we pick from our personnel base will be on their list. Yes, the list will be large, probably thousands. The hijacking is likely to gain national attention, and the hijacker will be described, maybe even with an artist's rendering from eyewitness accounts. It's too much risk for one of our guys, a guy who's jump qualified, a guy who might look like the artist's rendering, a guy who's been away during the hijacking. Friends, neighbors, relatives could raise suspicion. No matter how minimal the risk, we don't want someone on our team to be under suspicion."

I saw his point. The message was clear: the government, regardless of branch, wanted no part of this. They didn't want any connection or suspicion at all. There should be no hint of a trail that would lead back to them. If there were seven degrees of separation between people, they wanted ten for this job. They wanted deniability.

Anderson sat back. He had been using his serious and focused face. He was done, just as the girlfriend had been done when she had her orgasm. The similarity was starting to settle in. I had just been fucked. "Jonathan, you are a nothing. You're not Special Forces; you have no special training. You don't jump out of airplanes. In fact, you've only been on a plane once in your life, as a seven-year-old to see a rodeo in New York City. You didn't like it then, which may explain why you haven't flown since."

"How the hell could you know that? Did you steal Bullwinkle's Go Back Machine?"

His smiled broadened—a real smile, not a sneer. "For the record, it was Mr. Peabody's Wayback machine."

"Right" was all I could manage after being corrected. I had mixed up my Saturday morning cartoon characters.

"I usually am," he said matter-of-factly. "You're single and currently not dating anyone. We'd like you to keep it that way. You live in the Consolidated Barracks at Fort Myer. Mr. Mitchell, your roommate, also single, spends many nights away, at the apartment of one of several Mohawk and Allegheny stewardesses. He'll not miss you if you disappear for a few days before your time in the army ends in April."

He continued. "You don't have any plans when you get out, or for the summer or for the rest of your life. You're on the waiting list for the September class at Yale Medical School. Until you hear from them, you're in limbo, as your Catholic relatives are apt to say."

"So, because I've got nothing better to do, you think I'd like to steal an airplane and then jump out of it while I'm waiting."

"Not exactly. Some of your words are correct, but your sentence structure is wrong. I'm thinking you should be saying, 'If I agree to jump out of the airplane for Mr. Anderson, I'll get an invitation to join the September class at Yale Medical School. I can spend my summer preparing for the jump, for medical school, and for the rest of my life.'"

"Are you saying..."

"Yes. I couldn't have been any clearer. I will not repeat it. If you don't understand what we're offering, we have grossly overestimated your intelligence."

"That's it?" What I meant was something like "Is that all the discussion there is?" I say yes or no based on a ten-minute discussion. I had a lot of questions.

"Of course not. You probably have some questions. Let me answer one. We know you and your family don't have the money for tuition, books, and living expenses. Mere acceptance into the class won't do much good if you can't afford it. We'll treat you as a contractor; we'll pay you. Yes, a contractor, not an employee. A contractor without a contract." I nodded, waiting for him to continue. "We'll start paying you as soon as you get out of the army. Training will keep you busy during the summer. Through the NIH, you'll be awarded a fellowship that will pay your tuition and provide a small stipend for four years. Summers, we'll make arrangements for you to work for the government. In all, you'll get close to $200,000 over the next four years, but it will be distributed in a way that won't raise any eyebrows. If you're frugal, it will provide you with a solid financial foundation when you finish school, unless you blow the money on a car and other shit you shouldn't be able to afford as a student. Such behavior would draw unnecessary attention to you and maybe to us—we don't like either."

"Well, yes, the money is important, and it is appreciated. But how are you going to guarantee I'm in the next class at Yale? What makes you so sure I'll get into Yale Medical School with your help, and I wouldn't be able to get in without your help?" I didn't like my questions. They gave the impression I was leaning toward accepting their assignment, which I was.

"Addressing the first part of your question, we have several prominent Yale alumni who are sympathetic to the work we do to ensure the safety and security of our country. There are many graduates in the service of our country, and we call upon them from time to time to help us. The help they provide is not a risk to their positions, and they never know the deep background behind our requests. I have one such alumnus in mind. Someone on the national stage who I'm sure would help us. A word from him would go a long way at Yale.

"As far as you getting into Yale on your own merits, we think you might have a difficult time. Why? Because you've been out of school for a few years. You've done nothing to improve your academic qualifications for three years; you played minor league hockey, and you've been in the army. Yale may ask you to enroll in a graduate program to prove you can still do the work, still have the drive. This has a certain amount of risk because you might not cut it in graduate school. The dream may become too far removed to motivate you."

Anderson wasn't threatening me. He wasn't saying if I didn't agree to the jump, I could forget about med school. Rather, he was holding a carrot, not a stick, and he was very close to my own thoughts on this. I was worried about the time that had elapsed since I had last been a student. Was becoming a physician soon to become as remote a possibility as playing in the NHL? I too had thought about the graduate school route to gain entry. While I thought I could do the

med school bit, I had doubts about graduate school. The prize was still a medical degree, but graduate school was one step removed, one more obstacle in the
way. "You're asking me to become part of a clandestine illegal operation, and if
I agree, you'll assure my acceptance into Yale Medical School."

"Yes, a guaranteed acceptance and stipend if you help us. Are you confident you'll get in on your own? Are you confident you can afford it? Are you as
confident as you were about playing in the NHL?" He paused, his eyes still icy,
perhaps a little colder. He had just said what I was thinking about the NHL. Was
this guy a fucking mind reader?

I sat back and slid down in my chair a little, pretending to be as casual as
he was. "Come on! If you want to get on my good side—hell, even my neutral
side—avoiding hockey career comments would be a great place to start."

"Okay, no more hockey mockery." His response was instantaneous, and the
words just rolled out. No one could be prepared to say that, waiting for the
setup—hockey mockery. Mr. Anderson was very quick and a lot smarter than I
had given him credit for, a fault of mine in dealing with government employees.
Was my Harvard elitism showing itself—perhaps?

"So, you're saying if I don't do this, I might not get into medical school and
my future will be downhill from here?"

"No. I'm saying if you don't help us, we won't help you. The mission will
happen with or without you. With you, your contribution will be greatly appreciated by your country, and you will benefit. Without you, it'll still get done,
but you? Who can say?"

"This is un-fucking-believable! Is this how our country works?"

"It's what makes our country great," Anderson said, and he said it as if he
meant it.

"Go fuck yourself is my first reaction."

"I consider that as a maybe. A predictable reaction, but not an answer to my
question."

"You really don't leave me much choice, do you?"

"I'd like your answer. If you say no, we have to move on to plan B quickly."

Chapter 7

"There are still lots of questions. You'd be crazy to accept me if I said yes on the basis of school and money, right?"

Anderson asked, "Is that one of the questions?"

"No. Let's say I get on the plane and they give me the money. How do I get off before the second landing? I don't know how to use a parachute, and if I learn how to do that now, won't I show up on somebody's list as a trained jumper? And once I'm on the ground, how do I get away?" My voice was calm and confident. Inside, I was screaming. I didn't want to do this!

"Let's discuss jumping out of a plane later. Once you get on the plane, we have a planned route for you to take, with a specific time for you to jump relative to the time you take off. We want you to land in a specific area, where we'll have people ready to catch you and get you away."

"Catch me? That's how I'm going to get safely on the ground? You're going to have someone waiting to catch me? That's stupid."

"Poor choice of words. Catching you is just a term we use. It means we'll have several teams on the ground in a sixteen-square-mile area ready to find you, retrieve you, and get you out of the area safely and secretly."

"Have you thought this out? How are they going to find me? And, if you have enough teams to cover that much ground, aren't their families and loved ones going to be suspicious of them not being around at the time of the jump? Aren't that many people going to be missed? Don't they have someplace to be?" I wasn't being a devil's advocate. It made little sense based on what he had just said.

Anderson and Allen shared another look. This one I could read. It said, "You cannot ask us a question we don't have an answer for." "As far as finding you, you'll be equipped with a radio transmitter set to a specific frequency with a flat, short transmission range of six thousand feet. For the first five thousand feet of the jump, you'll be in free fall, tumbling. At thirty-four seconds you'll pull the rip cord. Four minutes after the parachute opens, you should be at about one thousand feet. At this point it will be safe for you to turn on the transmitter. Even if the plane turns around at once and starts looking for a transmission, they won't be able to detect it. They'd have to fly lower than six thousand feet to catch the outside range. Once you get on the ground, it'll be impossible for them to detect you from the air, but the signal will allow our people on the ground to find you. If you do the arithmetic, you'll see we can find you in that sixteen-mile square with four teams near the corners of that grid, and, using receivers, beam in on you." He paused, letting this sink in.

"As far as any suspicion on the catch-team members is concerned, they'll all be personnel who'll be 'working' at other facilities at the time. Yes, we will falsify records, something else I am quite good at. None—I repeat, none—of your catchers will have any parachute training of any type. They will not show up on any list of suspects. And, finally, the descriptions of you will vary a little, but this much you can be sure of: a white male, about six feet tall. Do you have any idea how many of our assets are five feet six to five feet eight; who are black, Hispanic, or Oriental, not to mention female; who are more than capable of being on the ground to catch you?"

"A lot?"

"More than a lot!"

"What if I just don't want to do it, which is pretty close to the truth? It's illegal!"

Allen smiled, more laughing with me now than at me as before. "Oh, we're always interested in the truth. The truth gives us a good point to start creating our story."

Anderson held up his hand to interrupt me. He had done it before. It irritated me then, and it irritated me now. "Covert, yes. Not necessarily illegal. Let me see if I can help you understand." Pinching the bridge of his nose with his manicured fingers and closing his eyes, he searched for words, working hard, his lips pursed.

He continued. "History is written by the winners. George Washington—you've been reading about him since you were a kid. Most of what you read was true; he was a great man. What if, early in his career—say, on his second surveying job into the Ohio Valley—he had a mission? What if someone said to him, 'George, we see a bright future for you, but we need you to do something for us'? The politicians in Williamsburg had a plan. 'We need you to lead a surveying party into the Ohio Valley.' George might have said he wasn't a qualified surveyor; he had only carried the gear and done some arithmetic on his first trip. Then they said, 'What we really want you to do is keep an eye open for the French ambassador while you're there. We're going to send an Indian scout with you who believes this Frenchie killed his brother last year. And if, just if, you run across this French ambassador, you turn your back and let the Indian get his revenge. We can't tell you what it means in the long run, but we'll make sure you have a prominent place in the future of Virginia.'"

"You're saying George Washington was the first CIA hit man? That's stretching it a bit."

"No, what I'm saying is sometimes history needs to be shaped. Men with vision need to do little things that have a profound impact on history, and history has a tendency to forget to record things that might have taken place in the shadows. Once George was asked, whether he accepted the assignment or not, he was in. He knew too much. He might have seen that his future depended upon doing this favor. He knew if he didn't accept the assignment, his future might not be as bright. If they could ask him to do this, they could ask someone else to do it. The point was, it would be done with or without him. George also knew if he did it, he was tied to these men. The secret was as much theirs to keep as it was his."

Staring at them, I thought for a minute, trying to study both of them. Nothing; they were stone faced. "Like Mr. Washington, I guess I have no choice but to take your offer. I'll do it," I said.

"Do what?"

"I'll do the hijacking." There was the motive of school and the money, of course, but there was also a sense of duty I hadn't known I had. I could make air travel safer. And there was adventure! "Oh, and I need to learn how to jump out of an airplane!"

"All necessary training will be taken care of in due time."

I was looking at Allen, the window, and the tops of the naked cherry trees over his left shoulder. I couldn't help feeling I had just been fucked. I didn't enjoy it, got no satisfaction. Would that come later, or would the money be enough? Anderson said nothing with either his mouth or his eyes. Being cold probably made him well qualified and good at this kind of job.

"Isn't Mom or someone else going to be suspicious when the artist's rendering from eyewitness reports describes a sandy-haired man with green eyes and the picture looks like me?"

Allen answered. "Sure, if the hijacker had sandy hair and green eyes. Hair dye and colored contact lenses will take care of that. We'll also try to age you about ten years. Mom won't recognize you. Hell, you might not even recognize yourself."

Chapter 8

Anderson ended the meeting, straightened his tie, flicked an invisible speck off of his Korvette blazer, nodded to Allen, and left the office. This wasn't his office, just a secure, convenient place to meet. Allen and I were left staring at each other, an uncomfortable silence between us, at least for me. "Let's go get you that cigarette you need."

"How do you know I need a cigarette?"

"I'm CIA. I know everything. Besides, everybody needs a cigarette after they've been fucked."

We walked in silence through the building, got coffee at one of the snack bars, and went out into the cold morning sunshine. The center courtyard of the Pentagon became known as Ground Zero during the Cold War because it was a likely target for a Soviet nuclear attack. When the café was constructed, it was formally named the Ground Zero Café. The café wouldn't open for lunch for another eight weeks, when it would be warm enough to eat outside.

We took our coffees to a bench on one of the sidewalks crisscrossing the courtyard. The day was pleasant for early February. The sun felt good on my face. My heavy class-A uniform felt comfortably warm in this protected place, as comfortable as Allen's wool sport coat. The high walls of the surrounding five-story building protected us from any wind. In colder weather this was a blessing. In August, the walls held in the heat like an oven.

Allen and I were alone except for the occasional person using the court-yard as a shortcut from one side of the building to the other. Taking a pack of Marlboros from his pocket, he shook one out for himself and offered me one. "Smoke?"

I took one. After lighting both with his chrome Zippo, he closed the lighter with its distinctive click. "A lot went on this morning, and it hit you very fast. If it's any consolation to you, we've been studying this problem for many months. We've had our eyes on you for most of that time because of the way you've handled yourself in the 902nd. We were going to approach you…"

"Don't you mean recruit me? That's what just happened, isn't it? Now I work for the CIA. From what I know, it's like working for the Mafia—there's no way out now. I'm in for life."

"All of this is very new to you, so I understand your concern. But let me finish, please."

"Go ahead."

"We're offering you the opportunity to help us, help your country on this project—this project only. A one-off assignment. Contrary to what you might think, doing a job like this for your country is not a lifetime commitment unless you choose to do so. There are many conscientious men and women who step up to use their unique abilities to help us and then return to their regular lives."

"What you're asking me to do is illegal, holding out the carrot of guaranteed acceptance into Yale. But you're also implying if I don't accept, my career in medicine may be more problematic."

"No, that's not our intent. We wouldn't impede your future; we'd just leave it alone. We wouldn't help, but we certainly wouldn't interfere. Whether or not you got accepted would be based on your own merits. If you think you can get in on your own and stay in without the financial help we're offering, walk away."

"You know my concerns, especially my financial limitations. I can't walk away from this."

"Look, I'm not going to try to blow smoke up your ass." Amusing because he said this as he was exhaling a cloud of smoke. I had to laugh, more of a short snort. He recognized the irony of his comment and action and laughed, a real laugh. "That was unintended. I'll have to remember not to put myself in that situation again. If I can continue?"

"Sure."

"We were going to recruit you slowly, but you were too aggressive at the joint meetings. You were the only military person pushing the agenda. The fear was that you would persuade someone on the air force team to change their mind and bring the issue to the front burner. If that happened, it would have gone political, and then our plans would be delayed. A delay could have had disastrous consequences."

"So, I was too close to your plans?"

"Yes, but don't let it go to your head. The plan for the hijacking is relatively simple. For our long-term goals to be met, the escape is the critical piece. The hijacker must get away. There are hundreds of men who could do this job for us, men who can jump out of an airplane and evade capture. Men who would have no difficulty with the mission. They would have no problem maintaining mission security. Most of what they do is dark, meaning they slip in, do the job, and then slip out. No witnesses. For this, there will be a planeload of witnesses." He paused. We both looked to the south, watching a helicopter descend to the pad near the mall entrance. When it disappeared below the wall, he continued.

"The problem is they all have friends, family, and colleagues who know what they do for a living, or at least suspect what they do. We don't want them to come under suspicion when the press puts a description or a composite drawing in the papers. The biggest liability is an ex-wife or girlfriend who wants revenge. She could recognize the drawing and blow the whistle. With you, that won't happen. Our assets will have legitimate alibis, and none will fit the description of the hijacker."

"You hope."

"No, we're sure. There is the highest degree of certainty for our success. The FBI can dig, but there'll be nothing there. And you're perfect because you're an unknown. We'll make you older and taller, dye your hair, change your eye color, and make you left handed. When they go looking, it'll be a dead end because the person they'll be looking for won't exist. We'll make you invisible to all who see you. They'll only see what we've created. Just like one of our normal missions, you'll disappear into the dark."

"But I still have to get away."

"You'll get away; that I can guarantee."

"It's still illegal."

"If you're concerned about getting caught and going to jail, let me repeat: you will not be caught. The catch team will get you out and return you to your earlier life, and you'll disappear from the radar of the investigation."

"Not getting caught doesn't make it legal. I'll be hijacking a plane for ransom, taking hostages. To some, it's an act of terrorism."

"Let me put this in a different light. We want to protect this country and its citizens from this type of terror in the skies. Yes, it's a terrorist act, a frightening terrorist act. Being at the mercy of a madman with a bomb, speeding through the sky in a metal tube at thirty thousand feet is frightening. We imagine this one act as having the potential to prevent it from happening to thousands of other people. On your mission, no one will be harmed. The passengers won't even be inconvenienced. They'll be on a flight that will land at their destination. They'll not even be diverted. Some may even consider themselves celebrities of sorts with the media attention they'll receive."

"The pilots will be forced to continue."

"Pilots always continue. Pilots are always delayed. We're merely controlling their delay. You don't see the bigger picture yet, do you?"

"No. Draw it for me."

"I can only repeat what Anderson told you. The mission is a way to ensure that our plan for the future safety of air travel in this country isn't derailed by the political establishment. We see this as a way to move our timetable forward, to accelerate security procedures. We see this as manipulating the politicians in this country to do what's right, not merely what's going to get them reelected. We see this as a way to wake up a sleeping, complacent country. We see this as absolutely necessary."

"Do the ends always justify the means in your line of work? Because here's what I don't get. Terrorism is not the act itself. Terrorism is the fear the act instills in all those not on the plane that night. It's the fear others will have in getting on the next plane. That's the basis of terrorism—to put fear into a fear-free, routine activity. The Palestinians and the Israelis have lived with terrorism for over ten years. A bomb or a shooting that injures or kills one or a dozen in a marketplace produces fear in everyone else the next time they go to a marketplace. A little act has big consequences."

"Sometimes it's not as clear as this, but yes, we do accept some collateral damage to achieve a higher goal. Most times, the risk is our people. Sometimes the risk is the innocent, and sometimes the risk is real but unknown. With this, I can tell you the risk is virtually zero. There will be fear, certainly, but no one will be hurt. If we don't do this, you can be assured sometime in the future, near or far, an event will occur and people will be hurt and killed, and the fear will be much greater. We are manipulating the fear, minimizing it for a greater good."

There it was! In Allen's mind, his CIA-trained mind, danger, even death, to nonhostiles, sometimes the innocent, was a calculated part of the mission. This collateral damage was always a consideration for them and every attempt was made to minimize it, but it was a risk and it was accepted. This was the most difficult part for me, both as a physician to be and as a human being.

He let this sink in, sipping his coffee and finishing his cigarette. He took his time field stripping the dead butt, letting the unburned tobacco fall from his fingertips and drift in the still air. It now made sense to me. I had no argument to counter him. "You should recognize there are two benefits from this mission. I've only talked about the security standards we want to introduce, but there is another benefit for the citizens of this country. They'll get an Ivy League–educated doctor out of the deal."

"You make it sound so noble."

"It is. It has to be this way. I'm pleased you're not just rolling over, that you're resisting, that you have a conscience. In a sense, you're validating our choice."

"I still have to learn how to jump out of an airplane."

Chapter 9

* * *

I went on with my army job as if nothing had happened, but the meeting with Anderson and Allen kept replaying in my head. The more I thought about it, the more comfortable I became with what I was going to do. They would probably say I was becoming a patriot. I would say I was accepting an opportunity. If I wanted to have the best chance of getting into and finishing medical school, this was the way.

True to his word, when I saw Allen at the joint FAA/air force meetings, he treated me in a manner that could only be described as less than neutral. While not openly hostile, he shut me up before the hijacking agenda item.

Allen and I met regularly. Partly, I think, to measure the temperature of my feet. If they were getting cold, he would probably have something to warm them up. To make it even easier, Allen managed to get us assigned to a group training Pentagon staff with the new security requirements.

Allen used our time together setting out a plan for my training. A lot had been done already, most of it parceled out to many individuals, each given only a small piece of the overall plan. Their careers in clandestine operations had been marked with these compartmentalized boundaries.

Over time, I was given specific details on the hijacking. It would take place on Thanksgiving eve. I would make my way to Portland, Oregon, over the course of two days, never flying directly northwest, never flying for more than three hundred miles on any leg, and flying as myself—that is, with my own hair and eyes. When buying a ticket, I would use cash. While it seems implausible now, in those innocent days flying was more casual than taking a city bus today. No eyebrows were raised when cash was used to buy a ticket because credit cards were in their infancy. Master Charge (now MasterCard) was just catching on, and VISA wasn't born yet.

There was a lot of thought given to each detail of the plan. Each time Allen went over the plan, he provided a little more detail, sometimes on his own, sometimes in response to a question from me. The questions showed him I was fully engaged and starting to think the way they did.

Routes from Washington to Portland were studied. Some I had to commit to memory. While this may sound daunting, it wasn't. It was general familiarization with the flights—for example, knowing there were three airlines in Topeka, Kansas, offering multiple flights going west. Knowing which flights were small intercity commuter planes, more likely to be late, versus the larger 727s that were more likely to be on time.

Allen took me to the Judge Advocate Generals (JAG) library and introduced me to the *Official Airline Guide*, or OAG, for North America, a very detailed book used by the travel industry to plan flights. It was a complete listing of every flight by every airline in the United States. There were two main sections; one section listed "flights from" and the other "flights to." In the former, every flight for every airline leaving every airport was listed. Besides listing every destination, it contained other information, such as the type of aircraft. The "flights to" was more valuable to me. With it, I could pick a destination and then do a back search to find originating flights—critical if I would be making a multistop trip from Washington to Portland.

The big blue book was substantial, challenging the New York City telephone directory in size and information. It was published monthly, and once the new one came out, the library discarded the old one. Allen salvaged an old copy for me to study and plan my flights.

Identification wasn't needed in 1971 to board a flight. However, I had to have an alias for the final leg. Allen explained that after I made the ransom demand, the airline crew would address me by name. I had to be comfortable with the name. They didn't want a flight-crew member calling my name and having me ignore them. When I suggested Charles Ignatius Anderson and then Francis Bernard Isaacson, they rejected them right away. CIA and FBI as initials would not do. Francis Albert Andrews was rejected for the same reason. I proposed Daniel B. Cooper. They agreed but only after scratching their collective heads for a couple of days trying to figure out what DBC meant. I didn't tell them and have told no one else. Don't know if I ever will.

They sent me to an eye doctor, probably one under contract with the CIA, to be fitted for brown contact lenses. The doc had to keep going for darker and darker colors to hide the green of my eyes. The brown part had to be larger than normal so the green wouldn't stick out the sides of the contact when I moved my eyes. If I moved my eyes too quickly, it was like wearing dark sunglasses. Everything on one side of my field of vision would go dark. Lucky there was no driving planned for me during the mission.

Contact lenses were glass at the time, they couldn't be left in overnight, and there was a long adjustment period for getting used to them. I started using them in the barracks when Mitch was away, but I could barely keep them in for an hour. While wearing them, my eyes constantly teared. When I took them out, my eyes were bloodshot. It took lots of fine-tuning by the eye doctor before I could leave the contacts in all day. Then I had to practice wearing them outside, in different kinds of weather—wind, rain, sunlight, you name it. Eventually I got it, but it was one of the more difficult parts of getting ready.

I tried dying my hair once on my own. Thinking ahead, I used a rinse so I could wash it out and get back to normal easily. The rinse didn't get the right color. I looked like a sandy-haired guy who had dyed his hair poorly. Allen arranged for me to be taught how to dye my hair at a beauty shop in Fredericksburg, Virginia. Fredericksburg was considered outside the DC commuting corridor at the time. The southernmost city that was considered a bedroom community of Washington was Dale City, so it was unlikely I would run into anyone who knew me twenty miles farther away.

On Saturday morning, I was the only appointment scheduled. The hairdresser lady showed me how to apply the rinse properly to my own hair, as I would have to do it in the motel the evening before the hijacking. Not only did she teach me how to do it, but how to do it neatly without making a mess of the bathroom. I had to use a hand towel for the initial drying of my hair, the only towel I was allowed to use on my hair. She also gave me a plastic hairnet I needed to wear to bed to avoid leaving hair color on the pillowcase.

"Hey, as long as I'm bringing a towel, why don't I just bring along an extra pillowcase? Then I won't have to worry about the hairnet."

She stopped dabbing the stuff on the back of my head and came around to face me. "No, this is the way we do things." Emphatic? Definitely! I said no more.

When she finished, she told me to go back to my room at the motel, stay there, and leave only for dinner at Bob's Big Boy next door. What little I had seen of Fredericksburg, I wasn't missing much by being confined to my room. She told me to wash my hair that night before I went to bed and again in the morning. After the second shampooing, I could see the lighter colors of my hair returning.

When I returned to the beauty salon, she washed my hair without comment. It was back to something close to my natural color. There was a slight difference, but I doubted anyone else would notice it. There was no conversation that morning. The training exercise was only to show me how to make my sandy hair black and then return it to normal. I guessed I would have to go to another specialist to learn how to normalize the rest of me after the mission.

Chapter 10

*   *   *

They were true to their word, and I received my acceptance to medical school just five weeks after I applied. Yale didn't ask for any additional information; they just sent the standard letter with the forms I needed to complete before I began in September. Mom and Dad received the news with an equal mix of joy and thankfulness, especially my mother. They were not as happy that I wouldn't be returning home for the summer.

The transformation into D. B. Cooper progressed steadily over the next two months. In addition to hair- and eye-color changes, mental transformations were started. Physical training for the hijacking began the day following my honorable discharge from the army.

Allen focused on getting me ready to jump out of an airplane. Before I could seriously consider going to jump school, he insisted I get back in shape, and by this he meant "end-of-basic-training shape." He got me a personal-training partner named Tex. Telling me his name was as personal and personable as Tex got. He was a small, wiry man with cold gray eyes and a white-walled haircut with a touch of gray on top. His arms and legs were tanned a deep bronze, probably not from surfing. He met me every morning at six for a run. At first, he ran and I jogged, but with time, I was running as far and as fast as I ever could, but never enough to challenge him.

Tex stayed with me for breakfast, making sure I stayed away from the pancakes and breads. He gave me the rest of the day to study the material Allen had assigned me before he returned for the evening edition of what I had suffered through in the morning. After three weeks of physical training, Allen met with me to discuss jump-school training.

I hadn't known the US government allowed the military of our allies to take training with our armed forces. The teaching cadre at the training centers didn't single these people out for special treatment. Only if the ally chose to identify himself as non-American did anyone know. Allen enrolled me as a lieutenant in the Canadian Army and arranged for me to attend the Basic Airborne Course at Fort Benning, Georgia.

The course was divided into three sections, each a week in duration: Ground Week, Tower Week, and Jump Week. Ground Week was pure hell. It was like basic training all over again, including the skinhead haircut and physical training—running, doing exercises, more running, doing more exercises, followed by more running. It weeded out half the applicants. Face it—Airborne is a fraternity, and, like any fraternity, they have standards and initiation rites. At Harvard, the Eye Ata Thigh boys didn't want new brothers to embarrass them. So too, the paratroopers didn't want some dumpy, dopey fat-ass walking around wearing wings, a beret, and jump boots. I had played hockey all my life—high school, college, and pro—and I found Ground Week physically difficult, but I got through it. Without all the running with Tex, I would have failed the first week.

Tower Week meant getting into the art and mechanics of jumping. There was a certain amount of fear that had to be overcome even in jumping off of a perfectly good platform fifty feet in the air to prepare you for jumping out of a perfectly good airplane. There were techniques to learn and a team spirit to be instilled. I didn't find it very difficult, either physically or emotionally. I thought it was three days longer than necessary, but it did serve to let some of the bumps and bruises of the previous week heal and get ready for Jump Week.

The big week was Jump Week—from airplanes. To get my wings, I needed to make five jumps, including a night jump. The jumps had varying amounts of equipment to carry. The week started with static line jumps, where a line connected to the airplane pulled the cord, and progressed to jumps where we pulled the cord. I was a particularly attentive student when it came to jumping with a load hanging from a strap around my waist and when jumping at night.

The last jump of the week was to be on Friday morning, the graduation jump. I had learned enough to safely jump out of an airplane, so when it came time to do the graduation jump, I feinted being afraid. This was in the plans from Allen. Said I didn't want to do it. Said I couldn't do it. Acted like a coward. I stayed in the plane and rode it to the ground, and they failed me. Because I was listed as a foreign national and had failed, there was never any record of my having taken parachute training. Something about not wanting to embarrass an ally. For us, it was just one additional layer of protection in the investigation that would follow the hijacking.

The plan required me to be on the hijacked airplane for many hours. I'd be touching many things, too many to wipe everything clean. The investigation after would match my fingerprints on file with the army. Rather than alter my fingerprints, the easy solution was to change my fingerprints on record. Allen's people took care of that. These were just a few of a small group of people, expert in their work, assisting and guiding Allen, who in turn guided me through the preparations for the jump. They didn't know who I was and I would never know who they were, but we were bound together in this assignment to the end.

July turned to August, and the heat and humidity in Washington became unbearable. I rarely spent any time outside. I continued with my morning and evening runs, but without Tex. The runs turned into times to think. I had had many talks with Allen over the summer and had convinced myself I was doing the right thing. The goal was to create a public outcry for better air travel security. As I waited for Thanksgiving and my jump, there were five separate hijackings to Cuba. Some involved fatalities at gunpoint; the press and the government seemed no more alarmed. The stories were buried in the back pages of the newspapers. How could I hope my mission would produce any different result? Allen assured me it would.

When not running, I spent a lot of my free time reviewing the previous month's *North American Airline Guide*. I learned there were airlines that kept certain routes sacred, never varying the type of aircraft or departure times. These, I committed to memory. I also spent time each day in the gym. I had worked hard to get in shape, and I didn't know what I would be up against after I landed in the forest of the Pacific Northwest. I wanted to be able to land safely, and if I had to hike out, I wanted to be able to do it.

Chapter 11

The week of Thanksgiving 1971 had been picked for the jump. No one told me why or who had made the decision, but it had been made long before I was on the team. I wondered if there had been someone else preparing for the jump before I came onboard, and if so, was he still in preparation mode as an alternate, or as a backup. Perhaps I was the backup, only to be pulled at the last minute.

During one of my meetings with Allen, I asked if there was a 100 percent chance I wouldn't get caught. He wouldn't say 100 percent, but he said the chances of getting picked up by someone other than the catch team were remote. When pressed, he hesitated, collected his thoughts, and continued. "We don't plan for failure, West. We plan for success. If you get picked up by someone other than our team, there's a plan to take you from them before they get out of the area. If they get you out of the area, there's a plan to get you transferred to one of our facilities. If that happens, you'll escape on the way."

There was a long silence before I responded. "But what if I do get caught? What if your guys can't get me? What if they lock me up and won't let you at me?"

He looked at me from under hooded eyes, his eyebrows crunched. "Are you worried you'll become expendable?"

"By expendable, do you mean am I afraid you guys will kill me rather than let me be taken into custody? If that's what you think I'm afraid of, then you're right."

He paused, looking at me with an icy stare. I could see he was choosing his words carefully. Finally, he spoke. "Jonathan, you can't get caught, dead or alive. If you get caught, we get caught. They'll run fingerprints and find they don't match anyone in the database. They'll see your hair has been dyed and you're wearing contacts. Whether you're dead or alive, they'll publish your real description and picture because you'd be even more of a mystery man than if you got away. Certainly, someone would recognize you, and when they did, they'd trace you right back to us. It wouldn't stop at the Pentagon. So we can't let you get caught."

"Wouldn't stop at the Pentagon! How high does this go?"

"You have no need to know, Jonathan, and no need to be read in on that information. Just know you'll not be caught. Know you will get away."

"Comforting, but not entirely. All you're saying is you can't allow anyone to recover my body. I could disappear, right?"

"Theoretically, yes. Practically, no. Your disappearance would raise too many questions. It might take longer to get back to us, but we think the trail would wind up there. That being said, if it were to happen, it would be acceptable for us to acknowledge this hijacking for all the right reasons rather than get caught in a lie that led to you being dead. Killing an American citizen on US soil and then trying to cover it up would be something the CIA, or the whole government, wouldn't likely recover from. Congress and the public would ask that every action we undertake be approved beforehand, and that would kill us. You will not get caught. You will survive."

Thinking about what he had said, I looked into his eyes as he looked into mine. He didn't blink. I had no training in being able to read people, but there was nothing that seemed to betray him. I nodded my acceptance and agreement. We were all in this together, all for the common good, and me for the money.

Thankfully, I left Washington and its oppressive mid-August heat, heading north to the relative cool of the Hudson Valley and home for a week with my family before heading off to New Haven. The visit became a reason to have a family picnic to celebrate my transition back to student life.

Both of my sisters lived at home, one enjoying her final summer of being a college student, the other preparing to move out after she got married. Their boyfriends were invited for a Saturday barbecue, as were aunts, uncles, and cousins. Dad got clams and a pony keg to complement the hot dogs and burgers. Aunts brought salads and desserts.

I wanted to buy a car in Connecticut, not New York. Sales tax and insurance were considerably less expensive. So my parents drove me to New Haven. I felt like a freshman starting college, but I did need a ride and it made them feel good. Allen arranged for a furnished apartment in Hamden, a suburb just north of New Haven and home to a number of Yale faculty, including several Nobel laureates. The apartment was part of the "fellowship" I had received.

The apartment had a spare bedroom set up as a home office. Mom and Dad were impressed. Dad had a concerned look and asked if I could afford it.

"Part of it is paid for by the fellowship, the room and board part. The little extra, I can make up from my stipend and the money I saved in the army." None of that was far from the truth, and it seemed to satisfy him.

They stayed in my room. It was a first for them, the first time they had stayed in one of their kids' places. It didn't hit them until the following morning, when it hit me: stayed in my own place for the first time, and I had slept on the couch!

Dad and I went out looking for a car and left Mom to do that mom stuff they like to do to make things homey.

As a student at Harvard, I hadn't had a car. Both Greyhound and Trailways provided bus service between Boston and Albany for visits home. When I played professional hockey, I had no money for either a car or insurance, so it wasn't even considered. The same can be said for my time in the army. In New Haven, I was itching to get a car. Money was no longer a concern with my money from Uncle Sam. But it wasn't just wanting a car; I needed a car to get to school.

I could have bought anything, but I didn't want to lay a lot of cash down, heeding Anderson's concern. I chose a two-year-old, lime-green AMC Javelin. It probably wasn't the wisest choice, but it suited my purpose. It was sporty, flashy, and fast. It had bucket seats and an automatic transmission on the floor.

The one concern I had about car ownership in New Haven was parking. Parking around a university, especially with a hospital, would be at a premium. Not so in New Haven near the medical school. The city was undergoing a revitalization that included a widening and extension of Route 34 through the city.

The proposed route ran one block east of the medical school campus. Phase one involved reclamation of some run-down housing. After an area about one half mile long and fifty yards wide had been razed and the ground leveled, the project was put on hold for funding issues. It proved to be a boon to downtown business, the medical school, and the hospital by providing free parking for hundreds of cars, including the Javelin.

Harvard and Yale shared similarities and differences. Both were isolated communities within their host cities, the original campuses built to keep the outside world outside. The outsides, New Haven and Boston, were so very different. The community surrounding Harvard was a continuation of the school community. What was needed inside and couldn't be provided spilled out and acted as a buffer—coffee shops, bookstores, restaurants, and a myriad of businesses catered to the college crowd. Even Ehrlich's, the venerable tobacco and pipe shop across the river on Tremont, was considered to be a colony of the Harvard Yard because the medical school was in the neighborhood. It was there I would go to get my tins of Dunhill pipe tobacco, trying a different blend, alternating with my standard My Mixture #10, or to stock up on Marsh Wheeling Natural Wrapper cigars at five cents apiece when there was a smoker to attend. While I had everything I needed in Cambridge, there was always the rest of Boston to explore when the mood struck. And I had the Bruins to cheer for!

Not so in New Haven. The medical school was also set apart from the main campus. While the main campus was up on the hill, the medical school could be said, and was said, to be on the other side of the tracks. Not literally, but figuratively. The main of downtown New Haven separated the two campuses, and around the medical school, the neighborhood was run down. Part of the required new medical student orientation included a talk by a member of the police department. While he welcomed us to his city, he also cautioned us that we were in a blighted urban community and it was not a good idea to walk around outside the campus alone after dark. He added, for that matter, it wasn't a good idea to walk around the campus after dark. We were fortunate at the medical school because some of the maintenance tunnels connecting the buildings were open to student and faculty traffic. These tunnels provided a safe way to get around at night and a warm way to get around in the winter.

I loved Yale and New Haven right away. I considered myself lucky to have had the experience of Harvard for undergrad and now Yale, probably the two most prestigious institutions in the country. As a kid growing up in a small town, I knew the dreams and aspirations of my friends. No one aspired to either Harvard or Yale. The goal was considered too lofty. Now I was Ivy League, two times over.

So, with my new apartment and new car, I settled into the routine of being a first-year medical student, commuting each day listening to Don Imus in the morning. His antics were a good way to start the day, and I grew fond of Moby Worm and the Reverend Billy Sol Hargis. I arrived at 7:00 a.m., picked up two newspapers in the hospital lobby, and read them while I had breakfast in the cafeteria. The timing was perfect for quiet reflection. The hospital staff working seven to three had left, and students and research staff wouldn't arrive until 8:00 a.m. At home, I studied without the distractions of worrying about money or noisy roommates. All was good.

Chapter 12

✳︎　✳︎　✳︎

At the beginning of November, I told my parents I couldn't come home for Thanksgiving because of my class and lab load. Predictably, it wasn't received well. I lied that most of the students weren't going home, something that seemed to be the norm for first-year students on this, just a long weekend. My mother reluctantly agreed but not before I promised to be there for Christmas.

In reality, the workload for Thanksgiving week was fairly light. The faculty understood first-year students would be anxious to get home for that first holiday. I would be able to leave New Haven in midafternoon on Monday and not miss any critical classwork.

Allen's team had picked a remote area east northeast of Portland for my jump and escape. The problem with the Pacific Northwest was trees—finding a large suitable landing zone was a challenge. In the plan, I would demand to be flown to Mexico. The 727 didn't have the range for Mexico, so they would have to refuel. I would insist on it being Reno, Nevada. Because of the terrain and forests in the early part of the flight and my insistence on refueling in Reno, we were sure the authorities would put most of their effort into trying to apprehend me north of Reno.

That was what we wanted them to think. The jump site would be on the flight path between Seattle and Reno, but in an area not far from Seattle. I would have to time my jump using nothing more than my wristwatch, so the closer to Seattle the better. A spot was found, a relatively wide, clear area that extended for about ten miles. It was part farmland and part grazing land. At each end was the remains of a clear-cut forest. The moon would be at the quarter on the night of the jump. The critical landmark in the area was the confluence of two rivers at a lake that ran perpendicular to my flight line. The water should be clearly visible as a sparkling band in the moonlight.

I went to see *Easy Rider* again at one of those dollar theaters to study Nicholson. Jack's eyes were remarkable in conveying craziness. But he also wore sunglasses, adding to his weirdness, so I got a similar pair. In the artist's sketches produced after the hijacking based on descriptions from witnesses, these sunglasses were a key feature and really did the trick. The rendering was quite good, kind of half me and half Nicholson, with my hair looking neat— businesslike, not military. I was still going to have hair shorter than most, but I could probably pass as an IBM technician or a conservative insurance salesman.

The first part of November passed quickly. I feared last-minute changes would occur, but none did. Allen's biggest task was to keep me calm. He started showing up at breakfast, initially in September, once a week. Then, in October, it became three times every two weeks. By November, he could see my grow- ing nervousness and urged me to calm down. This increased my concern. "If everything is going fine, why are we meeting more now?"

"Because you are so fuckin' whacked out. If you calmed down, you wouldn't see me. There's no need for us to meet, but you're worrying me and the rest of the team."

"I don't see the rest of the team. The only person I've seen has been you. How could the team know I was so fuckin' whacked out if I don't see any- body but you?" Verbalizing that made it clear: Allen was meeting with others regularly, reporting on me. "So, you think I'm whacked out, and you're telling them."

"Yes. Look, I understand your apprehension. You've never done this. I've never run an operation like this either, but I've managed a number of compli- cated missions. By comparison, this is not complex. The team is well drilled and capable. You've been prepared as well as you can be. You're ready."

"Rationally, I agree. But, as you say, I've never done anything like this."

"Don't worry. Remember, someone will be watching you at all times, except when you get on the plane in Portland. Up to that point, you'll not be out of their sight. If you get into any trouble, they're there to bail you out. The team will have credentials that'll trump anyone else. They'll take you into custody and return you to me. I'll debrief you, and then you can get back to your life."

"What about the mission if I need to be bailed out before Portland?"

"As you said, there is a backup. Read about it in the newspapers and watch it on television."

"I keep thinking I'll miss something and get caught."

"The only place you're vulnerable to a mistake is the last night in the hotel where you have to dye your hair and change clothes. Before then, just keep your briefcase locked so it doesn't open accidently. On that last morning, remember to leave your carry-on bag with all your old clothes, the towel, and the dye stuff in the room. It'll be picked up within five minutes of you leaving. After that, it's just a plane ride and a parachute jump."

I was still nervous, but he had made me feel better. "Yeah, I guess you're right. Piece of cake! You guys are the pros."

Chapter 13

Leaving New Haven on Monday after class, I had two days to traverse the country to Portland. There was a bus to Bridgeport, another to Hartford, and then short airplane hops, paying cash, using various names and different airlines. The short flights were cheap, and I paid for them without having to use a large bill or unfold cash from a wad. The circuitous route to Portland was necessary but boring. On a TWA flight from Dallas to Oklahoma City, I used the name Thomas William Anderson just to have fun and break the boredom. From Oklahoma City to Denver, I was Francis Albert Allen. When I gave the ticket agent that name, she looked up. "Francis Albert—just like Sinatra."

"My mother's a big fan," I responded. Clearly, my boredom and frivolous choice of a name was careless and against the instructions I had received from Allen. Now I was no longer a faceless, nameless passenger. To this woman, I was now a memory.

I spent Monday and Tuesday nights in no-name motels near the last airport of the day.

Tuesday night, I dyed my hair and put in my contacts for a while. In the morning, I put on my suit, shirt, and tie, grabbed my fedora and briefcase, and headed for the airport. As instructed, I left everything else in the room, relying on my shadow to pick it up.

I arrived in Portland on Wednesday, just before noon after a ninety-minute flight from Boise. I went to the Northeast Orient counter and bought a ticket for Seattle on flight 305 using the name Dan Cooper. The fare was twenty dollars, including tax. Later, when the press referred to me as D. B. Cooper, I was concerned. I hadn't used that name with anyone other than my team on that first day back in the Pentagon. Quite by accident, someone had used it when talking to the press, and it stuck. Was it an accident, or had someone on the team leaked the name?

With no luggage, just a carry-on briefcase, I took my ticket and went in search of the bar. I needed to feed my stomach because it was going to be a while before I would have the chance to eat again. A drink and a couple of smokes would help quiet the butterflies in that same stomach. And, I was hungry!

In preparing for the mission, I had to alter my appearance by losing weight. When I lost weight, the first place it showed was my face. If I lost ten pounds, my face looked as if I had lost twenty. The weight loss made me look gaunt and added years. Everything averages out in the end. As I got older, the reverse was true. If I gained five pounds, it looked as if I had gained twenty. Go figure! My prematurely receding hairline was exaggerated by the way I combed my hair. These all combined to add years, with witnesses describing me as being in my early to midforties.

I found the bar and settled in at a table near the window, avoiding the bartender. Bartenders are too observant, and they like to talk. They seem to be naturals at both, but it's all part of their job. They observe and engage the customers, trying to size them up, to see if an extra effort with service or conversation might pay off with a bigger tip. They look at the watch, the tie, and the haircut and can probably estimate within a couple of dollars the total amount of money a drinker has invested in those three items. A bartender might also pick up that my hair was dyed or that I wasn't a natural left-hander—maybe not at first, but, under FBI questioning, these little inconsistencies might be remembered.

The waitress, on the other hand, didn't even look at me when she took my order, a Budweiser, grilled ham and cheese, and fries. She slid the beer in front of me as she juggled a tray and then placed the sandwich without a word. Since

I was sitting at a table for four, if she remembered anything about me, it would be that I was wasting table space that could yield her a tip four times greater if the table were full. Maybe not; the lounge wasn't full. A few salesmen trying to get the last flight home before the holiday weekend. One was at a table, like me, with papers spread out, discouraging anyone from sharing the table. A few more salesmen were at the bar talking animatedly about the full weekend of football they planned to watch. Good. They had the attention of the bartender. Two elderly couples were having a light lunch, probably on their way to visit kids and grandkids for the holiday weekend.

Nibbling at my sandwich and fries, I tried to appear interested in activity on the tarmac below, beyond the big floor-to-ceiling windows. There was a fascination, much like that of a big-city construction site, as I watched the powerful little trucks move the giant airplanes around the gate area. And it was raining, drops running down the big pane of glass. In the Pacific Northwest, it always rained. We had considered that in our planning. What did it mean tonight? I'd get wet. I'd probably be wet after I left the plane, wet all the way down, and wet when the catch team met me.

Even though I was ravenous, I didn't wolf down my meal. I wanted to take it slow, avoiding any potential for cramping when I got on the plane. It wouldn't do if in the middle of the hijacking I had to excuse myself to use the toilet. Even eating slowly, I was finished by one o'clock. If I loitered with another beer, I might be conspicuous. I got the waitress's attention, got my bill, and paid it. A 15 percent tip would fade me into the background of all the other people she served that day. Grabbing my briefcase from the seat beside me, I left.

The men's room was my next stop, to wash my hands after the greasy sandwich and fries. I looked at myself in the mirror, a final check. I was startled at first, as I had been that morning at the stranger looking back at me. All seemed in order, the neat black suit and white shirt. The forehand knot looked perfectly left handed, as did the part in my hair. The water running triggered an auditory sensor that sent a signal to my dick that said, "Time to take a leak." Just as well; a nervous bladder was sure to come, and the emptier the better. Washing my hands again, I smiled as I went through this second washing. There had been a guy working in the Pentagon who was known for washing his hands only before he urinated, never after. When asked, he responded, "No need. My dick is clean, and I don't piss on my hands."

There were seats in the waiting area near the gate. Before this week, my time in airports and on planes had been limited to that one trip to the rodeo. The circuitous route this week had given me much more experience. I had watched the behavior of middle-aged men who had the air of seasoned travelers and had adopted their mannerisms of forced boredom. For them, there seemed to be less boredom today; perhaps they were looking forward to several days of not traveling and being with friends and family. I tried to amp my demeanor up a little to meet theirs without giving in to the anxiety that had been building all week. After all, I was getting ready to hijack an airplane and then jump into the night.

Under normal circumstances, I would have left New Haven early that morning and headed home to be with my family for the holiday. Checking my watch, careful to remember it was on my right wrist, I realized I would be sitting at my mother's kitchen table now, smelling apple pies baking. I could actually smell the apple pie. A vivid memory? No, the grandmotherly woman seated next to me had taken the top from her Tupperware pie transporter. "So far, so good," she said as she snapped the top back on, her worry lines temporarily turning to a smile.

To my relief, there were no kids waiting to take the flight. I didn't want to scare any kids. It made sense there weren't any. Being a short hop from Portland to Seattle, it was more likely a drive for a family than a plane ride. Most of my fellow passengers were probably making a final connection to Seattle from somewhere else. Well, they'd all be home tonight with a story for the dinner table tomorrow and for many Thanksgivings to come.

I forced myself to think about the other passengers because I didn't want to think about myself or what I was about to do. How had I managed to get myself talked into this? Or was it, how had I talked myself into this? Too late now? Maybe, maybe not. Could I just walk away, turn in my ticket and get one for Albany, join the family? Sure, but that would be followed by a fade into nothingness, no med school, no life. I got up and walked out to the American Airlines ticket counter. The big board behind the counter listed flights to the East Coast.

A hop to Chicago, then New York, then up to Albany. No need for short hops; I could fly direct, at least to New York. The flights to New York, Pittsburgh, Washington, Philadelphia, and Boston were all delayed. Why? Moving to the counter, I asked, "Is there anything direct to the East Coast?"

"Sorry, sir. Everything is delayed. The entire northeast corridor is shut down by a massive snowstorm. Can't say when it'll be opening up." The woman at the counter had not even looked up at me, busy on the phone with a half dozen tickets in front of her.

I walked away, my fate sealed by a Thanksgiving snowstorm. It shouldn't have been that simple. I should have been able to make a better decision, based on something other than the availability of a flight to New York. I should have been able to make a decision based on the rightness or wrongness of what I was going to do. But I didn't. Nothing left to do but go back to my gate and wait for them to call Flight 305 to Seattle. At least Mom would be happy. She loved it when there was snow on the ground for Thanksgiving.

Chapter 14

*   *   *

The flight was called at 2:20 p.m. I took seat 15D, an aisle. The grandmother with the apple pie had the window seat. With the flight less than half full, I moved back to 18C and had the row all to myself, putting me behind all the passengers and eliminating the chance of someone taking me from behind. This change in seats confused the authorities afterward because fellow passengers reported me in both seats. The plane took off on time at 2:50 p.m. As soon as the No Smoking light went off, I lit up a Raleigh. Pall Mall was my regular brand when I smoked, but I switched for the hijacking. Why Raleighs? My grandmother smoked them. Simple as that!

As the stewardess took my order for a bourbon and soda, I passed her a note. Without reading it, she put it in her apron pocket. When she returned with my drink, I told her she should sit down next to me and read the note. Poor girl, she looked as if she had been through this before, the horny traveler looking to hook up for the night. Before she left, I added "I have a bomb" and patted the briefcase. That got her attention, and she sat next to me to read the note.

The note was simple, printed in block letters using a felt-tip pen. Felt-tip pens were relatively new at the time and had a limited range of colors. The note used a black marker, and the printing was in large letters and wasn't written by me. Allen presented it to me and told me it blended with the persona they had developed, namely that I was left handed. A left-handed person had printed the note using his right hand. It simply read, "I have a bomb in my briefcase. I will use it if necessary. I want you to sit next to me. You are bein hijacked." The intentional typo of "being" was supposed to be consistent with someone focusing on the writing, not the message.

Florence Schaffner was the name on her tag, and, sitting next to me, she asked in a surprisingly calm and quiet voice to see the bomb. With the briefcase open, I showed her the eight red cylinders that looked like sticks of dynamite and the coils of red electrical wires wrapping them and connected to a large battery. To her credit, she remained calm and professional. The situation would have been so much more difficult if she had become hysterical, running to the front of the plane shouting, "He's got a bomb!" Well, difficult is an understatement. The mission would have been over. If I had been challenged, the hoax of the red toilet-paper tubes would have been discovered and I would be hoping I wasn't going to get shot by some cowboy.

As I closed the briefcase, I leaned into her. Speaking softly and calmly, I said, "I want you to go forward and tell the pilot what you just saw. Tell him I want two hundred thousand dollars in small used bills and four parachutes, and when we land in Seattle, I want a fuel truck standing by to refuel us."

She left for the front of the plane. When she returned she held out another drink for me. I declined. I had put my Jack Nicholson sunglasses on by then, adding to the strangeness of my persona and the situation.

Interestingly, when left alone, I became anxious. I had been alternately enjoying or dreading this up to now, but when Florence left me to go to the cockpit, the enormity of what I was doing settled in. I didn't become nervous in the crazy sense, just aware I was in the middle of something very big. Once the pilot radioed my request, there would be little chance of backing out without considerable notoriety and the consequences that would follow. I was surprised how a calm settled in when I put on the sunglasses. The glasses provided a shield, protecting me from the rest of the world. Is that the reason Jack wore them? Was he shielding himself from the world that had suddenly descended upon him and his celebrity?

The pilot came on the cabin speaker and announced we would be delayed in our arrival to Seattle. Florence returned to my seat to tell me Northwest Orient agreed to pay the money but needed a few hours to collect it from several Seattle banks. She told me they had acquired military parachutes from McChord Air Force Base nearby. I rejected these and asked them to get the parachutes from a skydiving club. I wanted them to think my parachute experience came from civilian rather than military training, and I also wanted to avoid the possibility the military had a secret stash of parachutes either intentionally defective or fitted with tracking devices.

The plane circled Seattle for two hours, and then Florence told me everything had been collected. We touched down at 5:39 p.m. The plane taxied to an isolated area of the airport with the interior lights turned off. The Northwest Orient guy in Seattle delivered the parachutes and the money to the back stairs of the plane, ten thousand twenty-dollar bills in a knapsack. Once I assured myself the money was not a bag of cut-up newspapers and the parachutes not someone's dirty laundry, I let all the passengers and crew leave the plane except for the cockpit crew and the other stewardess, Tina Mucklow. I would have liked to keep Florence, but she had already done enough. Tina seemed a little more nervous and avoided looking directly at me, so she seemed a safer choice.

At this point, I was the most nervous I'd be for the entire hijacking. Yes, I was concerned about jumping out of the airplane into the dark, but more concerned I wouldn't get that chance. We hadn't discussed what would happen to my money if I got caught. I had overlooked that possibility. Sure, I would be exonerated—maybe too strong a word. I probably wouldn't get shot when Allen came forward, but what about the money I needed for medical school? Maybe I wouldn't need it. Yale might deny me admission if I got caught.

I was nervous because things weren't going to plan. The issue with the military parachutes could have been an honest mistake. But then the tanker refueling the 727 reported having difficulties, difficulties that could be a ruse. A vapor lock in the pumper was the problem. I told them to bring in a different tanker. The second tanker didn't have a full load of fuel, and a third had to be brought in to top off our tanks. If I were the authorities on the ground, these were the kinds of things I would have done to slow progress until a plan to thwart the hijacking could be put in place.

I moved to the cockpit to give the crew instructions for leaving Seattle on a southeasterly course to Mexico City. There had been other hijackings before mine, but these were mostly freedom flights, demanding to go to Cuba. I didn't want to go to Cuba. What could I do with two hundred thousand dollars in Cuba? How could I get back to the United States? Of course, I didn't want to go to Mexico City either, but I couldn't tell them to start flying and I'll get out when I want to. That would make it too easy for them, although they must have known I intended to jump when I asked for the parachutes. If that didn't tip them off, then my flight instructions surely must have.

I told them I wanted them to fly as slow as they possibly could, about 120 miles per hour, at ten thousand feet, with the wheels down and the rear door open. Everything I wanted was agreed to except the rear tail door being open and the staircase extended during takeoff. No problem; I could lower it in flight, something that has since been corrected on the 727 by the installation of the Cooper vane. Their only problem was the need for a refueling stop to get all the way to Mexico City. I knew it didn't matter, but I reluctantly agreed, insisting on Reno, Nevada. Reno was a good choice, and I hoped the FBI team sent to interrogate the crew would treat them kindly. The crew members were good people, very professional, and they deserved to be treated well. Hopefully, they would be put up in a nice hotel, maybe one with a casino; get some good meals; and get to see a show.

During the time on the ground, a senior FAA official asked to come aboard for a meeting with me. There was no plan for any intervention on the ground. No contingency for aborting the mission. The critical part of the mission was getting away after. The FAA official was probably an FBI negotiator posing as an FAA official. I denied the request.

The plane left Seattle at 7:44 p.m. I noted the time and began my count-down. I sent Tina to the cockpit with the flight crew and told them to remain there with the door closed. As an extra precaution from prying eyes, I closed the curtain into first class. Military aircraft were probably all around us, but I couldn't see them. I could have checked the radar in the cockpit, but up there it was four against one. The risk didn't justify the little reward.

I put one of the parachutes on and strapped on the reserve. With my front and back covered with parachutes, I had no place to "wear" the knapsack with the money. It was heavy, and I didn't trust myself to hold on to it during my jump. Taking some of the lines from one of the other parachutes, I lashed the knapsack to my waist. All of this took time, doing it by myself—twenty minutes by my watch. I needed to jump soon if I was going to hit my target. If the pilot was on course, if the pilot was flying at 120 miles per hour, if he was at ten thousand feet, and if we had done the calculations correctly, I had a chance. I pressed the lever to open the tail door and extended the aft stairs. When this happened, a voice came over the plane's speaker system asking if I needed any assistance. Did they think I was some rank amateur? Well, I was, but I didn't need any of their help.

The timing of my jump was made after very careful consideration. The authorities knew I was going to jump. The only question was when. Having chase planes following me was a given, but cautious of changes I might dictate to the pilot once in the air, these planes would be at a distance until they were sure I was heading to Reno. The early part of the flight from Seattle to Reno would be when they were the least vigilant, partly because of the uncertainty of my final destination, but also because this area was much more populated and dense with forest than the areas farther south. For these reasons, I was to exit the plane sooner rather than later.

The jump target was an area between Portland and Bend, Oregon, about one hundred miles south southwest of Seattle. At 120 miles per hour, allowing for the initial climb at a faster speed and circling around to get on the flight path, I would be over the target area thirty-three minutes after takeoff. There was a fairly good-sized plain where the Cowlitz River met the Cispus River. In fact, the flood plane was actually a small lake, Lake Scanewa. There were open fields, no houses, and few trees. The water should be a clearly visible landmark for me.

I slowly descended the stairway after it was fully extended. Checking my watch, I jumped off into the dark exactly thirty-three minutes after takeoff. I had been a hijacker for thirty-three minutes. It had seemed like thirty-three years, the same age as Alexander the Great when he conquered the world and the same age as Christ when he was crucified.

Chapter 15

The night was cloudy below me, but the quarter moon was bright in the sky that held me. Orion was rising in the east, the belt one of the few star markers I knew. Below the clouds it was raining. Looking around as best I could in free fall, I saw the Northwest airplane continuing to the southeast. I couldn't see any planes following it. One of the lessons they'll learn from this will be to have the chase planes follow closer so they can see someone jump out of the ass end of the plane.

The plan called for a free fall of thirty-four seconds before I opened my parachute. Knowing I wouldn't be able to see a watch face as I fell through the sky, I had practiced counting—counting to thirty-four. Practicing under stress until I always got thirty-four seconds every time. During this time, I would descend to about five thousand feet, well below the altitude any chase planes would be operating at and maximizing the distance between my homing device and any possible detection from above, while at the same time getting into position for the catch team to detect the signal and prepare to extract me.

In my black civilian suit, I felt the dark, night cold immediately. No one had prepared me for that. It wasn't bitter cold like what I had grown up with in upstate New York, but it was cold enough, especially rushing by me at more than one hundred miles per hour as gravity pulled me down. Free fall was just long enough to keep me alert, thinking about keeping track of the thirty-four seconds, thinking about the cold. There was no time to think about the dark or the landing. That would come in a few minutes.

I pulled the cord on the primary chute and was relieved when it opened and started slowing my descent. There was a strong tug on the rope at my waist as the knapsack with money partnered with gravity and tried to continue its downward flight. The bag of money was heavy, and I doubt I would have been able to hold it if it hadn't been tied to me. The reduced speed of my fall made for an almost warming sensation. I wouldn't say I was comfortable, but I certainly didn't feel as cold.

With the parachute open, I had five minutes, more or less, to touch down, at the leisurely rate of about one thousand feet per minute. In the quiet of descent, I thought about the plane and the crew I had left behind. Could they land the plane with the aft staircase down, or would they have to retract it? If they had to retract it, would it pose a threat to them? When I activated the switch at the top of the staircase, I was surprised by the force of the air trying to suck me out. I had to hold on, first to the sides of the lavatory and then to the rails on the stairway as I descended the ramp. If they had to retract the stairway, would they encounter the same force trying to pull them out of the plane? I hoped they knew what they were facing and that one of the men would go back to do the job. Tina was not tiny, but she was certainly the lightest of the four remaining on the plane. I could see her opening the cockpit door and getting sucked all the way through the plane, bouncing off the seats and the floor, her limp body propelled out the rear of the 727. Pushing that image aside, I convinced myself there was likely a procedure for closing the aft door, probably even another switch in the cockpit. After all, they had asked me if I needed assistance.

The enormity of the sky above me amplified what I was doing. Nothing like hanging from a parachute around five thousand feet at night for a reality check. It was almost done. If I got down safely and the catch team was in place and I got away, would my life ever be the same? I hadn't thought of that in the planning stages. That was why the guys at the CIA were so good at what they did—they only thought about the mission. Was it training and confidence in their skills, or was it something else that kept them from talking about the rest of their lives? For them, the rest of their lives was the next mission, not a normal life. I don't know how they did it. For me, it was different, "One and done," as the expression goes. Still, their credo and bravado had enveloped me, and I was caught up in it.

The catch team—were they down there? Were they homing in on my signal? The flashing amber light of the transmitter was reassuring. I had taken it from my briefcase and strapped it to my forearm before I jumped, activating it only after the parachute was open. It was doing what it was supposed to be doing, just as I was doing what I was supposed to be doing, heading down through the night. Had the catch team picked up my signal yet? Were they moving toward me?

Through the clouds, I looked for the silver ribbons of water below but could see nothing. The clouds were too dense directly below me, but to the west, I could see them breaking up. When I came through the clouds, if I couldn't see the open fields, the edge of the water would be my target. Better to be a little wet than skewered at the top of a spruce. If the clouds masked the moonlight and everything was as dark as my black suit, I still might have time for a fast novena.

I watched the clouds as I approached them from above. They looked soft, yet thick and full, as if they could support me. There was no sound except for the rushing air as I descended through it. As I got closer to the clouds, I instinctively pulled my legs up to my chest, anticipating a landing. Silly and contrary to all reason, but nonetheless real. Just before I entered the clouds, I saw a shooting star in the late autumn sky—a lucky omen!

The clouds were wet—not like a bath, but like a cold steam room. It was a strange sensation being bathed in this mist while descending through the clouds in the dark. Not unpleasant, but not something to do again soon, if ever. As I moved through the clouds, the mist became heavier. I knew I was coming out of the clouds before I did because I could feel the raindrops. There was that "what the fuck" moment when I thought of myself as a raindrop. It passed when I came through the clouds.

I had thought parachuting in the rain would be like walking in the rain with the canopy of the chute above me acting like a huge umbrella. Not the case. I got wet, not from above but from below and from the sides. The parachute must have caused the air to swirl, and with it, the rain. I could barely see the river, but at least I could make it out. I had anticipated this and had been looking down into the dark the whole way to avoid losing my night vision.

A sliver of moonlight broke through the clouds. The storm was breaking, and the clouds above me were moving fast from the west. The wind pushed me and the clouds rapidly to the east. Farther east put me into an area with less forest. Too far, and I would be in danger of landing in a populated area and perhaps missing my catch team. The open area of pastureland or the clear-cut timber wasn't visible yet, but I knew it was there.

When I could see the ground, "clear cut" was really not an adequate description. There were a lot of fallen trees, branches, and stumps visible even from the altitude I was descending from. The landing, avoiding an injury, getting skewered on one of the few trees, now became worries. "Focus on doing what's right, not what can go wrong," I told myself.

There were still no sounds other than the rushing of air, but I started to pick up smells of planet earth. I would have thought the first smells would be of pine and spruce and fir, the trees that dominated the forests of the Pacific Northwest, but they weren't. It was rain. How could that be? Rain is just water. Water is a tasteless, colorless, odorless liquid—that's basic Chemistry 101. Hell, I had known that before I went to school. But let me tell you, suspended in the air a couple of thousand feet above the ground, rain had a smell. It wasn't the clean smell of summer rain. It wasn't the fearful smell of rain in a hurricane. I can't describe what it was, only what it wasn't, but for sure, it was pure, unadulterated rain.

Next came the smells of the forest. The evergreens dominated, and then the smell of grass, fresh cut. Not that of a suburban lawn, but the dustier smell of grass and hay in the loft of a barn, only wetter. Closer to the ground, earth and dirt took over my nose. Was it the wish to have my feet once again firmly planted where they were supposed to be? Was it the desire that once my feet touched the ground, the steps I would be taking would be the final steps in this adventure that had started six months ago? Whatever the reason, the dirt smelled great.

The parachute moved toward the open land east of the water. About one hundred feet above ground, everything went completely black. The instructors at jump school had said this would happen. The ground and everything around me was invisible. This was my signal the ground was near and I had to tug the lines of the chute to get a little lift and slow my descent. My legs came up into the landing position in anticipation of hitting the ground.

The landing was soft, the rain-soaked earth a cushion compared to the hard red clay of Georgia. Landing without incident, I gathered the chute and balled it up, covering it with the reserve chute pack to make it difficult to see. I took the radio transmitter off my wrist, noted it was still flashing amber, and placed it with the crumpled parachute. The knapsack came next, and after making sure it was still intact and contained the money, I hoisted it on my back and set off toward the wood line to await the arrival of the catch team. The catch team could focus on the transmitter without me attached to it. Watching from the tree line, I could be sure those who showed up focused on the transmitter and didn't arrive with guns and a pack of barking dogs. If they were on my side, they would be stealthy. I wanted to be extracted to safety, put on a plane, and sent home. I didn't want to be "taken out." A little apprehensive, perhaps. A little paranoid, definitely. The FAA person wanting to speak with me in Seattle had unnerved me and heightened my sense of caution. So, leaving the radio transmitter where I wasn't gave me some of the advantage back. I wanted to see the people who were coming to get me. They should be civilians, civilians who didn't look anything like me. We had agreed on a password like the old spy movies, but, more importantly, I wanted to see how they behaved when I wasn't with the tracking device.

Waiting in the dark, my senses had never been so alive. In the absence of city lights, the stars were bright against the darkness of the heavens. The night air was filled with the smells of the forest, especially the comforting smell of pine and spruce. Why was it so comforting? Was it because it was a smell associated with the holidays and fond memories of family and hearth? Or was it something more primal? Something ingrained in the genes millennia ago? I caught a whiff of musk. Was there a forest creature watching me as I waited?

The sounds were not intense, but my ears were sensitive to everything around me, sounds unfamiliar to me. Branches moving in the wind. Raindrops falling from the trees. A barn owl hooting in the distance.

I was more aware of my own body than I could ever remember. Respiration had returned to normal, but I was aware of every breath I took, paying attention to the exchange of cold air for warm. Taking in air I couldn't see, yet exhaling mist-filled air. Eye movements were silent, but I felt them. When I looked at the sky, I thought I felt my pupils constricting in the moonlight. As time passed, my heart beating and blood pumping through my arteries became louder. Could anyone else hear it?

There were four teams on the ground to pick me up. With overlapping sectors, the four teams could cover a wide area. All I had to do was land somewhere within a circle with a radius of five miles, and they would find me. There was also a search grid to follow if my signal didn't show up. If they didn't show up in an hour, I was to start moving north, back where I had come from, the route I would be least expected to take.

Two teams showed up within fifteen minutes. The dead-reckoning jump had been pretty close to the mark. They found the tracking device after a short search. There were no machine guns apparent, and there were no dogs. They huddled around, trying to figure their next step. There was no plan for my not being with the device. They looked legitimate.

I challenged them from the woods. "I'm glad I don't see any guns or dogs."

They all spun to the direction of my voice.

"Guns and dogs scare me, especially in the woods at night after I just dropped out of the sky." "Dropped out of the sky," was the code word.

A voice called out, "We don't like guns at night in the woods either. Let's get you out of here."

Emerging from my hiding place in the woods, I approached them. There were four of them, all in dark clothes and no with lights of any kind. As I got closer, I could see that none of them looked like me. All were shorter; one was Hispanic and one black. One of the dark shapes stepped forward as I approached. He extended his hand, I thought to congratulate me. "The knapsack." It wasn't a greeting or a question; it was a demand. I handed him the knapsack.

He examined the bag to make sure the money was inside and passed it to the black guy, asking him to count it. He turned to me. "We honestly didn't think you'd make it. We had prepared for both retrieval and recovery. Where's your parachute?"

"Next to the radio beacon, covered with the reserve chute. What's the difference between retrieval and recovery?"

He motioned one of the team to retrieve the chutes and indicated I should follow him. "Retrieval is what we're doing now. Recovery is when we come in and pick up the body. We don't like that. The body bag takes up a lot of room in the Suburban. It's more comfortable when you can sit."

We moved across the field and into the woods until we came to a dirt road. A dark Chevy Suburban C-10 had been pulled off the road and parked. The guy who had been asked to count the money was at the back of the C-10. The rear door was open, with piles of money across the cargo area.

"Four packages are missing—eight thousand dollars," he said to the guy with me, probably the team leader.

"You didn't keep any walk-around money, did you? The money is marked, and in spite of looking used and dirty, all the bills are sequential. It'll be easy to trace them."

"No, I didn't take any samples. If there's money missing, it either never made it into the bag or fell out on the way down."

The parachutes and the knapsack were put in the rear area, next to several rifle cases. Room was made for me in the backseat, where I was pushed to the middle by two of the other team members, one entering behind me and the other from the other side. I was handed a hunting jacket and hat, similar to, but not identical to, the ones the other guys were wearing. The driver and the man who had been doing the talking sat in the front.

The talker turned to me. "Why all the drama with hiding in the trees?"

"I wanted to be sure it was you and not some farmer or hunter citizen out for a late-night walk."

"Okay, that's good to hear. I'll be sure to pass it along." The sarcasm overpowered me. I was the one at risk. I had jumped out of the airplane while he waited on the ground.

"Here's a quick debriefing. There will be no discussion. It appears you got away clean. There were planes following the flight, but they weren't in a position to see you jump. They stayed with the flight for another three minutes before they circled around and tried to spot you. The pilot probably reported that he thought you jumped. They probably asked him to confirm before they turned the catch planes around to look for you. They're still circling around, and it doesn't look like they have a clue."

"Good."

"Right. We have a change of clothes for you. We're going to stop farther up the road to allow you to change. Your old clothes, including the sunglasses, will be burned with the money. Then we'll drive to Portland, where we'll board a private jet to Washington. In Washington, you're on your own. It's stating the obvious, but don't talk to anyone about this. There will be a lot of national press coverage. Do not collect newspapers or clip articles. If you must read about this, read one paper at a time and then throw it away before getting another. I shouldn't have to tell you to buy your papers at different places. If the authorities somehow manage to put you on a suspect list, we'll bring you in."

That was it. He turned to the front of the Suburban, looking into the night. I had completed my side of the contract. Medical school, the fellowship, my stipend, and my summer jobs with the government were the only physical reminders I would have. How long would the memories last?

He turned in his seat again, looking over his shoulder at me. "Oh, by the way, I had my man check the reserve chute for the missing money. Can't be too careful! The reserve chute you used was a dummy. It was all sewn up; the jump school used it to demo how to pull a rip cord."

Chapter 16

I settled into a forward-facing seat in the cabin. The plane was a Falcon 20, a French-made aircraft, tiny compared to the 727 but much more elegant. Set up to accommodate eight passengers, there were four plush seats, two facing forward and two facing rear on opposite sides of the tiny aisle. Behind these were two couches along the sides, facing each other. In front, by the pilots, was a small galley with snacks and soft drinks. There was no alcohol onboard.

The team leader offered me an apple juice, which I readily accepted. The plane rushed down the runway. As it lifted off, I felt as if it were going straight up, like the start of a roller coaster ride with a lot of noise, jet engines sucking air through the turbines and air rushing over the wings to lift us into the sky. I looked out the window, and the lights of Portland were behind us at a strange angle, confirming my sensation of a steep ascent. The plane leveled out, and the noise lessened. The interior lights had been turned off for takeoff and weren't turned back on—just the tiny lights on the floor, illuminating the aisle. After I finished my apple juice, I pushed the button to recline my seat and closed my eyes.

The mission was over. I had done it! Two thoughts, one terribly arrogant and one terribly wrong. The arrogance was thinking I was the most important person on this mission, the irreplaceable one. I would be reminded many times in the future that cemeteries were full of irreplaceable people. No, I was merely the guy who had bought the ticket, passed the note, and jumped out of the airplane. The reality: I was only one of many. They could have done it without me. I could not have done it without them, any of them. All the planning, training, and meetings were vital. Just the team that picked me up tonight probably involved dozens of people, most of whom I never saw. The terribly wrong thought was thinking it was over. They had a big investment in me and wouldn't soon let me go.

In my arrogant naiveté, I fell asleep.

Activity around me woke me. The plane began its descent. I looked to my right wrist for my D. B. Cooper watch, which wasn't there anymore. "What time is it?"

"Almost 0630. ETA in Washington National at 0712. The sun should be up by then. Some information came in for you. A task force has been put together to find and capture you. The FBI is in charge." My heart rate accelerated. "They have a composite description of you that makes you between five feet ten inches and six feet." That wasn't very comforting. "The suspect is a man in his midforties with dark hair and eyes, almost black. But the coup is—and they are not sharing this information with the press—their man is left-handed."

I smiled at that.

"The FBI is being very smug and self-confident about the left-handed bit. They feel it'll be the big break in the case. Left-handed men are only about 5 to 7 percent of the population, so they feel they've already reduced the number of suspects by over 90 percent and are expecting an early capture."

I was really pleased at this.

"You have time to wash your hair again before we land."

The Falcon put down at Washington National Airport just after sunrise. We could have flown into Andrews, landing at about five in the morning, but there we would have stood out, having to pass muster as a civilian airplane on a military airbase. Landing at National, we were just one of many flights, private and commercial, trying to get on the ground as soon as possible after the airport opened in the morning.

I was supposed to make my way back to Connecticut on my own, passing myself off as a college student or young professional heading for a Thanksgiving dinner somewhere. The snow that had grounded the flights to New York had fallen as far south as Washington. The snowfall was just a dusting by my standards, but travel north was at a standstill until road crews could clean up the mess. Before I left the plane, the team leader gave me a message from Allen, providing me with the address of a place to stay until I was able to travel.

Outside the private terminal, I grabbed a cab to Georgetown, then another to the address of an apartment building near DuPont Circle. I got the key from the building manager and let myself into the apartment. A quick look around confirmed I was the only occupant. Fresh linen was in the bedroom closet to make up the bed, and there were towels for the bathroom. I threw my bag on my freshly made bed and took a shower, washing my hair again. The color was almost back to normal, and there was no telltale dye on my white towel. I dressed and went out looking for a place to have breakfast.

The snow was still falling, one of the worst Thanksgiving storms the DC area had ever had—up to an inch was expected! Where I grew up in upstate New York, this storm would be considered a light flurry even if it occurred on May 1, as it did in 1962. Only the wind made the short walk uncomfortable. There was an open coffee shop on the ground floor of one of the new buildings on Massachusetts Avenue. It was almost empty because of the holiday.

Inside, my nose was bombarded with the smells of breakfast. Bacon and coffee dominated. I was hungry, having not eaten anything since yesterday noon. Without looking at the menu, I ordered pancakes, eggs, bacon, and biscuits, adding an orange juice and a coffee. I found a discarded copy of the *Washington Post*, or, as it was known then, the *Washington Post and Times Herald*. Waiting for my meal, I busied myself looking at the paper. There was nothing on the front page, and, after twenty minutes of reading during a casual, relaxed Thanksgiving breakfast, I realized there was nothing at all about the hijacking. It shouldn't have surprised me. This edition went to bed before midnight, just about the time things were developing on the West Coast. The afternoon edition of the *Washington Star* would probably have full coverage.

The front page was about the snowstorm in the Northeast. Snow would make my mother happy and put her in a good mood. She loved a light dusting of snow for the first holiday of the season. Said it got her into the Christmas spirit. With the blizzard, she'd be really happy.

I was grateful for the weekend by myself because I needed time to become comfortable with what I had just done. Needing more coffee, I grabbed my empty cup and the read newspaper and headed back up to the counter. As I put the newspaper back on the counter, I scanned the other papers lying about—the *New York Times* and a weekly rag published in Alexandria—there was nothing about the hijacking. I got another coffee and returned to my table to enjoy the winter wonderland view.

With nothing else to do, I stayed in the coffee shop until 10:30 a.m. If I went back to the apartment, I'd either pace all day or watch television, waiting for the local news at noon. If something happened overnight, it might be covered in the early local news broadcast. If it was of national importance, it would be covered on *The Today Show*. Once *Today* signed off, there would be no scheduled news until noon. I wanted to ease myself into the coverage, preferably with a newspaper, but that wasn't possible until later this afternoon.

After nursing a second coffee, I went back to the apartment and fell asleep, right through the noon news. I called my mom and dad around two thirty. Thanksgiving dinner was usually a four o'clock start, so they'd be sitting around the kitchen table getting ready. As she always did on holidays, she answered the phone cheerily with a holiday greeting. "Happy Thanksgiving."

"Happy Thanksgiving, Mom."

"Hi, sweetie. Oh, it's so good to hear your voice. We miss you. Oh, Johnny, you wouldn't believe what a wonderful Thanksgiving this is. We have snow. It started last night, and it's still snowing. Can you believe it? They say this might be a record for Thanksgiving."

"Yeah, I read about it in the paper this morning. They said you might get twenty-four inches."

"Dad, Uncle Jack, and Ted have been going out every hour to keep the driveway and sidewalk clean." Uncle Jack was one of two uncles I had, married to my mother's sister. They lived in Pennsylvania, and Thanksgiving with my parents had been a tradition for almost ten years. Ted was my little sister's boyfriend—had been for a couple of years now—and was considered a future son-in-law already.

Dad had always had a thing about shoveling the sidewalk. It had something to do with being afraid someone would fall on our unshoveled sidewalk and sue him. In the new house for five years now, he still had the same need to shovel even though there were no city sidewalks on his property—just the short walk from the driveway to the house.

My other sister and her husband-to-be, Dick, would be joining the family later in the day. Dick was a local boy who came from a large Irish family. She and Dick were learning the balancing act of splitting time between families on the holidays, families that both had longstanding traditions of being the center of holiday activity. With so much snow on the ground, he'd be tested today, with twenty miles of snow-covered road between the families.

"Do you think your old army job would have anything to do with that hijacking in California?"

Mom's question floored me.

If you are searching for an answer or trying to buy time, answer a question with a question. Stalling won't work with cops or wives, who suspect you've been drinking or cheating or both, but it might work with your mom long distance on the phone on Thanksgiving Day. "A hijacking in California?"

"Well, I saw the news this morning about a hijacking that took place in California, or out there someplace, and I know you said you used to work with the FAA sometimes. They said the FBI and the FAA were investigating it. I thought they might be the people trying to solve it. That would be so exciting."

"Mom, I don't think so, but I haven't talked to anyone since I got out. In fact, I've been so busy, even working today, I haven't heard about this. When did it happen?"

She tried to fill me in and had most of the details correct except for California. What it told me, though, was that it had caught her interest. Mom wasn't what you'd call a current events expert. In fact, she had no interest in current events. What news she did get was from the television. To have gotten her attention, the news must have been saturated with the hijacking.

I headed out for dinner about five o'clock. Food wasn't what I hungered for. I was hungry to see what the *Washington Star* had to say about the hijacking. The streets were as deserted in the evening as they'd been in the morning. I had to walk around a bit, first to find an evening paper and then a place to eat. Not many choices for Thanksgiving, but I found a place that advertised Thai food. I'd never had Thai.

If I had been under suspicion, being watched, I'm sure my reaction when I saw the composite sketch on the front page would have sealed my guilt. My arm stopped with the paper halfway up. The paper had two artist's sketches on the front page above the fold, one with sunglasses and the other without. The witnesses described me as more gaunt than I had become during my self-imposed weight loss program. Nonetheless, I knew it was me and was shocked. The shock lasted only a second or two, but to me it seemed an eternity. I couldn't move the paper. Then my conversation with my mom flashed through my head. I was sure these pictures were on television, and she hadn't said anything. The fact that she hadn't was the force I needed to unlock my arm at half retrieve and finish picking up the paper. If my mother thought the hijacker looked like me, she would have said something. She didn't, so I felt safe. Of course, mom hadn't seen the gaunt me. My food came, and I occupied myself with eating, now a purposeful act of ungaunting.

After ten minutes, I picked up the paper and started reading. The newspaper articles were very complete, considering less than twenty-four hours had passed. Either the reporters were very good or the authorities wanted the information out in the public domain—probably both. They were too far to the west in their estimate of my drop area. In our planning, we anticipated a response that would try to intercept me when I landed, but we also figured they would be expecting me to jump farther into the flight, south of the dense forests and severe terrain in Oregon. The authorities just hadn't expected me to jump as soon as I did. There was no report of a group of men in a Chevy Suburban fleeing the scene or a suspicious private jet leaving Portland. Best of all, there was no mention of a left-handed suspect.

There was a special holiday table set up to the side of the cashier, with paper cutouts taped to the wall depicting turkeys and Pilgrims. A paper banner declaring Happy Thanksgiving ran from one end of the table to the other. Seemed out of place in a Thai place, and I hadn't noticed it earlier. Now, the visual impact triggered thoughts of Thanksgivings past. I felt my mood changing. I felt thankful. I had the holiday spirit.

Of course, everyone knows the rest of the story. No trace of me, or the money, was ever found until some of it showed up on the bank of the Columbia River ten years later. Everyone involved in the investigation got excited thinking they had a new clue. They'd been wrong about where I exited the airplane and wrong on where I landed. When they found the money on the Columbia, it seemed to reinforce their initial error. All sorts of experts came forward, postulating I must have landed in one of the tributaries of the Columbia and the money had drifted down. There is no doubt the packets of money fell out of the knapsack when the parachute deployed. The force of the parachute opening was significant and tugged hard at the cord around my waist. Given the drift and the geometry of the jump, coupled with the wind and rain that night, the money could have gone anywhere.

Only three of the four lost packets of ransom money, two thousand dollars each, with two hundred dollars missing, were found. The rest of the money was never found because it was ashes within twenty-four hours of my jumping out of the plane.

They never found me because the government people who were looking for me were misled by the government people who had helped me escape.

My job in the 902nd MI Group had finally become a James Bond experience—exciting, dangerous, and full of intrigue. I had done something good for my country, and, viewing it through the retrospectroscope, I had enjoyed it. I had also earned admission and enough money to go to medical school and was ready to put all of this behind me. Or so I thought.

Chapter 17

∗ ∗ ∗

When I awoke Friday morning, I was ravenous. After a month of watching what I ate, the gorging yesterday must have triggered that ancient survival piece of DNA, telling the rest of my body the lean times were over and the time of plenty had returned. Today, I was as anxious to see a plate of breakfast as I was to see the newspapers. The journalists had had time to collect information and analyze the story, and it would be interesting to see what they had to say. One thing for sure: they hadn't captured the hijacker yet.

The temperature was still hovering around the freezing mark, but the snow was gone except in those places in shadows. The area around DuPont Circle was more alive today, with more choices open to me for breakfast. I found a diner and went inside, assuring myself first there were papers on the counter. I grabbed a *Post* and headed for a table. A happy waitress was at my table right away, pouring coffee without either of us asking. "What can I get for you this morning?"

I smiled, turning to the almost-empty room, and jokingly asked, "I don't need a reservation this morning, do I?"

She got it and smiled back. "No. This is my first year here, but they tell me the Friday after Thanksgiving is the least busy day of the year, especially for breakfast."

"There aren't many people working, and with the folks who go home to celebrate..." I added, trying to add a reason to her explanation.

"Yeah, that's part of it."

Again, I chose my breakfast, heavy on those items that were considered excess calories, including biscuits, gravy, and pancakes. I added cream and sugar to my coffee and grabbed the *Post*. Most of the front page was about the hijacking, but none of the articles had any more information than yesterday afternoon. There was speculation the hijacker was probably dead, and efforts now were to recover the body and retrieve the money. While there was a detailed description of the hijacker, as well as the reprinting of the artist's sketch, there was no mention that the search was limited to a left-hander.

It looked as if I had gotten away with it. A calm settled in, but I was still troubled by the comment made by the catch team leader, who said they were surprised I had survived the jump. I was grateful I didn't know that as I was preparing for the jump because I probably would have tried to back off the mission. I didn't want to think about the consequences of such a move on the CIA. These were pretty serious guys.

Enough about the past and the "shoulda, coulda, woulda" thinking. It was over and behind me. Time to think about the future—my next four years in medical school. Get back to New Haven and dive in. Dive in! A funny choice of words for a guy who had just dived out of an airplane.

The hijacking shared the front page with the weather. The storm had crippled the Northeast. While Washington was relatively clear and the paper was reporting cabs and buses were getting people around, there were stories about deep snow still blocking roads north of Philadelphia. There was no sense trying to get back to New Haven today. I'd stay put and give them another day to get things cleared out.

I spent the rest of the day doing a lot of nothing. I walked a lot, feeling the tension of the past months leaving my body with every step. When I was preparing for the hijacking, I knew the tension was building within me; it was to be expected. But the training and preparing for the unknown, together with getting into the routine of school again, had built thin layers of tension. I was just now realizing how many of these layers there were as I walked them off. I forced myself to eat lunch and dinner, not being hungry for either. Lots of carbs for both. I could feel my cheeks starting to puff up.

In spite of spending all day outside, walking in the cold of Washington, I felt well rested, had caught up on all the news, and didn't want to spend another night alone in the apartment. I needed a night out.

In my Pentagon days, a night out meant heading into the District, which really meant going to Georgetown. While some would argue whether it was in fact the District, it was the center of nightlife for the young adults, particularly those of college age. Tonight, I didn't feel like being with college students. Instead, I felt like being among the junior government employees who hung around the Hawk and Dove on Pennsylvania Avenue, behind the Capitol.

The Hawk and Dove was home to Washington's politicians, junior politicians, and politician wannabes. The Capitol was nearby, as well as office buildings that were home to the Senate and the House. After work, it was a place where these workers congregated and drew others from government offices farther away. It was always interesting to go there. When someone walked in the door, those at the long oak bar would look to see if it was a person of interest. There was always an early trip to the men's or ladies room in the back to see who might be seated at the tables or booths. Everyone at the Hawk and Dove was on the make, not necessarily for a bedmate for the night but sometimes for a career-advancing connection.

Chapter 18

When I walked in, it was no different. Most of the people at the bar stopped drinking, talking, or smoking and looked up. Content or disappointed that I was a nobody, they returned to what had been making them happy before. The front of the Hawk and Dove was all glass, the bar up front, off to the right. Beyond, there were booths where people wanting to be seen could be seen and people wanting to see people could see people. For those not interested in the spotlight, there were tables to the rear where a meal could be enjoyed in private.

I surrendered my coat to the coat-check girl and went to the bar, where I had no trouble getting the attention of the bartender. The crowd was light. When asked if I had a beer preference, I shrugged indifference. The beer was delivered and placed on a coaster with a flourish. I lit up a Pall Mall, and, with the smoke in one hand and the beer in the other, started people watching like everyone else, including a look over every time the door opened.

Unlike everyone else, I wouldn't recognize a political celebrity unless it was Nixon. When ladies came in, I did spend extra time watching them take their coats off. Even with bulky sweaters, women can't hide a nice chest when taking off a coat. They tend to thrust their chest forward when taking their arms out of the sleeves.

Three ladies about my age came in. The patrons at the bar took a quick look and then returned to drinks and conversation. Not me. I watched the coat-taking-off process. One of the young ladies caught me watching and rather than turn away or minimize the chest thrust, she faced me and threw her chest out with a smile. I caught both the thrust and the smile and raised my glass in a toast. Grabbing her purse, she said something to the others and then came straight to the bar.

"What were you toasting?" she asked.

"What makes you think I was toasting?" Always answer an uncomfortable question with another question.

She moved closer, thigh pushing against my knee. "Oh, I just thought maybe you liked what you saw and toasted me."

Now, I've never been what anyone would consider a ladies' man. Not knowing what to say, I had always felt awkward around them. Well, I knew what I wanted to say, but I could never speak without sounding like an idiot. So I generally kept my mouth shut. Women like to talk and I didn't talk, so the ladies usually moved on. Not so tonight. Maybe I was emboldened by my recent adventure, or maybe the lady was special, but I felt playful.

"I liked the way you took off your coat. First, you thrust one arm, and then you thrust the other."

She moved her thigh from my knee and came closer. Her right breast brushed against my arm as she put her purse on the bar.

"So, you like my arms," she said, brushing her breast against me again as she moved back into the thigh-against-knee position. "Buy me a drink, and we can talk about my…arms."

Ordering a Merlot, I got up to offer the seat.

But she gently pushed me back. "Thanks, but I'm comfortable right here," she said as she shifted just a little so my knee was more straight on, if you get my drift. "How about you? Are you comfortable?" she said as she did a little grind of her crotch against my knee.

"I'm really quite comfortable, but I hope you don't change your mind about the seat and ask me to stand up."

"Good. Now let's talk about my…arms. What do you like best?"

"Well, I really can't see much of them because of the bulky cardigan sweater, but I do like the way they stick out from your body. They don't just hang there like a lot of arms do."

"I like the way they stick out too," she said, doing a little adjustment on my knee. "But arms are supposed to stick out. It's not until later in life they start to droop." She handed me her wine glass and slid one arm, then the other, out of the cardigan. "There. Now you can really see my arms a lot better." She was wearing a long-sleeved, white turtleneck shirt, the perfect complement to the sweater, and looked fine without the sweater. The turtleneck wasn't tight, but it wasn't loose either. It was tight across the neck, shoulders, and chest but hung baggy from the breasts down. Her breasts were full, with just a bit of separation and the hint of nipples straining against the fabric.

"You're right. I can see your arms so much better now. With the sweater on, I didn't realize how big they were. Do you work out?"

"Yes. Lately, I've been working out by myself, but I do so much better with a partner."

"Partners are so much better. I'm Jonathan, by the way."

"And I'm Brooke with an *e*. And now that we know each other so well, Jonathan, I think I can tell you that I'm very horny and I want to get laid tonight."

"Does horny have an *e* in it? Doesn't matter, Brooke with an *e*; I'm horny too."

Was her name really Brooke, or was that just a name she used for a pickup at a bar? I used DB when I was hijacking airplanes.

Brooke had the most fantastic blue eyes, the blue that God seems to have reserved for the Irish. The predominant blue was Carolina blue, named for both the sky and the home-team jerseys of the athletes at the University of North Carolina. Her eyes also had the blues of the waters of Bermuda—not just one blue, the full range of blues like those seen from the outside bar at the Pompano Beach Club. Then there were some flecks that tossed around light, be it sunlight, moonlight, or candlelight. The effect was the same, just dazzling. Eyes like these always prompted the question, "Your eyes are fantastic. Are those your real eyes, or are they contacts?" A silly question. Kind of like asking, "Your tits are great. Are they real?" It didn't make any difference with either; the effect was the same—they got your attention, and you could look at them all day without getting tired.

Brooke was about five feet three inches with long brown, almost auburn, hair. I guess that meant she had auburn highlights. She had a beautiful face, but, more important, she had a confidence about her. She was not a woman who shrank away. She was an equal; she took it to me. Well, equal is taking a lot more credit than I deserve. She was the pursuer that night, and I was glad of it.

"I have to ask you a favor," she said, leaning a little closer. "Will you give me a kiss? Nothing passionate, and not a peck on the cheek. Just a gentle kiss on the lips; no tongue. I want to feel how warm and soft your lips are."

I must have looked puzzled. We had been talking about having sex, and now she wanted me to back down and give her a gentle kiss.

"It may sound silly, but I want to know about your lips. We could leave now and go and have wonderful sex, but that's just sex. I also like the foreplay, the kissing and stroking. If your lips are hard or cold, we'll just have quick sex and I'm sure it'll be good, but if your lips are soft and warm like they look, we'll have a wonderful experience."

I leaned forward and looked at her face. She truly was a beautiful woman. I brushed a strand of hair that was falling over her face, held it to her cheek, and kissed her gently. A kiss as if we were longtime lovers and had just agreed where to go for dinner, a couple in love, nothing sensuous to the casual observer. As I was about to break it off, she flicked her tongue across my lips. It startled me. She smiled when she saw she had surprised me. "Surprise! I didn't say I wouldn't slip a tongue in there. That was a little reward for an excellent kiss."

"The kiss was okay?"

"It was excellent. That's better than okay. Let's get out of here, and I'll let you put those lips and tongue to good use."

"I don't have a place to go. I'm staying with a friend."

She kissed me again, probably just to shut me up, because I was breaking the spell even for me.

"We have two rooms at the Shoreham. You don't think I'd go off to the apartment of some guy I just met, do you? We have a plan that keeps us safe. The first one back gets her choice of room. Second one back gets the other. If one comes back alone, one of the guys is going to have a dream come true."

"You are something, aren't you? Let me finish my drink, have a cigarette, and calm down a bit, if you get my drift, and then we can grab a cab. Go over and talk to your girlfriends for a few minutes; it'll help me calm down quicker."

She smiled at my embarrassment and need to stay seated. She was anything but cooperative. She pushed gently against my knee. "But I want to leave now," she said, playfully pouting, handing me her sweater. "Carry this over to our coats, please. I don't want you to calm down."

I did as instructed, self-conscious and with a little artificial limp. There was a cab at the curb. She told the driver to go to the Shoreham. Getting in, I managed to slide my still-mostly-erect dick into a more comfortable position in my boxers.

During the ride to the hotel, Brooke ran her hand on the inside of my thigh. I thought it was a good move, so I returned the favor. Neither of us went for third base, both content to keep the other interested.

"So, Brooke with an *e*, where are you from, and what brings you to Washington?"

She told me she was originally from Nova Scotia, had gone to nursing school in Chicago, and was now working for a pharmaceutical company in Philadelphia, working as something called a clinical nurse associate.

I nodded knowingly and said, "That's nice." I had no idea what that meant and didn't care because as she was talking, her hand was sliding farther up my thigh. I again returned the favor.

"Yes, that is nice." She shifted, separating her knees a little. We were having one conversation about two different topics, one about what she did and one about what we were doing. As I shifted my legs to relieve the building pressure, she explained she was involved in the clinical studies necessary to get drugs approved. She visited doctors' offices on the East Coast, checking records and making sure the files were in order. She leaned into me as she finished talking. "It's really not that hard. What do you think?"

"I think it's hard enough."

She continued, explaining the other two women worked for the same company and were also not American, both being from England. Having no interest in the US holiday, they had decided to descend on the American Capital and party for the weekend. They were new to Philadelphia and didn't want to risk partying where they might be known, feeling it might be bad for their careers.

I paid the driver in front of the Shoreham. The entrance was just as impressive as when I had last been there as a twelve-year-old with my family. Chilly November was more comfortable than hot, humid August. The doorman smiled and welcomed us. I had to pause in the lobby area to take in the truly magnificent view. The large lobby with the atrium was even grander than I had remembered. Comfortable chairs and couches were set about in multiple conversation groupings. Ferns, flowers, and large potted plants added to the welcoming feeling. Some Christmas decorations were up already and added a festive air.

Brooke led the way to the elevator bank. Two other couples got on when the car came. Brooke pushed the button for the eleventh floor and settled back, leaning into me. I was in the corner with my left side to the wall. She reached around with her left hand, hidden by both of our bodies, and started rubbing me. It wasn't an attempt to get me off; just a reminder of what was to come. The elevator stopped at our floor first. Had we had to stay on through many more additional stops, I think would have been the first to get off.

Brooke stepped forward, looking over her shoulder with an "I'm in complete control" look, and said, "This is where we get off." The double meaning was so obvious I had to look away from the others in the car, sure they knew what she meant. As we walked down the corridor, she took my arm. She was continuing the foreplay started at the bar. She rubbed her breast against my arm—first the side, and then, when we got to the door, she turned such that my arm brushed across the nipple. She still had her coat on, so I felt nothing but the vague shapes; I'm sure she found it more pleasant. The move had an effect on my mind, sending needles of anticipation through me. Once in the room, she took her coat off. She stood in front of me, kissed me hard, and pulled my coat back, pinning my arms in the sleeves behind me.

"I'll be right back," she said going into the bathroom. "Don't start without me."

I sat on the bed waiting, looking around. The room wasn't as grand as the lobby area. Of course, I didn't have much of a history in hotels to make any kind of comparison.

Brooke came out of the bathroom. I had thought she'd do the "change into something more comfortable" bit, but she still had on the same clothes. Her turtleneck was now outside her slacks, but that was all that had changed. She sat next to me on the bed. "Miss me?" she asked as she wiggled closer and kissed me. She had brushed her teeth. Tasted like Ipana, the same brand I used.

"Yeah, I did" was the correct response. She was going to get all the correct responses tonight. She leaned back, stretching out on the bed, taking me with her. She was on her back. She had one arm around my neck, and the other was spread out on the bed. She pulled me closer, and we kissed again. Her lips parted easily, taking my tongue. She started squirming and moaning immediately, moving to roll me on top of her.

The rest of the night was a blur of squirming and moaning. When we were both sated, she got up, went to the bathroom, and brushed her teeth again. She crawled back into bed, gave me an air kiss, and was immediately asleep. I lay there for two or three minutes, not doing much more than catching my breath before I rolled over and fell asleep.

The next morning we made love again and then showered together. It was playful and erotic, with neither of us expecting anything more. I combed my hair without drying it with a towel. I didn't want to answer any awkward questions should there still be residual dye. A kiss at the door, a note from her with a phone number, and I was gone. We promised to stay in touch.

Chapter 19

*　*　*

I returned to New Haven on Saturday, taking a regional train into New York's Penn Station and then going across town to Grand Central to take another regional to New Haven. The Javelin was in the apartment parking lot, and I spent the rest of Saturday digging it out.

Nothing happened with Allen for most of that first year in school until he showed up one morning in early April during my breakfast in the cafeteria. Cordial, even friendly with a big smile, he shook my hand and sat down without asking or being invited. He filled me in on a few details of the investigation.

The hijacking was still being handled by the FBI, and they were nowhere close to the truth, partly because they were blindly following the evidence suggesting a left-handed hijacker. There had been a couple of unsuccessful copycat hijackings that ended poorly for the hijackers, death being their fate. This further convinced the FBI that I hadn't survived the jump either. We enjoyed a smile when Allen told me about a black clip-on tie found on the plane. The FBI must have been confused, having evidence of both a left-handed forehand knot and a Windsor knotted clip-on tie. Allen said they thought the tie had been left to deliberately confuse them. The mission had accomplished everything it set out to do. Everyone—the airlines, the government, and the public—now wanted to improve airplane security.

Except for that one visit from Allen, I led a typical life as a student, including time to go to Philadelphia and meet Brooke for a few weekends. The end of my first year found me near the top of my class. While others prepared for summer down time, I got ready for my first summer as a contractor for the CIA.

The job was in the bowels of some minor division of the State Department. I didn't realize it, but I had started my training in a very secret, formal, yet subtle CIA indoctrination program that would lead to me becoming an assassin.

Beginning with the Korean War, the CIA had become concerned the Soviets were using brainwashing as a weapon. How else could they explain how patriotic, captured American airmen denounced the United States and the Korean War? If the communists were using brainwashing as a weapon, the CIA wanted it too. They initiated a program called MKUltra to investigate and weaponize mind control for use by assassins. Dr. Sidney Gottlieb, a chemist who had joined the CIA in 1951, headed the program.

The government in general, and the CIA specifically, recognized the need for deniability for any covert action. The best deniability would be a covert agent not remembering anything he or she had done. Gottlieb got free hand, and his first experiment was a success. He hypnotized a young woman, instructed her to kill a sleeping woman, and told her she wouldn't remember any of it. She accomplished the task, albeit with an unloaded gun. Even when shown a movie of her pulling the trigger, she couldn't remember or believe she had done it. The initial experiment couldn't be repeated.

Gottlieb and his team of scientists moved on to drugs, including the use of LSD on CIA employees. The most notable subject, Frank Olson, plunged to his death from a ten-story building while on an LSD trip. Gottlieb moved his experiments to a more controlled location and patient population, shifting research to Vermont State Hospital, a psychiatric facility in Waterbury. Here, Dr. Robert Hyde, working for Gottlieb, treated institutionalized patients with metrazol, a drug known to cause convulsive seizures, and with shock therapy, sometimes in combination, in an attempt to erase memories. The experiments were successful in getting someone to kill but unsuccessful in erasing memory.

The program came to an end in 1975 when the Senate's Church Committee and the Rockefeller Report revealed that the CIA had been involved in several assassination attempts, including attempts on the life of Fidel Castro, and that in 1960, Gottlieb had personally been involved in a plan to assassinate Patrice Lumumba, the newly elected prime minister of the Congo.

This was the world I entered in the summer of 1972—a shadow operation to train assassins who wouldn't be a liability to the government if caught. Of course, I didn't know this, and I didn't know I was in a program, code name Enterprise. The CIA developed me differently from the Gottlieb program. If I didn't know anything that would tie back to the government, I couldn't tell anything.

I obviously had an adventurous streak, or I wouldn't have done the hijacking. But I also had discipline and a sense of direction. I had goals and knew right from wrong. This was where they got me. While they let all the other attributes sit on the back burner for a while, they attacked my sense of right and wrong. They gently led me into discussions that tested my sensitivities and started me down the slope where the ends always justify the means. The goal was to get me to where I could eventually see right and wrong in the same way they saw it, to where whatever I did was right as long as I eliminated a larger wrong.

After a three-day orientation program, the training started. They paired me with Frank, identified as another summer intern at the State Department. Frank was a nickname. He introduced himself as Walter Jackson but asked me to call him Frank. I don't know why and didn't ask. I just did. Frank looked more like a chemistry student. He was tall, with an athletic body going ovoid prematurely, and wore a sport shirt with a pocket protector. He told me he was a history graduate student from Georgetown interested in the Third Reich. I thought of myself as an amateur historian, but American history. While I tried to impress him with my knowledge of the Erie Canal and the Butterfield Express, he remained focused on the Reichstag Fire. He didn't care about American history and didn't engage in any discussion. As soon as I finished talking about anything American, he would continue his monologue about the Third Reich.

"Why all the interest in Germany?" I asked.

"Many people think of World War II as the worst tragedy to have ever taken place. They are wrong, dead wrong! Everything—and I repeat, everything— that led up to the start of World War II was the tragedy. Why? Because people watched it develop and ignored it. Some have argued that people and nations stood around and did nothing. I disagree. They ignored it as a conscious act. If they had acted differently, World War II could have been avoided and the millions who died and the millions more who suffered would have gone on to live productive lives. Can you imagine the state of the world today if the war hadn't happened? How the economies of the European nations and the United States could have been different? Just think of the impact Hitler had. If he hadn't become chancellor, think of how the world would have been different."

I took his bait and responded. "Isn't this one of those discussions that usually involves history majors in a bar after the fourth pitcher of beer? Isn't this where someone says the world would be different if Hitler had been killed in the trenches of World War I? Or someone says the United States would never have gotten out of the Depression if not for World War II?"

"No, those are asinine discussions. Hitler didn't have to die in World War I. Hitler didn't have to die. But there could've been events that took place that would've changed the course of history."

Over several weeks, Frank explained his position on Hitler and fed me with his ideas—a belief that small changes, short of assassination, make profound changes in the course of history. He began by stating the obvious. "Hitler became a problem with the Beer Hall Putsch in November of 1923. He attempted to overthrow the government, for Christ's sake. He should have been on someone's radar at that time. After all, it was only a few years after the end of the First World War. The Allies had supported a new government in Berlin, and this nobody comes in and tries to disable it. Sure, he got put in jail for treason. The world was tired and just put him away and forgot about him until it was too late."

"So you think he should have been executed then?"

"Why do amateurs always think killing is the solution? It doesn't have to be killing, but the solution has to be well thought out. Here's a what-if for you. What if the court decided Hitler should serve his time in solitary confinement? What if he didn't have Rudolph Hess as a cellmate? Could he have written *Mein Kampf* on his own? There are really no other documents he wrote that have stood out as significant. Hitler provided some thoughts and ideas, but Hess contributed a lot to getting those thoughts into the message Hitler wanted."

"If Hess was the brains behind the Third Reich, how come he wasn't in charge?"

"Don't interrupt. Your ignorance is getting in the way of your understanding."

"Jawohl, Mein Fuhrer," I said mockingly.

His look told me he didn't appreciate it.

"What if Hitler had someone else as a cellmate? Someone not as malleable as Hess? What if that guy said, 'Hey, Adolph. I don't think you can get away with blaming everything on the Jews. How about the Italians? Or how about the Americans? Germany might have won the war if they hadn't gotten involved at the last minute and tipped the scales.' Without Hess as a cellmate, would he have risen to such power?"

"Yeah, I can see your point."

Frank felt the German government had dropped the ball. They could have put a spy in the cell with Hitler, assisting him with the book but reporting everything back to the authorities. They could have retried him for the things he said in *Mein Kampf* and put him away for a long time. Little things like that could have changed the course of history if someone had been thinking.

"What if Heinrich Himmler had been successful in his attempts to breed pure white chickens and had become the chicken king of Europe? Would he have been receptive to Hitler's message for the Third Reich? He would have been a success and may have seen Hitler as a threat to his chicken business. Again, you must ask if Hitler would have been as successful without Himmler at his side. Would the Final Solution have gotten off the ground without him, or with someone else? Those little changes could have been orchestrated by someone or something if they had been paying attention and thinking ahead. The whole Nazi thing may have fizzled out in the early 1930s." Frank had made his point, and I acknowledged it.

Frank admitted it would have been very difficult, not impossible, to predict the havoc Hitler was capable of early in his career. But he even offered some what-if scenarios after Hitler rose to power, none of which involved assassination but all of which involved manipulating events and opinions that could have changed history.

Hitler had something other than a normal relationship with his niece Angela Raubal. After she became involved with a young man, Angela was found dead in Hitler's apartment as a result of a gunshot from Hitler's gun. The story at the time reported she committed suicide. Neither the police nor the press challenged this theory. Since then, some historians have argued Hitler was responsible for her death. If this information had made its way into the German press and been discussed in the manner that it would be today, there is little doubt it would have put a significant dent in Hitler's career, maybe even ending it.

Hitler never married. He claimed the country was his family, his wife, and his children. He felt as a single man, he had the hearts and minds of all German women. If he married, he speculated, he would be looked upon less favorably by them. Therefore, he and those around him kept his relationship with Eva Braun a secret. Again, an opportunity where someone with foresight could have done things that could have altered the course of history.

Frank was a masterful teacher, using bits of trivia to flavor pieces of history. He claimed all of his facts were accurate and supported by documentation. At the end of several weeks, he convinced me that small, seemingly insignificant, nonviolent acts could have altered Hitler's impact on history. It was all a setup. I had to be convinced before he moved on to the last offering in his what-if alternate history.

Hitler suffered from several afflictions, both real and imagined. He was a vegetarian and abstained from alcohol for reasons unknown. Frank speculated that he might have suffered from gout, known to be aggravated by both red meat and alcohol. There was a tremor in one of his arms that became more pronounced as the war went on. Hitler was also an abuser of drugs. It is well documented that his personal physician, Dr. Theodore Morell, injected him many times each day with various medications, including a mixture of amphetamines and barbiturates.

I made the mistake of interrupting Frank at this point. "I see where you're going with this. If someone got to Dr. Morell, this would be an opportunity to inject Hitler with something that would, how would you say, be incompatible with life."

Frank looked at me like a disappointed teacher. "West, you are just not getting it, are you? First, it would be difficult to get a physician to do that with that oath you guys take that starts with 'Above all, do no harm.' Second, if Hitler was poisoned, Morell would be the first person under suspicion, and it would cause more harm than good. Hitler would be venerated as a martyr. No, it would be better if Dr. Morrell gave him nothing, a placebo. Even better if Dr. Morrell didn't know he was giving him nothing."

"Aha. Someone, a third party, switches the medicine."

"Yes. Maybe Hitler doesn't get the amphetamines he needs to get through the day and starts acting crazy agitated. Or he doesn't get the barbiturates he needs to sleep at night, and it throws his whole system off. The High Command he surrounds himself with see the aberrant behavior and questions the way forward in something other than the silent manner they had been doing. Some of his staff had concerns about his ability to lead. This may have convinced more."

"That makes sense. Exposure is one person once removed from the activity, and Morell would be genuinely frantic," I said, starting to believe it.

"Yeah, it makes a lot of sense. As with anything, there is an element of risk. Hitler was thought by many to be suffering from bipolar disease. A review of the medications Morell gave him suggests some of the drugs aggravated the condition. There is the risk that removing the amphetamines would stabilize Hitler. But then you can always hope he would see he was doing wrong. Not likely, but certainly a justification for those seeking the high moral ground."

I had completed Frank's course. He had shown me multiple nonviolent ways to discretely and indirectly eliminate a threat someone posed to the harmony presumed to exist in this world. I didn't know it at the time, but this was a critical part of my recruitment by the CIA. For the hijacking, they had convinced me that doing harm for the greater good was acceptable, provided I felt the harm I did was less than the harm that would happen if I didn't act. Frank took this one step further, tapping into any future reservations I might have if my oath as a physician seemed in conflict with a task they assigned—sometimes placebos work. He masterfully used history to make the case after the fact. He set me up for the final stage of my indoctrination, which would convince me that when asked to do harm for the greater good, the request was made based on solid, irrefutable knowledge that there was no other way.

Frank was reassigned after a month. Before he left, we had lunch with his replacement. Frank finished first, made his farewells, and left me with the new guy. "So, you survived a week with der fuhrer?" he asked.

"It was more like a month, and I wouldn't call it surviving. I learned a lot."

"Did he get on his pulpit on the Reichstag Fire and how the world would look if someone had knocked off Hitler in World War I?"

"You might be confusing some of the historical facts. Frank did mention the Reichstag Fire, but I don't recall him trying to work it into his hypothesis."

"Whatever. You have my sympathies."

"None required. I enjoyed my time with Frank. He's brilliant and has an interesting look on history."

The new guy stopped beating up on Frank. I learned later the little discussion was my oral examination for Frank's course. I passed by defending him and his views.

The new guy continued my indoctrination. He got me interested in current affairs. As a member of the community known as scientists, I shared their lack of interest in most things nonscience. By working with me, he would make me more knowledgeable, if only in self-defense. He might start the day with "What do you think about the White Panthers bombing the CIA office?" If I didn't know, I'd have to read up on it or listen to his lecture. His lectures were intentionally boring. The only way to avoid them was to get up to speed so I could have a discussion and not listen to his monologue.

He didn't limit himself to domestic news. We discussed Vietnam. What would happen if we lost? What would happen if we won? Would Vietnam, divided into North and South, present us with the same problems as North and South Korea? East and West Germany? What about the UN sanctions against Israel? What do you think about the Gaza Strip problem? What do you think about Lebanon? What are we going to do about the Middle East? We need their oil, but we support the Israelis. A dilemma! What about the Chinese and their ICBMs?

In the years before the Internet, it was much more difficult to find information quickly. There were limited resources; books in the library were good for background but failed the test for up to date. Television and radio news only gave news in small, easily digestible sound bites. Newspapers and periodicals provided more depth. Fortunately for me, the State Department had a fourth source available.

The State Department provided a daily service that screened dozens of newspapers from around the country for news of interest to the business of the State Department. These articles were clipped, photocopied, and distributed throughout the building, usually twelve to fifteen sheets of paper with printing on both sides. These were a godsend and enabled me to get up to speed quickly. I enjoyed becoming a news junkie. The habit continued when I returned to New Haven. Without access to the news clippings, I focused on just three newspapers: the *New York Times*, the *Washington Post*, and the *Herald Tribune*. I found the *Herald* politically most neutral but continued with all to assure I didn't miss some nuance.

Chapter 20

B ack in New Haven for my second year, I settled into the familiar routine. Brooke and I got together every three or four weeks, either at her place or mine. Neither of us was ready for a serious relationship; she was deeply involved in her career and I in my studies. We would be polite when we got together, inquiring about each other's lives, but we would usually be in bed within fifteen minutes. At that time, it was good for us. Hormones urged us to mate. Having each other, we didn't spend time on the prowl trying to get laid, which left us time to pursue studies and careers.

I got home for both Thanksgiving and Christmas. The funk I had imposed on Mom had disappeared. Many of her friends stopped by for a drink or coffee and dessert. She regaled them about me and my accomplishments as an all-American and professional hockey player (it embarrassed me every time she mentioned this), my very secret and important job at the Pentagon (I cringed at this), and my soon-to-be medical career. Yes, all was well, and I seldom thought about the CIA except when the check came at the beginning of each month.

In late February, I went to my usual quiet table in the corner with my tray, books, and newspapers, prepared to eat and read in silence as I always did. Not so this morning; my usual table was occupied. Seeing the beard and longish hair, I didn't recognize him. As I turned toward another table, he said, "Jonathan, please join me."

Allen's voice quickened my pulse. "What the fuck!"

"Good to see you too, but I would expect something a bit more articulate from a Yale physician in training."

"Sorry; you caught me by surprise. I never expected to see you again." When we parted last year, I assumed we were both in the other's rearview mirror. Then the surprise turned to curiosity. "How did you know where to find me?" The words hadn't left my mouth when I knew the answer. Allen must have been watching me to know where I'd be at seven o'clock on a Tuesday morning. Not only where, but my favorite table. Shrugging one shoulder, he reached for his coffee.

Knowing he monitored me was bothersome. "How long have you been following me?"

"Let's just say we never stopped having an interest in you. Had to make sure our money was being well spent."

"You spent your money by having me jump out of an airplane. Remember? You're paying on the installment plan."

"I came to talk to you about some ideas for your summer job this year. We thought you might enjoy a change of scenery from New Haven."

"I haven't given it much thought. Too busy with school. Maybe I should take the summer off, relax. Go to the Cape and learn how to surf on Marconi Beach."

Allen smiled. "You have a contract to work for us during the summers. It might be a poor career choice to take the summer off. Consider what it would do to your financial situation without the income each month, not to mention what you'd do next year for tuition."

"If I may remind you, I jumped out of a fucking airplane for you guys. That was the deal, with the payment spread out to reduce the possibility that I would get caught with a lot of cash from doing a job for the CIA. I didn't jump out of the plane for one year's tuition and stipend." My voice had risen above the whisper we had been using.

"A contract is a contract, regardless of the fact that you think you completed all of your obligations by jumping out of the plane." The latter he said with a sense of irritation. "There are things we want you to become familiar with this summer." He paused to add emphasis. "And next summer, and the summer after that."

Then and only then did it strike me that the CIA had me for the rest of my life. That was the reason for the contract and the four-year payout. The summers were to train me. For what, I didn't know, but they had their hooks into me and wouldn't let go. They could have let me win big at Saratoga, or I could have been transferred to a real NIH predoctoral fellowship. None of that had happened.

"Are you my handler? Is that the correct term? Okay, handler, here's the story. I don't want to be in the CIA. I want to finish school and get on with my life."

"Johnny…"

"Jonathan!"

"Jonathan. When you did the jump, you didn't do it for the money or the tuition. You did it for the adventure and to help your country overcome the potential obstacles politicians could throw in the way of increased airport security. That's happened! We're years ahead because of the intervention you were part of."

The words struck home with me. I had committed to the hijacking before any discussion of money occurred. Oh, I liked the money and the guaranteed place in medical school, but he was right. Initially, the excitement and adventure attracted me. Yes, I had been moved by being part of something that could make a difference—a chance to play secret agent.

"I've been following the news, and the cooperation among everyone in improving airline security is impressive. Every time I read something about it, I experience a sense of pride. That being said, I still don't want to be in the CIA. I was a fool to take such a risk then, and I don't want to do anything like that again."

"If I can go out on a limb and tell you some things I shouldn't…"

I raised my eyebrows, tilted my head, and gave him my best "you're full of shit" look.

He stiffened at my reaction and continued. "All right, I never go out on a limb. I'm prepared to lay a lot of things on the table for you today, and I have authorization to do so. You're a bright young man with a good sense of what's right. You did a good job during the hijacking, and Frank gave you the highest marks possible as a patriot. He also gave you pretty good marks as a quick-study historian."

Allen continued. "Jonathan, you already understand there are times when well-intentioned men and women help the decision makers make the right decisions. We do this by being vigilant, collecting information, and having resources that help us see problems before they develop. This puts us in a position to intervene, preferably indirectly. Directly, if there is no other choice. We like to do things at a distance and with deniability. All of this requires the use of different assets, from multiple backgrounds and with multiple skill sets. Yes, we have the secret-agent types, but there are also accountants, farmers, college professors, foreign nationals, and yes, physicians. Name it, and we have someone like that working for us. You've even met a few. The hair dresser in Fredericksburg and the eye doctor who fitted you for contact lenses were contractors."

"What you say is true. I believe in what you do. As a citizen of this great country, I am grateful there are people like you and yours out there doing what you do. The point is, I don't want to be a CIA doctor, spending four years of my life training to be a physician and then use my skills stitching up CIA spies. If the truth be known, I can't see myself yet as a physician, treating people, making split-second life-and-death decisions, telling a young family their mother died as a result of injuries from a drunk driver. There, I've said it. I'm not sure I want to be a doctor, and I don't want to be in the CIA."

Allen had his head down. I imagined him regretting what he had told me, developing arguments to turn me back to his team. Instead of despair on his face, he had a smile when he lifted his head.

"Jonathan, Jonathan, Jonathan. I've been waiting for you to be honest with yourself, so we could be honest with each other. A new chapter in your life is ready to begin."

My turn to stare now, a look of incomprehension reflecting the incomprehension I felt.

"There's an hour before class. Let me get us more coffee, and we can talk. Get a start, as they say."

Without waiting for my response, he went over to the big stainless-steel urn and returned with two coffees; a paper travel cup for his, mine in a cup with saucer. He knew a lot about me, such as I always drank my coffee from a cup or a mug if I had the choice over a paper cup. He placed the coffees on the table and retook his seat.

"Jonathan. Yes, I am your handler, as you called it. Before you arrived at the Pentagon, I'd been watching over you. I picked you from the soldiers at Fort Dix and started your top-secret security clearance during your first month in the army. I had you assigned to clerk school, the Pentagon, and then to the 902nd. Yes, I am career CIA, and no, I will not tell you if I've ever killed anyone."

"Thank you for the clarification, and thank you for watching over me. The biggest fear I had when I got drafted was winding up in a jungle, either killing or being killed. It would have been nice to know my fate when you guys decided it."

"Nice, but it wouldn't have been a real test for you. I had to know how you'd react under certain circumstances. We knew you could handle the physical part of basic training, but could you handle the mental part? Giving in and taking orders? For that you couldn't know our plans. Another thing: you're not CIA. I'm not recruiting you for a full-time job in the CIA in any capacity—not as an agent, not as a physician. You are and have been operating as a CIA contractor. I'd like you to continue as a CIA contractor." He lifted his coffee cup and stared at me over its rim. He sipped without taking his eyes off of me.

Now I felt on the spot. It was out in the open, lying right on the table between us. I was in the CIA, but not as deeply involved as I had suspected and feared, being asked to continue that relationship. "This is a lot for me to take in at one time. Can I have time to think about it?"

"Jonathan, surely this isn't a complete surprise to you. You're smarter than that, and I'm smarter than you're giving me credit for if you think I believe you're stunned by this. Let me tell you a few more things that may help clarify the role we have in mind for you."

"Sometimes you say 'we,' and sometimes you say 'I.' Which is it?"

"Both. I switch between the two when speaking to you. If it makes you more comfortable, I can stick with one, but for the record, they're the same. Which do you prefer?"

"You."

"The CIA is a large organization, a very large bureaucracy with many arms and many layers of management, all controlled by politicians. The director is a political appointee, and we're overseen by at least two committees in Congress, one in the House and one in the Senate. We're a rich target for the press, who are developing an intelligence-gathering mechanism equal to that of many countries. Fortunately for us, the various press groups are very competitive, looking for the scoop, and they don't share information. Reporters get help from foreign intelligence agencies who understand the process and the power of the press in this country. They often tip the press to something they've uncovered. It's generally not critical information, just stuff intended to embarrass us or make us use a lot of resources to counter."

Allen took another sip of coffee and continued. "Sorry for the digression. Congressional oversight, as well as our director, attempts to control what we do and how we do it by having a direct say on the number of people we employ. They can do this in a couple of ways. They can limit the number and size of the buildings we're allowed to use. The thought process is simple: if they give us a building for one thousand staff, they're limiting our staff to one thousand. The committees also control our budget. Part of the budget is kept secret in the name of national security, but the line item for salaries is available to them and therefore vulnerable."

"Interesting," was all I could manage.

"An understatement. To continue to operate, let alone increase our activities, we had to be creative. There's a part of our budget that's considered 'dark,' meaning it's not disclosed and can't be disclosed per the National Security Act. Congress and the White House recognize, for example, that we pay informers. The amounts of the payoffs and everything about these informers are protected. Just a big bag of money over which we have total discretion. When they tied our hands on staff hiring, we became creative. A couple of examples will help you understand the role of the contractor and why contractors are necessary. This is classified information intended to help you, and it's all you'll be allowed to have, so don't ask questions. I won't answer. Do you understand?"

I nodded that I understood.

"When we looked at our organization in Langley, we saw we had head count and budget for cleaning the building and offices. These cleaning people had high-security clearances, as high as our analysts and agents in the field. The head of the cleaning unit was ready for retirement. We approached him and asked if he'd consider being a contractor, essentially doing the same thing but running his own company. He jumped at the chance and hired his own crew, many former CIA maintenance staff. We shifted about half of the cleaning head count to this contractor, allowing us to hire more analysts and computer people. The bean counters believed we were doing the same cleaning job with fewer people."

This was an interesting insight. The few questions I had were more of curiosity and wouldn't be answered. Again, I nodded my head in understanding.

"Contracting out the cleaning for Langley proved successful and got us looking for other ways to maximize our resources. In the normal course of our business, we forge documents, passports, and visas necessary for our personnel to gain entrance to or egress from foreign countries. There's a normal workload, but sometimes a large number of documents are needed on short notice. In the past, we overstaffed to prepare for such bursts of activity, leaving us with talented people sitting around underutilized until the need arose. Using the same contractor model for our document needs, we identified individuals within the CIA and put them in the printing business, freeing up both head count and budget for use in other areas."

Allen paused, sipped his coffee, shook out a cigarette, and lit it. Through the exhaled smoke, he continued. "I know there are questions, and I appreciate you not asking them. These two examples illustrate restrictions we've overcome to carry out our mission. One of your questions has to be how you fit in as a contractor. A good question. Besides the examples I've given, we have part-time contractors in all walks of life. Highly placed individuals in academia and business watch for and gather information in their areas of expertise. We also call upon them to analyze information. In some cases, we ask them to intervene. Jonathan, you have done all of this already."

My puzzled look asked the question I wasn't supposed to ask.

"In the hijacking, you sat on the joint committee and analyzed information collected prior to your joining it. You collected your own data in preparation for the jump. And finally, you intervened by hijacking the plane." Allen remained looking at me, but his expression changed, a subtle change but one that took on new meaning.

"In the future, I'd like to be able to ask for your help. Not to the extent of anything as dangerous as you did in the Pacific Northwest. There's too much invested in you now, and we don't want to risk you getting hurt. More will be invested in you because you're a valuable asset who can fill a unique niche."

"Will I get a chance to speak today?"

"Yes, but later. I hope to able to answer most of your questions as I go through my agenda, so you get the information in a systematic manner. Asking questions, even innocent and personal questions, will be distracting."

I nodded again.

"Now, the big question that got this going this morning relates to your summer employment. Three different jobs have been chosen for you this summer. All are important for your development, and they'll give you insight for the future as well as provide you with an interesting summer. Would you like me to go ahead?"

Nodding yes, I knew this would make it or break it for me. Allen knew it also. He as much admitted it by having this orchestrated presentation prepared. A helter-skelter back-and-forth punctuated by questions and objections from me was not in his plans.

"You're going back to Washington. It won't be necessary to take your car, because you'll be working most of the time in the District, within walking distance of your apartment. If you're more comfortable having your car, I can arrange to get a parking pass at Fort McNair. Parking in the District is either impossible or expensive. I might add that it's dangerous. A lime-green Javelin is an attractive target for theft by a pimp."

He continued, getting no reaction from me to the slur against the Javelin. "On paper, you'll be assigned to Walter Reed Army Institute of Virology for the summer. After the first week, you'll go over to the Department of Energy in the new Forrestal Building. There, you'll be working alongside one of our people. I say 'working alongside' with caution. You'll not be working. You will not be speaking. Rather, you'll be watching, listening, and learning."

How long will I be in a nonspeaking role? I thought.

"I only want you there for a week, with a group whose name is still evolving. What they do is more important than what they're called. They're a science and technology group working in an area that's coming to be known as 'futurism.' Specifically, they're looking at revolutionary technology in the earliest stages of development, or, as it's termed, 'disruptive.' Disruptive is not a negative term. It means the technological advance is so profound it'll render the technology it's replacing obsolete. This is in contrast to advances that are evolutionary or sustaining, which are merely modest improvements. There are examples of disruptive technology in the last decade.

"In the early 1950s, televisions and radios had vacuum tubes. With the introduction of the transistor, radios and televisions got smaller. The transistor was disruptive to the vacuum tube because it rendered it obsolete. Now the transistor is being challenged by the integrated circuit, which is at least an order of magnitude smaller. The integrated circuit is a disruptive technology because it will make the transistor obsolete. Your objective at the Department of Energy is not to learn what they're doing, but to get a sense of how they're doing it. Understood?"

"Yes."

"After Energy, your assignment will be at the State Department, in a small section that's also looking to the future. They're not attempting to identify new technologies but rather to identify changes in the geopolitical environment that may change the world or be threats to the security of the United States. You'll be surprised to learn they're looking not only at our enemies, but also our allies. A threat is a threat! Again, I'm interested in your learning how they do the assessment rather than focusing on any threats.

"Finally, you'll spend a week in Atlanta, at the Centers for Disease Control, or CDC. I have three reasons for sending you there. First, it's good cover for a medical student. Second, they're doing futurist modeling on disease threats. Then, when you graduate from medical school, we want to retain you as a consultant. The easiest way for us to do that without drawing attention to us or you is having you as a consultant to a sister agency such as the CDC. Did I leave anything out?"

"Where do I live in Washington and Atlanta?"

"Good question, but I forgot something. After you finish at CDC, you'll return to Walter Reed for another week. It won't be much of an assignment, but we can't risk your meeting someone in New Haven who's been to Walter Reed and quizzes you. You should be able to answer questions about the commute, the weather, the campus, the food. That's why you'll start and finish at Walter Reed. Okay?"

"Sure."

"Now, as far as your living arrangements in Washington and Atlanta, we have apartments in both places. When you commute to Walter Reed, you should take the bus—something you'll be able to bitch about if the subject comes up. And yes, you will bitch about using the bus to get around the District in the summer."

Chapter 21

Allen picked up his napkin, crumpled it, and put it in his paper cup. Standing, he moved his chair back to the table, grabbed his coat from the back of the chair and said, "I'll be in touch. You take care." And then he left me with my thoughts.

Those thoughts were simple. I was a CIA contractor not just for the foreseeable future, but maybe the rest of my life. There were no illusions now of putting the hijacking behind me. That mission had merely been the first step. I had done a job for them, and they'd paid me. Was it a clean slate? No, it was like the Mafia: in for life. The only escape was death. Even the code of silence bound me. As I looked around at the familiar surroundings of the last year and a half, they were now oh-so different. I'd never sit at this table again without seeing Allen across from me, hearing his voice sealing my fate.

The reality of the present broke my mood as I looked at the clock. I needed to get to my first class of the day, a biochemistry class. I grabbed my books and jacket and walked from the cafeteria knowing my life had changed this morning. I was down in the dumps. Not even a cheery greeting from Marie, the in-house schoolteacher for the chronically ill children, could brighten my day.

I struggled through the next week, the routine broken by a lecture by a Nobel laureate on the main campus, a leisurely twenty-minute walk from the medical school. Turning into the lecture hall, I saw Allen. No longer in grubby med-school attire, he wore a respectable suit and tie. I don't think he saw me. Was he visiting another of his contractors?

In February, I received a bill for sixty dollars from the Connecticut Personal Property Tax Department for my Javelin. I had never paid a personal property tax and was curious about it and even more curious about what would happen if I didn't pay it. My neighbor Jerry had an interest in cars, and we would often talk. I had met him in the parking lot when I came upon him looking at my Javelin. When I had the opportunity, I asked him about the tax.

His first answer was the important one. If I didn't pay the tax, I wouldn't be able to reregister the car. Also, I wouldn't be able to get a Connecticut driver's license when my current one expired. Good to know. I paid the tax.

Jerry also told me a bit of trivia about this particular tax. The tax had been the brainchild of Peter Falk, the actor. Before becoming an actor, he worked as a low-level analyst in the State Budget Bureau in Hartford. Falk saw the large number of expensive toys owned by the rich in and around Greenwich and proposed a personal property tax on cars, boats, and planes to make up, in part, for a budget deficit. He left government service soon after, moving to New York City to begin his acting career. I don't think he ever returned to Connecticut to live and be subject to his tax.

Allen showed up again around Easter with some details about my summer in Washington. Assuming I wanted my car in Washington, he arranged for a parking tag at Fort McNair. He also got me an apartment in a residential neighborhood behind the Capitol. Convenient, it was about a ten-block walk along the mall to the Department of Energy in the Forrestal Building. It was also near Union Station, where I could get a direct bus to Walter Reed, assuming I chose not to fight the traffic and parking after I tried driving it once.

When exams were over at the end of May, I loaded the car and headed for Albany to spend a few days with my folks. While excited about the new things I would be exposed to this summer, I was on edge because of what it meant: I was getting deeper and deeper into the heart or the bowels of the CIA, I knew not which. I'd have to see how the CIA job smelled.

My parents were curious about my returning to Washington for a summer job rather than someplace else, preferably nearer them. I told them it was part of my NIH predoctoral program, emphasizing the assignments at Walter Reed and CDC and avoiding any mention of the others. To them, the hospital and CDC made sense for a medical student, and we left it at that.

When I left Albany, I stopped in Philadelphia to spend a few days with Brooke. Arriving late in the afternoon, I got there just as she was getting home from work. We made it into her apartment but not to her bedroom, christening the stairs between the first and second floor of her duplex. It was uncomfortable but quick. A more leisurely exploration of each other's bodies followed in her bed, and we allowed the tension to build until we released it together. After a long shower together, we went out to dinner.

Brooke didn't like the Javelin, feeling it was too flashy. Then she rode in it. It was one of those cars you had to experience to appreciate, both comfortable and sporty. It handled well and responded to the foot when called upon for acceleration. Now she liked it. Or, as she put it, "You can't see much of the shitty green from inside."

Brooke and I enjoyed Italian food—good Italian, not the run-of-the-mill spaghetti joints. Friends had told her of an upscale Italian restaurant on the east side of town under the expressway. When we arrived, we had our choice of any table. An empty restaurant was supposed to be a red flag. Turns out it was so upscale, we were early at six o'clock. Most of the reservations were for seven and later. The recommendations were well founded. It had great food. The restaurant, Panorama, was one of the fine-dining establishments in the city. It gained national notoriety twenty-five years later as the last place a secretary who worked for the Delaware governor had had dinner before a prominent Wilmington, Delaware, attorney murdered her.

I congratulated Brooke on her choice of restaurant. Brooke appreciated those little things and showed me later when we got back to her place. Of course, I then had to thank her for her token of appreciation. We thanked each other again in the morning before I left to continue my trip to Washington and the summer of new experiences.

Chapter 22

I found the furnished apartment on the 300 block of C Street NE easily and parked in front on the short block. The street was not what I had expected in Washington so close to the Capitol—tree lined, quiet, and a sense of neighborhood. A seller would call the houses brownstones, and a passerby would call them row homes. They were more accurately upscale row homes. There were only seven on this street, all two stories, all brick faced, and all with a basement with separate entrance. That was my apartment—a basement unit in the middle of the block.

Before unloading, I went in for an inspection, retrieving the key from the lockbox. The apartment had a large living area with a separate bath in the back of the unit. The unit had areas dedicated to kitchen and sleeping—not a separate kitchen or bedroom, but better than an efficiency. Being in the basement made it dark and damp, which was remedied easily by turning on the air conditioner and lights. I decided it would do for the summer.

Throughout the summer, I heard people upstairs. Their appearances were sporadic, and I never saw them. The few times they were in residence, the quiet I had come to enjoy was disturbed. I was happy their presence was limited.

Sunday I spent becoming familiar with the neighborhood, did the grocery shopping, found the nearest Laundromat, and checked out the restaurants. Everything was convenient. As promised, it was a short walk to Union Station for the bus to Walter Reed.

The tour of the neighborhood included a walk around the Capitol and down the south side of the mall to test my supposed short walk to L'Enfant Plaza. It seemed a long way to walk to start or end a workday; even more so in the uncomfortable summer heat of Washington. Worse was the humidity, hanging in the air, so thick I could drink it. That's weather in Washington—cold and damp in the winter and hot and humid in the summer. Comes with building a city on a swamp! A walking commute would leave me drenched in sweat, a condition I didn't enjoy. Walking would be my mode of travel only on the nicest of days, when I could take my time, perhaps strolling with a cup of coffee in the morning, stopping at a bench to read the paper. I knew that on most days, I would take a cab.

On Monday, I walked to Union Station and took the bus to Walter Reed. All told, the commute took about one hour—not bad for Washington, DC. I didn't think I could do any better if I drove, proving Allen right. I found the facility map, located the Army Institute of Virology, and did more walking.

The Walter Reed campus was magnificent, red-brick Georgian buildings on over one hundred acres of park-like land with stately trees as old as the sixty-year-old hospital in the middle of a rather pricey neighborhood on Georgia Avenue. Finding my way around proved more difficult than finding the complex. The buildings didn't seem to be numbered in any particular way. In fact, while there were perhaps twenty buildings on-site already, construction had just started on what they referred to as Building 2. I eventually made my way to where I had to report.

I spent the first part of the day filling out paper work, getting a photo identification card, and undergoing an orientation briefing required for all new hires. Orientation took place in a large, under-air-conditioned conference room and included all the new hires for the week, from orderlies to physicians—and one guy from the CIA. Thankfully, the briefing was brief.

They gave me instructions to report to my duty station in midafternoon. With a couple of hours to kill, I walked around the campus and found a cafeteria. After lunch I reported to the Walter Reed Institute of Research in Building 40 to begin my week. An information officer gave a familiarization tour. He wore the uniform of the Public Health Service, like that of the US Navy. A trained pharmacist, he carried the rank of a lieutenant junior grade, or first lieutenant in the army. He didn't seem to enjoy his assignment as a tour guide, spending the rest of the afternoon giving me a history of Walter Reed as a medical facility.

For the rest of the week, he showed me around and introduced me to people on a list on a clipboard. Drawing a line through a name as we left an office or laboratory was the only thing he seemed to enjoy—one step closer to the end. I felt sorry for him, but I didn't want to be doing the "waste some time" tour any more than he did. Each day, we agreed to start a little later, with a little longer lunch on our own and an earlier departure. By Friday, we agreed to change our routine. We had morning coffee together, and then I left.

I had seen Brooke the previous weekend, and we had no plans for this weekend. I could have called her and driven up but decided against it. While we were becoming closer, we hadn't talked about being exclusive yet. Part of me resisted calling her for fear she wouldn't be available because she had made other plans. The vague generic term of "other plans" carried the possibility she had a date. I wasn't ready to face that yet, to see how I might react to those words. So I decided to stay in Washington for the weekend.

On Saturday, I drove over to Fort Myer—just a visit for old time's sake. There was no warm and fuzzy feeling. The historic grounds registered merely as a place I had once lived. I thought because the whole CIA thing had started when I was stationed here, there would be an emotional connection. There wasn't. After the week at historic Walter Reed, I viewed the new buildings at Fort Myer in a new light. The modern buildings were functional and well suited for their purpose, but they stood in contrast to the other buildings built a century earlier, when the horses weren't ceremonial. As I looked at the sandstone-and-chrome Consolidated Barracks and the Consolidated Mess Hall, I appreciated the older buildings more. The newer ones were almost an eyesore. Familiar, yes, but out of place, like putting a McDonald's next to the state house in Colonial Williamsburg.

I spent the rest of the weekend being lazy. The apartment had a big twenty-one-inch television, so I watched a little baseball, a little golf, and some sitcoms on Saturday night after dinner at a local Mexican restaurant. Sunday morning came and went with me missing church again. I chose to vegetate in the cool dark of my cellar apartment rather than venture into the hot and sticky day outside. The day drifted by until evening, when I had to start preparing for my next assignment.

Monday morning looked as if it would be a magnificent day. I turned on the television for the local weather, and they confirmed my initial impression. A cloudless night and high pressure from the northwest had chased away the heat and humidity, at least for a while. After a leisurely shower and shave, I dressed and had two hours to kill before I had to report for work. Today I decided to walk—or, rather, stroll—to work.

I walked past the Capitol on the south side. The Capitol grounds crew was hosing everything clean for the day. The gardeners were in the flower beds, tidying things up. Young people, officious in their dress and manner, hurried about, on their way to work in the Capitol or the federal office buildings that serviced it. Farther down the mall began, at this end only grass and trees that would give way to the reflecting pool on the other side of the Washington Monument. The morning was still comfortable, the sun shining but no humidity. You didn't have to feel the humidity in Washington; you could see it. But today was clear, no hazy humidity.

The paths and sidewalks around the mall were full of people. More serious young people headed toward the Capitol. Others walked with equal purpose to the buildings that framed the mall. In contrast were those moving at a more sedate pace, generally older. They were also headed off to work but were less obsessed with the perception that the work they did, or who they did it for, would change the course of history—or perhaps aware that it wouldn't. Some probably took the slower pace to relish the final quiet moments before hectic, high-powered jobs would consume the rest of their day, and perhaps evening.

And, of course, there were the mall joggers. I could never understand joggers or the jogging craze. I hated running and couldn't see the attraction of running along a congested path with others also intent on putting miles of dusty running behind them while pounding along in the dust created by those who had gotten there earlier or ran faster. Dust sticking to their damp bodies, mixing with the sweat, making sweaty mud that dribbled down, collecting in the tops of fancy jogging socks. Getting up early to suffer this self-abuse made even less sense. Maybe my thoughts merely reflected how much I hated the running part of basic training. In basic, we had to run everywhere. No, it wasn't just that. Even as a kid, I hated running. That may sound strange coming from an athlete who had competed in a very physical sport at the highest level for most of his life.

To compare jogging and running with skating and hockey was absurd. Running was pure punishment to the feet, the ankles, the knees, and the hips. These delicate joints are not meant to take a pounding, and to do it daily, in extreme cold or heat, defined insanity for me. Hockey is art compared to the self-induced beating of jogging. Skating, even skating for hockey, is a gliding motion, serene with nature and gentle on the joints. Even the frantic moves necessary in hockey are choreographed motion compared to the drudgery of pounding the pavement. One never punished the body by skating in excessive heat. Quite the contrary. Hockey is done comfortably, on ice with warm clothes. In hockey, the damage is done by others, not self-inflicted.

I had been walking the path but moved over to the sidewalk on Jefferson Drive. Being close to the moaning, sweating, struggling joggers was not the way I wanted to start my day. At Fourth Street, I found a kiosk selling coffee, juices, doughnuts, and other breakfast items. Getting in line with nonjoggers preparing for the workday, I got a coffee, a hard roll with butter, and the morning paper. A bench on the path in the shade of a tree beckoned me. It was about halfway on my foot commute to work, the perfect place for my breakfast. As I was spread out on the bench, the joggers bothered me less than they had just a few short minutes before. I was doing everything they weren't—sitting in the shade, eating carbohydrates, and smoking. Some moved to avoid my smoke. They frowned. I smiled. The mall had been the site of many protests. Sitting, eating, and smoking were my protest to the insanity of jogging in Washington in the summer.

Chapter 23

After finishing my light breakfast, I continued my walk to work. At Ninth Street, I turned left to the Forrestal Building, which housed several government agencies, including the Federal Energy Administration, my host for the week. At the information desk, I got directions to the third floor, where I met my contact for the week, the lovely Monika Baumgarten. Lovely was an understatement. Monika was beautiful, movie-star beautiful—about five feet six in spiked heels, long blond hair, blue eyes, and a body that could only be described as magnificent. From top to bottom, she was a welcome treat after the dirty, sweating joggers. I couldn't keep my eyes still. Her face was perfect save for a little crooked nose, probably the result of a childhood fracture that didn't heal properly. This little imperfection only amplified the rest of her beauty.

"Hi. I'm Monika, and I'll be accompanying you while you're here at the Federal Energy Administration." Her smile looked a little crooked too because of the nose, and her voice had the hint of New York City. None of this detracted from her beauty.

"Jonathan," I said, offering my hand to her. "But you already know that."

"Yes, Jonathan. I do. There's a full week for you. Let's get started. Would you like to stop by the cafeteria for coffee?"

"Thanks. I've had one already, but I can always go for another."

"I know what you mean. I need a couple of cups before I can get started in the morning," she said as she turned and walked away. Not moving, I just watched her. She wore a light summer dress. Sort of silky, but probably not; I don't know fabrics. When she walked, it shifted from side to side, anchored at her waist. Oh, did I mention her waist and hips? Her waist was tiny and then swelled out to perfect hips that rode on great legs connected to nice, tiny ankles. Monika stopped after a half a dozen steps and turned. Having not moved, I was still watching, and she knew it. A woman like her had a lot of experience with guys watching her. Her legs shifted, beginning a turn she continued only with the top half of her body, her breasts in profile. She had nice breasts. Not huge, but definitely large. With a smile, she nodded, indicating she wanted me to follow. I did.

"I'm not supposed to ask you anything about what you're doing. That's operational security, and it discourages you from asking me what I do. Conversation should be limited to small talk and to things you see during your stay here in Energy. Let's get our coffee and then swing by my office for a short briefing about what happens here. As a visitor, you must leave your briefcase there. You shouldn't bring anything into the building for the rest of the week. Anything you need while you're here, I can provide. Also, it goes without saying you can't take anything out of the building."

After we got coffee, we went up two flights to her office. I liked walking up stairs almost as much as I liked jogging, but I had to admit, following her up the stairs, I could have gone for a few more flights with no complaints.

Monika's office was small and could have belonged to anyone, with no personal effects. The only thing of hers was the scent, her perfume—Shalimar, I think. Inviting me to take a seat, she sat behind her desk.

"This week, you'll spend a lot of time sitting in meetings. You're not allowed to take notes, nor are you allowed to ask any questions directly. If something isn't clear, ask me. If I don't know the answer, I'll ask someone to explain it to you. Clear?"

"Yes, ma'am."

"Please call me Monika." Before I could correct myself, she continued. "You'll hear a lot of information that may be above your level of understanding. Some of the science is very advanced. It's not your job to understand all of the science, but you'll understand enough to appreciate what's going on. The assignment this week is to understand the process. That process is probably beyond anything you could imagine.

"In academia, scientists claim to work openly for the sake of advancing science. In reality, they don't. Many work for tenure or notoriety. Most work for publications and research grants that lead to tenure and notoriety. If they have an edge on their competition, they don't share. In industry, nobody shares. Confidentiality agreements have significant penalties if someone gives away corporate secrets. Even the rest of the government, like the scientists at NIH, don't share, probably for a combination of reasons they have in common with academia and industry. Here, you will see sharing. Here you will see challenges to ideas—not for the purpose of embarrassing the speaker but to advance understanding. Usually, it takes about a year for the good scientists who join us to get into the spirit. Even though you're a newcomer, unknown to them, the fact you're here means you're entitled to be here. No one will restrict their discussion because you're in the room."

After I provided my nodded assurance that I understood, Monika continued. She described the group's search for technological advances. She used the same example of vacuum tubes, transistors, and integrated circuits Allen had used to illustrate disruptive technology. However, she took the discussion further, describing the work product of the group. "There's no science done here. This is a think tank. Scientific advances are evaluated through literature review and discussion. There are multiple disciplines looking into physics, chemistry, and the biological sciences. There are other scientists who look into areas that might seem unusual—for example, science fiction. Everyone is familiar with the gadgets in the James Bond novels and movies. The gadgets are the fun part. The technology behind them is what's important."

I nodded again.

"Every group has a monthly report, mostly an administrative exercise to justify their existence to the GAO and Congress. These are toned down in the science terms, with just enough to be credible. The important findings and recommendations are passed though different channels. The reports highlight areas of interest. What's an area of interest? I've already told you about vacuum tubes, transistors, and integrated circuits. In spite of these rapid advances, all examples of disruptive technology, there's another in the works, the chip. This is a significantly smaller and more powerful advance. While the report addresses the technological advance of a chip, it also addresses the potential impact of such a disruptive change on energy and commerce in this country. Just as the transistor reduced the size and energy requirements in its applications, the chip is expected to have orders of magnitude of change in this area again. The chip will reduce electrical usage, not only because of the power needed to use it, but also the auxiliary power needed to cool it. Being significantly smaller, it will require less energy to produce and less energy to transport. These improvements have the potential to have a significant impact on the commerce of this country. If these advances are made outside of the US and we're not on top of it, we could find ourselves at a significant disadvantage."

Monika was as impressive for her intellect as she was for her beauty. She'd been talking to me without notes, and I got the sense I was getting the toned-down version. She continued. "I've addressed only the economic and energy consequences. There are national security consequences as well. If our enemies get the jump on us, they could be in a position to produce advanced weapons that are cheaper, lighter, and capable of carrying larger payloads."

I had wondered why Allen wanted me here. It hadn't made sense until now. "That's quite a responsibility. How many people are charged with doing this?"

"The exact number is classified. There are enough to do the job. You'll meet many of them this week. There are others who are traveling, visiting colleges, universities, and industry, both here in the US and abroad, and attending scientific conferences to listen and talk to the leaders in all these fields. The bottom line is if an alert comes out of this group, the likelihood it will become real in the future is very high." Monika stopped talking, gave me a crooked smile, and continued. "If they say someone is building an escalator to the moon, don't question it."

I smiled. "This should be quite an experience."

With that, Monika reminded me to leave my briefcase in her office, and we set out to meet with the futurists.

I walked to work most mornings, stopping for breakfast halfway at the kiosk, enjoying my coffee, roll, and newspaper each day. The routine was nice, almost comfortable, something I could get used to easily. Two afternoons proved too warm and humid to walk, especially the slight uphill at the east end, up to the Capitol. They called it Capitol Hill for a reason. You couldn't ski it, but it became a challenge in the heat and humidity.

The workweek was a blur. Much of what the futurists were talking about was well beyond me. They were looking at lasers with implications all across the board, including military uses. The interest in microwaves had both consumer and military applications. They always looked at the technologies that had an impact on energy, as would be expected in the Federal Energy Administration, but their discussions always seemed to include a look into military applications.

I had a little more understanding about the emerging use of chips replacing transistors. This had everyone's interest, and not just for the energy implications. The discussion focused on the use of these chips as integrated circuits in computers. The ramifications of this advance, while by definition sustaining, could prove to be disruptive.

Computers had been around for many years. Originally they had been large, bulky devices, housed in rooms, powered by vacuum tubes. The heat generated by these early computers required air conditioning to keep them from overheating. Transistors allowed the units to be smaller and run cooler. Integrated circuits allowed even more advances. Now, chips had the potential to revolutionize the computer. They were predicting computers would be the size of typewriters, with more power than the largest room of computers currently available.

Monika and I went to lunch by ourselves in the cafeteria. For a woman with a beautiful figure, she had a great appetite. Her order to the counterman was specific—very rare roast beef on rye with mustard, a pickle, potato salad, and carrot cake for dessert. I hoped she wasn't a jogger, burning those calories off early in the morning.

During lunch, she offered a clarification on some of the finer points from the morning. She probably thought me very attentive. When she spoke, I always looked at her face and gave her all of my attention. I watched her eyes, how they would sparkle when she got excited about a subject. And I watched her mouth. I loved watching her lips move as she spoke. I let her talk without interrupting because she'd have to wet her lips, and then I could watch the tip of her tongue slide across those lips. On her, the New York accent was sexy. I learned she was from Queens, but I noted something else in her accent.

"Are you originally from New York? I hear something a little different in your accent."

She smiled. "Everyone can tell I'm from New York. I feel self-conscious about it, and I'm trying to work on it."

"Well, it sounds like you've made a great start on it."

"Not really, but thank you. What you hear is a bit of a German accent. My parents are German, and as a child, I spoke only German. It wasn't until I got into grammar school that I spoke English. In fact, I would come home and teach my parents English. We still only speak German at home."

"Were you born in Germany?"

A big smile, a little more crooked this time. When she was being playful, her smile would be just a little more crooked than normal. I don't know if she did this intentionally, but it was enchanting. "I like to say I was made in Germany."

My confused look amused her. She laughed—a natural laugh, but very sexy with that crooked smile.

"Mother was pregnant when they left Germany. I was born here. So I was made in Germany and born in the United States." No doubt a practiced line, and she enjoyed delivering it.

Monika continued being friendly and attentive all week. She sat next to me in the meetings, making sure I understood the process. She seemed to know when to ask if I understood the science. If I gave a puzzled look, she'd either seek clarification from one of the scientists or tell me she'd explain it at lunch. As the week went on, she used fewer of the toned-down explanations. We spent every lunch together, and as the week passed, I found myself very attracted to her. I wanted to ask her out but held back. What would Brooke think? Easy solution to that question: I wouldn't tell her. What would Allen think? More important, what would Allen do if I hit on one of his people? I thought the attraction was mutual. Maybe I was just hoping.

During lunch on Friday, Monika asked if I had plans for the weekend. I had none. Brooke and I had made no plans because I wasn't sure how much free time I'd have.

"Some friends and I are heading over to the beach for the weekend. We like to go over at least once before the season starts to avoid the crowds. You're welcome to join us."

"The beach?" I asked.

"Rehoboth Beach. It's a small town on the Atlantic about one hundred miles east of here. Takes about three hours to drive over. We go for a short weekend, leaving early Saturday morning and coming back Sunday evening. Melissa, my friend—her family has a big house on the south side of town. Her mom doesn't see much of her and loves to spoil her, and us by association. During the day, we do the beach-and-swimming thing. Her dad likes to have a cocktail hour before dinner, and her mom likes to cook us a big meal. After dinner, we go out for drinks and dancing, either in Rehoboth or Dewey, the next town south. It's very informal except for the cocktail hour and dinner. Just young folks hanging around together. There are no boyfriend/girlfriend relationships in the group, just a group of friends. One word of caution, though: her mom is a Catholic and insists we all go to church on Sunday. I'm not Catholic, but I go to her church. A small price to pay for dinner and a bed."

"Sounds wonderful. How will we get there?"

"If you could drive, it would help. Melissa has a car, but there will be five of us. That might prove uncomfortable for a four-hour drive. It also gives us an option if someone wants to leave early or stay late. We're not all tied to one car."

"I thought you said three hours."

"If it's a nice weekend, there can be a lot of traffic. Plan on four hours, and then if it takes less, we'll be pleasantly surprised. I should ride with you because I'm the only one who knows you. I'll give you my address, and you can pick me up at seven thirty on Saturday morning."

"Can I bring anything? Wine? Beer?"

"No. Melissa's mom and dad do everything. Just bring your suit and some nice clothes for cocktails and church."

"A suit? At the beach?"

She laughed again. "A bathing suit."

Chapter 24

✳   ✳   ✳

Monika lived a few blocks from the apartment on C Street. When I pulled up, she had the same initial reaction to the Javelin Brooke had had. As I put her bag in the trunk, I said, "It's a lot nicer on the inside when you're riding in it."

"That I believe," she said as I opened the door.

The trip over was an easy drive on uncongested roads under a clear blue sky marked with wispy white clouds. As we headed east, the sun was in my eyes, so I drove with the sun visor down, looking into the narrow slit between it and the hood of the car. The next car I got would have tinted windows. Monika saw my discomfort. "That's the problem going over in the morning. The sun is in your eyes, but it's even worse coming back. Everyone tries to stay as late as possible, but then the sun is low for most of the trip. The traffic will be heavier too." Something to look forward to!

The landscape surprised me. The land was flat, which I suppose should have been expected on a coastal plain. Another surprise was the well-tended farms with acres of corn separating the small towns and hamlets along the way. With Washington so densely populated, these small rural communities, some within an hour of the capital, seemed very pleasant. Monika became more comfortable as the miles rolled by. Conversation was limited to small talk, with some background on Rehoboth, the friends we would meet, and Melissa's family. The others had arrived by the time we got there.

Rehoboth proved to be a pleasant little town, more similar to the small seaside communities of New England than I would have imagined. The main street ran straight to the boardwalk, with the beach and ocean beyond. The majority of lots in town were fifty feet frontage and one hundred feet deep, with small cottages that shared a similarity in design.

Melissa's family home occupied two lots in the second block from the ocean, and, at three stories tall, it was the largest in the neighborhood. Two large oaks shaded a porch in front. Comfortable wicker chairs with plush, colorful cushions decorated the porch, perfect for people watching—or, as I would learn later, cocktails. Parking for six cars was available on a grass area to the side and rear of the house.

Monika's friends introduced themselves and made me feel welcome. They seemed to be genuine friends with no pretenses, as if they had known each other since being kids.

Everyone was eager to change and get to the beach, but Melissa's mom wanted to feed us and talk. Melissa stepped in and told her there would be lots of time for talking over cocktails and dinner. "Mother, you know we have to go to Gus and Gus for lunch. It wouldn't be a Saturday at the beach without that."

The house was huge, at least seven bedrooms and six baths. Melissa had her own room. Monika and the other girl shared a large room on the third floor, while the other guy and I each got a room on the second floor. When I changed and came down, the others had already assembled with beach chairs from the back of the house. The bath towel I had brought from home was considered unacceptable and replaced with a large blue-and-yellow beach towel.

We had most of the large, sandy beach to ourselves. On the ocean side of the boardwalk, it extended as far north and south as I could see. Shops lined the boardwalk—pizza and burger joints, more than one arcade, mini golf, and what looked like an old Woolworth's. South, past the shops on the boardwalk, I saw houses, large and small. On the sandy beach, a few other groups clustered together around umbrellas, blankets, and chairs used to define their territory. There were couples sharing a beach blanket and the occasional solitary sunbather, reading or just enjoying the sound of the waves crashing on the beach.

Melissa selected an area near the water line, advising the tide was going out and, therefore, we were safe from having to move. Chairs were unfolded and blankets and towels spread, now defining our territory. Monika put her towel next to mine. "Stay close to me until you get used to the gang." She seemed more intent on isolating me from the group, keeping me on the periphery. Soon we were by ourselves as the others ran to the water. Monika had worn a wrap covering her from neck to ankles for the walk to the beach, a flowing, swirling, dress-like thing. Standing in front of me, she took great care in undoing the tie at the neck, talking the entire time to ensure she had my attention.

"Did you see how Melissa's mother looked at you? First at you, then Melissa. Seems to me, she would like an Ivy League doctor in the family." The wrap drifted from her body to the sand. She knew she was beautiful and sensuous. Monika knew what she was doing was erotic. And she knew the effect of her actions on me. As she bent to pick up the wrap at her feet, her breasts hung heavy, straining the top of her peach-colored bikini. Her eyes never left mine, and I lost the struggle to maintain eye contact. She asked, "Do you like my suit?"

"Yes."

"Even the color? In early summer, I wear peach or coral. Once I get a little color, I can switch to white to accent the tan."

"I'm sure that's nice too." I sat with my knees up, elbows resting on them, but I was struggling and uncomfortable because I could feel an erection growing, making me self-conscious on a public beach with only a bathing suit keeping me from embarrassment. She folded her wrap and crawled onto her towel after moving it closer to mine, overlapping the edges, a sign of growing intimacy.

"The beach is great, but I don't like the water. I could lie here all summer and not once go in the water. Maybe, when it's hot, I'd go down to cool off, but just up to my knees. The ocean water's sandy, and the salt dries my skin." She said this as she started putting Coppertone on her arms. She sat on her towel, on the edge closest to me. Leaning forward, she rubbed the oil on her legs, spreading them to get high on her thighs. She squeezed a little more oil into her hands and rubbed it onto her shoulders. Leaning back, she applied the oil to her waist, fingers sliding along the top of her bikini bottom, fingertips just inside the fabric, and then up to the bottom of her bikini top. When she did this, her breasts pushed up, making them even more inviting. A final dab of oil, and she started on her chest. Very erotic, and she knew it. Then she rubbed the oil over the tops of her breasts, first one and then the other, never losing eye contact with me. As her hands went inside the bikini top just a fraction, she said, "I hate tan lines." This was an invitation to watch her, which I accepted.

"Jonathan, you should put some oil on, especially your shoulders, or you'll burn." She sounded sincere until she added in a playful manner, "Lie back, and I'll do your shoulders and chest while my hands are greasy." Pushing me back, her eyes moved to the front of my bathing suit, still hidden beneath my folded arms.

"No, I'm okay for now."

"But, you look…I don't know, a little uncomfortable." She couldn't have been more direct. "Let me know if I can do something for you," she said as she rolled over on her stomach, handing me the Coppertone. "As long as you're sitting there doing nothing, put some oil on my back, please."

This I could do without revealing my growing problem. As I took the Coppertone, she reached behind her back and undid the clasp of her bikini top. "I hate tan lines." When I started on her back, she asked me to do her legs first. Her calves felt both firm and supple as my greasy fingers slid along the smooth skin. I hesitated before starting on the backs of her thighs. "Come on. There's only a few good hours of sun. Can't waste any of them." I moved up her thighs, and, as I did, she spread them a little, inviting me to apply the oil between her legs. I did. She moaned, "Oh, that feels so good. Jonathan, you have great hands."

Oiling my hands again, I started on her back. First the shoulders, and then down to the top of her bikini bottom. She reached behind and pulled it down a bit.

"I know, you don't like tan lines." As she lay on her stomach, her breasts pushed to the sides, spilling out of what remained of her bikini top.

"Do the sides, please."

Starting at the top of her bikini bottom, I moved up both sides, stopping before reaching the sides of her breasts. She reached around and took my oiled hand to the mound of the side of her breast. "That's the spot. There can't be any tan lines at all. If I could, I'd be lying here naked, letting the sun tan my whole body."

I wiped my hands on the corner of my towel, crawled over to my side of the towel, and lowered myself onto my stomach, carefully pushing my erection to the side. If I could have done it without being obvious, I would have slid my hand under my towel to dig a hole under my groin. Someplace it could rest without having the weight of my body on it. I was uncomfortable and had to take the pressure off. I tried thinking about anything but Monika and her silky smooth body in the peach bikini alongside me. I thought about the joggers on the mall, the sweaty, puffing, struggling joggers plodding in the summer sun of Washington. Imagining myself as one of them. It worked. Tumescence was in remission.

Monika was serious about sun tanning. Once she got fully oiled, she quieted down and "worked" on her tan. Before long, I heard her snoring softly. I turned my head to look at her, wondering what it would be like to fall asleep in bed beside her, listening to her breathe like that. My eyes got heavy.

Just as I nodded off, the others returned from the water. Ready for lunch, they didn't bother taking orders but set off. They returned with burgers, fries, and soft drinks for all of us. When I opened my fries and asked for ketchup, they all laughed. "Rookie! This is the beach, and at the beach, we eat beach fries. No ketchup on beach fries, only vinegar." I watched as Melissa dunked a fry into a cup of vinegar. Hesitating, I tried a fry dry. Not bad; different from any fry I had ever had. Gus and Gus used only Idaho potatoes, fried in peanut oil, the temperature a trade secret; drained; and then fried again. The result was a fry slightly crisp on the outside but fully cooked on the inside. I tried one dipped in vinegar. While I would have preferred salt, pepper, and ketchup, the beach fry with vinegar tasted pretty good.

During our lunch, it was apparent the other three were happy I was there. Monika never went in the water, and the others felt bad that she spent the day by herself on the beach. With me keeping her company, they didn't worry about her. They also talked about what they would do this evening after dinner. Talk turned to clubs in Dewey that had live bands and dancing. They asked if I danced. While I like clubs, especially those with live music, I had to admit I wasn't a dancer.

Melissa spoke first. "Now I know why Monika brought you. She doesn't like the water and doesn't like to dance. You're her beach-and-wall-flower buddy."

Everyone was thrilled they could do their thing and again not worry about Monika.

It made me wonder, if Monika didn't participate in any of the things they liked to do, why did they bring her?

"Do you go to church?" asked Melissa.

"Not as a general rule. Is that something else that Monika and I have in common?"

Monika nodded yes and smiled sweetly. With her hand on my leg, she said, "It doesn't make any difference. Melissa's mom insists we all go to church together in the morning. Remember, I told you? Not far—St. Edmond's, just down the street."

"No problem. We can sit in the back and watch."

Melissa hustled us off the beach at five o'clock and told us to shower, change, and be ready for cocktails at six o'clock, followed by dinner at seven. As I got ready for a shower, I saw I had gotten quite a bit of sun, with my shoulders, legs, and face red. The bathroom had little bottles of shampoo, conditioner, and body lotion, like a hotel. It looked as if someone was a regular traveler, but Monika told me later Melissa's mom liked the idea and reused the little bottles, feeling it was a nice touch and reduced waste. Hoping I wouldn't suffer later, I put lotion on, with an extra dab to my face, hoping to avoid a peeling nose.

Everyone dressed smartly for cocktails, sort of beach casual. Gentlemen had on long trousers and sport shirts, and the ladies all wore light dresses. The ladies had planned on getting sun today, and the colors chosen complemented their slight sunburns. A very handsome group of young professionals and a successful middle-aged couple. While Monika may have been considered on the outside at the beach or on the dance floor, she was the center of attention during cocktails and dinner. She was dazzling, directing the conversation, being the bridge between the young people and our hosts. She had a grasp of the most complex issues and was current on what was popular with the different generations. Sensing when a discussion became contentious, she skillfully guided the conversation to a different subject.

As I watched and listened to her, she became more fascinating. Except for the autonomic response of my dick, I had been neutral to her advances on the beach, but now she had my full attention. Then the hammer struck! She was so good, it was if she had been trained, fitting in everywhere with great interpersonal skills. She had been my guide all week. She was a plant by Allen, to test me, see if I could be seduced. See if I was a risk. Perhaps trying to get me in bed to see if she could wring a secret out of me. The realization caused me more than a little disappointment. I thought she was attracted to me as much as I was to her, but she was merely working. Disappointed, I knew I had to keep my guard up.

The more I watched and listened to her during dinner, the more convinced I became of my notion. She would turn to me and become the seductress again, moving so easily in and out of those roles.

After dinner, we all helped clean up, over the protestations of Melissa's mom. The talk turned to going to a club, and Monika declined. Said the sun had made her tired, and she didn't want a late night. "I want to be fresh for church in the morning."

Well, that did it for me. Clubbing with three people I hardly knew didn't appeal to me—three people who would leave me at a table or at the bar while they danced. If Monika planned on turning in early, I had a book I could read. Not surprising or disappointing to anyone, I too declined the invite to the club.

After they left, Monika suggested a short walk to see the town, it being my first visit. The early evening was beautiful. A fresh breeze come off the ocean, scented with the clean smell of the sea. Flowers and bushes were in bloom, and the air held some of their fragrances. When we had descended to the street, she took my arm. The small talk continued as we made our way toward the board-walk, enjoying the evening.

Couples, families, and groups of boys following girls crowded the board-walk. Monika caught me smiling and said, "What?"

I told her I had enjoyed the smell of the ocean and the flowers when we were on the porch. Now, closer to the ocean, all I could smell was suntan lotion.

Laughing, she said, "You should come back on the July Fourth weekend. The place is mobbed, and you can smell suntan lotion as soon as you turn into town off the highway, a mile out."

An old-fashioned bandstand occupied a central area where the boardwalk met the main street. We turned west on the main street and walked one block, crossed the street, and came back down the opposite side. All the buildings were one or two stories—T-shirt shops, an old-time photo place, ice cream joints and pizza restaurants, and, of course, a Dolle's salt water taffy store. Nothing special, nothing different, but they fit together well. The one exception was Carlton's, a very high-end clothing store that seemed more likely to be found in Palm Beach. When we got back to the boardwalk, I turned to the south, ready to retrace our path back, but she stopped.

"It's such a beautiful evening, and I don't know if I'll get back again this summer. Can we walk back on the sand, down by the water?"

"Sure."

As soon as I said that, I envisioned Allen sitting on her shoulder, smiling at me. She took off her shoes and held me tighter, brushing her breast against my arm. We walked on dry sand, still warm from the afternoon sun. The beach had a different feel at night. Not just the absence of people. The water crashing against the shore looked and sounded more natural. At water's edge, there was a ledge where sand had washed out. Without speaking, Monika moved us toward it and sat down, patting the sand alongside her for me. "I know the sun sets in the west and we're facing east, so don't think of me as stupid or silly, but I love to sit here on the beach at sunset and watch the sky and water blend at the horizon."

"No, not at all. My last time at the ocean was a family vacation. Must have been twelve or thirteen years ago. Sundown meant the end of the day."

"You didn't go to the boardwalk for the rides and ice cream?"

"No, it was Virginia Beach, and I don't remember a boardwalk. The hotel was kind of small and right on the beach."

"That's right. Virginia Beach doesn't have a boardwalk like we do here." Sitting close now, her arm still grasping mine and her leg close, almost touching. As she snuggled a little, she said, "You'd be surprised how fast the temperature can go down when the sun sets. You'll be happy you have me keeping you warm." The sensuous woman of this afternoon had returned.

The light left the sky, and we watched the shadows grow, the horizon losing definition. We talked, but of what, I don't remember. I was just aware of her closeness. The smell of her. I couldn't place the perfume. It wasn't Shalimar. "Did you change perfume?"

The comment seemed to please her. "Jonathan, you are attentive, aren't you? Yes, I did. I brought My Sin for dinner and tonight. It's a better after-sun perfume than Shalimar—not as sweet." As she spoke, she turned her head to the side, catching the last of the setting sun. I could see she had that crooked, playful smile.

I agreed with a nod of my head. Looking up, she took my face with one of her hands and kissed me, gently at first. Something the bards would call a chaste kiss. Then her lips parted, and I felt the tip of her tongue sliding across my lips as her free hand came around my neck. Her hand slid down my chest and rested on my leg. "I've wanted to kiss you since that first lunch we had on your first day at Energy. You didn't talk about yourself, Jonathan, and you have a lot to talk about. You were attentive, watching my eyes, not my chest."

"There are probably a lot of guys you meet who wouldn't be able to tell you what color your eyes are," I said in an attempt to lighten things up, to change the subject, maybe to back her off a bit.

"It is nice, isn't it? I tried to get your attention today in my bathing suit, but you didn't take the hint. I think I caused what the Scots call 'a tilt in your kilt,' but you backed off."

"Monika, I had a very hard time keeping my eyes off you today, and when I put the lotion on you, I thought my hands were so hot I'd give you a bad burn. You did get to me." A fleeting urge to just shut up, kiss her, and stick my tongue down her throat and my hand up her skirt overcame me. No, I would have to go for her breast first. In my mind, the argument was almost won and the rutting DNA taking control, but I saw Allen sitting on her shoulder, smiling. Only now, he had a camera aimed at her chest, waiting for me to grab a tit. He bobbed his head at me, saying, "C'mon, man. I'm getting hard just watching this. Go for it."

I wanted her badly, but I felt it was a trap. A trap where I wouldn't get laid and would lose my tuition and stipend. Yes, ridiculous thinking. The last time I had seen Allen, he did everything he could to keep me working for the CIA. The last thing he would do would be to bounce me out. But the big head doesn't think well when the little head is getting all the blood. "Monika. I can't. I'm seeing someone." Not really a lie; I was seeing Brooke twice a month, and we were intimate. That should count for something.

"Then why did you come to the beach with me for the weekend, not spending it with her?"

"She's traveling on business, and I came here because I didn't want to sit around by myself. I'm sorry. I hope I didn't do anything to lead you on. If I did, it wasn't intentional."

"Forget about it." She got up and waited for me to stand up. When she did, Allen fell off her shoulder. He fumbled around in the sand looking for his camera. "Let's head back."

We had no more discussion on our way back to the house. A bright moon in a cloudless sky with the scent of Midnight Jasmine in the air. A romantic night wasted. Monika went straight to her room; not even a good-night from her. I took a long, cold shower and went to bed.

Breakfast, church, and the rest of Sunday were strained, and the others noticed it. Everyone stayed away from us. I was in a terrible mood, probably a bad case of semen backup. Monika was forced to ride home with me by her friends. "You came with him; you go home with him." Perhaps an attempt on their part to give us a chance to heal our relationship. It didn't work. Silence filled the space between us until we passed Annapolis. I tried to end the silence as the Javelin took us into the last hour of our trip.

"Monika. I'm sorry. I should have told you I was involved with someone. I thought you were just being friendly."

She started tearing up. "I've just spent so much time working on my career. In school, I was disciplined, no doubt the strong German work ethic combined with American hustle. No dating. No parties. No social life. I missed the whole sexual revolution. I had lots of chances. Then work, buckling down. I avoided any relationships at work."

Looking at her, anyone would know she had lots of chances. She was gorgeous and smart and probably hit on more times than anyone. I said that out loud, hoping it would be taken as a compliment.

It wasn't, or, at least, she didn't say thank you or smile. "I thought you were different. I really liked you, Jonathan, and I wanted you to know how much. I was wrong. I feel like such a slut for my behavior and what I said."

I reached over to pat her leg and provide reassuring words. She flinched at my touch. "I'm sorry. If I wasn't involved with someone, I would have been very receptive. You are an incredible woman. If things don't work out, maybe we can get together." Wow, that was the wrong thing to say.

"That's even worse, being someone's rebound girlfriend. How could you think I would find that attractive? Makes me feel all I am is a pretty face with nice tits."

"Well, not really nice. More like great tits." Saying that with a crooked smile made me think I could connect with her at a level she would understand.

Again, the wrong thing to say. "Shut up and drive this ugly piece of shit. Not another word. Do you hear? Not another word."

The silence between us returned, all the way to her apartment. She grabbed her bag from the backseat, turned, and walked away. True to her word, not another word.

Chapter 25

The next week, I was off to the State Department. The commute was about the same distance as Energy, but on the north side of the mall. A middle-aged man met me at the reception desk and introduced himself as an information officer who would be my escort—an escort who didn't seem pleased to be babysitter for me. I learned one of the reasons. Allen had rearranged my schedule, and I would be at State for two weeks. The feedback from my week in Energy had been positive, and they wanted me to get a broader exposure to State. In addition, the first week included the Fourth of July and would shorten my time in the building. Allen felt the time with State couldn't be condensed.

In a Spartan office, my escort went through the agenda for my time in State. Like Energy, I was exposed to disruptive analysis thinking, although they didn't call it that. In fact, I never learned what they called it. Unlike Energy, I would spend time with people who specialized in evaluating existing and potential threats in defined geopolitical areas.

The group that evaluated Europe included Russia and East Germany and had the largest staff and projects under review. Vietnam, of course, had almost as many resources and as much activity. China and Korea were evaluated by a single group and the impact of China in Vietnam shared. The Middle East was staffing up, not limited to Israel anymore but including Iraq, Iran, and Saudi Arabia. Yes, Iran is not technically in the Middle East, but the government considered it a strategic part of the region. A small group looked at potential threats from India and Pakistan. Central and South America, which included Cuba, had a group, as did the continent of Africa. Even though the threats in each of these areas seemed different, the analysts spent a lot of time sharing information. State also had a desk devoted to internal threats within the United States.

None of this became clear until I met the people who monitored worldwide problems. I initially thought the biggest of these would be communism, but I was wrong. While it did represent a big threat, in their minds, international drugs and the threat of religious upheaval, specifically militant Muslims, presented a much larger threat.

They took some time to explain these seemingly unrelated threats. The profits from drugs spawned an increase in the numbers of people supplying the drugs. This included areas in Central and South America, the Far East, and the Middle East. Drugs and money had profound implications for the United States. The drugs funneling into the United States had undermined the very fabric of the country. More of a concern to the State Department, the monies from these drug sales could be used to finance increasingly more aggressive militant Muslim groups. These groups currently targeted Israel, but the fear was that interest would shift to the bigger targets of Europe and the United States, the principal allies of Israel.

The time with State, after my time with Energy, gave me an appreciation of the work being done and the potential threats existing in both the technological and the geopolitical arenas. More importantly, my respect for the people doing this work increased dramatically. They may have been meek-looking, pocket-protector-wearing geeks, but they did first-class work. At the end of my week with Energy, I was excited about the future and the technological advances coming forward. After my time with State, I was scared, apprehensive the world would not be able to enjoy the future.

I ended my two weeks in the State Department with a view of the world that was on the negative side of neutral. I read the newspapers with eyes now colored with skepticism. I trusted the news reports less because some of what they reported seemed at odds with what I now felt obvious. Why didn't they get it? The guys in State understood it. Why didn't the politicians and press get it? Why weren't they doing something about it? I didn't have kids, and it made me question whether I wanted to see kids grow up in such a dangerous future. If it was just me, I could handle it. I'd run and hide in the hills and get by on very little, but that's not the future you have in mind when you bring a kid into the world. You want something better for them. I should have asked one question of each of the people I met at State: do you have any children? If they did, I'd feel a little better. If they didn't, then I might just start looking for some land on the top of a mountain in West Virginia, scrape a free-fire zone of about one hundred yards around it, and stockpile food and ammunition.

The same routine was presented to me when I arrived to begin three weeks at the CDC in Atlanta. A middle-aged woman, pleasant but officious, in the uniform of the Public Health Service guided me through the weeks. My familiarization with the work of CDC exposed me to teams working on geographical areas but had the overlay of diseases, which really know no boundaries. The present and existing conditions got more attention than in Energy or State. The future, as CDC dealt with it, could be very short term due to the potential for the spread of disease and the potential for epidemic or pandemic disasters. There was a heavy emphasis on infectious diseases and control either by treatment, isolation, or inoculation. In all the discussion, there was the undercurrent that these infectious diseases could be weaponized. As such, they would present a much larger threat, as the normal spread could be intentionally accelerated and broadened by malicious men. All of this led to interactions of CDC with foreign governments and our own State Department, for obvious reasons.

During my assignment at CDC, I became more aware the bureaucratic process, at least the observation of it, as it operated on a daily basis. I asked more questions at CDC than I had at Energy or State and learned I was in a new program informally referred to as Friends of, or FO. It had been designed to be a broad introduction to CDC. The participants came from a number of sources, but most had an interest in health care. Being sponsored by the State Department, I was a FOS, or Friend of State. Others were sponsored by the NIH, the FDA, or foreign health organizations, either individual countries or large sponsors such as the United Nations or the World Health Organization (WHO).

While this was interesting, I had been spoiled by the wider scope of the analysts at Energy and State. This was applied medicine, and I began questioning my chosen profession. Still, I had to be realistic. I had only finished my first year of medical school and still had a lot to learn. The next three years would put me in contact with patients, and my view toward medicine might change. And this was only my first summer in Allen's training program. Surely he had orchestrated this first summer to pique my interest and test my resolve, especially with Monika.

Brooke wanted to come to Atlanta for a weekend. We talked a couple of times a week, and, as the time approached for her trip, I looked into things to do in Atlanta. While it wasn't what you would call a tourist attraction, I thought there might be enough to do as a couple that we would keep busy. We had a good time on Friday night when she arrived. We rushed back to my apartment and went straight to bed. After a great start on the weekend, we decided to go out and sample the nightlife. The evening looked perfect from my window, a clear, moonlit sky.

Outside, it wasn't so perfect. The heat of the day was having a difficult time dissipating, and the humidity was a permanent fixture. We ate at Romeo's, an Italian place on Peach Street. We both enjoyed the meal, but it was more of a family restaurant than a romantic café. After dinner, we tried one of the clubs in the area offering jazz, but it proved too noisy and crowded for our tastes. We decided we were more interested in the cool of my bedroom and the company of each other.

The heat and humidity had already exceeded uncomfortable when we left my apartment in the morning at ten o'clock. We did a late breakfast and then a couple of hours driving around in the Javelin, the air conditioner cranked up to the max. We drove through and past the few areas of interest, not wanting to get out and sweat. Having seen all I had scoped out, we went back to my apartment. It was a good thing we liked each other, because we spent a lot of time in bed. While I enjoyed seeing Brooke, Atlanta in August is not romantic. Sure, we spent a lot of time naked together, but after a while, that isn't romantic. She caught me a couple of times when my thoughts drifted to Monika, distracted, far from her nakedness next to me. She asked, and I lied about the poverty and sickness I had become aware of around the world through my visit to CDC.

I felt bad thinking about Monika while lying in bed with Brooke—or did I?

Chapter 26

✳ ✳ ✳

After completing my month at CDC, I drove the Javelin up the Interstate on a Saturday. Traveling on a summer Saturday was not my best decision. Traffic was heavy with vacationing families heading to or from the beach or mountains. The rest stops were packed, and there were long delays at the tollbooths. At least it wasn't the Garden State Parkway, with tollbooths every ten miles. That would double the time of my trip.

On Monday, I went back to Walter Reed, taking the bus from Union Station. The heat and humidity were brutal. In the five-minute walk to Union Station, my shirt dripped with sweat, and the bus had a faulty air conditioner. August in Washington was worse than Atlanta. For the rest of the week, I wore shorts and a T-shirt for the commute and changed when I got there. I still sweated, but at least I didn't have to sit in damp, smelly clothes all day.

There wasn't anything planned for the last week, so I walked around, familiarizing myself with the layout. I went to a couple of seminars and spent time in the cool of the library to keep up on current affairs, a habit picked up in the Pentagon and one that would continue into old age. Allen sent a message saying he would meet me for lunch on Thursday in the hospital cafeteria.

He wore khaki trousers and a short-sleeve sport shirt. Not looking the least bit frazzled by the heat, he looked as if he had been delivered by a private car, or at least an air-conditioned taxi.

"Jonathan. You're looking well. How are you holding up in the heat?" he said as he reached across the table to shake my hand.

"Washington in the summer is like a sauna. I don't see how people put up with it."

"Imagine what it was like twenty years ago, before air conditioning became so widespread. Makes you wonder why our Founding Fathers chose this place for a capital."

"Right. What brings you to Washington?"

"Came to see you. Came to find out how you liked the program this summer." I was glad he remembered I preferred him to individualize the responsibility for me and didn't use "we." "I thought about what you might need and what you might find interesting. How did I do?" Allen was here to have lunch but made no attempt to leave the table for the serving line.

"I enjoyed it. Very interesting!"

"How so? Be specific and be brief."

"I understand what you were trying to do. The government isn't the president or the laws passed in Congress. It's not the IRS, and it's not the bureaucracy I dealt with at the Pentagon. Partly that, but there are also hardworking, dedicated people watching out for us, for the present and the future. They aren't working for a paycheck, and they aren't working for the glory or for the next election. Rather, they're working because they believe what they're doing is important. Many will never get any recognition. Some are looking so far into the future they'll be retired in Florida when they're proven right. There'll be nobody around to slap them on the back, no attaboys, just the satisfaction of having done a job well. The experience was refreshing, and I thank you."

He studied me as I spoke, looking for something.

"Well, thank you for having the open mind. Some folks don't get it, but you did. The people who count gave positive feedback. Not everyone you met evaluated you, but you impressed those who did. Well done! Any negative feelings?"

"Yes, but more a result of what I saw and heard. A lot of the stuff was classified, but now, when I read where some senator or congressman mouths off about something I know he doesn't believe and it's contrary to what I've learned, it makes me want to scream. There are reports that filter up, and I know they're sanitized, but the truth has got to be pretty evident. It's the politics and politicians that are the problem."

"That's one of the downsides of doing what we do. I feel that way all the time. The only truths come from those we work with. The reports that get issued by the people you met are clear, complete, and crisp, defining the potential threat with precision. It's unfortunate, but as they move up the management ladder, they get sanitized. If there's the possibility the findings may be too critical of our allies, the report is toned down. If the report has the possibility of inflaming our enemies, it's toned down, especially if the reports will be viewed by Congress. Congressmen seem to care more about making headlines than making headway in solving problems. Management knows information gets leaked to the press by Congress, so it's made more neutral. It amazes me anything gets accomplished on the world stage with the information that's being used by senior administration personnel.

"We try not to be too harsh on them and just keep doing our job. Someday, something big will happen, and someone will ask for the background information. Then and only then will our work be appreciated. Remember, I told you we only need Congress for our manpower and budget. The people who need to know all the information to do their jobs have the information they need to do their jobs. A politician will confess that his most important job in Congress is to get reelected because he can do good only if he's in office. Therefore, he spends more time working at getting reelected than doing the job he was elected to do."

"Thanks for the clarification. All of my experience has been with bureaucrats, like motor vehicle and IRS—not the best examples of public relations for civil servants. When I listened to the politicians making promises, I believed they'd make laws that would make the impact of the bureaucrats minimal. Now I realize politicians aren't public servants. They're just politicians, and our country is great in spite of what they do."

Allen smiled and said, "I'm glad you got that understanding from your summer with us. It's all I could hope for. When I need something from State or Energy, I see the raw information, and I talk to the analysts. I hope you understand that if I ask you to do something, I'm basing my request on real information, not a sanitized version."

"Yes, I do. But what do you mean by 'if I ask you to do something'? I'm not signing up for anything as dangerous as jumping out of airplanes again."

"I won't ask you to do anything that dangerous. But you can still be a tremendous asset to your country. You've shown a concern about a career in medicine—or, rather, practicing medicine. The profilers think you have a bright career ahead in the private sector, such as the pharmaceutical industry—not in the lab, but on the business side, where you could rise to a position of worldwide responsibility in drug development. As such, you'd be required to travel all over the world for your job. That would be valuable to us. I'd like you to finish school so you have the option of doing something like that with me."

"But I thought my value was being invisible. How can I be of value with a high-profile job?"

"You'd still be invisible to the people we deal with. Sorry to disappoint you, but your celebrity status would only be within a narrow band of your specialty, and the work I would ask of you would be out of the spotlight. I'd ask you to collect information or talk to people in what would be a natural part of your job. Any action I would ask of you would be indirect. I could ask you to provide misinformation to someone that would have the high likelihood of slowing or misdirecting something we view as a threat, or to drop a few words of clarification that would be helpful. For example, there's an informal recombinant DNA symposium in Boston in October. Are you familiar with the science?"

"Yes. The first papers were published in 1972, and there's talk of commercializing it in the pharmaceutical industry." The newspapers in New Haven had been full of stories for over a year. There were research labs at Yale doing recombinant DNA research, and there was an unwarranted fear that a monster bacterium would escape into the water supply.

"Precisely. The symposium is at MIT and will attract an audience from many disciplines and from around the world. There will be formal presentations, but the value will come from off-the-record discussions over coffee or during breaks. I'd like you to study up on the technology. There's a briefing package for you that provides the correct level of information for someone like you to understand what's going on. It'll also give you enough information to think up your own follow-up questions should you get a chance to ask the questions we have."

"Why don't you send the people who prepared the questions to the meeting?"

"We'll have a presence there, but their credentials will identify them as government employees. Some of the academics and foreigners are reluctant to talk candidly with government employees. The folks doing the research in this field now are basic scientists, working with bacteria, viruses, and what they call vectors. Nobody is doing any work with people yet."

"Don't you have others like me, meaning consultants, working in academia?" The question sounded cranky, even to me, but we had agreed to meet for lunch and there was no attempt yet to move to the cafeteria line.

"Yes, we do, but I want you. We understand there will be a group of students there—or at least they'll be operating as interested students—who are part of a group who claim to be children and former students of the original Manhattan Project scientists. They claim these early nuclear scientists were fraught with physical and mental problems for the rest of their lives because they didn't realize what they were doing. The group will raise a conscientious objector argument during the symposium. There will be a group outside the building protesting, and they'll try to disrupt the meeting from the floor. I'm not asking you to stop them, just to get close to them and find out what makes them tick. Don't misunderstand me; I'm not asking you to solve the problem. I would be happy for you to provide one piece of information we don't already have."

"How am I supposed to do that, and what do you know?" My stomach growled.

"You don't have to know what we know. Just ask the questions I provide and see where it goes. You're an outgoing guy. Ask them what the problem is. Ask them what their objections are. Just seem interested and sympathetic. They'll talk. Keep an open, receptive mind, and you'll be surprised at how well it goes. I don't want you to solve it, but you can point them in the right direction." Smiling, he leaned forward. "Just don't join the demonstration and get arrested. I can't bail you out."

"No problem with that. Maybe I'll just meet them over lunch," I said, hoping he'd take the hint.

"The symposium starts with a reception on Friday night, more of a beer and pizza party. There's a full day of meetings on Saturday and a wrap-up on

Sunday morning. You'll only be there on Saturday afternoon. During the afternoon break, keep your ears open. Then engage one of the protestors in a discussion. One of the reasons you're important for this meeting is you're not involved. A critical point on the protestors' agenda is requiring class IV labs for the research. Class IV is too restrictive and expensive and would eliminate a lot of the research in this area. The protestors are asking NIH to impose this restriction, and they have a grassroots effort with local civic groups. The fear is that a monster bacterium will be created in the labs that will spread rapidly and end civilization as we know it. Sounds similar to some of the concerns that the early atomic scientists had—once the reaction starts, it can't be stopped and the world will end."

"I remember reading about that."

"When the protestor brings this up, you ask what the current precautions are and state, 'Certainly the scientists working on these new bacteria won't want to take it home to their wives and kids. With the awareness the protestors are raising, won't that be enough to ensure nothing will escape from a lab?'"

"Okay, but why my interest? And why should they pay any attention to what I say?"

"Good point. The answer for both is the same. You are in Boston for something else and saw the notice for the demonstration. You're not a recombinant DNA guy, just a med student who plans on specializing in infectious diseases, where the pathogens involved are real. Why is current practice for working with diphtheria or staph not enough for recombinant research?"

"I'll see how it goes. Let me ask you a question." I got a nod from Allen. "I know I'm not supposed to ask why, but the scientist in me is curious. What's the connection to national security?"

"You're right, but in this case, I can answer you. The technology is brand new. There was a paper published last year by an academic in California. Before that, it wasn't on the radar. Academia has a big jump on this. The commercial implications were evaluated by industry, and they're moving ahead. We're trying to catch up. The honest answer is we don't know yet. We're on offense and defense on this. The technology could be a quicker, easier way of doing genetic transfer, or it could be disruptive. For example, if there's an oil spill, it's possible to have bacterium engineered to eat the oil. Currently, that would take years. With this new technology, it could be done in days. Big impact as Energy sees it, economic and environmental."

"I can see that." The mention of bacteria feasting on an oil spill only made me hungrier.

"Suppose one of our enemies uses the technology to create a monster bug. We have to know how to create a monster bug to counter it. There are also some interesting by-products. For instance, science has the capability of allowing the production of big pieces of DNA from little pieces of DNA. DNA is unique to each individual, more unique than fingerprints. The technology could enable us to identify bodies in a major disaster, war or natural. There's the potential that there'd no longer be an unknown soldier. It would be useful in criminology. For these and lots of other reasons, we want this research to continue at the basic science level, and we don't see the need for class IV laboratories."

"Thanks for the explanation. If the guys in the think tank at Energy believe it's worthwhile, that's good enough for me. One more question."

"Shoot."

"Did you ask Monika to test me?"

"Two questions back at you. Monika? And test you about what?"

"Monika, my contact at Energy. Did you send her to test my morals? Check me out to see if I could be seduced? Check me out to see if I'd give her a toss while I was in a relationship?"

Allen nodded recognition when I mentioned her name, then had a look of curiosity as I explained the second part of my question, and followed that with an amused look. He sat back in the chair, shrank down, and said, "I've never met Monika. She works in the Information office at Energy. One of the analysts works for me, not her. People say she's really smart, good at her job, and a real looker. I didn't have to test you. Already had everything I needed. Now, if you're telling me she made a move on you and you declined, I may have to send you in for some tests—maybe your eyes, maybe your sanity. As I said, I heard she is really something."

I sat staring at him, glassy eyed, filling with disappointment and then anger with myself. After several weeks, I knew the major reason I had avoided her advances was because of Allen. It bothered me that Brooke wasn't more of a factor, but she wasn't. "Fuck me!" was all I could manage. I didn't shout it out, but it was loud enough that the lady at the table to the side looked over.

Allen laughed. "Sorry. I'm not laughing at you. Just laughing at what you said and the reaction of the lady. One advantage of my job is a lot of exposure to field operatives who've worked all over the world. I've picked up cuss phrases in about eleven languages. If you want to avoid looks like that again, you either whisper or learn a language. For your future reference, it's *ne khuya sebe* in Russian."

There wasn't much I could do in response to that. I felt ridiculous.

"You're thinking too much. I wouldn't do something like that to you. You've been watching too many spy movies. If I wanted to test you with a woman, I would have put you in the program. Yes, we do have a course that teaches you how to seduce, how to recognize you're being seduced, how to resist seduction, and how to be seduced without giving up any top secrets. I'm afraid all that happened was she found you attractive. You turned her down for the wrong reason."

"Ne khuya sebe."

The lady still looked at me. I think it must have been the way I said it.

Chapter 27

＊　　　＊　　　＊

As requested by Allen, I went to Boston for the conference and talked with several demonstrators, including the chief organizer, the son of a minor player in the Manhattan Project. He was passionate! He ranted but only had a meager science background, turned off, I supposed, by his parent having been corrupted by science. When I brought up the similarity to working with infectious diseases, it made him pause. He had an answer for everything else but no answer for that. I didn't know if he was unprepared or if I had managed to reach him on an intellectual level. Allen was pleased with my report, and the urgency of class IV labs disappeared from the popular press.

The rest of the year passed with nothing out of the ordinary. Most second-year medical students would say the second year is hardly ordinary. For me, being able to focus on my studies was a welcome return to normal. Focusing on my studies forced my internal conflict about Monika and Brooke into the background, along with the work I had done for Allen.

Allen showed up in mid-March, again in the cafeteria, again for breakfast. He sat at my table, a paper cup of coffee in his hand. No beard or grubby look this time, but no suit and tie either. This must be his CIA-casual look. "Good morning, Jonathan. Hope you've managed to get through the winter reasonably well." Connecticut was coming out of one of the worst winters in years. The hills in Hamden near my apartment had been a challenge for the Javelin. On two occasions, I had had to park in the supermarket parking lot at the bottom of the hill and walk home. Fortunately, both times were Friday nights, and the city had sufficient time to plow and sand the hilly streets before the workweek began again on Monday.

"It was bad, but I got through it." Allen had a dark tan. "Looks like you spent the winter in south Washington."

He smiled, and his white teeth made his tan appear even deeper. "I got away for a few weeks of warm weather. Are you ready to talk about next summer?"

As I sat down across from him, I said, "If it's going to be anything like last summer, I can't wait." I had had no breakfast yet, or even coffee. He made no offer to get me any but got right to the point of his visit.

"This summer, it might be good for you to get some exposure to the pharmaceutical industry. If you still feel only warm about treating patients and would prefer to be on the business side, it might be a good time to try it. In September, you'll be going into the clinic. Having the pharmaceutical business experience will give you a chance to make a fair comparison."

"What have you got in mind?"

"I can place you in any top-tier pharmaceutical company, in several different capacities. However, there are two problems. The first is most are located in New York City or New Jersey. I'd prefer to have you in Washington, where we can meet. The second is a bigger concern for me. If I place you with a single pharmaceutical company, you'd be at the mercy of what they decide to expose you to. I'd have little input. For them, you'd just be another intern. I want you to get a fair exposure to the industry because I think it would be good for you. All of my concerns can be addressed by offering you a ten-week internship at the PMA. The Pharmaceutical Manufacturer's Association is the Washington-based trade association for the industry. In Washington speak, that means the PMA is their lobbying group."

"What does a lobbying group do?"

"They spend a lot of time on the Hill, presenting the case for their members, determining if there's legislation pending that would either help or harm them. If they view the legislation favorably, they help get the bill passed. If it would hurt, they support the opposition. A lot of help is in the form of contributions to get the congressman reelected."

"I'm surprised that's allowed."

"Everything is above board. Has to be. The Congressional Ethics Committee watches over things closely. There's a first-term congressman from Connecticut. If he nominates you for a summer internship at PMA, you'd be accepted."

"Why him? Why Connecticut? Didn't you say that most of the pharmaceutical industry is in New York and New Jersey?"

"Yes, I did. Here's the rationale. This guy is a freshly elected member of Congress. He doesn't have a lot of political capital yet. He's looking for allies. Connecticut is home to Pfizer's major research facility in Groton. Bristol Meyers also has a big facility in Wallingford. While they're not in his district, there's a significant spillover effect throughout the state. If he has ambitions for the Senate or for governor, they're a nice ally to have. Plus, he's a graduate of Yale. He'd be happy to help out if someone from Yale asked him to help a Yale med student."

"And someone from Yale would do that?"

"Today, if you say yes."

"So, back to Washington for the summer. Housing?"

"Same as last time. It'll be convenient. Is that a yes?"

"Yes."

"A word of caution. We've done some research on the congressman. He's into exotic cars. We don't believe he'd consider a lime-green Javelin as an exotic car, so don't bring it up. There's a meet and greet this weekend in Westport. You'll go down to meet him. I'll drive."

I nodded okay.

The turnout for the meet and greet was lower than I had expected. Allen reminded me of his low political capital. I nodded as if I understood what that meant.

When I told Brooke I was going back to Washington for the summer, she was pleased because it meant we were only two hours apart. We had tried to keep seeing each other during the academic year, but it proved difficult. Time was limited because her work schedule had her traveling on weekends. I found the trip long and tiring. It was at least five hours by car, and the middle of the trip meant traversing the Cross Bronx Expressway, which was a parking lot no matter the time of day. That meant ten hours out of my weekend traveling with no studying. I tried the train, but it was over five hours each way when I counted the time to get to and from the station. I gained some study time on the train, but the noise of other passengers was distracting. I even tried flying once.

Ocean Airlines, a small commuter, had a limited number of flights from New Haven to Philadelphia. It used a Beechcraft 99, a sleek-looking, uncomfortable, twin-engine commuter plane. The interior was minimal, to say the least. There was no upholstery on the walls, and the thirteen seats were barely upholstered. Yet the flight time was only ninety minutes. Seemed like a great deal until I tried it. The plane arrived late. The pilot circled a few times before he could get it on the ground. If the plane arrives late, it makes sense it leaves late. Still, I could live with it until I learned why it was late.

Most airlines let pilots bid on flights according to seniority. The long hauls, coast to coast, were picked first. Get a big chunk of time in one flight—one takeoff, one landing. They also picked the airports that were easier, with easier defined as gate availability, on-time record, and ease of takeoff and landing. New Haven was not on any list of favorite airports. In fact, because of the difficulty in landing at the airport, any route that included it was consistently the last one chosen. That's not too alarming until you consider "most senior pilot" translates to most experienced pilot, and the natural extension of that is the least senior is the least experienced. Simple inverse equation: least experienced pilot gets most difficult airport.

After getting airborne, we made it to Philly without any problems. The landing in Philly was rough. The guy across the small aisle sighed and said, "That was easy compared to what happens in New Haven." I had just landed, had two days to look forward to with Brooke, and I was thinking about a landing forty-eight hours in the future. As the weekend passed, I found myself counting down, getting more anxious as the time grew closer. I was distracted, to say the least—not just by the thought of the upcoming flight but by my anxiety. Strange behavior for a man who had jumped out of the ass end of a 727. Brooke picked up on it, and I told her of my fear.

"Last summer, after you went to the beach for a weekend, you were distracted. You've been distracted ever since. I think it might be more than that."

Could she see into my soul? Yes, I thought of Monika, but I didn't think it was intruding into our relationship. Women are said to be more perceptive and sensitive than men. Perhaps there's some truth to that.

The flight back was as bad as I had anticipated. The plane was late arriving in Philly, so we were late taking off. It was winter, and the weather was bad. The pilot circled the New Haven airport twice on his approaches, but he couldn't get it down.

The plane diverted to Hartford, sixty miles to the north. We flew over Hamden on the way to Hartford, and the bus from Hartford to New Haven went right through Hamden. Both times, all I could do was wave. The bus returned us to the airport, and I retrieved the Javelin and went home, arriving ten hours after I had left Brooke's apartment. So much for flying! Brooke thought it was an adventure and laughed about it. I told her she could fly the next time, and she took that as a sign I didn't care for her as much as I had. She got no argument from me because I don't think I did at that point.

Chapter 28

The second year of school ended and had been good for me; I was near the top of my class in just about everything. Next year the emphasis would be on clinical experience, with a minimum amount of time in the classroom. The second year had proved to be easy, but getting top marks was tough. The medical student part of my brain needed to relax during the summer. I was looking forward to going back to Washington and starting a new learning experience with PMA. Allen had provided me with a rewarding experience the previous summer, and I expected nothing less this year.

While I arrived a week later than the previous year, Washington was August hot and humid already. With the Javelin parked in front of the house on C Street again, I moved in. Lights and air conditioning drove the dark and dampness from the basement apartment. The neighborhood was still convenient, and I took advantage of the local market and stocked up. I had dinner at Dos Locos, the Mexican restaurant on the next block. There were few other people dining when I arrived. Surprisingly, some of the staff remembered me and welcomed me back. A nice feeling for sure! A book kept me company over dinner. When the place started filling up with the Sunday dinner crowd, families and couples, my book and I left.

Even though it was still warm and humid, I sat on the porch. Reading until dusk, I remained, sitting and watching what little traffic there was, either walking or vehicular. When for the fiftieth time I found myself looking up the street in the direction of Monika's house, I stopped kidding myself and admitted I hoped she would walk by. Why didn't I call her? Why didn't I walk over toward her house? I gave myself the same answer my father gave me when I asked a question he didn't feel deserved an answer—"because."

Monday, I took a cab to PMA. The office was in a building next to the *Washington Post* on Fifteenth Street at the corner of L, five blocks from the White House. The building directory listed PMA on the fifteenth floor; easy to remember—Fifteenth Street. fifteenth floor.

A pleasant-looking woman at the reception desk smiled as I approached and told her my name. The area had no seats, so I stood waiting, examining the various posters in the lobby area. Within a few minutes, someone came to collect me. While I expected a secretary or an information officer, I was greeted by the senior vice president of government affairs with a smile much too large for a summer intern. "So, you're the summer intern from Congressman McDonald." That explained the smile. It wasn't for me, but what I represented. Too used to the honesty of last summer, Allen was treating me to the other side of his world this summer. "Hi, I'm Russ Higgins, and you'll be spending most of your summer with my people learning how the pharmaceutical industry works with the government."

Russ took me to his office, a nice one near the corner. Looking out, I saw McPherson Square, one of the parks that dot downtown Washington, below me, only a block away. From his office, the green of the park looked deceptively cool compared to the heat and humidity I had just encountered. I wondered if that was also the real Washington—deceptively cool to the casual observer, hiding the real intensity.

Russ explained what PMA did and some of the problems they were facing.

In 1962, the thalidomide crisis struck. Mothers who had taken thalidomide during their pregnancy had babies with deformed arms. The crisis, while significant, had been minimized in the United States because the FDA had withheld approval of the drug. Congress and the public called for stronger laws for drugs before they were allowed to be sold in the United States. Since then, the FDA had been issuing new regulations to implement the laws passed by Congress in

1962. The industry struggled with the interpretation of these regulations, often written by lawyers with little training in science and hence no idea of what was practical or, in some cases, even possible. Rather than have twenty voices talking to the FDA, the PMA represented the industry with a single, well-thought-out voice.

For the rest of the first week, I spent a day being introduced to each section within the PMA. Besides the Government Affairs group, there was a Legal group, a Science and Technology group, a Public Affairs group, and an Administrative group. None of them were particularly exciting, and I felt a dread setting in about spending the summer with these people. That changed at the end of the week when I sat in on a meeting of the Science and Technology group.

At that meeting, I learned there were the people who worked at the PMA, and there was the PMA. Through this, I also learned something valuable about people and organizations that would help me for the rest of my career.

The interesting part was the dynamic of these people within the organization. The people of the PMA had two masters, their bosses and the member companies. For those who had to deal with the FDA or members of Congress, they also had to "work and play well" with them. I initially felt sorry for them. Not so. These were the people who knew the game and played it best. Most were there because they enjoyed the work and the balancing of the conflicting priorities and egos of people. These were the people who taught me the most because they showed me how to manage from the bottom up, not the top down. They were managing people, and the people didn't even know they were being managed. I tried to spend the most time with them. Allen wanted me to have my impact from a distance, to be removed. What better way than to learn how to manage the people who thought they were managing me?

Each night, I spent some time on the front porch of my apartment, reading a book or the paper, or just watching the comings and goings of the neighborhood, but every time, looking for Monika. Hoping she would walk by. Then, it happened.

One night, as the heat was leaving the day and the humidity was being driven out by a high-pressure ridge coming in from Canada, I was not the only one on the street. Everyone was out, enjoying the brief reprieve, storing up fresh air and pleasant thoughts of summer evenings for when the heat and humidity of Washington August would return with a vengeance. And it would. Average temperature and humidity in Washington meant just that, average. If we got a pleasant evening, we were trading it for one that promised to be extremely unpleasant. I had just returned to my stoop perch and hadn't sat down yet. Rather, I was looking at the building. I could smell the fragrance before I saw her. I thought my mind was playing tricks on me. I wanted to see her so badly. I thought of her so often.

"Pretty car." I heard from behind me.

I turned. There she was with the crooked smile. Remembering our last conversation coming back from the beach, I replied, "Pretty face."

She made eye contact. "Ugly color!"

I was hoping I wouldn't get the next line wrong. She was saying the things from the Rehoboth trip. It was almost like a code, a code of apology without saying I'm sorry. If I got it right…well. If I got it wrong, I would kick myself. "Great tits!"

She smiled. I had gotten it right.

"You remembered our last conversation."

"I've remembered every word and regretted every word. There was so much I did wrong that weekend. Our conversation was just the last thing. I wish I could do it all over again."

"How sweet of you to say that. Do you still have a girlfriend?"

Chapter 29

For the rest of the summer, I learned everything I could about the pharmaceutical industry. It was where I wanted to spend my career. What better place for a doctor than to have a job where the impact was not just on a few hundred patients in a private practice, but being able to have a positive impact on the lives of thousands, maybe millions?

Much to my disappointment, I didn't see Monika again. Was she waiting for me to show up at her front door and tell her I no longer had a girlfriend, only to remind me she didn't do rebound relationships? Women! I still had a lot to learn.

Allen, I did see—several times, in fact. Our relationship was changing. Not that we were becoming good buddies, but just more familiar, less formal, me less on edge. He was interested in how my summer was going at the PMA and not surprised when I told him of my interest in a career outside the practice of medicine. "Great, but you still have two years of clinical medicine ahead of you. The first time you save someone's life may change your mind, and if you do, I want you to know it's okay. But I'll still try to work with you."

"And convert me?"

"No, not convert. More like try to work you into the bigger plan."

"You don't seem concerned. Is it because this summer has given me an interest in business?"

"No, I'm not concerned because I know you'll do the right thing, something I've known from the first time we met. The clinic won't change your mind. Even if you save dozens of lives, you won't change your mind. Why? Because you'll see the practice of medicine is overmarketed to the medical students. You're always on duty, even when you're off duty. The only time you're free from your doctor responsibilities is a week vacation you get to take twice a year. Even then, you'll dread the possibility of hearing the cry go out, 'Is there a doctor in the house?' No, Jonathan, you don't like being controlled 24-7. The future I've shown you has more freedom and flexibility than the routine of a physician practicing medicine." He smiled, more of a grin. Absolutely sure what he said was true. He read the future as if it were already a record of the past.

The grin remained when I told him of my initial impression of the PMA, the people, and the lesson in management I had learned and how I might apply it.

For lunch, Allen had picked the Rib Room at the historic Mayflower Hotel, just one block from the PMA office. Had we been a few years earlier, we would have likely seen J. Edgar Hoover having lunch there, as was his habit for over thirty years. The conversation shifted to current events. He was aware I followed the news regularly. He used our talks to help direct me, not quiz me, in areas that should be on my radar. The news that summer in Washington was all about Nixon and Watergate. Other than the obvious, he said little.

Allen took particular pride in the progress made with airport and airline security, citing the recent antihijacking pact between the United States and Cuba. "Jonathan, this is a direct result of the work we did, and it's important on two different fronts. The first is obvious. It was within the broadest scope of our objective. Even the nuisance factor of the Cuban hijackings is gone with the changes taking place. Second, and not in our original plans, it opened a dialog with Cuba. This fundamental change in foreign policy was totally unexpected. I hope you can see the benefit of the things we do; do you?"

"Admittedly, I felt a surge of pride and accomplishment when I read the story of the pact with Cuba. Would it have happened without what we did?"

"Who can say? We did what we did. The pact was signed. Both dealt with hijackings. One followed the other. So, my answer is yes, we had an impact."

Changing the subject, he continued. "It's not something where I see you having a role, but I can share with you a major concern of mine, for now and for the future. I've had discussions with the think tanks at Energy and State, and they're also studying this. The trouble in the Middle East is going to explode again soon. If you think Watergate is dominating the news now, the Middle East will dominate in the future, providing problems in every sector of national and international life—economics, energy, politics, religion, and military—you name it."

"Are you talking about the Israeli trouble?"

"The problem is more than Israel. Most of the countries over there have three things in common. The Arab world shares the Muslim religion, which Israel does not. They have oil, which Israel does not, and they have a dominant military presence, which Israel almost has, thanks to US training and arms support. It's this US support of Israel that will cause problems. The US is at the mercy of the Middle East oil-producing nations. The US economy is based on their cheap oil, and they're getting really pissed at us. They're four thousand miles away, yet we're very vulnerable to them. Not their military, their oil."

"But there are vast reserves of oil in Texas and other parts of the Southwest."

"US domestic oil is a piss hole in a snow bank compared to what we import from the Middle East. The stuff in Texas is more expensive to produce, so we rely on OPEC oil. Right now, it's cheap and plentiful. However, we see both a short-term and a long-term problem. There will be conflict in the area before the end of the year. There have been wars with Israel in the past, the most recent 1967. Israel defended itself with our guns and planes. Now, in 1973, we foresee a coalition of Arab states attacking Israel, at least two countries allying themselves in war with them. It won't make any difference if Israel wins or loses; we'll lose."

Allen's forecast of the immediate future looked grim. He was projecting an armed conflict with Israel. Israel could respond and defeat its aggressors as it had in the past, or it could be wiped off the face of the earth. The might of the United States could certainly save Israel from destruction, couldn't it? How could we suffer?

Allen continued, answering my unasked questions. "Our economy will get crushed, or, at the very least, be at the mercy of OPEC from now on. Oil is currently selling at less than two dollars a barrel. OPEC will raise the price to over ten dollars a barrel before the end of the year. Gas prices at the pump will double or triple overnight, and that's if we can get it. It'll come at a bad time for the northern United States, at the time when refineries are shifting from gasoline to heating oil. In addition to high-priced gas, we'll get high-priced heating oil. High prices are bad enough, but short supplies of oil complicates matters. The fuel needed to run our businesses and factories could cause many to close their doors, temporarily for some, permanently for others. Fuel needed to get groceries to the market will be in short supply. The only bright spot is we'll still be able to get oil from Iran. The shah has increased his production capacity. When it happens, he'll benefit the most, and we'll get our oil from him at the inflated price. It'll get worked out, but the Arabs will have sent their message to us: support Israel at your own risk. The economy will adjust and rebound, but we'll always be under their control. As we adjust to the higher costs, they'll continue to increase the cost of oil to us, to the world. Our economy will change forever, led by a demand for smaller, more energy-efficient cars."

"And if we let Israel fall?"

"Same thing. They know they have us by the balls, and they'll squeeze us. But that's not the only bad news for the future. Let's say the price of oil increases tenfold to twenty dollars a barrel. The oil-producing nations already have more money than they know what to do with. In the future, they'll have ten times as much. What are they going to do with it? They'll buy airplanes and tanks and guns, probably from the Chinese and Russians. They may even attempt to buy a nuclear bomb. I say attempt, but I doubt the Chinese or Russians will be stupid enough to sell to them. They could become targets as easily as us."

"Jesus!" was all I could manage.

Allen paused, looked at me curiously, and then smiled. "That's kind of funny, considering the situation. We've got the Middle East in turmoil, with the Muslim and Jewish worlds ready and capable of setting that whole region on fire, and your only comment is 'Jesus.' If there's any way to unite them against us, that would be the most inflammatory term."

"I..."

"There's more. The shah will continue to sell us oil at the inflated prices, which will piss off the rest of OPEC—not just because he continued to sell oil but because he sold oil to the US, the same US that's supporting Israel. It'll also inflame the radical Muslims in Iran who have been trying to oust him for years. This will unite all the factions against the shah, and he'll be overthrown. When? Who knows? But sooner rather than later, probably within the next five or six years. The current regime will get replaced by an ultraconservative religious leader, a radical Muslim leader. The official policy of that type of government will be against anything Western. Iran will become a magnet for the radical militant groups that have already been terrorizing the West. Just think of the Munich Olympic massacre happening anywhere in the West, not just to the Jews. We don't want this to happen, but it appears it's inevitable."

"If this is going to be the biggest problem facing the West, I'm assuming you mean North America and Europe. Won't there be some type of coalition formed to fight them?"

"There might be, but it'll be useless. The West has a difficult time understanding and combating anything other than another Western mind or culture. Just look at Vietnam to understand this. We didn't understand the culture. We tried to bring democracy to Vietnam. They had no fuckin' idea what democracy was. We had to learn how to fight a war we invented. Do you realize our country won its independence from England by fighting a guerilla war? We invented guerilla warfare, and we couldn't win one in Vietnam. The guerilla war in the Middle East won't be fought in the desert or in the towns and cities of Iran and Iraq. It'll be fought in the cities of North America and Europe. It'll be a war of terrorists, bombing like the IRA did, only worse because all the extra money we'll be paying for oil will pay to arm these terrorists. We'll be paying for this war against us with our own money."

"What can I do? I don't see myself going house to house fighting terrorists."

"No, this'll be a war where we must excel in intelligence. We're developing sophisticated equipment to help us gather and analyze intelligence, but human intelligence will still be the coin of the realm. The oil money has allowed the Arabs—and I use Arabs in a generic way to include the Iranis—to enjoy a very Western lifestyle, the same life they profess to despise. They drive their expensive cars right into their tents or bathe their camels in the swimming pools of their palaces. I don't know if they use swimming pools to bathe their camels, but the image of it gives me perspective on their attitudes and helps me cope with the insanity of it all." He looked at me for understanding. "The Middle East is a powder keg. There are so many enemies over there. If we could identify them and eliminate them, the future would be bright and safe for our children."

"I understand. The visual image is profound." Allen sometimes had a way with words: a Bentley in a tent or a camel in the pool. I got the message.

Chapter 30

Allen stopped talking when the waiter came to clear our table. Nothing for unintended ears, as was his habit. We watched as he removed the remnants of our meal.

"There's part of this I don't understand. If the West is so bad in their eyes, why are they trying so hard to be Western, with the cars, the planes, and the houses?"

"Don't be misled. I'm focused on the conflict that will have the worst impact on the West. Some of that is being fueled by those who are trying to have the best of the West. Make no mistake; this is the internal conflict in the region. The very religious are ultraconservative and hate those who embrace even the slightest bit of the West."

"But there must be good people. Isn't the shah, in spite of his greed about oil for money, a friend of the West? Aren't there some who are trying to improve the Middle East by introducing some Western ideas?"

"Yes. Part of this westernization has been sending sons off to university in Europe and the States. The more prestigious the school, the better. The more prestigious the degree, the better. Smart ones go off to MIT and Caltech for engineering degrees. When they come back, they'll build an infrastructure that doesn't depend on camels and tents. Some go off for business degrees. These are the really forward-looking ones. The smart ones know the oil won't last forever and they have to use the oil money now to build an economy for the future. There are others, most often the son far down the succession line, who'll go for medical degrees. Medicine is a high calling in the Arab world. A healer. As with the others, they seek their education in the elite universities, such as Yale."

"Is there any harm in that?"

"No. For the most part, they take their education and go back to make the country better, building roads, bridges, and the infrastructure needed to support a new economy. They start businesses and build hospitals and schools, providing employment, education, and a future for many people in their country. These are the good guys, albeit good being defined by us. But there are also the bad guys, and they too find their way into the US and European universities. The bad guy engineers learn much of the same things, like how to build a bridge, but also how to destroy it. Some learn how to build bombs and how to weaponize a bacteria or virus. The biggest fear is they learn how to build a nuclear bomb. They're even more dangerous because in our open society, they're free to move around, find clusters of the disenfranchised, and preach their brand of religion. American freedom allows them to build an infrastructure within our boundaries that may, in the future, take us down."

"Jesus!"

Again, I got the look. "We have a pretty good handle on the good guys and the bad guys. The guys in the middle are the ones we're having trouble identifying. Most of them are okay, just royalty without the possibility of ever ruling. Sure, they raise some hell; who wouldn't? They come over here to get an education, but they also want to drink, party, and get laid as much as they can before they have to go back. I think you can help us with this middle group of guys."

"I've got a pretty full plate now. There just isn't any time to party with a bunch of guys I don't even know."

"No, no. Nothing like that. It may never pay any dividends, but I think you should start to cultivate some Middle Eastern friends. Not just in your medical classes, but throughout Yale. Your interest shouldn't be seen as political or partying. There are strict rules where you could do more harm than good. Music? Not likely. It seems a credibility stretch to say you have an interest in Arab music. Art or food might provide opportunities."

To a casual observer, Allen was a picture of calm, sitting there smiling, relaxed in posture and face, at ease with himself and the world. From where I sat, he was the most tense I could recall seeing him. He usually controlled himself well. It was part of his job, and he was good at it. Today he was acting disturbed, becoming more tense as he spoke, knowing something was going to happen, something he had no control over. The other look he gave was determination. He'd find a way. He wouldn't be defeated.

"I don't know what I can do. I'll look around, but I just don't think there's anything I can connect with."

Allen started to answer but stopped when the waiter approached our table.

"Gentlemen. Can I offer you dessert? Coffee?"

"Coffee," I said, my eyes lighting up. I leaned forward across the table toward Allen. "Yes. That's it. Coffee!"

"No, I don't think so."

"No! Coffee!"

"No, Jonathan. Would you prefer no, thank you?"

The waiter, obviously confused by our discussion, just stared at us. "I'm sorry," I said, "I don't want any coffee."

With a backward glance, he walked away.

Waiting until the waiter left us, I said, "No, I mean coffee might be the answer. I had Syrian coffee once, in New York. I was looking for a place to get a good cup of Portuguese coffee, my favorite up to that point. An Arab grad student at Columbia talked me into trying Syrian coffee. It was wonderful, but more important to me at the time, I didn't need all the expensive coffee-making paraphernalia necessary for Portuguese coffee."

"That's it! They love their coffee. They must meet someplace just to sit and talk over cigarettes and coffee from back home. Don't forget tea. They drink a lot of tea."

"At least it's a place to start."

Allen looked at me from across the table, a pleasant look. He smiled at me. "You'll do just fine, Jonathan." I'd managed to calm him.

Chapter 31

✳   ✳   ✳

The rest of the summer was fascinating, especially the time spent in committee meetings with the Science and Technology representatives from the member companies. At first, they were reluctant to be candid in my presence, but Bert, the PMA staffer in charge, shared sensitive information, and the talk flowed more freely. The summer cemented my desire to work on the business side of medicine and not the clinical side. The people were better rounded and not focused in a narrow specialty of medicine. I found talking about world events more stimulating than discussing the latest hot article in the *New England Journal of Medicine.*

Brooke and I spent several weekends together, alternating between her place and mine. The time we spent in Washington was uncomfortable for me because I feared we would run into Monika.

During my last week in town, I screwed up the courage to walk through Monika's neighborhood. Passing her house on the opposite side of the street, I hoped to see her but feared she would see me. I didn't know what I'd do if I saw her, and I didn't know why I feared seeing her. Retracing my steps, I walked back slower, stopping across from her apartment. If I still smoked, I could have stalled, stopped to fish out a cigarette, fumbled with the pack, made a couple of attempts to light it, and inhaled slowly to enjoy that first hit of nicotine at the back of my throat and in my lungs. But I didn't smoke anymore.

The main door to her building opened. Out she came, stood at the top of the stairs, and looked straight across at me. She beckoned me, one hand holding onto the railing and the other motioning me to her. Stupid as it might seem, I looked around and pointed at my chest. Both of her hands went up in exasperation at my sheer stupidity. "Yes, you." I walked across and stood at the foot of the stairs, looking up at her. God, she looked wonderful—white tennis shorts, a blue oxford shirt with the sleeves rolled up and the tail out, and delicate sandals on her feet. She had her hair up against the heat of late August, as she had worn it on the beach. Her legs, face, and arms were tanned. Yes, she looked wonderful. "What are you doing here?"

The question caught me by surprise. "I could say my car was missing, and I was out looking for it" was all I could manage.

She knew it was a lie.

"First, I'd say good. Tell the police someone stole it. Tell them to look for someone with terrible taste. Second, I'd tell you you're looking in the wrong place. If it was parked here, the neighbors would report it, saying a pimp had set up business in the neighborhood." I knew she meant that. She came down the steps and sat, patting the step next to her for me to sit down. I did. The concrete step was hot.

"I hoped to see you before going back to Connecticut."

"When?"

"Tomorrow. I finished up today, and school starts next week."

"No. When were you expecting to see me?"

"Kind of hoping to run into you on the street, sort of casual and, you know, surprise. Talk a little, maybe get some ice cream."

"For a guy who's a couple of years away from being a doctor, you're such a little boy. What about the girlfriend? Are you seeing her on the way home?"

"No. I saw her two weeks ago. Things are different between us. Have been since the weekend at the beach with you."

"Let's get some ice cream," she said, standing up and brushing imaginary dust off the seat of her pants. As we walked, she spoke. "I'm sorry I was so rough on you. All that not wanting to be a rebound girlfriend—it wasn't very realistic of me. Everyone our age is on the rebound. That's what we do—date lots of people until we find the right one." Stopping, she turned. "Last summer, I was on the rebound, attracted to you and at the same time looking for a reason to push you away, because I was mad at my old boyfriend. Look, I didn't mean to get between you and your girlfriend..." Pausing, she waited for me to add a name so she could stop saying "girlfriend."

"Brooke."

"Nice name. One I would have picked. Anyway, that was a crazy way to start, first a working relationship, then taking you to the beach. Shouldn't have done it."

"No, I'm glad you did. Monika, I'm attracted to you too, but there was something else going on that weekend, not just Brooke." I told her as best I could about the test I thought Allen was doing. Because I was vague, not wanting to reveal the CIA contractor-in-training thing, it sounded lame. Why did I feel and act like a teenager around this woman?

"So, you thought I was a test to see if you would become involved with someone you worked with? Why should that matter? Here in Washington, half of the people are dating someone they work with." She had stopped walking and turned to face me while she said this.

"Working in Washington, the government security and all—it was all new to me. I don't know, I just thought..."

"Jonathan, you overthought. Life is a lot simpler in Washington than you're making it. People here are just normal people." She believed what I said but probably thought me naïve. Thankfully, we arrived at the ice cream place. The interior was cool and bright. Monika ordered a banana split, and I ordered a chocolate cone. "Really? An ice cream cone? You *are* a little boy!" She turned to the clerk making her sundae and told him to make it for two and canceled the cone order. We took our split to a table and sat across from each other.

"Here's the deal, Jonathan. We can date, even though you're seeing Brooke. The rules are no sex while you're dating Brooke. No, that wasn't clear. You can have as much sex with Brooke as you want, but while you're still dating her, no sex with me. I'll trust you to tell the truth on this. Don't show up at my door in an hour and say you broke up with Brooke and expect to jump into bed with me. For now, I'm sharing a banana split with you—not my body, not my bed. We're going to get to know each other."

The rest of the evening together wasn't long, maybe another hour, but a wonderful hour. There was no sexual tension, no worry about the right time to make a move. Even with Brooke, there had always been some apprehension. With Monika, it was different and felt better. I was making a friend, an important lesson. After I left Monika, I wondered if I would apply it to my relationship with Brooke.

Driving had always been relaxing for me. Once I got past the drudgery of getting ready for a trip, the tension flowed out of my body as the miles rolled by. The drive back to New Haven was also a good time to think, and think I did, about both Monika and Brooke. I didn't love either yet. For Monika, it was too soon. Yes, it was an infatuation with both her mind and body, but it was also her presence and personality. Monika was strong. The emotional release of sharing ice cream and conversation was as rewarding as sharing Brooke's bed. I wondered about a deeper relationship with Brooke, one that would expand on our sex life to include the other aspects Monika had shown me. The one thing I knew was I couldn't continue to see both of them. If I had a strong physical and emotional relationship with both, it would hurt two of us when I made the ultimate decision. It would hurt the one I left, and it would hurt me. Neither deserved to be hurt.

Back in New Haven, I struggled to get into my study routine. A month went by before I remembered my assignment from Allen. I studied my classmates, anyone with dark skin subject to a closer look. Soon I realized I wasn't very good at identifying students from the Middle East by merely looking at them. I introduced myself to three students for closer examination, finding two of them from India and one a Pakistani, born in Minneapolis.

Then I found what I needed on a notice board, an announcement for a social club meeting, the Arab League Coffee Club. The mimeographed sheet invited students to get together for coffee once a week at an Arab-sounding restaurant in East Haven, over by the airport. That would be a good place to start.

The group met on Wednesday nights at seven o'clock, after evening prayer for those Muslims who prayed six times a day. The place was in a rough-looking neighborhood, but I had come to learn the lime-green car was not an attractive target for car thieves—it was too conspicuous.

When I walked in, conversation stopped and eyes turned to the sandy-haired me as I closed the door. Inside, it was like most seedy ethnic bars, the only difference being the exotic smells of unfamiliar foods and tinny, unrecognizable music coming from the jukebox. Those there for the meeting were as apparent as I was not. Young men with olive skin, black hair, and dark eyes gathered at the side of the restaurant in front of a banner that declared Arab League Coffee Club in English and in squiggly script that probably said the same thing in what I assumed was Arabic. As I walked over to the sign, a young man with a beard stood to greet me. "How can I help you?"

"I'm a bit embarrassed. I might be here under false pretenses." He stiffened, and his dark eyes widened. "Recently in Chicago, I went out for dinner with friends at one of the numerous ethnic restaurants the city is known for, a Portuguese place. After dinner, we had coffee, without doubt the best coffee I had ever had. I raved over it, and the owner invited me to watch a cup being brewed. The process was complex and conducted at an elaborate chrome-and-brass machine. While I was enjoying my second cup, a colleague, a student from Syria, told me Syrian coffee was much better. He offered to take me to a Syrian restaurant the next night, but I was leaving the following morning. Then I saw your notice in the Student Union, and what can I say other than here I am, and all I want to do is try the coffee."

The tall, bearded gentleman facing me lowered his head, shaking it gently side to side. "I am Ahmad, and I am sorry, my friend, but you were misled." Was I misled by the notice, thinking this coffee club was open to all? As I wondered, another man who had been close enough to hear what I had said stood. Were they going to ask me to leave? Were the two of them going to physically remove me? "Your Syrian friend was wrong. Turkish coffee is better than Syrian coffee."

The other man stood. "Neither Syrian nor Turkish can compare to coffee made in the tradition of Lebanon." Both were all smiles. Others joined in spouting their preference.

"One thing is sure: all the coffees of the Arab world are better than the Portuguese. After all, is not one of the most popular coffees named Arabica? And, my friend, you do not need a big, expensive coffee pot to make any of the coffees of Arabia. How we make it is important, not what we make it in." With that, they called for more coffee and welcomed me.

For the next two hours, I drank coffee and listened to several of these young men extol the virtues of the coffees of their homelands. Through their bragging, I learned the differences, subtle on the surface, that made these coffees unique. All had in common a finely ground coffee made in small pots, usually copper. Just the preparation allowed for certain distinctive flavor changes. For some, the water was brought to a boil and then sugar was added for a sweet coffee. The sweet water was put back on the fire and brought to a boil again, and then the coffee was added. The process of bringing it to a boil could be repeated, adding to intensity, but also to the bitterness of the coffee. In some, a portion of the brew was saved and used to start the next pot of coffee. I marveled how cultures so far removed from one another could have customs so similar. Sourdough bread and sour mash whiskey also used a portion of the previous batch in the next.

Other differences between the coffees were the use of cinnamon, cloves, or cardamom. With each, the option of milk was available. I needed neither milk nor sugar in the three cups I tried that night. I also refused to declare which coffee was better, claiming I would need to come back again with a clean palate. To endear myself, I agreed all I had tasted that night to be better than Portuguese, but I kept to myself that the reason was all were easier to make.

When I got home, I was wired! I was so full of caffeine I couldn't sleep. Next time, I'd have to limit my intake. I wondered if they made decaffeinated.

I only got to the coffeehouse every three weeks, so it was difficult to establish friendships beyond our love of coffee during those two hours. When I reported this to Allen when he showed up for breakfast just before the Christmas break, he said, "Don't worry. Don't rush it. It'll come with time. If you can get some names and countries, I can find out who's who and help guide you as to where to spend your time. I'll try to stay in touch more often now."

After the first of the year, a new face appeared at the coffee club, Shapour Hamidi, an Iranian graduate student in engineering. He explained he had lost his student visa and had to return to Iran. The reapplication process had delayed his return. After he introduced himself, he set out trying to catch up learning what others already knew about me. When I mentioned the Pentagon and my summers in Washington, he became more interested than the others had been. This made me much more alert to him than to the others. As soon as Allen showed up again, I provided him with Hamidi's name.

Twice a month, I tried working on my relationships with Brooke and Monika. With Brooke, we shifted from the mostly physical relationship to becoming more friends. She seemed less pleased with the change in our status than I had thought she would be.

Although more difficult, I also stayed in contact with Monika. She didn't want to come to New Haven. However, she felt comfortable inviting me to Washington. If I didn't want to pay for a hotel room, I could stay on her couch, but she made it clear she was still not ready or willing to share her bed with me. The first trip, I stayed at a hotel, which proved awkward for both of us and set us back. Part of it was an element of distrust that crept in that we both recognized but couldn't understand. Was it she didn't trust me, or she didn't trust herself? On the second trip, I stayed on her couch.

Arriving late on Friday night after the long drive from New Haven, wiped out, I was asleep within an hour of arriving. On Saturday, we had a great day. It was just a little awkward when it came time to go to bed, but we got through it. The next morning, as I made up the couch, she came in. She stood in the archway, arms crossed. "Comfortable?"

"It was okay. Friday night, I was so tired, I could've slept in the tub. But last night, I felt all the slats of the sofa." She had one of those Danish Modern things built for style but not comfortable for sitting, let alone sleeping.

"If we ever get together and live happily ever after, remember last night. That can serve as an additional motivator to make sure we never go to bed angry with each other."

Joining her happily-ever-after scenario, I said, "Maybe you'll be the one to sleep on the couch?"

"Never happen. I'll always get the bed. Remember that." And she turned and went into the kitchen.

The third time I visited her, she took pity and invited me to share her bed, but with the reminder there would be no sex. That was easy for me on Friday after the long drive. I had no desire for anything but sleep. But we had such a good time together on Saturday, it was hard on Saturday night, and by hard, I mean hard. After a chaste kiss good-night, she turned away from me. She tossed and wiggled, inching closer. Soon, she pulled on the covers, drawing them to her. She appeared to be asleep, and I assumed this cover hogging to be normal for her, sleeping by herself for so long. To keep covered, I had to move toward her. I could feel the heat of her body on my back. We weren't touching, but with a final wiggle, we did. "Hold me," she said. "I want to cuddle."

Rolling over to face her, I put my arm around her but kept my pelvis almost six and half inches from her back. Then she took my hand, kissed it, and brought it up to her neck. I could feel her breast on my arm. She wiggled one more time and backed into me, eliminating the distance between us, my erection pressing against her. "That's better. Now go to sleep." Her breathing quieted, the rising and falling of her chest became slower and more rhythmic, and she was asleep. I, on the other hand, was not! It took me a while. I had to wait until a lot of muscles relaxed. Not wanting to move, afraid I would wake her and she would move away, I just lay there, my nose close to her hair, smelling the mix of shampoo, conditioner, and her perfume. There was something else too: her. I could smell her. I fell asleep.

When I awoke, we were facing each other. She had rolled over during the night. Our faces close, we were breathing each other's air. When she woke up, she didn't move, just her eyes opened. I was self-conscious of my morning breath but couldn't smell hers, just the smells from last night. "Good morning," she said, a sweet sleepy smile. "How did you sleep?"

"Better," I said. "But I had a hard time falling asleep."

Giggling a little, she moved her leg between my legs, wiggling to get it high between my thighs. "Yes, I could tell you had a hard time of it. You're a good man, Jonathan. I'm glad we waited until now to have sex," she said as she pulled me closer.

"Now?"

"Now! I don't want Brooke to have the advantage any longer."

"Brooke?"

"That's good, Jonathan. Just think of me."

Chapter 32

✳ ✳ ✳

The year in the clinic was now an obstacle to overcome to reach my new goal. I still had the desire to excel at everything, but I didn't see my studies as I had in the past. Education is based on building blocks, looking forward, and applying basic information to learning the intermediate and advanced levels. Not so for me anymore. The knowledge continuum in medicine no longer existed. Each course was an entity in itself, to be mastered and then shelved.

Allen was waiting for me in the cafeteria on Tuesday morning the week after I returned from visiting Monika. All business today. "Jonathan, I've got some preliminary information on Shapour Hamidi that we have to talk about."

"I have forty-five minutes before I leave for class. If you need more time, I can meet you for lunch."

"Forty-five minutes should do. More information should come in later today, so don't leave without me giving you a way to get in touch with me." Allen was serious. So different from the more relaxed, casual relationship that had developed between us over the past years.

"Does this mean I'll get a trench coat and a piece of chalk to make markings on a mailbox?" I joked.

"All you Ivy League nerds have trench coats and carry chalk," he teased. Nonetheless, the seriousness of the meeting was obvious. As he leaned forward, his smile was gone. "Iran is a mess, and it's getting worse. I'd hoped you'd make contact with someone, maybe an Iraqi, who had a friend of a friend in Iran who could help us dot a few of *i*'s or cross a *t* or two. But you may have gotten more than that, like someone who's writing the book."

"Literary references, *i*'s and *t*'s, writing the book? Are you saying I made contact with someone important?"

"Maybe. Here's what I've got so far. Hamidi's uncle is likely a high-ranking member of the shah's intelligence service, the SAVAK. He might as well be Hamidi's father. The uncle's married but doesn't have any sons, a big embarrassment in Iran—hell, in the whole Middle East, for that matter. When his wife didn't bear him a son, he divorced her. He remarried, but his second wife didn't have any sons, a shameful situation for him, a challenge to his manhood. So he has taken on his brother's son, Hamidi, as his own."

Allen continued. "The shah was the first of the ruling class to be educated outside of Iran. Went to a school in Switzerland. Since then, it's been considered the thing to do. Hamidi has been in the US a couple of times, first at George Washington in DC. The whole Washington scene overwhelmed him. He behaved foolishly and got into a few embarrassing situations. His uncle brought him back home, gave him additional training, and sent him to Columbia in New York. Still too much intrigue there for him, with the United Nations. As a last resort, they moved him to New Haven. He seems to have kept a lower profile here."

"I can't say. Just met him."

"That's the point. From what you said, he took an interest in you when you said you'd been in Washington and in the Pentagon. Hamidi may think you're connected, or maybe even an agent."

"Well, I am, aren't I?" I shouldn't have smiled when I said this. The look he gave me let me know. My look back let him know I shouldn't have smiled.

"When he was in Washington and New York, he hung around the places the Western diplomats frequented. He was pretty open that he was from Iran and asked a lot of pointed questions. At one point, he told people he was a reporter and actually asked if he could record conversations. It was comical."

"Yeah, he was certainly interested in me, what I did, and what I was doing. Everyone else at the coffee club seemed focused on coffee. After all, we only got together for about two hours, and I only went every three weeks."

"If my information is right, he'll seek you out and try to get more time with you. Be on your guard with him. He may try, at least in his mind, to recruit you. Might figure it would be a way to get back in good graces back home. If that happens, you'll be a name in Tehran, and so much for being invisible, at least for that intelligence agency."

"What do I need to know?"

"You'll need to bone up on Iran. I've got some stuff to get you started. The US and Iran have been working together for years, openly and undercover. The relationship started over oil and communism. But now, there's a wider interest in Middle Eastern stability. To be frank, we may have created a monster with the shah, and now he's holding us hostage."

Allen paused to take a sip of his coffee and light up a cigarette. "US involvement started in the early fifties, when we were worried about the spread of communism. Remember, we saw communists everywhere then. We helped the shah return to power after a couple of coups, primarily because of our self-interests, and those of England—oil and a fear of communism. When he returned to the throne, he established an intelligence organization within Iran to prevent the dissidents from trying to oust him again. The CIA helped him set up the SAVAK. Even at that time, it was clear it wasn't the best situation to be in, but it was better than losing access to the oil and having Iran come under communist control."

"But I thought the shah was popular in Iran and the United States."

"He was, and he wasn't. When he first took over from his father, he was welcomed by us and his countrymen. The father was a tyrant, and the shah seemed determined to import democracy and a Western standard of living. He appointed a prime minister who promoted democracy. All was good until he proposed nationalizing the oil industry, essentially taking it away from England. Then all hell broke loose. He alienated the West by this move but gained favor in Iran. The prime minister went for a coup, supported by the conservative Muslims who were unhappy with the Westernization sweeping the country. With the help of the US and England, the shah retained power. There were a lot of pissed-off people in Iran—those who just didn't like the West involved in their affairs, those who resented the loss of the oil back to the West, and the conservative Muslims who saw the potential for further decline in their control and a return of the decadence of the West. Add to this the potential threat of communism, and the country was a mess. Iran's neighbors were also wary."

Allen continued. "The shah wasn't a fool. He saw what was happening, so he was more than happy to get CIA input in establishing the SAVAK. At the same time, he was adopting radical changes in his country, trying to be more democratic. The White Revolution in 1963 inflamed the most significant religious leader, the ayatollah Khomeini. It called for land reform, rights for women and non-Muslims, and the sale of a few state-owned industries. Khomeini protested, and they threw him out of the country. He went into exile in Iraq, where he remains today, but he still exerts an influence from afar with followers in Iran. The more things the shah changed, the more people he pissed off. The more people he pissed off, the more intelligence he needed from the SAVAC. He kept expanding their powers to the point where it's a feared entity in Iran today. The only thing I can liken it to is the Gestapo. It does the same things and instills the same fear in the populace."

"I'd never heard of the SAVAC until you brought it up."

"Why would you? It's not getting much attention in the press. The US government isn't going to bring any attention to it. Can you imagine the headlines for a US-inspired gestapo operating in Iran?"

"That's good background. I can assume Hamidi will try to get close the next time I go to the coffee club meeting. Should I stay away for a while?"

"No. Don't do anything different. Stay with whatever pattern you've been using. He'll try to monopolize your time, but don't let him. He'll push; it's his nature. But stay with the others as much as possible. Chances are they know who and what he is. If you stay with him, they'll cut you out and avoid you. Everyone in that group has the potential to be important."

"Okay, but what should I say? Won't he continue to pump me about Washington?"

"Stick with coffee. Stick with the things you've been talking about with the others. If you haven't mentioned Energy, don't. If you have, I'll get you a cover story."

"I don't know if I talked about Energy. Don't think so. I had no reason to go into those details. If I did, I'll just…"

"No, don't say anything until I get back to you. We don't know what he knows, and if you say the wrong thing, you could scare him off."

"Wouldn't that be a good thing?"

Showing some frustration, Allen said, "No, not yet. First, we must decide if he's any use to us."

Time was running out, and he knew I had to get to class. As we collected our things, I asked, "How will I know when you have something else? Will you show up here again?"

"No, you need to be able to get information to me. If Hamidi doesn't see you at the coffee club meetings each week, he'll come looking for you. You must let me know if that happens."

"How do I do that?"

"Have you been to Louis' Lunch yet?"

"No, I've heard about it. Isn't that the place that invented the hamburger?"

"That's one of the places that claims to be the first. I have a tendency to believe their claim over the others. You can get in touch with me through Carl, who works at Louis'. I'll brief him today. He knows about you. Let him know if you need to talk. He can find you if I need to get in touch with you in a hurry."

I shook my head and stared at him over an armful of dishes and books.

Allen answered my head shake. "What? You thought I'd leave you here by yourself? Carl is the modern-day equivalent of a chalk mark on a mailbox."

Allen was waiting for me when I left the building after my last class. "Coffee?" he asked.

"Do you know where I am all the time?"

"You're a student; it's not a secret what the schedule is. Med students are all in the same place at the same time. Nights and weekends are more of a challenge." The playful expression was back. We went to a coffee shop near the medical school campus and took a booth near the back. Allen took the side of the booth where he could keep an eye on the door.

"Hamidi is the nephew! There's nothing else on him other than what I've told you already. People are making inquiries, but that will take a while. It's nighttime over there. In the meantime, just do as I said. In the course of normal conversation—and I stress, normal conversation—see if you can find out what he's doing here. What's he studying? Has he seen much of the country? Don't sound too interested. A few of these guys have been sent out of Iran because they like to fuck guys. It's the next step up from goats. Kind of, get out of here and sow your wild oats someplace where you won't embarrass the family. Tell him you have a girlfriend, but not Monika. Maybe a girl back home who's waiting for you to finish school. I don't want him snooping around her and Energy."

"Thanks. No need for her to be involved. I'm okay with the small talk. Science and medicine should be the areas I focus on. I'll tell him about my summer at CDC."

"If you can, find out if he has any friends, either here or elsewhere in the country. See if he tells you about George Washington and Columbia."

"Got it. Anything else?"

"No. Sorry for the two meets in the same day. I got ahead of myself when you told me about him. This guy could be important to us, and I wanted to make sure you were comfortable and remind you I've got your back."

I stuck to my routine. I went to class, studied, and didn't return to the coffee club for two weeks.

As soon as I opened the door, Hamidi walked toward me. "I thought you gave up on the coffee club. Where have you been?"

Moving deeper into the room, he remained at my side. "I don't come here every week. My studies keep me busy. The coffee is a treat for me, and I don't want it to become routine. So every three weeks works out well for me." By now, I had reached the back of the room, and the others greeted me with less attention than Hamidi showed. Perhaps Allen was right, and they knew his background. I had to be careful. I had to cultivate Hamidi's friendship—an overstatement of the relationship—without alienating the others. They made room for me at the table. Hamidi had to grab a chair from another table if he wanted to stay close. He did.

The featured coffee for the evening was Ukrainian, a surprise for me. Ukrainian coffee in a Middle East coffeehouse? They laughed at me. Ukrainian coffee was popular with Westerners, and they had anticipated my coming tonight. Being located just north of Turkey, the Ukrainians had adopted some Turkish things, such as coffee. They felt it was a nice change of pace for them, more of a dessert type of coffee, good for evenings when less serious discussions took place. Was this a message to Hamidi that they wanted to avoid anything serious tonight?

The coffee was brewed in the traditional way but included all the condiments associated with Middle East coffee: sugar, clove, cinnamon, and cardamom. This coffee was wonderful! I told them so, and they were pleased with their choice for the night. They cautioned me, however, it wasn't their favorite, and the next time, they'd return to the more traditional coffees of their homelands.

One of the more interesting observations I made during the short two hours was their complete avoidance of anything dealing with their homelands. Usually, someone had received a letter or a visitor with news from home. Earlier discussions had touched on several aspects of life in Iran, and almost always there was the air of dissent—not profound, but it was there. Tonight there was none of that. When they spoke to Hamidi, which was infrequent, it was polite but not friendly. When Hamidi tried to engage me, they would draw me away with questions about the coffee. It was interesting to watch, as if they were trying to distance themselves and me from him.

Chapter 33

Within a week, Allen was back, waiting at our table, coffee in front of him, nothing for me. The crap on the table suggested he may have been there awhile—several newspapers, an empty plate, and several crumpled napkins. "Good morning, Jonathan."

"Seeing you again so soon, I can guess the subject of our discussion this morning."

"You'd be right if you said 'the uncle's monkey.' I have more information on this guy. He is who we thought. Forgive me if I repeat things I told you before, but you need the complete picture to understand the situation." At least he waited until I had taken my coat off and sat down before he continued.

"His uncle is a senior officer in the SAVAK. The organization wasn't bad when it started in the fifties. It almost had a noble purpose back then, at least as far as US interests were concerned. The Iranis fooled us to the point that we helped train them. Yes, the CIA and the US Army. The US sent a guy over to Iran in the midfifties to train them. One of our heroes. Norman Schwartzkopf, a West Point graduate best known as the guy who led the investigation of the baby Lindbergh kidnapping case in the thirties."

"The CIA set up the SAVAK?"

"Yes, and from the beginning, the shah used it to remove his political enemies. We condoned this in the beginning because it included the communists and any other radical group that wasn't moving toward the democratic government we wanted. Over time, it took on a life of its own, rounding up anyone they wanted, whenever they wanted. In addition, they're starting to make enemies outside of the country, including the US. None of the other nations in the area are happy with what they're doing, with the possible exception of Egypt. The discontent has to do with power and money and oil. And there's still the religious issue. The exiled ayatollah is building quite a following in Iraq, and his teachings are still finding their way to sympathetic ears in Iran. There are some in State who think he could return to Iran if the climate gets much worse. If that happens, the country will become a theocracy and return to the Middle Ages."

"Where does that leave us with Hamidi?"

"I want him out of New Haven. I really want him out of the country, but I'll settle for New Haven for now. We've identified several people in that coffee club who might be valuable to us in the future. We fear Hamidi will scare them away if they think he's spying on them and reporting back to the SAVAK, putting their families at risk. There's a plan that needs your help."

Allen then outlined his plan and my involvement. It was critical that I not alter my habits and that I stick to my visits with the coffee club. The next time, I would bring a guest.

As I was readying myself for the next coffee club meeting, predictions by Allen during the summer became facts. Egypt and Syria were preparing for an attack on Israel. Some would say it was a complete surprise to Israel and the United States. I would disagree—Allen knew. History would record that Israel also knew, or strongly suspected, but was advised by the United States not to fight until attacked. On October 6, the Israelis were able to do just that when Egypt took their military training exercise live and moved east into the Sinai at the same time Syria tried to regain the Golan Heights, beginning the Yom Kippur War. Less than three weeks later, it was over, and again Israel had prevailed, with modest help from the United States. A tentative cease-fire was promoted by the United States and the Soviet Union. While the intense fighting stopped, the tension remained and was felt by the rest of the world. Saudi Arabia persuaded OPEC to start reducing oil output, initiating the oil embargo. My respect for information provided by Allen, while high before, increased significantly.

Over the next two weeks, I stayed with my routine. I thought I saw Hamidi lurking, perhaps waiting to intercept me and engage in conversation, but I avoided him. I hoped I wasn't obvious. If I was, I might have to get Allen to schedule training in this if he expected me to do any more of it.

Wednesday afternoons were relatively light for me, which was one reason I could free myself up for the coffee club. On the day of the coffee club meeting, I went to the train station to await the arrival of a "friend of an old friend" Allen had arranged to visit me. As the train from New York unloaded its passengers, a tall, blond, middle-American-looking young man strode across the passenger lounge. He could have been mistaken for a cowboy if he had been wearing a Stetson. He waved as soon as he saw me. I waved back and moved toward him. We shook hands and greeted each other not like long-lost buddies but as friends of friends. As we walked to the Javelin, he kept the conversation going but really said nothing. Once inside the car, he put his fingers to his lips, cautioning me not to speak. "Can we stop somewhere so I can get something to eat and take a piss?"

"Sure, there's a Howard Johnson's on the way to my house." The ten-minute drive to the Ho-Jo was punctuated with the light conversation about the train ride, the weather, and hopes for the Red Sox.

Once inside, he spoke more directly. "We have to be careful. If Hamidi is as interested in you as we think he is, he may have bugged your car. Same thing could be true of your house. We won't get much of a chance to talk except for now. Tonight, I want you to introduce me as Lance, a friend of your former room-mate at Harvard. I'm on my way to Boston, but I wanted to stop, say hello, and have a meal. During our discussion, I learned about your coffee club and became interested. You invited me along. You don't have to do anything else. After that, I'll carry my own conversation. If you're questioned about me afterward, you'll only say it was a surprise visit, that you had only met me once before. When they check with your old roommate, the road will end there. Got it?"

"Yes. Do you need an introduction to Hamidi?"

"No. It'll work out better if you don't. Just a general introduction to the group as a fellow coffee lover."

After we finished our late lunch, we went to my apartment until it was time to leave. Lance left his overnight bag in the spare bedroom in anticipation of returning. Again, in the Javelin, our conversation was light.

Chapter 34

＊　＊　＊

As soon as we entered the coffeehouse, Hamidi was in my face, placing himself between me and Lance. "So good to see you again, my friend. There is much to catch up on. Perhaps you should come here more often. If you cannot, we can meet for lunch."

"Shapour. Hello. Time is limited because my studies keep me busy. In fact, tonight, I'm doing two tasks at once. A friend is passing through town. I've brought him so I wouldn't miss it yet still be able to visit with him."

"And, of course, to introduce him to our fine coffee and your many friends."

"Nice to meet you. I'm Lance." Lance extended his hand to Hamidi. He was no longer the cowboy; he had taken on a less masculine demeanor. A subtle difference I wouldn't have noticed except it was in contrast to the Lance I'd been with for the last three hours. But Hamidi picked up on it and was beaming. The three of us moved to the back of the restaurant and joined the rest of the group.

The evening progressed with the usual talk about coffee, Hamidi, always at my side, wanting to talk about my days in Washington, contributing as a starting point his memories of the city. An hour into the evening, Lance left for the men's room, announcing he wasn't used to so much strong coffee. When he left, Hamidi made an excuse and followed him. The rest of us returned to our conversation.

What followed was bizarre and unexpected, although looking back, it must have gone strictly according to plan. Sounds came from the men's room, loud shouting, two voices. Then the crash of metal against the wall or floor, probably a garbage can. Hamidi came stumbling through the door and fell to the floor, blood from his face dripping down his shirt. Lance came through the door and stood above him, fists at the ready. He was angry. Everyone had turned to look. Hamidi attempted to get up and in doing so reached for Lance's leg. Lance pounded him in the face, a vicious blow that knocked him to the floor again. "I should break your hands, you filthy pervert. Isn't that what they do in your country? An eye for an eye and cut off the hands of someone who tries to touch someone's dick."

Everyone in the room stood, no one more shocked than me. Some were smiling. No one moved to help Hamidi. I thought Lance would hit him again, but instead, he spit on him, walked over to retrieve his coat, and said, "I'll get a cab. I'll send for my stuff." And with that, he left the building.

Still, no one moved to help Hamidi. As I started to move, Ahmad grabbed my arm and turned me back to the table. With the others, we sat and returned to drinking our coffee, leaving Hamidi sitting on the floor, leaning against the service bar.

The owner called the police, who arrived shortly. Hamidi managed to stand himself up, leaning against the wall. The police spoke with the owner and then with Hamidi, who looked as if he wasn't talking at all, just shaking his head. He reached into his pocket and showed the police something from his wallet. One officer led him to a chair at an empty table.

A police officer approached me. I don't know if the owner had told him Lance had come in with me, or if he approached me as the only non-Arab-looking person in the room. "What happened?" he asked.

"I was sitting here, and then I heard a noise coming from the men's room. It sounded like arguing and then a crash, like a garbage can fell over. Next thing, Hamidi came flying out the door, all bloodied. The other guy was standing in the door saying something that sounded like 'pervert.' Then he left."

The policeman looked to the others and asked if anyone had anything to add. He asked if anyone knew the guy. Before I could answer, Ahmad spoke. "I've never seen him before tonight." Which was true. No one was pointing the finger at me, saying he came with me.

"Can you describe him?"

Again, Ahmad replied. "He was about medium height, very strong looking. I don't know, but he looked Mexican to me."

"Why do you say that?"

"Because he looked like the actor who played Ben Casey on television and I think he was Mexican or something like that." As Ahmad said this, the others nodded in agreement. I couldn't believe it. These guys had taken a tall, blond-haired, American cowboy and described him as looking like Ben Casey. Nothing could have been further from the truth.

"Any idea of where he went?"

"Probably back to where he came from. Hamidi spent some time with him. Can he tell you anything?"

"He's not talking. Said it was a misunderstanding. Showed me a card that says he has diplomatic immunity and doesn't have to talk to police. He's the guy who got beat up. He doesn't want to press charges. From what the owner said and what you said, it sounds like he got what he deserved. I'm just trying to get something to put into my report. All I can do is what I can do. Gentlemen, enjoy the rest of your evening. Sorry for the disturbance." And with that, they helped Hamidi to his feet and out the door.

Ahmad took my arm. "The coffee has gotten cold. Let us get some fresh coffee and sit and talk." At the table, he poured two fresh cups from the pot. The familiar Syrian coffee, which had become my favorite, along with Ahmad's soothing voice, calmed me down. He settled in, lighting a cigarette, blowing the bluish smoke upward, watching it rise. "Your friend—Lance, that was his name?"

"Yes, Lance." I was going to add he wasn't my friend, but it didn't seem important at this moment.

"This friend Lance has done us, and probably our families back home, a great favor tonight. Perhaps, in a way as yet unknown, he has even helped you." He looked at me, his black eyes serious, full of expression. "Hamidi, as you might have gathered from the questions he asked of you, is not really a student. Yes, he is registered as a student at the University of New Haven but claims allegiance to Yale. He never says he goes to Yale, but when asked, he says he goes to school in New Haven. Some who have just met him think he is humble saying New Haven. They assume he is at Yale. So be it. But he is neither humble nor an Eli. Most likely, he is in the employ of the SAVAK, the vicious Iranian secret police."

"The Iranian secret police! What would the secret police want here at Yale?"

"There are two answers to your question, my friend. They are mainly interested in the Iranian students and faculty but also those from many countries in the Middle East. The faculty is of less interest because they are most likely to remain in the United States. They have good lives, and most are on the way to becoming citizens. Yes, there are some dissidents to the shah among the faculty who sometimes are vocal, but for the most part, they have no families in Iran to use for leverage. Those with families in jeopardy are not outspoken."

"If the secret police are as bad as you say, that certainly makes sense."

"Believe me, they are. Which leaves the students as Hamidi's main target. He has managed to infiltrate a few student groups, this being one. Two hours, several times a week, is hardly a full-time job."

"That's the two answers—faculty and students?" I asked.

"No, the second reason is Hamidi himself. The secret police are not interested in what either the faculty or students at Yale say or think. But Yale is the last stop for Hamidi. The SAVAK is watching him, not the students or faculty. Hamidi first came to this country to Washington, DC, not because of any talent he had but because of his uncle, a high-ranking member of the SAVAK. Talent does not follow bloodlines. He was an embarrassment in Washington, so they sent him back to Tehran for additional training. They sent him next to New York as a student at Columbia. He was an embarrassment there as well. I should add that I know none of the details of the so-called embarrassment, but it is rumored he has always liked the boys more than the girls. Once again, they sent him home for more training. Perhaps they taught him the pleasures of a woman's body." Ahmad smiled, blowing smoke again in the air, a memory flashing through his mind. "A shame they would have to teach such a thing.

"Yes, a shame. So, in the terms of your national pastime, he started in the majors, did not do well. Got traded to another major-league city, but he still did not perform. Then he got sent down to the minor leagues in New Haven and, once again, he failed. He has three strikes, so he is out." Ahmad hadn't gotten the analogy right, but he got his message across.

"Now, what happens to him?"

"The diplomatic immunity card he showed the police is his ticket back to Tehran. Because he showed it, the police are obligated to call his embassy to report his altercation. Those in New York are familiar with him from his time there. The embassy will ask about the circumstances. The police will report the facts and may provide a copy of the report, which includes the owner's and your description of the incident, including the word 'pervert.' Hamidi will be on a plane to Tehran tomorrow night, or at the very least, the weekend. After that, who can say?"

"Wow!"

"What can be said is he will not be here anymore, and we have you and your friend to thank. So I think you will be drinking coffee free for the next year. Lucky for us you don't come every week. It would be expensive." He said this with a toast and a sardonic smile. I accepted his toast and would certainly drink his coffee.

"I had no idea about Hamidi. I thought he was just being friendly. Now I don't know if he was spying on me or hitting on me."

"Why would you say he might be spying on you? Are you a government agent?"

"No, but I told him I did my military service in the Pentagon and I had worked a couple of summers in Washington. That was when he became interested in me."

"Ah, that is probably the case. He probably was not hitting on you. You are not an attractive man." Ahmad then added, "But what do I know what an attractive man is? I love women, especially American women. Let us talk about women now, Jonathan. Always we talk about coffee. Let us talk about women. Do you have a woman?"

"Ahmad. That's a very direct way of changing the subject from talking about coffee to the women I date."

"No, Jonathan. We went from talking about an Irani who had the power to hurt my family. And I asked you if you have a woman, and you responded 'women.' Do you think perhaps a poor, unsophisticated camel jockey cannot tell the difference in these two words?" He was having fun with me now, all of his teeth participating in his smile.

"Wow, I thought that was a derogatory term. Are you really a camel jockey?"

We were both laughing now. The others had been listening to our light banter, and everyone was laughing. It felt good. I felt one with these men for a while, forgetting I was here for a different reason. Reservations would arise later if I ever got asked to do something that would harm any of them.

Allen stopped by the following week to tell me Hamidi had been put on an Iranian Air flight to Tehran on Thursday night. Someone had driven up from New York to pick him up at the police station. They kept him inside the embassy until they took him to the airport. He also told me there were others in the coffee club who might provide valuable information. With Hamidi gone, they were likely to speak more freely, and he suggested I consider moving my participation up from every three weeks to every two. I told him I'd have to think about it. Before he left, he told me he'd be back in two weeks for breakfast. This was the first time he'd ever scheduled a meeting with me.

As he was leaving, I asked if I was in any danger from Hamidi or the SAVAK for the role I had in setting him up. "You didn't set him up, Jonathan. Hamidi made the mistake of making a pass at Lance in the men's room. Lance doesn't go for that shit, so he pounded him. Nothing to do with you."

"Right" was all I could manage.

Chapter 35

✳ ✳ ✳

Allen was waiting at my table just as he always did. He was a creature of habit, and his habit was to be waiting at my table.

"Good morning, Jonathan." Two coffees were in front of him. "Coffee?" he asked, pushing one at me.

As I accepted the coffee, it occurred to me we seldom shook hands at these meetings. Rather, each meeting was a continuation of an earlier meeting and required nothing more than a greeting. "Coffee is fine, but I'm more interested in hearing what you have to say."

"There's quite a bit. First, we've gotten a much better line on the others in the coffee club. Among the Iranis, most are sons and nephews of important government officials, some who are in support of the shah and some who aren't necessarily so. Both of interest to me. Ahmad, who seems to be your main contact in the group, is the son of a midlevel member of the oil ministry."

"Ahmad is studying economics, not engineering or anything to do with oil."

"That's what makes him interesting. The Iranis and most of the powerful in the Arab world send their sons off to study engineering in the West. At first, we thought the goal was to maximize the level of internal expertise and reduce the need for the West, giving them the foundation to nationalize the industry. That's always seemed to be their focus. With Ahmad focusing on economics, it raises a couple of questions. Are they at a point where they have enough expertise in engineering? Are they at a point where they're thinking in terms of changing the economics of oil? Regarding the latter, it only means one thing to us: an increase in price. Why would they do that? Are they considering using the extra money as a weapon, directly or indirectly, to conquer the West? We don't know, and we don't know if Ahmad knows. Just keep your ears open. If given the chance, probe a little."

"Yeah, got it." I wasn't quite comfortable using a friendship with Ahmad to probe. I would have to see how this played out.

"We're working on the others, but it's difficult to assess the level of the parent in the bureaucracy and the position of the son in the family. There's not a lot of potential value for us in the fifteenth son of a low-level minister in the Agriculture Department."

"Right. A number-two son of a general trying to get into the Skull and Bones would be of interest. Or, the nephew of a high-ranking member of the SAVAK would also be on your list," I said, the latter a reference to Hamidi.

"Jonathan. Hamidi is dead!"

"Dead?" I had been sipping the coffee Allen had gotten me, and the shock of hearing the news made me spill some of it on the table. Allen passed me a handful of napkins with a sympathetic but not surprised look at my reaction. "Jesus, that's terrible! How did it happen? When?"

"Sometime in the last week. A cable came in last night. The government reported it as an accident, but it looks like an execution. A bullet in the back of the head is hardly an accident."

"Execution? How could that be, with his uncle so high in the SAVAK? Won't there be retaliation? After all, he was like a son."

"The uncle ordered the kill. At least that's what our man in Tehran heard from his informants. The report is being spread wide and openly. The uncle wants everyone to know no one is beyond the arm of the SAVAK, even favorite nephews. It's part of the fear campaign they wage. If he did order it, it's consistent with what we know about him. Everything is for the state—no exceptions."

"Did we have something to do with the murder?"

"If you're asking if we killed him and made the finger point someplace else, the answer is no. An emphatic no! If we'd done it, it would have looked like an accident. Most certainly, we wouldn't allow his death to be used by the uncle. We would've used it to make someone else suspect. Someone we couldn't touch. Let the SAVAK go after them. No, this was the uncle's work."

"Did we have anything to do with it, by putting him in that embarrassing situation at the restaurant and having him sent home?" I needed to ask the direct question and not allow Allen to move around it again.

"Jonathan. All we did was expose one of Hamidi's proclivities. We didn't send him back to New York, and we didn't have him flown home to Tehran. We certainly didn't have him killed."

The evasive answers were irritating me. "I repeat: did we have anything to do with his death? No more bullshit. Did we know this would happen?"

"Let me tell you what I know for sure. Yeah, I knew he liked the guys. He'd been arrested in both Washington and New York in men's rooms. Here's what I'm less sure of: would he follow Lance into the men's room? Don't know. Did he ever follow you into the men's room? No. If he followed Lance into the men's room, would he make a pass? Don't know, but probably. If he made a pass at Lance, would Lance beat the shit out of him? Yes, it was part of the plan. If all of that took place, would he be removed from New Haven? I don't know, but most likely. Would he get sent back to Iran? Again, I don't know but, most likely. Would they kill him? I don't know, but I can tell you, if he kept screwing up, he was going to die young."

I felt as if I'd been involved in a murder. Oh, I probably couldn't be convicted in a court of law, and a priest might laugh me out of the confessional, but in my heart, I felt I'd been a participant in Hamidi's death. "You knew it would happen, or at least that there was a good chance it would happen, didn't you? And you made me part of it by having me bring Lance to the club."

"That's what this is all about, isn't it? Feel as if you somehow led to his death. Well, you didn't. Hamidi didn't have to follow Lance into the men's room, and he didn't have to hit on him. They didn't have to bring him back to Iran. Those were decisions other people made, he and his people, his government, his uncle. But I can tell you this. I've seen his whole file. He was one sick son of a bitch. Sooner or later, someone was going to kill him, but before they did, he'd cause a lot of people, some of them Americans, a lot of grief. And it wasn't just the sex stuff I'm talking about, and it wasn't the sex stuff that got him killed. Hell, those guys have four wives and a hooker anytime they want. Call them temporary wives. They even fuck goats. Hamidi's problem was he got caught, lots of times. That's the embarrassment. He was going for the bigger score each time. Who knows, maybe next time it would've been a little boy or girl. Shit, I'd love to take credit for him being removed from the face of the earth, but the only credit I can take is I got him out of that coffee club so you could do your job."

I hadn't seen Allen angry before. He was angry and passionate. Passionate about his work. Passionate about protecting Americans. Passionate about taking the garbage out. Now vented, it looked as though the air was being let out of him. He sank back in his chair, head hanging a little lower, his arms on the table, right hand fiddling with his paper cup of coffee. I felt sorry for him. But then...but then I realized he was a master handler, and he was handling me now.

"Well played; you almost had me. I thought maybe the anger was you coming through. It was you all right, but it was staged. Staged for me."

Allen stiffened, no longer slouching in the chair. No longer the self-reflecting patriot. Hands moved closer together, touching, forming a unit from the two, he looked at me with clear eyes, not cold, but not containing a lot of warmth.

"I appreciate it. Believe me, I do. If I left here today without it, I'd dwell on my role in the death of that young man. I probably will spend some time thinking about it, but I'll also think about your performance and wonder more about that. You knew it would have an impact on me, and you were prepared. Means I'm still predictable, which, if I stay in this game, would be a liability."

Allen's expression remained neutral, but the right side of his mouth twitched, an acknowledgment of what I was saying. Whether he was agreeing or disagreeing, I couldn't tell.

"Look, I know there are bad guys in the world. I want to help, but I don't want to pull the trigger. The work you do helps keep America safer, maybe even the world. I learned that in the run-up to the hijacking. You reinforced that lesson during my summer in Washington. Did I wonder why you asked me to take Lance to the meeting? Yes. Did I think it was part of the plan to keep America safe? Yeah. Would I have still done it if I knew Hamidi might be killed?

Probably, but only if you told me he was a bad guy. You don't have to give me the details. Everything you guys do is based on solid information and is well thought out. You asked me to accept that, and I did. If you want me to continue helping you, you have to promise not to blow smoke up my ass. If someone is a bad guy, tell me."

Allen was staring at me. There was a look I had never seen before, a darkness reflected in his eyes and the shape of his mouth. I was asking to enter that same dark place he lived in. He was thinking about it. Did he want me in there? Would he open the door?

"I'm not finished. When you guys picked me to do the hijacking, you were using me, using me to do something the FBI or someone else couldn't or wouldn't do. I was a means to an end. You used me to get Hamidi out of the country, something that clearly stepped on the toes of another agency, probably the FBI. I have no problem with what I did in the hijacking. I can see the changes that have taken place already, and I'm convinced those changes will save American lives. When I have time to think about Hamidi, I'll probably feel the same way. The problem I have, besides smoke up my ass, is a feeling I'm being used to work between the cracks in areas where the CIA disagrees with the FBI. I think the FBI had eyes on Hamidi and had him identified as a potential threat. Why? I don't want to know. Whatever that threat was, you—and I mean the collective you—decided you couldn't wait for them to respond and took things into your own hands, my hands. So, as your contractor, what protection are you giving me against being picked up by the FBI for questioning or being charged with something?"

"Jonathan, I understand what you feel. You understand the big picture. I've known that from the start. If you didn't, I wouldn't have taken you so far. I'll take what you've said into consideration, but you've got to remember, part of why you're so valuable to us is the deniability we have about you. I can't promise you'll be given access to operational plans. Agency policy runs on a 'need to know.' You didn't have to know what we knew about Hamidi to do what I asked you to do. You didn't have to know what we suspected would happen to him if they brought him back to Iran. Maybe you should have known he was a bad guy. That I'll think about for anything in the future. But even if I don't say the words 'bad guy,' you have to understand I'm not dealing with saints. Nobody I'm interested in will ever win the Nobel Peace Prize. Threats to the security of the US must be removed. If that means removing them from this country or embarrassing them or wrecking their credibility or killing them, that's my job. I hope you'll never have to pull the trigger, but as time goes by, I can guarantee there will be times when you'll want to."

"What about the other thing?"

His eyes focused on my face, but he wasn't looking at my face. Rather, he was looking through me, at the back of my head. I could feel his eyes piercing me. "Yes. The simple answer is yes. Like the hijacking, there are times when action—not words, not processes, not meetings with Congress—is required. Yes, we—I—will use you to do things that could eventually be done differently if we go through the process. The process takes time, though. That time, sometimes, is critical. Waiting can allow time for something bad to happen. Waiting can sometimes remove the opportunity for action. So yes, I will ask you to step in. If it helps you any, we do this because we can and because we have to."

"What if I get caught?"

"You won't!" Allen was emphatic, no doubt in his voice. "You won't because, while there's no agreement between us and any other US agency, there is cooperation. We both see the same problems. If something like Hamidi has to be done and they can't, we do it. They cover their ass. If it's wet—"

"What's wet?" I asked.

"Wet means there's blood involved—a hit, an assassination. They make sure they're covered. It doesn't mean they set up alibis. That would be too obvious. It means they're prepared with an alternate explanation, another enemy the target had, diverting attention away from us. The job gets done. There are no congressional inquiries. Clean. The same thing happens overseas. The FBI has a line on someone wanted for a crime in the US. The target flees to Whogivesafuckastan, where they can't get him. We find out. We get him. Everyone is happy. Sometimes we even work with other foreign agencies, doing the same thing. It's the way we make the world safe in spite of our government."

I hadn't expected any of that from Allen. Now the smoke had cleared, and none of it was aimed at my ass. For the first time, I felt a member of a team, a team much larger and more complex than I could have ever imagined. "Thank you. I had reservations when I started, I admit, but following the world news on a daily basis has given me a deeper appreciation of the evils in the world. I'm glad to be part of making it safer. Can't say I'm on the side of the angels yet, but I definitely know I'm not in the field with the devil. I know the role you have for me is specific and out of the danger. I'm just happy now you recognize my concerns and will take me more into your confidence—recognizing, of course, the need to know."

"Good. With that understood, I'd like to make it easier for us to be in contact. My showing up unannounced every few weeks or months isn't good for you. If it's any comfort to you, you're being watched out for on a regular basis— not around the clock, but we try to make sure you don't get into any trouble. I'll give you a telephone number where you can reach me. Most of the time, I won't be there, but someone will know how to get in touch with me. Call from a pay phone and leave a detailed message. The person who answers has the need to know anything you say. I'll get in touch with you as soon as I can. If you have an emergency, someone else will get in touch, in person. They'll give you my name, and you do whatever they say."

"Okay, but what if you need to get in touch with me?"

"We're lucky in that regard. We've modified the Bellboy pager, like the pagers you use in hospitals. It's identical to the one you have, so it won't raise any suspicions. If it beeps, call the number I gave you. I'll be waiting on the other end."

I was relieved, but didn't know why. Nothing had changed. I would probably have felt bad if I was away from the influence of Allen. He had a powerful personality. I could see why he was doing what he was doing. "What now?"

"Just keep doing what you're doing. When there's more information on the members of the club, I'll let you know, and we can figure a way forward. In the meantime, keep your ears open. They'll be more talkative around you now. I'm sure they don't have a clue as to what happened. They're just pleased Lance beat the shit out of Hamidi and he left town. They might know he's dead. You'll be able to tell the next time you see them. They'll either be overjoyed and try to thank you, or they'll be scared shitless of you. Hell, if they know your routine, there might not be anyone there the next time you show up. Regardless, this was a successful mission. Anything else is a bonus."

Chapter 36

I returned to my routine. It may sound redundant to keep saying that, but being a successful medical student means having a routine. It means getting ready for class, going to class, studying, getting some sleep and a bit of food, and starting over again the next day. Weekends are for catching up, with an occasional break to keep your sanity and allow the mind and body to heal. I included two weekends off each month, one with Monika and one with Brooke, and two hours every three weeks for the coffee club.

The routine still included reading three newspapers every morning at breakfast. The more I read of the troubles in the world, troubles created by the greed or arrogance of men, the more comfortable I became with my decision to go all in with Allen. There had been a time when I thought of myself as a criminal. Well, not really a criminal, just someone outside of the law, if that makes sense. Not so anymore. Now I was a facilitator of good, using means that might be considered by some to be questionable.

It had taken the last two years to become comfortable with this new understanding of myself. Both my experiences as a medical student and my summers being trained by Allen were the key. Medical training is basic—learning about the structure and function of the human body, a curriculum shared by every medical school in the world for over a hundred years. Over this course of rote study, there is a subtler but more important lesson being taught. A lesson to make decisions quickly, life-and-death decisions. Not yet, but in the clinic beginning in September, I would be exposed to these decisions. They wouldn't be my decision yet. Rather, I would be observing others making them. In the ER, diagnose quickly and treat. In surgery, cut more to stop a bleeder. In the delivery room, save the mother or save the baby? Above all, make the decision quickly. The training in medicine helps make the quick decision the right decision. The guiding principle of first do no harm is best served with quick decisions.

So too during my summer with PMA. I sat in many meetings listening to difficult, multifaceted problems being discussed. Some argued for a delay in the decision until more analyses could be analyzed or a consultant consulted. The true leaders forced a decision. They argued the worst decision is no decision. These decisions often sought to avoid harm, or at least perceived harm.

Allen was training me in a similar manner. The hijacking overcame the inertia of no action by bureaucrats and politicians. It was a decision to avoid harm and foster good. The same could be said with Hamidi. Some could argue with me, as I had with myself, that taking a life was wrong, worse for me as a physician-to-be. Now I disagreed. I valued life dearly, and protecting and saving lives was the right thing to do. Allen, if he was involved with Hamidi's death, had done the right thing; he had facilitated the elimination of potential evil and protected good. Evil is like an infectious disease or cancer. If left untreated, it consumes the organism. Sounds simple when said like that.

In all of my internal debates over the past two years, one thing had become clear. It ultimately came down to the risk of doing something or the risk of doing nothing. When presented with these alternatives in the future, either as a physician or a contractor or as a businessman, the risk associated with doing nothing is usually high.

The year passed. The gray skies of winter gave way to the warmth and green of spring. With spring came the end of the school year and plans for the summer.

Allen came to New Haven a couple of times. He had background on several of the members of the coffee club, but there was still much to learn.

"We have information on about half of the members. For the most part, they appear to be sons of middle-level government officials, here to get an education, go back home, and make a contribution to the government or an allied family business. There's a couple we haven't finished yet, including Ahmad."

"Why Ahmad?"

"Well, he's the fourth son. His father's not in the Oil Ministry as we originally thought, but in the Iranian Foreign Service, serving as a trade attaché in Paris. There are a few questions about him we still haven't answered."

"Ahmad or the father?"

"Both. Being the trade attaché in any embassy usually means government agent. I was a trade attaché. Don't get me wrong; it's a real job, and there are real people who do the job, but a lot are spies. The outstanding question about the son is, why is he so interested in you? We have solid information he's been making inquiries about you."

"Why would he be interested in me?"

"That's the question we're trying to answer. There are a couple of possibilities. He could be interested in what you can do for him. He may think of you as completely neutral but a potential asset for information he can milk from you. He may be interested in the contacts you made in Washington. Hell, he may even be evaluating you to see if he can turn you. The other possibility is he may think you had something to do with getting Hamidi. If that's the case, he may think you set Hamidi up with Lance. Either way, you should be okay."

"Should be?"

"Don't worry; you're okay. Now you're informed that he may try to use you. Pick your brain or turn you. You can be on alert, and if you find he wants to use you that way, we can feed him. If he thinks you were involved with the Hamidi thing, we'll know by how deep he goes trying to get a line on you—the people he asks and the questions he asks. We'll make sure the answers he gets show Lance has been a longstanding homophobe and has a history of getting into fights with guys like that."

"Is Lance really like that?"

"Lance is whatever is required. That's his job."

The conversation switched to where I would work during the upcoming summer. Allen had arranged for an internship in New York City working for a large multinational pharmaceutical company. Summer would start with a few weeks at CDC, again working with the Infectious Disease Branch, but the majority of the time would be in New York. The choice was not random. The company headquarters was on the east side of Manhattan. It was to be my initiation into the broader range of activities that were to be my life after medical school.

I had had some association with the company, American Pharmaceuticals, during my previous summer at PMA. It was one of the largest drug companies in the world and had a significant influence on PMA policy. Most of their sales came from the United States, but they were one of the first to recognize the potential of foreign markets, with offices in seventy-six countries, a major player in Europe, South America, and Japan.

After sweltering again for two weeks in Atlanta, I arrived to the relative balminess of summer in New York. Allen provided me with an apartment. At American Pharmaceuticals, they assigned me to a general intern program for the first week. It was basic and boring, but it was important that I be treated like any other intern, so I tolerated it. After the first week, they assigned us to areas where the company thought we could best be utilized. I was the only medical student, and they assigned me to the medical department, learning about pharmaceutical medical and business processes in the United States and foreign countries.

The intern program gave me a keen insight into the problems a multinational drug company faces. I became familiar with the regulations being created to guide the development and marketing of drugs domestically and overseas. Contrasts became immediately apparent, with the US FDA having a much stronger control of all elements than their foreign counterparts. The biggest contrast was the amount of hard science required. The FDA mandated unequivocal proof in the form of what they called adequate and well-controlled clinical studies, while the Europeans were more trusting by giving credence to testimonials as acceptance of proof. The Japanese didn't trust Western data in Western patients and demanded all work be repeated with Japanese patients.

After the overviews, they assigned me to a team where I worked as a clinical study monitor, or as close to it as I could with so little training. Interestingly, it was the same kind of work Brooke did. I accompanied people who talked to the doctors who conducted the clinical trials for the antibiotic drugs that American Pharmaceuticals had in development. Most of these trips were to large teaching hospitals. The first few trips weren't exciting, but they were interesting. After I got the hang of it, they became routine. It was just a question of checking the progress against a plan, making sure the hospitals had adequate drug supplies and checking paper work collected for the company. There was always an obligatory expensive lunch or dinner at a restaurant of the local doctor's choice. We always let them choose the wine, and I always wondered if they would pick the same expensive wine if they had to pay for it.

There never seemed to be any free time. The work dictated the travel schedule, so we might visit six cities in a week, leaving New York on Sunday evening with stops in Chicago, Kansas City, Denver, and Tucson, with a red-eye back on Friday. If we hosted a dinner, it generally ran until about ten o'clock. Then it was off to bed to catch the first flight in the morning to the next city. If an evening was free, it was used to travel. We often arrived at our next destination around midnight and were up at dawn for an early meeting.

Chapter 37

* * *

I enjoyed my time in New York, especially when I stayed in the office. The work was something I could imagine as a career. Each week presented a new task to be learned, new people to interact with, and new problems to be solved. The internship exposed me not only to a different side of medicine, but to finance, with budgets for the projects, managing the project, and coordinating the various inputs. Even the drudgery of travel took on meaning once I learned to look on it as part of the adventure.

New York City was exhilarating, full of life, and vibrant. At first, the noise bothered me, but with time, it faded into the background, the sirens and horns just as natural to the city as the wind and chirping birds are to the country. The restaurants, clubs, and theaters could have overwhelmed me, but I practiced a lot of control, especially in the restaurants. When I traveled for work, I had to entertain. If I ate the same way back in New York, I'd have to buy a new wardrobe every couple of weeks. Weekends became a time for restraint, both eating and drinking. Walking around the city also worked off some of the calories.

New York is many different cities, depending upon who you are and what you want. As big as Manhattan is, it's a collection of neighborhoods, not visible during the workday but clear in the evening and on weekends. Each has its own restaurants and bars frequented by the locals. Things taken for granted in small towns but not thought about by visitors, these neighborhoods have their own dry cleaners, tailors, drugstores and hardware stores, giving each a distinct flavor.

Most people experience it as a tourist, doing the tourist things and eating tourist food. New Yorkers don't own or need a car. Cabs and subways are the way to get around town. A true New Yorker doesn't go to Momma Leoni's for Italian, he goes to a place like the Trattoria Gatti on the East Side. In summer, the only time tourists and New Yorkers are on the same page is at a ball game, either Yankee or Shea Stadium. They ride the subway to the game together, cheer together, and eat cold hot dogs and have warm cold drinks together.

When in town, I tried to keep lunch hours to myself, one more way to control my weight. There weren't many gyms around, the closest being six long blocks west on Forty-Second Street, across from Bryant Park. East to west, the blocks are long compared to the relatively short blocks that run north to south. Most days, I brought an apple and took a walk at lunch. I had my favorite haunts.

At the east end of Forty-Second Street, just before First Avenue and the United Nations, was Tudor City, an apartment complex built in the 1930s on an area reclaimed from a rough Irish meat-packing neighborhood. With time, it became gentrified, reaching its peak with the construction of the UN. Tudor City included an elevated park stretching across Forty-Second Street. The park was gated, available only to residents, but that didn't prevent anyone from walk- ing around the park. The park was truly an oasis in the heart of Manhattan, with the sounds of the city muffled and distant. On warm days, the shade was cool, and, being elevated, there always seemed to a little breeze.

The other place I frequented was the grounds of the United Nations. There's a nice park behind the main building, formal to a degree, with well-tended gar- dens, trellised roses, and paths extending down to the river. It's not as cool or relaxed as the park in Tudor City, but the energy of the city can be felt watch- ing boat activity on the water. It was here I was surprised on a beautiful early August noontime on an incredibly mild summer day.

I was leaning on the railing, watching the river traffic, when a voice from behind said, "Excuse me. Would you know where a camel jockey could get a good cup of Syrian coffee?" I knew at once who it was before I turned.

"Ahmad. You're the last person I thought I'd run into here. What brings you to New York?"

"Like you, I finished my studies for the summer, and I am working in New York. I am doing low-level administrative work at the Iran mission to the UN.

Well, not really administrative. If I were to get promoted, I would be a junior administrator. Right now, I guess you would call me a gofer, or today, a takefer."

"Takefer? Is that an Iranian term?"

"No. Today I took something from the mission to our ambassador's office at the UN. So I was a takefer. What are you doing here? Do you work at the UN?"

"No. I've got a summer job in town with a drug company."

"That is great. Which one?"

"American Pharmaceuticals."

"Ah, that is just down the street. Perhaps we can get together for lunch."

"Sounds good, Ahmad, but being in town during the week is unusual for me. The job requires a lot of travel, and when I'm in town, there's a lot of luncheon meetings. Today's unique; I have a free hour. They canceled a meeting, so I came over here for some decompression." Most of that was true—not all of it, but enough.

"That is no problem, my friend. I will not tie up your infrequent lunch hours. Perhaps it might be even better. I can take you to a nice Iranian restaurant on a weekend when you are in town. That will be better. Then we will have more time, and you will sample something more than coffee from my country."

Now I regretted pushing him off for lunch. With lunch, I could limit my time to an hour. By turning him down, I've left myself vulnerable to a much longer period of time, and on less-than-neutral ground.

"Ahmad, that sounds good. I'd like to try Iranian food. When I get my schedule for the next couple of weeks, I'll call you. Can I reach you at the mission?"

"I understand. You are a busy man with multiple women, if I remember. Here is a number where I can be reached. It is not the mission, but it has an answering machine if no one is there."

I extended my hand and took his card. "Ahmad, it was good to see you, but now I must get back. Work in the business world is more regimented than being a student."

"Yes, and nothing like working for the government," he said as he shook my hand. Were his eyes looking for a response to this comment about government work? I declined the invitation to respond.

I thought about this encounter with Ahmad as I walked back to the office, grateful he had not walked back with me. It disturbed me that we had run into each other here, far from New Haven, and that he was spending the summer working just a few blocks away. Had he followed me here, or was it serendipitous? If he followed me, why? I needed to call Allen and fill him in as soon as I returned to the office.

Allen called back within the hour. "Jonathan. I got your message. You sounded a little unnerved. And, before you ask, we record all calls that come in. Hearing the tone of someone's voice is sometimes as important as the message."

"Yeah, it was unsettling to be approached by him. Totally unexpected!"

"Before I called you back, I did some checking. Ahmad arrived from New Haven yesterday. This was his third trip to the Iranian mission this summer. The other trips were day trips, associated with a relative visiting and an educational function sponsored by the UN. The mission hasn't listed him as an employee, and there's nothing on the agenda at the UN, so we have to assume he came for you. I've asked someone to keep an eye on both of you for the next week or so. We'll see what he's doing."

"You said 'both of us.' Why me?"

"If we follow him, we've got to know if he's following you. To do that, we have to know where you are. Nothing sinister, just good tradecraft."

"Can I learn how to determine if someone's following me?"

"Already in the works. I'm trying to schedule something for you with one of our contractors. I don't want to send you to the Farm. It would be a link back to us. There are lots of people teaching these techniques to the corporate types, and some of them are our people. Get me your travel schedule so I can set something up."

"Can you get me a gun?"

"No!" Allen was emphatic, didn't even have to think about it. "It would be too dangerous for you to carry a gun, especially in New York City. If you insist, which I think you will, we'll wait until you get back to New Haven and schedule time with one of our contractors to give you some of the basics at a shooting club in Connecticut. Then we'll see about getting you a gun. You won't be able to get one legally. There's too much risk with the background check."

It was one of those unusual weeks when I remained in New York. At lunch-time, I still went out, but I avoided the area around the United Nations and Tudor City. The Iranian mission was on Thirty-Ninth Street between Second and Lexington Avenue, with Tudor City Park on a direct line between it and the United Nations. If Ahmad was following me or trying to run into me, that would be a logical place. Instead, my noontime walks took me to Park Avenue, and I enjoyed the high-end shops that called it home. As I walked, I sensed being followed. Allen had someone on me. Was Ahmad there too?

I got a beep on my pager from Allen the next day. When I got to a phone and called, a lady put me on hold. When the line came live again, Allen said, "Ahmad's following you for sure, tagged along behind you when you went up Park Avenue, but never got closer than half a block. Looked like he was just trying to see if you were going someplace, and if so, where. After work, he followed you home. I don't know if he knew where you lived before, but he knows now. Time for you to change your schedule and route. Avoid a routine. Leave earlier, go west a bit, get a paper and some donuts for work. Buy a dozen for the folks in the office."

"Why is he following me?"

"Jonathan, I think he's SAVAK, and he might think you're connected to us. I've checked and double-checked everything on our end, and there is absolutely no connection to us, no loose ends. It looks like he might be good at his trade, very intuitive. Regardless, you've got to stay on the safe side. It might work to our advantage. Remember, you went to the coffee club to make some contacts. You've exceeded your goal. You've got them coming to you. We can play this to our advantage, but you need preparation before you meet with him again."

I expected Allen to say I should lie low, don't draw attention to myself, avoid Ahmad. Now he was telling me to go forward. "Meet him again? In New York? No way!"

"Yes way, but don't worry. I'll have you prepared and have you covered. We'll have someone watching you around the clock now, and I'm bringing you in for some conversation management."

"Conversation management?"

"Yeah. A way of engaging Ahmad that makes him think you're being open but not really giving him anything."

"Excuse me for being just a poor old medical student and not a secret agent, but if he's so good, won't he have had the same training in his spy school and know what I'm doing?"

"Good question, Jonathan. Very perceptive, with a hint of sarcasm—or is it sardonic? I don't know; I always mix those two up. But I like it in you. You think a couple of steps ahead."

"And you avoid answering questions."

"No, I just didn't get to it yet. The training you'll get will take that into consideration. Trust me. Have I ever let you down?"

If he were here, my look would have been enough of an answer. My silence should send the same message. I simply didn't know if he had ever let me down. He set me up with Lance, but let me down? Who knows? Add silent skepticism to sardonic and sarcasm on his list of *s* words.

Allen scheduled conversation management training with a public relations consultant, the contractor he had mentioned. The man was very likeable, a big smile on a big man with a mane of big gray hair and a British accent. He had a walking stick, which I thought was an affectation to amplify his English presence until he stood and had to lean on it. He caught my look and apologized, saying he had done a bit of automobile racing in his youth and had not done it well enough. Later, I learned his apology was an understatement. His name was Nigel Radcliff, and he had been a promising Formula 1 driver for the McLaren Team in England. An accident ended his career and left him with a stiff leg he couldn't bend. But, as they say, when one door closes, another opens. During his racing career, he was the darling of the British press, and he used that to launch a second career in public affairs.

"I'm told you need to be taught how to control a conversation. Well, that I can still do. Have you ever paid close attention to a politician giving a news conference?"

"Can't say I have," I said, which was the truth. I didn't listen to their bullshit anymore.

"Well, if you did, you'd see they never answer a question they don't want to answer. They answer a difficult question with an answer they have to another question. They divert. They manage the conversation. I will teach you how in one short day. I apologize now."

"For what?"

"From now on, you will not be able to watch any politician giving a news conference without saying 'That cheeky bastard is ducking the question.'" He ran his hand through his big hair and flashed a smile.

Nigel spent the day explaining and demonstrating the art form he practiced. In an interview, he said I must have some key messages I want to get across. "Watch *Meet the Press*, and you'll see this done skillfully every week by professionals. They keep coming back to their message, regardless of the question asked. So too it is in our conversations. Stick with areas you are comfortable with, areas you have knowledge of, and keep diverting the conversation back to those areas. Don't speculate. You give your opponent—yes, he is your opponent—openings to probe. Stick with the truth. The truth is easier to remember with fewer discrepancies."

"What if he comes out and directly asks me if I'm a spy for the CIA?"

"Answer truthfully. 'I'm not a spy for the CIA.' That is true. I understand you are a contractor who sometimes works for the man who set up this training. So you can say you're not a spy with credibility. Even if you were on a lie detector, your body wouldn't betray you."

"What if he asks me what I did in Washington?"

"Great question, because he probably will. Tell him you worked at Walter Reed, which is true. The records there show you were there all summer except for the time you spent at CDC."

"What if he knows I spent time at Energy and State and asks questions?"

"Again, stick with the truth. Oh, yes, they sent me to Energy to learn what they're doing about big changes in energy needs. Same thing for State. They sent me there to learn about what's going on in the world. All of it relates back to the CDC experience. CDC is worldwide. You have to understand the geopolitical climate in case you get sent to Africa for Ebola. Many of the diseases of Africa are due to the primitive living conditions, including a lack of energy in an area with potentially large energy reserves. Disease can be eliminated if conditions could improve." Nigel was making this up as he went along, and, while he didn't have an in-depth grasp, he showed me what he meant about telling the truth and linking everything back to the main experience at Walter Reed and CDC. We worked on it for the rest of the day. When I left, he seemed satisfied with what I was doing, and I was less worried about pulling it off. Less worried does not mean not worried.

Chapter 38

*   *   *

I spent the weekend upstate. I was going to visit my parents but worried I might be followed, and if the shit hit the fan, they might be at risk. Instead, I opted to go to Saratoga for the car show. The American Legion took advantage of crowds descending on Saratoga in the summer, lured either by the sport of kings or by the toney atmosphere of the super-rich who made the area a summer retreat. They all shared a love of sport and the smell of money. The Legion wanted some of that money and hosted a car show. Some visitors flush from a big score at the track might drop some serious coin if a particular car caught their attention. I had always loved cars, but this was the first time I had gone to the show.

Whether it was the show, the majesty of the mountains, or merely the time and distance from my problem in New York, I had lost a lot of anxiety by the time I returned to the city late on Sunday.

The following week, I was on the road traveling and didn't worry about Ahmad. Imagine a city as big and populated as New York and having the worry that I would run into Ahmad. Of course, the chances of that happening increase dramatically if the other person follows me and wants to run into me. Nonetheless, the silliness of the situation struck me. After all, hadn't I asked for this? Hadn't I taken the training offered to handle it?

It didn't take long. Tuesday of the following week, Ahmad was waiting when I stopped for coffee and bialy at the Chock full o'Nuts shop on Forty-Second between Second and Lexington. The little shop was a busy place in the morning. Not only folks getting ready for work in the neighboring buildings, but the night shift from the *Daily News* building across the street. They were noisy, transferring their end-of-shift enthusiasm to those just starting the day, making it a nice way to start the day. Was it nice, or just different? I didn't care; I liked it.

"Jonathan. How lucky for me to see you! Are you in town this week?" Before I could respond, he added, "We must make time for a meal. It has been so long since coffee in New Haven."

Surprised, I hesitated, and in response to the clerk asking me if he could help me, I said "Yes," which Ahmad mistook for accepting his invitation.

"Good. Finally, we will have some time together. I will make a reservation for tonight and call you with the time." Stuck! Nothing I could do about it now. I would see how well I'd been trained.

The restaurant was on East Thirtieth Street. Ahmad was waiting, and we went straight to our table. The place was dark and had Middle Eastern music playing softly in the background. "Softly" might not be the right word. Soft I associate with romantic. This music, to my mind, could never be romantic. Best to say it wasn't loud. Ahmad offered to order for both of us. I didn't object, telling him it was my first time in an Iranian restaurant.

The waiter brought us water and tea. After Ahmad ordered, a plate of hummus and pita arrived, with yogurt on the side. I wasn't a fan of any adult food that looked like baby food. Even to this day, I don't like it. People ask if I like guacamole. Sure I do, but it must have chunks in it so I know it's an adult food. While he spoke, I picked at the pita. I didn't know if it was seeing him again, the foreign feeling of the restaurant, or my recent training with Radcliffe, but I was wary, carefully measuring each word he said, watching him for gestures, and hoping I wasn't obvious.

"I've been looking forward to talking with you for quite some time now, even before the incident with Hamidi. There may be things we have in common that we should explore."

"Yes, there is a love of coffee. That's for sure."

"No, I think there is more."

"Oh? Like what?"

"I will not make the small talk and get diverted by American women and American cars. Rather, I will get straight to the point, as you Americans say, especially in New York. We are more alike than you may think. Perhaps we are more than we pretend to be." This he said with a calm voice, his dark eyes staring at me. Breaking the stare, he grabbed his glass of tea. "Do you like the tea with mint, Jonathan?"

"Yes. What do you mean we're not what we pretend to be? I'm not pretending to be anything. I'm a medical student, something I've wanted to be for many years. If I were pretending to be something, I wouldn't pick medicine, and I wouldn't be pretending at Yale. The regimen is too rigorous. What are you pretending to be? Are you really a student?"

While I felt uncomfortable, Ahmad stayed relaxed. His posture didn't change, nor did his expression. Was he still comfortable, or was he well trained? "I will not pretend to be modest, Jonathan. I am an intelligent man, what they call a mensa as are you. Like you, I am a man of many talents. In addition to being a natural scholar, I am a gifted athlete, as are you. And, like you, I am a patriot. But more than a patriot for my country, I am a patriot of the world. There is good and evil in the world. It is true in my country as in yours. I serve my country to keep the evil out by learning where it is and watching it. Watching to make sure the evil outside does not attach itself to or try to undermine the great young minds of my countrymen living in the West."

There it was, laid right on the table. All but admitted he was SAVAK. Ahmad was controlling the conversation with the truth.

Radcliffe's words were in my head: stick to the truth. "Ahmad, do you mean you work for your government? Are you spying on the students at Yale? Are you SAVAK?" I asked about SAVAK before he could ask me if I was CIA. Was I controlling the conversation, or was I being controlled?

He kept his eyes on me, blinking slowly, still pulling off pieces of pita and dipping them in the hummus, still sipping his tea, remaining calm. I had just asked him if he was part of the most vicious intelligence agency since the Gestapo, and he was remaining calm. "Jonathan, I could answer, I could lie, or I could ask you if you are CIA, but I won't do any of that. It is not important what I am, or who

I work for, but it is important what I work for and what I believe." As he spoke, he seemed to get calmer, almost serene. "I know, better than you, there are evil people in my country. There are those who want to reverse the changes that have taken place under the shah. There are others who want to embrace all the changes made and become fully Westernized. They would abandon our culture, which is thousands of years old, and adopt yours, which is two hundred years old."

"Ahmad, it can't be that simple." Had I managed to avoid the reference to the CIA, or had he let me avoid it?

"No, my friend, it is not. The two groups I described are the extremes in my country, and, as in your country, the extremes make the most noise and the most trouble. There is a large group in the middle who subscribe to neither of those views. The people in the middle are afraid the conservative extremists will persevere, and then they will be declared enemies of the state and be prosecuted. These moderates are patriots who honor our long history and culture but also see the advantages offered by the West, and they look for ways to meld the two. I am in that latter group. Like them, I do not want to abandon my culture. Rather, I want to embrace it, preserve it, but move forward with the rest of the world. The Japanese did it. In Tokyo, one can walk the streets and see kimonos and business suits, sushi and rice alongside burgers and fries. The past and the future can live peacefully together in the present and enrich a nation."

"You are a powerful speaker, Ahmad. You have a future in politics."

"Only in a free society that does not punish such thinking or speaking. It is unfortunate, but in my country, it is becoming more difficult to speak openly. There is time, while the extreme conservatives are still a minority, to make a change. The large middle will move to support a new Iran. But they will hide and disappear if the extremists rise to rule. There is much the shah has done that is good and he has won the support of many, but he is moving in a direction no longer considered benevolent and is losing support."

"Interesting" was all I managed to say. Radcliffe had not prepared me for this type of discussion. I had prepared to dance and dodge around my work in Washington. This was coming right out of left field.

Ahmad smiled at me. "This is a surprise to you. I did not expect you would be prepared for this type of discussion. Certainly you need to discuss this with others, but they will ask you many questions, and if you leave now, or end our discussion now, you will not be able to answer them." He said the last bit with his finger moving back and forth, first pointing to himself and then to me. Pausing, he let this sink in. "Allow me to tell you some things so you will be able to answer their questions."

Conversation was interrupted by the waiter coming to take our appetizers away and bring the main course. Without missing a beat, Ahmad continued as if we were two old friends talking about last night's Yankees game. "Ah, I have ordered a meal that will ease you into the flavors of the Middle East. We like to say we are Iranian, Syrian, or whatever and define our food that way. In the broadest sense, our food is Persian, with subtle differences for each nation, and within each nation, even more subtle differences. But you are not familiar with our food, so you would not appreciate the differences. Tonight's meal should appeal to your Western palate but still serve as a proper introduction. I have selected a platter of grilled meats, lamb and what you call Cornish hen. The meats are only mildly seasoned and accompanied by cold tomato and cucumber in a yogurt sauce. Yogurt is very popular, and you will find it in many of our dishes. A meal would not be complete without rice, and for us we have baghali polo, a green rice with fava beans and dill."

The meal smelled wonderful, reminding me of the aromas of the coffee-house. The plates were colorful and the meats browned and golden, the vegetables red and green and floating in a white sauce and the green rice. "Looks and smells wonderful," I said, glad to be moving to more comfortable conversation.

"One thing the West has contributed that I cannot do without is eating utensils. To eat a meal in the countryside now without a fork or a spoon seems uncivilized and unsanitary. Of course, it is not, but to me it is not a cost of progress; it is a benefit."

Sampling each of the dishes, I focused on the food, our earlier discussion hanging in the air, waiting to resume. After the waiter cleared the table, Ahmad leaned forward, more conspiratorial now. "Jonathan, let me tell you what I think. I think you are more than a medical student who likes Middle Eastern coffee. While I do not think you are a CIA agent, I think you are under their control, or at least their instruction. What they have in mind for you, I do not know. Nor do I know why they had you infiltrate a group of Iranian students.

There is no one there who should be of any interest to the CIA, except perhaps me, and my guess is until you tell them, they do not know I am important. In their eyes, I am possibly a government agent sent to remind the students of their families back home and to make sure they do not stray or form any alliances with people who may try to harm my country."

The waiter brought coffee to the table. Ahmad made a ceremony of pouring my cup and his. He held his cup in two hands, something I had not seen him do before, blowing gently across the top.

"Jonathan, you had me fooled at the start. You were just an American living a little dangerously, hanging out with foreigners from the Middle East and at the same time enjoying coffee. You didn't show up every week, and you made no effort to make friends. In fact, you tried to avoid the only man there who wanted to be your friend, Hamidi. Perhaps you sensed he made the others uncomfortable. He did, and he was becoming a problem I would have had to deal with sooner or later." Pausing, he looked for me to say something. I didn't.

"But I did not have to deal with him. You made it easy by bringing your friend Lance. That alerted me at once. It was not that you brought a friend; it was who you brought. He had a menacing air about him, at the same time sending friendly signals to Hamidi. He pretended to be gay, to be interested in Hamidi. You did not see it; I did. Yet when he walked to the men's room, he walked like a predator, not prey. As soon as Hamidi followed him, I knew. As it unfolded, I watched you and saw your surprise. You were either a very seasoned agent, or you had trusted someone explicitly when they told you to bring Lance to the restaurant that night. Probably the latter. Only later did I remember where I had seen Lance. It was in Tel Aviv. Then I knew you were associated with the CIA and was sure I could trust you."

Ahmad paused, letting the accusation sink in. "You do not have to answer. If I am right, you will be able to tell your people enough to answer many of the questions they will ask you. If I am wrong, you will probably never see me again. But I think I will see you again. Why?" He looked at me to engage him in conversation.

"Why?" seemed a proper response. There was nothing to add to that one word, and I was saved from an awkward long silence by the waiter returning with our dessert.

"Again, I have attempted to blend the tradition of Iran's past with the contributions of the West. We have Bastani Akbar-Mashti, an ice cream with the flavor of saffron and pistachios, and zolbia, a crunchy, fried Persian doughnut with saffron and cardamom. Both will be excellent accompaniments to more coffee."

"No yogurt?"

"There is yogurt in the ice cream and the doughnut. I told you we are very fond of it."

Nibbling on the tasty doughnut, I thought about taking a couple in a doggy bag for breakfast tomorrow. It was good to be distracted for a few minutes.

"Jonathan, what I have said to you will be very interesting to your superiors. They will have much to speculate about but will be able to do nothing but ask more questions. What I am about to propose to you will expose me and give them reason to send me back to Iran. I would not be able to explain my ejection from your country. I will not speculate on my fate."

"Don't try to make me—"

"I am not attempting to do anything but make you aware of the seriousness of what I am doing and the personal risk to me for doing it. I hope that means something to your superiors. I said there are evil people in my country and in your country, and I think you agree." I nodded yes. "These evil people are from many countries as well as Iran. These same evil people have compatriots in the US. In my country, there are enough Irani extremists to keep things upset, yet agents and elements from other countries are agitators. In some cases, the same agitators are acting both for and against the shah and for and against the extremists. Their only goal is to cause unrest in my country. Why?" He paused, looking at me. I had no answer. I was waiting for him to provide the answer.

Ahmad continued when I didn't respond. "There are many reasons. Some of them are communists looking for opportunities. Others are capitalists, believing unrest will benefit them financially. Ironic, is it not, that both capitalists and communists are fighting for the same thing. They do not know they are fighting together, Jonathan, but the result is the same. Neither will win in my country; only the extremists will win. The future success of my country, and perhaps the stability of the whole region, lies with the moderates, not with either of the extremists. You smile, and well you should, but the same thing is happening in your country."

"Ahmad, c'mon," I said as both a question and a comment, showing doubt that capitalists and communists were fighting together in the United States.

"Who will win in your country, I cannot say. But the communists are here. They might not be called communists in your country, but the result is the same. There are people who want everyone to be equal, with free everything and little work to earn it, sowing the seeds of a welfare state. The capitalists are profit motivated—fight the government, pay as few taxes as possible, tie the courts up with frivolous lawsuits, fleece the defense budget with weapons that are not needed and not wanted. Don't you see the similarities?" He didn't wait for an answer this time. "And to add to the problem, there are agents of Iran, both those in favor of Westernization and those opposed, operating in your country, aiding both the communists and the capitalists. How can this be, you say? They grab the ears of your Congress and whisper for support for, or overthrow of, the shah. There are agents from the US doing the same thing in my country. How are we ever supposed to resolve our issues with all of these agitators?"

"Ahmad, I don't know what to say."

"When you meet with your supervisors and tell them what I told you and answer the questions they have for you, all will be clear. Then you and I will be able to work together for what is right. That is more than enough for tonight. Did you like the food?"

"Unfair question, Ahmad. With all you said distracting me, I didn't give it the attention I should have."

"Then we will do it again, when your mind can focus on the food. Here is a number where you may reach me. It is best you call during the work hours."

With that, we left the restaurant. Even though we were heading in the same direction, Ahmad chose to separate himself from me and walked off alone, leaving me to find a payphone to call Allen.

Chapter 39

A llen answered on the first ring. When I finished telling him about my din-ner with Ahmad, an uncomfortable silence followed. "Are you still there?"

"Yes. Just taking a minute to process all this. Jonathan, this is something I wasn't expecting. This guy is full of surprises. I'd like to talk to a couple of people. Can you call back in a half hour?"

"Yes." Thirty minutes seemed like thirty hours. During dinner, listening to Ahmad unwind his story, I had become anxious. My anxiety heightened in anticipation he would ask me questions I wasn't prepared to answer. After relat-ing the story to Allen, I was almost frantic. Now I was in the middle of a real spy story, being led into a conspiracy by a member of the fiercest intelligence agency in the world. After twenty-nine minutes, I redialed Allen. Halfway through the first ring, he answered.

"Jonathan. Sorry you had to wait, but I needed the time. There's a team digging into Ahmad, trying to find out who he really is. When you met him in New Haven, we knew he was SAVAK, but the early indicators were he was only a low-level operative watching the students, keeping them in line, like he told you over dinner. The more we dug, the more information we got. That's a red flag for us. A lot of information usually means a background has been created for just that purpose. With real agents, the background is scrubbed; anything that can be used for pressure is erased. No family, no friends, nothing. His was all out there for the taking. It took time to find the truth beneath the story. No doubt, he's a bad guy, disguising himself as a low-level babysitter."

"But everyone in New Haven liked him, or at least no one in New Haven was afraid of him. How much of a bad guy could he be?"

"Very bad. Anyone he has disciplined disappears. Sometimes the discipline is an accident, or it may be indirect, on a family member. The incident at the coffee club actually helped to enhance his reputation by taking out Hamidi."

"So taking out Hamidi was one of the considerations in our plan?"

"Yeah, but not to enhance Ahmad. Now he thinks he knows something about you, and he wants to use it to manipulate you. Through you, he wants to manipulate us to work for him. The good thing we've got going for us is he's pretty much a lone wolf."

"Meaning?" I was by no means less frantic, but I wanted to get a fuller picture.

"Meaning he doesn't report to his supervisors often. While he's good, he likes his superiors to think he's even better. Doesn't ask for help; just gives them results. As long as he's producing, they leave him alone. That means you're probably not on any radar back in Tehran. The only one who knows about you is him. That's a big plus."

"Yeah, you can't imagine how comforted I am by that. Wait, what do you mean by 'that's a big plus'?"

"Ahmad wants something from you, Jonathan, or he wants you to do something. That something will seem reasonable, even highly moral, based on what he said at dinner. He'll want you to be a coconspirator on something. I want you to meet with him again and find out more."

"And then?"

"And then we'll figure out what we're going to do about it."

"Any rules?"

"Be honest. Always the best policy and easy to remember. Tell him we think he's a bad guy, wants to recruit you, but we don't know why. That ought to get him talking more."

"I'll call you when I'm done. Any chance he'll hurt me?"

"No, he wants you. Doesn't make sense to hurt you just for asking questions."

Hanging up the phone, I stood looking at the normal people in the world around me, a world that seemed comfortable with itself, unaware of the drama playing out around it. A drama that could spill onto the front pages. A drama that included spying, murder, and the nastiest people on the planet—the SAVAK. And I was being asked to play games with them. As I walked back to my apartment, I was envious of those I passed. Envied them their innocence. Envying even the homeless I saw. Life couldn't get much worse for them. It could get a lot worse for me.

The rest of the night was a waste, spent tossing and turning, walking around my apartment. I sat by the window. A three-quarter moon dominated a cloudless sky. If I weren't in the middle of Manhattan lights, I might have seen some stars. Tiring of the moon, I watched the traffic on the street, seven stories below me, until I fell asleep in the chair, a dreamless, unrefreshing sleep. The alarm was my enemy and friend that morning. Although I needed more sleep, I wanted the day to begin so I could call Ahmad. As soon as I got into the office, I called him.

"Ahmad, Jonathan. We need to meet. No lunch, no dinner, no drinks, just a meet to talk."

"Jonathan. That is good. How's lunchtime? You pick the place."

"How about the UN park, on the promenade, down by the rose trellis?"

"Twelve fifteen, UN park near the rose trellis. See you then." There was no smile in his voice; it was all business. I suppose he was reacting to my voice.

The morning dragged as I tried to look busy. The more I focused on the paper work in front of me, the heavier my eyelids got from being up most of the night. I was getting soft, I thought, and I shifted into medical student mode, reverting to my sixth food group. It wasn't on the USDA list; it was mine and used for staying awake when my mind and body were numb. A cup of coffee, a Pepsi, and a glazed doughnut got all the vital systems alert with the infusion of caffeine and sugar. I left the office at noon and headed east to the river.

Ahmad was already there. As I approached, he walked forward and intercepted me. "Do you have anyone watching you?"

"Not that I'm aware."

"You picked the place, so I have to make sure there is no one listening to us. Let us move to the park in the front and north of the UN. We can walk together, but I prefer not to talk." He was practicing his tradecraft, making sure Allen and his people were not in a position to listen. When we got to the street, I stopped.

"Now it's my turn. I don't know that you didn't plan this and have people waiting for us up the street. We're going to walk down to Forty-Second Street, then west, and find a nice place to talk." We walked south until we got to Forty-Second Street, then west. There was a small patch of grass, flowers, and a single tree in front of the Ford Foundation, an empty bench inviting in the shade. As I pointed to the bench, he looked at me and grinned—not his normal friendly smile, but a menacing grin.

"Good choice, Jonathan. Did you have help to pick this out, or is this spontaneous?" My nod told him it was only me. "Good. You are inexperienced, but you have good instincts. A spot in the open, little chance of a listening device, lots of traffic to muffle conversation if I should be recording this, and lots of people around. Did you convey our conversation to your superiors?"

Ahmad was right—the pedestrians on the sidewalk near us would insure a nonhostile discussion, and the traffic would be a test for any listening device. As I thought this, the air brakes on a passing truck sent a blast of noise echoing off the buildings, followed by car horns blaring. All part of the symphony of New York City streets. "Yes, I told them. They asked what you want. You were open to the point of saying you wanted something but fell short of what that is."

"Did they agree there are agitators in both of our countries?"

"There was no discussion about anything other than you, and I'm not privy to the information you or they have. But a rational man would assume that statement is correct. So what?"

"With the removal of Hamidi, you have shown your ability to rid your country of an agitator who had the potential to harm it and mine, something beneficial to both of us."

"I'm not agreeing that—"

"You do not have to agree. It is a fact; you know it and I know it." His face and voice were stern. His eyes were burning into me, his nostrils flared, and his shoulders were back and straight. Ahmad was the aggressor now. I tried to maintain my neutral posture, not being submissive. "That is what I am proposing: more of the same. I could not touch Hamidi, but you put him in a position where they had no choice. If left here, he would have fucked up even worse the next time. I am saying there are others, both your targets and mine, where the same creative solutions can be used."

I didn't back down or shrink. Leaning forward, I asked, "Like what, for instance? Clearly, you've benefited from Hamidi being sent back to Iran and claim your country has benefited. Seems to me all the benefit is going one way. How can you help us?"

Ahmad sat back, crossed his legs, and watched the traffic for a moment. Then he spoke more softly, more measured. "I have told you of the concerns in my country about the direction the shah is moving. If he continues, he will be overthrown, most likely by the extreme Muslims. If that happens, the exiled ayatollah Khomeini will become the head of the government, a minority government, a theocracy, and all the reforms will vanish. The theocracy will throw everyone in government out, the good and the bad. Most of those thrown out will be executed, along with their families. Foreigners will be thrown out or executed, including Americans. Life in Iran will revert to the Middle Ages. There are few options open to us and the world if we are to avoid this. One option is to temper the shah. It will outrage the extreme Muslims even more, but the rest of the country would stand up. The US exerts a strong influence over the shah but seems reluctant to do anything about him. They sit back and watch him destroy the country. If that remains their position, the only option is to take things into our own hands and eliminate the shah now."

"Are you fucking kidding me? You want to assassinate the shah, and you want our help? Are you out of your mind? If you want him gone so bad, why don't you do it yourself? How could you think we'd help you?"

"Jonathan, you are so new to this. You do not understand."

"Right you are on that. But wait. Let me call up my superior, and you can explain it to him. He's been around for a while, and he'll understand. Then he can explain it to me, and we can set up a time and a place for me to shoot the shah." I was being sarcastic, my voice was rising, and I was becoming animated, with my head bobbing and my arms flailing. I must have looked like a crazy man, but then in New York, crazy is relative.

"Please calm down. People are watching. Let me finish, and you will understand. The shah will not change. If he continues with his plans for rapid

Westernization, there will be a rebellion and the ayatollah will return and assume power. That cannot happen. Such a threat must be eliminated. It may be too late already. The clerics in Tehran are already talking about his return. We must eliminate the ayatollah also to give democracy a chance. I cannot do it myself, and I cannot seek others to help me." He was pensive, staring to his left, past me, toward the East River.

"You're asking the US to help you eliminate the shah and the ayatollah?"

He turned to look at me. "In spite of strong support for such actions, I cannot trust anyone. Every aspect of our life in Iran is infiltrated with spies from both the shah and the ayatollah. I would be betrayed, and the cause would be lost. The outside, the CIA, could do it. There would be no need to let anyone else know. The people would rejoice; the shah would be gone. Everyone would think the coup came from within, from the large middle group. There would be turmoil within the religious group, but there would be no one else to step forward. There would be a call for elections. The middle would be strongest and be elected. Do you not see what that would mean for the world?"

"No. As you said, I'm new to this."

"The rest of the region would come in line. There would be fear the same might happen in their country. Stabilizing Iran would stabilize the entire region. It would be like springtime in the Arab world. There may even be a chance to rework some of the boundaries of the countries in the region. The country borders now mean nothing. They do not define ethnic regions or tribes. The British, French, and Russians drew the borders at the end of the First World War with no regard for any local or regional needs, only with an eye to their colonial interests. Straight lines drawn on a map defined countries. There was another, better solution available, but it was ignored. Major T. E. Lawrence, known in the West as Lawrence of Arabia, was a scholar who studied the people of the region. He made a map that the Arab world agreed to but was ignored by the Allies. Those boundaries could work today. The Western powers have no colonies there anymore."

"I'm not an expert, but I think you're insane. What am I supposed to say?"

"I want you to take the message back to your superiors. I want to meet with them, but I fear they will not meet with me. You will have to be the go-between. I want you to convince them they must do it."

"I don't believe in what you're doing. I won't be an effective advocate. They'll laugh at the naiveté of your plan. Then what?"

"Jonathan, you must convince them. Let me help you to become motivated. I think Monika or Brooke would be disappointed if you didn't. They are safe and comfortable in their homes in Philadelphia and Washington now, but that could change in the time it takes me to get there."

I was on my feet, standing in front of him. "You crazy motherfucker. If you even look at either of them, I'll hunt you down and tear you apart. They have nothing to do with this. Leave them alone."

"I will. All you have to do is get me a meeting with your boss. Merely getting me a meeting is the first part; he must agree to the plan. If he doesn't, what can I say? He might not care about your lady friends, but he will care about his role in Hamidi's death. It would be easy to change the documents in Tehran to put suspicion on the CIA." The iciness returned to his dark eyes, sending a shiver through me in the August heat of midday. He held all the cards. He wanted a meeting with Allen and had threatened Monika and Brooke. He knew what he was doing. He'd get the meeting, but then what? Allen couldn't agree to his plan. He was a madman, a lone wolf.

As far as I was concerned, the meeting was over, so I turned and left, going west toward the office, leaving Ahmad sitting on the bench. He called after me, "Call me at the number I gave you—tomorrow, no later."

After I passed the Ford Foundation, I stopped and turned. Ahmad was gone. He couldn't have gotten to the corner yet; he must have gone up into Tudor Park. I was furious with him, with myself, with everything. I had to get to a phone to call Allen. I got to the corner of Forty-Second and Second Avenue and turned north. Allen was waiting, leaning against the building on the east side of the street, one leg on the ground, one leg behind him, up on the building.

Chapter 40

"Need a beer, sailor?" Allen spoke in such a relaxed manner that I came down a bit in my anger. Seeing him, I knew I had an ally. The cavalry had come to the rescue.

"That son of a bitch! You should have heard him." Once I started talking, the anger returned at explosion level.

"Heard it all. We had the whole area covered with long-range microphones and lip readers. Didn't figure he'd go for a meeting place you chose and he'd want to go someplace else. The park in front or Tudor Park were the logical choices. Didn't figure the middle of Forty-Second Street. Was that his idea or yours?"

I nodded my head. "Mine. I didn't know if he had a crew with him, watching, recording. Figured the middle of Forty-Second Street would throw them off."

"It was a good figure. There's no need to worry about him having a crew. Remember, he's a lone wolf on this one, at least in New York. Don't know about anywhere else, but we'll know more later."

"That crazy fucker threatened Brooke and Monika."

"Yeah, he's a crazy son of a bitch, all right. As soon as I heard that, I sent people to watch over them. Don't worry; they're both safe."

"How soon before someone's in place?"

Allen looked at his watch "Five minutes."

"Thanks. The next five minutes will be the longest of my life until I know they're safe."

"Five minutes ago. Teams have already checked in. Both ladies are safe. Same goes for your parents, just in case. Let's go someplace quiet and get that beer."

I looked at my watch, wondering how much of my lunchtime I had left, and then realized how stupid that was. Ahmad wanted me to assassinate two world figures, Monika and Brooke had been threatened, the CIA had put guards on them and my parents, and I was thinking about my lunch hour. While it felt like the middle of the afternoon, I had left the office only forty minutes ago.

"There's lots of time. You're free for a couple of hours. One of your investigators at Mt. Sinai called and needed you to check something. I know a quiet little place that has cold beer, where we can talk." Allen gave me a reassuring grin, and we set off walking.

We walked silently in the direction of my apartment. "Are we going to my place?"

"Yes. It's got the beer."

"How do you know? No, let me guess. You've been in my apartment. Why? How long?"

"Someone's been watching you for a few days now, in case you needed help. A crew went over this morning. After last night, I wanted to make sure you had a safe place to go and that no one had bugged it. We changed the locks to make it more secure, and I've put someone in the apartment across the hall."

"How could you arrange that so fast? Oh, let me guess. That building is a CIA safe house, isn't it?"

"Only the end of the floor you're on. The unit across from you is ours, as are the next two. When you're at home, you're safe from the bad guys."

"You've had people in all those units?"

"No, they were empty. After we cleared your place, I put someone across the hall. We have a lot of people, but not that many."

"You must be worried about something now."

"We'll talk in a minute."

"If you knew we'd go there, why didn't you have your guy this morning get another six-pack? Those two Schaefers are mine." I didn't get an answer, just a look.

We got to my building and went up to the seventh floor. As we walked down the hallway, I noticed the building was quiet during the day—no televisions, no radios, and no talking. Just the sound of the elevator descending and the lingering smell of last night's dinners and this morning's coffee and bacon. Allen handed me two keys. It wasn't home, but it was familiar, yet it felt different now. I looked for cameras and microphones but saw nothing. Allen went to the fridge and came back with a beer and a Pepsi. I reached for the beer, realizing it wasn't a Schaefer but a Budweiser.

"The Pepsi's for you. You can't go back to work with beer on your breath. You're supposed to be at Mt. Sinai. You can keep the rest of the Buds, but save a couple in case I come over again. When I found out all you had were a couple of Schaefers, I had someone pick up some Bud. How can you drink that shit? Schaefer's for college kids." He took his sport coat off and sat at the dinette table, his gun in a shoulder holster under his left arm.

"That motherfucker threatened Monika!"

"In case you weren't paying attention, he also threatened Brooke and indirectly threatened you." Allen was right. He had threatened both women, and I had focused only on Monika. "Jonathan, we knew he was one of the bad guys, but we didn't know he was crazy. I'm sorry you've gotten involved with him. This went on too long. We should've had a handle on him sooner. It is what it is, and we have to deal with it."

Struggling with my hatred for this man allowed me to ignore the choice I had subconsciously made between Monika and Brooke. "And why's that?"

"Ahmad's gone over the edge. Kind of explains why he was in New Haven babysitting Hamidi, and it also explains why we understood so little about him. Yeah, he's SAVAK, but not a major player. More important, he knows this, or at least suspects it, and resents the life in front of him. The future he faces is full of low-level assignments, with little chance of moving up. Like all SAVAK agents, he's one mistake away from being recalled to Tehran and disappearing. High risk, very little chance of reward. Realizing this seems to have pushed him over the edge at some point. As he went further over the edge, he concocted that scheme of getting rid of the ayatollah and the shah. In his demented mind, I suspect he sees a big role for himself in the void that appears after both are gone."

"Yeah." I wasn't agreeing to anything more than Ahmad being a crazy fucker.

"What's more important now is making sure he's alone on this, both here and back in Tehran. He's asked for a meet with me, and he'll get it." Allen was pensive, his lips thin across his teeth and his eyes clear and sharp. He was serious; he was on a mission.

"Mike." As I used his first name, his eyes jumped to me, and I held his stare a long time. I had broken one of his informal rules. When on a mission, he was Allen, his last name. Everyone on his team called him that. It helped him depersonalize the team and make them a machine to do a job, much like a shovel or a hammer. Shovels and hammers don't have first names, just shovel and hammer. "Two things can come out of this. One is he's alone, here and in Iran. The other would be that he's not alone. Regardless, he's threatened me and my friends. What do we do?"

Allen went to his jacket and retrieved a pack of Marlboros. He lit one and looked around for an ashtray. I didn't have any but got a dirty coffee cup from the sink. I took it to him and grabbed the pack. As I shook one out, he looked at me and asked, "Did you start smoking again?"

"I don't, just in times of stress. Seems I only smoke when I'm with you."

We sat in silence for a few minutes, filling the room with smoke. The apartment would stink tomorrow.

"We're pretty sure he's alone, but we have to make sure. If he is, he's no longer of any use to us. If he's got help someplace, we've got to find out. I can get that information from him at the meet. It's Friday. Set up the meet for Sunday night." He gave me the time and the place, a dingy Irish bar on the West side of town.

Taking a drag on the Marlboro, I paused. The smoke burned my throat and stung my eyes. I exhaled, watching the blue smoke rise and disappear in the breeze from the air conditioner. "If he's alone, do we take him out?"

Allen looked at me, multiple questions telegraphing from his eyes and the fidgeting of his fingers with the Marlboro. "What do you mean 'we'? Do you realize what you're saying?"

"Yeah. We both know this is going to happen someday if I stay in the program, and we both know you guys aren't going to let me get out of the program. Let's get it over with. This guy is a piece of scum, and he threatened me."

"Now you're crazy. No, that's not what we have in mind for you. You're supposed to be invisible, our man in the background, setting things up so we can do our job. Maybe sometime in the future, after you've been on a few more assignments, we'll talk." Allen had said no. As far as he was concerned, the matter was closed. Not for me.

Allen's beeper went off. "I have to use your phone." I nodded yes and pointed him to the phone hanging on the wall. I listened as he spoke, shaking his head, pacing as far as the leash of the phone cord would allow him, running his fingers through his hair. "Good. Don't lose him, and call the other end."

After taking his time to replace the phone, he came back to the easy chair, grabbed another Marlboro, lit it, and spoke through the smoke blowing from his nose and mouth. "Ahmad just got on a southbound train. One of our guys is on the train with him, and they alerted the people in Philly and DC who are watching Brooke and Monika. Everything will be fine."

"How could you have missed him if he's this crazy?"

"We dug up everything we could on him. We got little as a danger signal. He had a neutral background. So we went to the simpler rule: if there's nothing to find, then there is nothing. Might simply have been an intelligence officer. Intelligence officers are not operatives. The skills they have make them too valuable to risk in the field as an operative. This guy was a nothing, a political appointee who thought he was James Bond Assad, an intelligence asset and a field operative. We messed up. But, I repeat, Brooke and Monika and you are safe. We'll know more after the Sunday meet, and then we'll decide what has to be done."

I had already decided on one course of action, and as he was talking, I made up my mind on another. "Are you sure Brooke and Monika are safe?"

"Absolutely. We'll have eyes on them 24-7 until there's no more risk."

I nodded agreement. While my body said yes to him, my mind was far away. "I have to get back to work. It'll help keep my mind busy. I'll call his office and set up the meeting for Sunday night."

Chapter 41

* * *

As soon as I got to the office, I called Ahmad. The woman who answered said he was unavailable. I left a message about dinner on Sunday, saying I wanted to repay his generous hosting of Iranian cuisine with one of Irish fare. The woman laughed and said it was a nice gesture.

The rest of the day was a waste of time, time spent moving paper from one side of my desk to the other. Since it was a summer Friday, I had no meetings. There were few meetings in New York on Monday or Friday, leaving time for long weekends in the mountains or at the Jersey shore. Just after three o'clock, I left the office and went west on Forty-Third Street and into Grand Central at the Depew Street entrance. At a newsstand on the far side of the terminal, I got a copy of *Guns and Ammo* and an afternoon paper to wrap around it. I exited on Forty-Second Street and went to my apartment. Once there, I grabbed one of Allen's Buds from the fridge and sat down at the dinette table. The smell of the cigarettes from our earlier visit still lingered, the air conditioner not having removed it all yet. Taking a long pull on the beer, I opened the magazine.

Allen didn't have to teach me how to shoot. Dad had started me with a .22-caliber rifle in the woods behind my uncle's house. When I became proficient, they taught me how to shoot pistols. Both of them preferred pistols to rifles. The dominant memory I have of the three of us is going out every Thanksgiving morning to the gorge just outside of town. Each of them would have a holstered pistol under his cold-weather gear. If cold enough, we'd shoot at pieces of ice. Warmer, we might help the neighborhood by doing some "ratting." Ratting was a city-dump sport, but ours was too close to the city, and fear of a stray shot ricocheting limited us to the gorge.

Dad had a .38-caliber Smith and Wesson police revolver, while Uncle Chuck carried a .22 Colt Woodsman. After about an hour of shooting, we'd return home and spend an hour in the basement, talking while we cleaned and oiled the pistols. As I got older, they sat and drank coffee, and I did all the cleaning—by choice, not by default. I longed for the day when there would be three pistols, me carrying mine in a holster under my jacket. When my uncle died, he left me his Woodsman. The gun was still registered in his name even though he had been dead for four years. Transferring a pistol meant getting a pistol permit in New York State. Not too difficult, but I wanted to have a carry permit, an almost impossible task at the time.

Not so in Virginia. In Virginia, it was possible to buy any kind of gun. Many guns changed hands at gun shows every weekend. "Gun shows" was probably an exaggeration. These were flea markets that emphasized guns.

The back section of *Guns and Ammo* had a listing of gun shows. The shows were all over the country but predominantly in the South. I found what I was looking for, a gun show that weekend at the fairgrounds in Fredericksburg, VA. I had gotten into the habit of keeping lots of cash on hand. Between what I had in my wallet and what I kept stashed in the apartment, I had over $600. I walked to the Avis rental office on Forty-Third Street in the parking garage near Lexington and reserved a car for Saturday.

By seven thirty on Saturday morning, I was through the Lincoln Tunnel and on the Jersey Turnpike. Traffic was heavy with the Jersey shore vacationers heading south to start their vacation week, but it thinned out when the vacationers moved toward the shore on the Garden State Parkway. Driving was easy to the Delaware Memorial Bridge. The huge span dwarfed everything around it. I stopped for a late breakfast at the first rest area in Delaware and topped up the gas tank. Two and a half hours to get here, and then another two hours down to Fredericksburg.

I skirted Washington on the Beltway, going around on the east side. Fredericksburg was only about forty minutes south on I-95 from there, with the fairgrounds clearly marked as an exit. I parked the car and went into the large white exhibit hall.

The hall had no real order. Shotguns were in a section to the left. Military weapons were at the back of the hall. Beyond that it was chaos. Most dealers dealt with multiple types of firearms—rifles, shotguns, and pistols. For the first hour I walked around, getting familiar with the place. I stopped, looked, and listened to customers talking with dealers. Some dealers focused more on the money than the paper work. I found a pistol dealer and watched as he made several sales. When the customer made a selection, he handed him a clipboard and asked him to fill in the information. When the customer returned, he didn't ask for any identification to confirm what was written.

I wanted a .25 Beretta. A Beretta was easily concealed, with its short barrel, but still useful up close. I also wanted something more powerful with a little more range, but still small. The ideal pistol was a .30-caliber Walther PPK. I had looked at these pistols at other vendors earlier and felt comfortable with my choice. Now was the time to buy.

I made eye contact with the guy behind the counter. I had watched him for a while and knew he wouldn't want to spend a lot of time with me. Nodding, he asked if he could help.

"Yeah. I need two pistols, a .30-caliber PPK for myself, but I need something for my wife. She's a nurse and sometimes has to work nights. With the drugs in hospitals, I'm just afraid someone will wait for her in the parking lot thinking she might have some."

"My daughter's a nurse, and I have the same fear. Those fucking crazies don't know they don't carry dope in their purses, but then again, they're crazy. I gave her a .38 revolver. Have to say, she didn't like it at first, but now she doesn't go out at night without it."

"If I could get her to carry one of those, it would be great. But I know she'll resist having a gun, and if I give her something that big, she'll just say no. Something smaller for her. Maybe a .22. If someone gets close enough, it'll do the trick. When she gets used to that, then she'd be ready to move up."

"Most of the .22s are big, but you might consider a small Beretta .25. Fits in her bag. Should be easy to learn how to use. I taught my daughter to aim low and just keep pulling the trigger. Makes lots of noise, might hit a foot or a leg, but scares the shit out of any guy cuz he thinks he might get his balls shot off."

I laughed. "You should send that in to the Beretta people. Let them use it in their advertising."

He left the Beretta and the PPK on the counter for me to examine while he went off to help another customer. He was smiling, hopefully bonding with me over my comment about his cleverness.

When he returned, he said, "What do you think?"

"I think these are excellent choices. The PPK is just a step up from the Beretta. I think she could handle it. I might let her try it when I'm teaching her to shoot. Okay, I'll take them both."

He handed me two clipboards. "Fill out both forms, one for each pistol. Technically, you're the buyer for each, so sign your name." He left me to fill out the paper work and went off to help his other customers. He had an assembly-line routine for his booth, and it worked well, getting the most out his one-man shop. I completed both forms using the name of a high school classmate; the street address in New Haven; and Hampton Beach, VA, as my hometown. When he returned, he looked over both documents. Satisfied that all the blanks were filled in and both were signed, he asked if I needed ammunition.

"Sure. I was going to wait and get it at the range, but I suppose I could get it here."

"Two boxes of each should get you started. You'd be surprised at how fast you go through ammo at a range. You should start with wadcutters for her Beretta. They've got a lighter load cuz they're used at the range. She'll get less recoil when she shoots, but it's still pretty effective up close if she needs it." With that, he put the guns and ammo in a brown paper bag, and I paid him and left. As soon as I walked out of the building, I was a felon, having used false information to buy firearms. At the car, I transferred the brown paper bag to a gym bag I had in the trunk.

On the way home, I violated similar laws in Maryland, Delaware, New Jersey, and New York, as well as federal law for transporting illegal guns across state lines. Pushing these thoughts and thoughts of the laws I might violate in the future out of my mind, I focused on the drive and the ribbon of smooth concrete, or as smooth as a poured concrete road can be. The spaces between sections of concrete, whether overfilled with tar or left as constructed, contributed ka-thumps that I both felt and heard as the Goodyears went over them. The soothing rhythm might have put me to sleep if it had not been competing with my increased heart rate.

I returned the car to Avis and grabbed the gym bag, grateful I didn't have to walk through New York with a gun in each hand. The guns and ammo went under my mattress when I got home.

Chapter 42

Sunday morning came much too soon. After I had finally nodded off, the sun woke me at dawn. Unable to get back to sleep, I went out for the papers, coffee, and a bagel.

Around noon, the ringing telephone startled me. Ahmad confirmed our meeting, making sure I would be bringing my superior. Then he asked about the Irish bar and why I had chosen it. I told him it was my turn at ethnicity. It was also dark and out of the way, a place none of us were likely to accidently run into anyone we knew. By his silence, he seemed to accept this. Continuing, I added that he should bring a sweater or sport jacket, as the Irish were much more sensitive to the heat and tended to keep the place cold. The sport jacket ruse was to reduce his curiosity when I showed up wearing a sport coat in the summer to conceal my pistol.

The phone rang again with a call from Allen. With a friendly, almost casual tone, he asked if I was ready for our meeting. "Yeah, he just called to confirm. Seemed curious about my choice of an Irish bar." I didn't tell him about the sport coat discussion; it might tip him off I now had a gun.

"We had an eye on him this weekend. Avoided Philly and went to Washington for the day. He knows where Monika lives and seemed content to just take pictures of her on the few occasions she was out. Probably a good idea you didn't stop to see her on your way home from Virginia." Allen went silent, waiting for me to comment.

"There was someone following me?"

"Yeah. Told you I'd keep all of you safe. Didn't you believe me? You felt it necessary to get a couple of guns?"

"You talked to the dealer?"

"No, we had eyes on you. With so many people, it was easy. What do you plan on doing with those guns?"

"Protection, just in case you guys aren't around when I need you," I said, hoping I didn't sound arrogant.

"Well, I'll be around tonight, so you can leave them at home." As he signed off, saying he'd see me later, I mumbled something.

What I had mumbled was "no fucking way" was I going to meet with Ahmad tonight without a gun, maybe two. The more I thought about Ahmad, the angrier I got. This was the big leagues now. Unlike hockey, this wasn't a game. This was real life, and I had been treating it like a game. Jonathan West, super spy.

Over the past several months, I had learned something else about myself. The difference between good guys and bad guys wasn't black and white. Sure, bad guys were basically bad with no redeeming values. Maybe their mothers saw something good in them, but I didn't. The big learning experience was about good guys. Good guys did bad things, mostly to bad guys. But sometimes the innocent got hurt—sometimes a little, sometimes a lot. Still, I wanted to be one of those good guys, and if I had to do bad every once in a while, so be it. Doing a little bad was better than the guilt afterward if I could have made a difference and didn't try.

Hearing that Ahmad had watched Monika unleashed a curious mix of emotions. It infuriated me he had gone to Washington and knew where she lived. Ahmad had taken pictures of her! In my mind, he had violated her by taking her picture. I was consoled only by the fact that Allen had people watching out for her—comforting, but it would have been unnecessary if I hadn't made her vulnerable. All of this made me miss her. I couldn't even look at a picture of her; I didn't have one. Ahmad did, and that made me angry again. Thinking of her smell, the smoothness of her skin, and the sound of her voice, I had to hear her voice, know she was safe.

Half expecting her to be out, I called. Monika answered on the second ring, surprised to hear from me because it wasn't my habit to call during the day. "Glad you were home. Thought you might be out, enjoying a summer day."

"No, not today. If I felt better, I would have gone out, but I've spent most of the weekend in bed."

"Sorry you're feeling poorly, but happy to be talking to you. I miss you and wanted to hear your voice."

We talked for about thirty minutes, thirty minutes that changed everything. Thirty minutes that made me realize I loved Monika and wanted to spend the rest of my life with her, and I told her. When she told me she felt the same way, I was in heaven.

I left for the meeting early, wanting time for my emotions to cool down. It was a bad day to walk across town to cool down. The city was hot. A humid haze hung over the city. The Beretta was in an ankle holster I had picked up in Fredericksburg. Lucky for me, or I would have had to suffer the heat with my jacket on. Unlucky for me, I hadn't practiced walking with a pistol in an ankle holster. The holster was awkward, and I walked with an unnatural gait.

The steep canyons between the buildings provided welcome shade as I walked on the north side of Thirty-Ninth Street to Fifth Avenue. Running east and west, the narrow street amplified what little breeze was blowing from the river. At Fifth, I turned north and found my way into the shade of Bryant Park.

Bryant Park was one of those oases in the heart of Manhattan that had multiple personalities. During the workweek, it was surrounded by hustle, people going to or from work at the beginning or end of the day. At lunchtime in the nice weather, office workers sought patches of grass to sit and eat lunch, choosing either the sun for their tan or the shade for what little coolness it offered. The vibrancy of the city was just outside the park; people were on the sidewalk, cabs, buses, and trucks crowding the streets. Even in the park, some of that energy could be felt. People used it as a shortcut, fast walking their way to or from someplace else. The picnickers ate their lunch on the grass, in a hurry, eating quickly to get back to work or do an errand.

At night, it was a typical big-city park, not safe for anyone. When the sun went down, the drug dealers, hookers, and hoodlums reigned. Normal people avoided the park, walking on the far side of the adjoining streets, hoping the multiple lanes of traffic afforded them protection from, or at least warning of, any threat. Without the innocent to prey on, those with criminal intent preyed on one another. Every night there were fights.

Only on the weekend did the park take on the personality that its architects intended. It became a place of leisure, a place where city dwellers found grass to lie on and look at the blue sky. Here, they communed with nature as best they could, feeding the squirrels and pigeons.

I took a seat on a bench in the shade, still with plenty of time before the meeting. If I narrowed my vision to eliminate the surrounding skyscrapers and tuned out the sound of the traffic, I could imagine myself in Mayberry. There were young families having picnics, blankets spread out, kids with balls and balloons. There were young lovers also having picnics but perhaps with wine and cheese replacing the peanut butter sandwiches and fruit drinks of the young families.

The ones who drew most of my attention were the elderly, for the most part alone. Yet each acted like a regular visitor to the park. Each had a favorite bench and a routine. Many of them fed the pigeons and chased the squirrels away, or vice versa, with scraps from bread bags saved during the week. Most wore their Sunday best clothes, the women in their fanciest house dresses, pearls, hats, and, of course, gloves. The gents wore suits that had seen better days, shiny from too many pressings or wrinkled from lack of the same. Shoes shined but equally shabby. White shirts that had faded to yellow, ties so far out of date they may be back in style soon, and the occasional fedora. While most sat and fed their pets, some just sat and stared. Those in the shade moved when the sun moved in on them. Those in the sun moved to stay in its warmth, even those with sweaters.

These were the poor, forgotten souls who had managed to stay in Manhattan in rent-controlled apartments, living on small pensions. Some, I was told, might be quite wealthy, having acquired their fortune by saving and investing. Yet they remained frugal, fearful they would outlive their money and be put in a "home", a fate worse than death for people of their era. They had retained their independence and were proud of it. They were both alone and lonely but were used to it, as evidenced by the solitude they choose with so many of their peers around them. Or, perhaps, it was living in New York, where being aloof was protection from being hurt, both physically and emotionally.

As the shadows lengthened and the afternoon passed into early evening, different noises replaced the soft music from the portable radios and the squeals of the children. It was the noise of the rebel young and their loud shouts and even louder music. At the first sounds, the young families were the first to pack up their kits and kids. The music was coming from the northwest corner of Bryant Park. The young families went east to leave. The older people had been gravitating toward the east end of the park for the past fifteen minutes, a sign they were used to the drill. As the noise and the noisemakers moved from their corner into the park, the elders vacated their benches and left the park to them. Before long, I was the only one remaining in the park. All the people I'd been watching had departed. I didn't move. It wasn't time for me to leave yet. As I sat, a reality hit me and saddened me. The bad guys had taken over the park, chasing the good people away.

The bad guys were the young toughs, a gang dressed in T-shirts and dirty jeans. All wore engineer boots, big, heavy, and black. Cigarettes hung from their mouths, and most were carrying beers, or bottles of some kind, not even taking the precaution of hiding their drinks in brown bags. They were flaunting their power. The cops who drove by on Forty-Second Street continued to drive by, not stopping. The thugs walked in my direction. Was it my imagination, or had they turned up the volume of their music? Not that it mattered; I perceived it as louder, so it was louder. They walked in an exaggerated tough-guy shuffle, bobbing greasy, long-haired heads left to right, front to back. Their laughter got louder. Was it an announcement of their approach or a threat? I moved the Beretta from the ankle holster to my pants pocket and felt the comfort of my fingers closing around it. They would not chase me away. I would stand my ground.

What was playing out in Bryant Park now was a micro drama of the rest of the world—the scared, helpless, or weak being preyed upon by thugs. The thugs were these hoodlums who had taken over the park, or the thugs like Ahmad, who wanted to take over a country. They were cut from the same cloth. Watching this happen, watching poor old women and men being driven from one of the few places where they could find sanctuary in their final years convinced me I wanted to do good. Not just the good of being a physician who heals. The people I saw being run out of their park seemed healthy. They didn't need medical help. No, I realized I wanted to do good like Allen and the rest of his organization, help create a world where these old people could sit in the park without fear and watch the sun go down.

In my pocket, my hand felt the smooth, cold, polished steel of the Beretta as the thugs came closer. I wanted them to try something. I wanted to be the vigilante tonight. I want them and their kind to fear Bryant Park after dark, the same way the old people feared it. They came closer. By now they had seen me, and they were closing in.

"What have we got here?" said one of the thugs, only it didn't sound as I've written it. I had to listen hard to understand because the words were covered by accents and slang, unchanged by education or exposure to the rest of society. "I think we got someone who's lost. Looks like we got someone who don't know this is my park, and he has to pay admission when I'm here. How much you got, boy? Cuz how much you got is exactly how much is what it's gonna cost you." The others laughed and echoed guttural yeahs.

In my pocket, I gripped the Beretta, my hand closing around the butt, my index finger on the outside of the trigger guard. They weren't close enough to touch me before I could get it out and fire, but they were close enough to see the outline in my pocket. They stopped. They'd heard of Bronson and the vigilante; everyone had. Made the New York City streets safe. I smiled and said in a voice that was remarkably calm and measured, "All I got is what you don't want. I'd really like to give it to you." I raised my left hand, made a finger gun, and pulled the trigger twice. "But you have to earn it. Can't just give it to you."

The looks on their faces changed. I wasn't the easy mark they had thought I was. Could they overcome me before I took whatever was in my pocket out and used it?

The talking thug shrugged. "This sorry-assed boy don't got nothin' we want. I wouldn't be caught dead wearing those threads."

"Dead's a good word," I said, becoming more surprised with each minute at what I was becoming. I wanted them to attack me. I wanted an excuse to pull the Beretta and shoot them. They must have seen it in my eyes. I felt it. I was doing that Jack Nicholson thing again. The thought crossed my mind that this was what it must be like to be temporarily insane. I could get away with it. The district attorney would ask, "But why did you have a gun when you went to the park if you didn't intend to shoot them?" The image of the district attorney faded, replaced by that of Ahmad. I looked at my watch. Time to go. I held my left wrist up, showing them. "Cheap watch. Not worth being dead to wear it."

I rose, my right hand still in my pocket. Ahmad and Allen would be waiting at the bar west of here. Go through the thugs, or go around? I decided to go through them. They recognized my resolve and parted, leaving a corridor between them. Would they jump me as I went through? They didn't. I moved through the park toward the corner they had entered. As I left the park and entered the real world of New York City again, I could feel the shakes coming on. "What the hell did I just do?"

I went to a bench at the entrance of the park and sat, putting the Beretta back in the ankle holster. The shaking subsided in a few minutes. I realized I was the man Allen thought I was. I could kill and would have killed. The feelings that had led me to medicine, helping others, were the same feelings I had just had when I wanted to kill. A few deep breaths and I knew who I was and what I wanted to do for the rest of my life. I wanted to help others who couldn't help themselves, be it through medicine or with the Beretta.

Chapter 43

✳ ✳ ✳

The bar was on West Forty-Sixth Street, between Tenth and Eleventh, on the edge of Hell's Kitchen. An Irish neighborhood that was still tough but becoming gentrified due to the publicity as the home of the Jets in *West Side Story*. The locals resented the popularity, preferring to continue their illegal crafts as they had for over a century, out of the spotlight. Rumor had it there were still hit men who could kneecap someone cheaper than the Italians. The bar was attempting to cash in on the notoriety while trying to retain the loyal locals. They welcomed outsiders, but not in the evenings or on Saturdays, times reserved for locals. Outsiders were welcome for lunch and on Sunday, any Sunday, unless the Jets were on television. The Jets, in kelly-green jerseys, were still the local favorites.

The bar was one of those dark places that overwhelmed the senses. First, you were completely blinded going from sunshine to darkness, even with all the lights on inside. The shock of dark coolness lasted as long as the first breath, and then you were overcome with a century of smells—stale beer, stale cigarettes, and sweat dominated. As you became accustomed to these, the subtler sights and smells took over. The well-worn wooden floor and bar with nicks and gouges from beer mugs, boots, and bodies making contact for the last one hundred years. The smells of thousands of cabbage dinners were part of the tapestry of the wood now. Then there was one peculiar odor I didn't recognize that first day but would only years later in England, when it came to me again. It was the smell of roasted mutton impregnated in damp wool, food and a fabric fond to both the British and Irish.

As my eyes adjusted, I saw Allen and Ahmad in a dark booth deep in the corner. Both had pints of Guinness. I took the seat next to Allen, across from Ahmad, after restrained greetings. Allen delayed sliding over, his hand remaining on the bench seat, his left hand bumping my side and my sport coat pocket. He reached across the back of the booth, then slid his hand down my back. A professional pat down looking for a gun in my pocket or the telltale feel of a shoulder holster.

A waitress approached and asked if I wanted a Guinness. I couldn't stand Guinness. I didn't like the taste, and I didn't like warm beer. "If you have Boddington, I'll take one of those. If not, a Bud."

The waitress returned and placed a beer in front of me without a word. As she left, she looked at Ahmad with the same disdain as when she took my order. Looking at the head on the beer, I knew I'd gotten a Bud. The head wasn't the creamy, tiny bubbles of Boddington. Didn't matter; I wasn't there to drink.

"I don't think she likes me," said Ahmad.

"She hasn't known you long enough," I said. "She should wait until she's known you as long as I have before she says she doesn't like you. But maybe she's smarter than I am." I turned to Allen. "That's sardonic!"

Ahmad's eyes went wide, and his nostrils flared. He hadn't been expecting confrontation.

Neither had Allen, who jumped in. "Gentlemen, we're here to see if we can work together in a way that benefits us all. That doesn't mean we have to like each other, but it does mean we have to respect each other."

Ahmad raised his glass in an insincere toast and nodded. Allen's glass went to touch his. I hesitated and earned a hot stare from both of them. Raising my Bud, I touched glasses. Allen invited Ahmad to talk.

Ahmad repeated all he had told me about the shah as a far-left liberal and the ayatollah as a conservative right-winger. He went through his arguments why neither was fit to lead Iran and how the majority of the moderates wanted both extremes to exist in a modern Iran not led by either group. He was candid in his desire for CIA help in eliminating the shah and the ayatollah, and he wanted direct intervention, not just assistance.

Allen broke into the lecture. "Let me be clear. You want us to assassinate both the shah and the ayatollah. Not merely overthrown the shah and keep the ayatollah in exile, but to assassinate both of them."

"Yes. That is the only way. Without the possibility of either being in power, then and only then will the moderates feel comfortable and confident going forward with the new Iran."

"And you want us to do both assassinations. Not help you, but do it ourselves, by ourselves, with no help from you and your fellow moderates."

"We will offer intelligence. We will provide access into areas that would be difficult on your own. But we cannot assist with the actual assassination."

"Why not?" I asked. Ahmad wasn't telling us everything. As I asked, I felt Allen shift next to me. With his arm across the back of the booth, his hand shifted to touch my shoulder. A calming motion meant to tell me to cool it. Too late; the question was already on the table.

"If it is learned the moderates were working with the Americans, it will not be viewed as truly an Irani coup. There will be those who will feel we are being manipulated by the Americans. No, it is better this way."

Now it was time for Allen to speak. "I'm assuming there's a group within Iran, within this large moderate group, who are preparing for the transition once the shah and the ayatollah are eliminated. Who are they, and how far along are they in their planning? Have they selected a leader? Is there a plan for running the country after these men are gone?"

"There have been discussions with many of them. Once the obstacles are removed, they will move forward quickly. They will make a wise choice for leader."

"And if one or the other fails? What then?"

"Allah will show a way."

"No, my friend, you are too transparent. You want all the benefit and none of the risk. If the plan is successful, you plan on promoting yourself as the savior, the man who single-handedly worked the magic to eliminate both threats. You have grand visions of yourself as the new ruler of Iran."

"There is some truth there. And, if it happens, the United States, as well as the rest of the Western world, will have a true friend in Tehran. Think of all the good that could be done."

"And if it fails, you'll be able to stand off and blame the CIA. That's not enough for us."

"Do you not like the plan?"

"Oh, I like the plan plenty. If the shah stays on the throne much longer, he'll manage to piss off just about everyone in Iran, all the Middle East, and the rest of the world. If the ayatollah ascends to the throne, it'll be even worse. On that we can agree. What we disagree on is how we get there and who is on the bus."

"On the bus? I do not understand," said Ahmad.

"An American expression. For you, it means if you want a better Iran, you must earn it. An idea and intelligence aren't enough. If we agree to help, we get to pick the new leadership of Iran, and right now, it's not you. There might be a position of responsibility, but you can't have control. You're not equipped to lead."

"How high a position in the new government would we be talking about?" Ahmad sounded interested, and he sounded realistic, but I had my doubts. More likely, he was stalling for time, still using us until he could figure out something else.

"That's not for me to say, but once everything's done, if your role became known, I think the new government would want to reward you. If it fails, who can say?"

"Then we will work even harder to make sure it does not fail. However, you sound like you are threatening me, Mr. Allen. If you are saying it is your way or there is no way, that is unacceptable to me." Ahmad turned to me. "Reason with him, Jonathan. Tell him what we talked about. Tell him how good it would be for America if I were to lead the new Iran."

I looked to Allen for guidance as he continued to stare at Ahmad. No help came from him. I tried anyway, but my words were as hollow as Allen's. "Ahmad. Neither Mr. Allen nor I are equipped to decide who is good or bad for these positions. Yes, the shah is bad, and I agree the ayatollah would be worse, but who would replace them? That determination must be left to those more expert than I am. As far as you as a leader, I don't think you're any better than I would be, and I wouldn't pretend to be qualified to lead."

Allen continued staring at Ahmad. His eyes didn't move. This upset Ahmad. He had looked to me to endorse him, perhaps reminding me of his threat. What a fool he was. How could he think I would endorse him? "I will tell the world about what you did to Hamidi, an Irani national beaten senseless by an American CIA agent and then sent back to be executed by CIA confederates in Iran."

Allen broke his silence. "And I will tell the world you are a liar."

Ahmad turned to me. "Cannot we work something out?"

Allen answered for me. "Ahmad, you are naïve expecting a plan of such magnitude can be put together on such short notice. A plan this complex will take months of preparation and planning, selecting the men with the right skills to infiltrate, execute, and escape—not for one objective, but for two. Surely you understand what's at stake. This cannot be entered into casually. Will you continue talking with us and help with the plans? At the very least, we have to evaluate the intelligence you can provide, determine if what has to be done can be done. Then we have to identify who can lead after the shah and the ayatollah are gone. Every detail of this plan has to be foolproof. We'd also like to talk with your superiors, or the other moderates in your country. We have to identify a role for you. Is that possible?"

Now it was my turn to be shocked. I looked at Allen and drew nothing. The expression on his face was stone again. Was he waiting for Ahmad's answer? I was waiting for Ahmad's answer.

Ahmad's personality changed in front of my eyes. The arrogance was gone, and he adopted an air of humility. "I am sorry." His head was bowed, eyes looking at his shoes through the heavy table. "I want so much for my country and expect everyone to want it as quickly and as much as I do. Of course, a good plan that takes time is far superior to an ill-conceived plan. I am grateful for your help, and I will do whatever you require to assure the correct outcome." As he finished, his head came up. There was no smile, just evil on his countenance. Yes, he was playing us. We were the only game he had. He needed us, and he thought he had us.

Allen was reaching into his pocket. Leaning into me, our shoulders touched. He was up to something, and he didn't want me to interfere. He was sending me a message that said, "Stick with me." When his hand came out of his pocket, it was wrapped around folded cash. A fifty came off the top, and he passed it across the table to Ahmad. "Ahmad, Jonathan and I need a few minutes. Can I ask you to get us another round of drinks and settle our bar tab? See if you can get that cute little waitress to like you a little better. She'll ask you for a smaller bill; they always do. It's her way of trying for a bigger tip. Tell her it's the small-est bill you have, and as she gives you the change, tell her to keep it. Watch her eyes light up. She'll start liking you a little more."

Ahmad smiled, took the money, and confirmed our drink requests. When he got to the bar, Allen started talking.

"That man is dangerously insane. We can't let him go on any further. Time is on our side now. Nothing will be agreed tonight. He knows we need time to work out a plan for him. We'll tell him we need another meeting."

Ahmad returned from the bar, three drinks held in two hands. He smiled broadly.

"You were right my friend, she likes me now that I gave her money. American women are so fond of money. She almost made me think she likes me, but it is just the money. With a little more money, I could fuck her in the back room. A toast to American women. With enough money, I could fuck any of them." Ahmed raised his glass and extended it across the table for a touch. Allen and I raised our glasses but stopped short of the touch. We were merely drinking at the same time he was, not toasting his boasting.

"How long will it take to work out an adequate plan, my friends?" Ahmad had leaned back, comfortable for some reason. He was at ease, perhaps thinking we were all friends.

Allen leaned forward, pulling his shoulders up to his neck, elbows on the table, fingers of both hands locked together under his chin. I couldn't see his eyes, but my guess was that he was trying to hide his revulsion for the man he was looking at. "Ahmad, my friend, I live and work in a bureaucracy, and, by definition, bureaucracies mean wasted time and money. I'll do what I can to speed up the process and share with my superiors your plans for the future, and we'll pull together a group to work on a plan and a timetable. Can we get together again in two weeks to discuss what we have? I'll probably have some questions for you also about the intelligence we'll need and our needs on tactical aspects we would expect from you and your team. Will you agree to that?"

Ahmad was pleased. His face was all smiles. He stayed leaning back in the booth and nodded agreement. "Good. If it is the will of Allah that we wait two weeks, who am I to question him?" He leaned forward, reaching for his beer, but stopped short. "Jonathan, I hope we will be very good friends for many years to come. When all of this has been accomplished, you will come to my country and be my guest. I will be married and have many temporary wives. When I select my temporary wives, I will try to choose some who will be pleasing to you. That way, when you visit, you can choose one, or several if you wish, to enjoy while you are there. I know your taste, so I will be able to pick them with some degree of certainty."

"Ahmad, that's not necessary. First, I don't need a temporary wife. I don't want to insult you or your culture, but it's not my way. And secondly, I doubt you know my tastes."

Focusing on me, his voice lowered. "It is not a cultural thing I speak of, Jonathan. It is a friendship thing. I know your tastes, and they are quite varied. You date two young ladies, both quite beautiful, but very different. One is a blonde with a magnificent body, and the other has darker hair, not black or brown, but what you call auburn. This darker-haired woman is very nice, but I prefer the blonde. I have pictures of both, but it is the blonde I look at most." As he said this, he raised a cupped hand and moved it up and down, simulating masturbation.

My body tensed. Allen sensed it and put his hand on my shoulder, then slid it down to the small of my back, completing his casual frisk for a gun. His touch reminding me to cool it, telling me it was just talk, nothing would happen, cool it.

Ahmad continued, with his beady eyes narrowing. "Perhaps someday you can introduce me to the blond-haired woman and encourage her to be nice to me. I would very much like to enjoy her as a temporary wife. Very simple—I will share with you, and you will share with me. The way of true friends in my country."

"I don't think so, Ahmad..."

"That is okay, my friend. I know where she lives. Perhaps I will introduce myself to her."

My jaw clenched. I wanted to reach across the table and rip his throat out. This fucking guy thought he could do anything he wanted.

"It may not be as pleasant as if you introduced me, but in the end, she will enjoy it. There is a saying in my country: 'Every woman should enjoy the pleasure of an Irani man's body.' I have tried many times in this country. Some women are excited by the mystique of a man from the Middle East. Many years ago, they introduced us with that silent movie—the name escapes me, the sheik of something. Others are interested in the wealth we have. I never pay, even when they protest. A woman has no rights, especially when a man wants her body. As long as they are not married, they are available. Neither of your women are married, are they, Jonathan?"

By now, I was on the edge of my seat, with Allen's hand now locked on to my shoulder. Ahmad knew he was pissing me off, and that seemed to spur him on. The more pissed off I got, the harder he pushed.

"Ahmad, two things to remember. The first is the mission. If you want my cooperation, back off the sex thing, or I will not cooperate. The second is personal. Leave Monika and Brooke out of this. If you even talk to them, I'll break your fucking legs."

"Jonathan. Jonathan. You are angry. I was just talking. In my country, we do this all the time. It is considered a compliment for me to want your girlfriend. It seldom leads to anything." He was sneering now. "But, because it is you, if I meet them, I will fuck them, whether you or they like it."

I slid forward on the booth seat. Allen's hand on my shoulder couldn't hold me. He spoke before I could say or do anything. "Ahmad, we have cultural differences. Let's not let these get in the way of the mission. Jonathan is new to this business. Give us a few minutes, would you? I'd like to talk to him. Calm him down. Explain these differences to him. I know what you mean. Leave it to me. Okay?"

"Yes. I will talk to the waitress." Ahmad gave me a look that said "Pussy," slid out of the seat, and headed to the bar.

Before I could speak, Allen said, "Jonathan, we can't work with that man. The plan stinks, and I don't think he has anybody behind him. After this meeting with us, he could go back to Iran and start something, and when I say start, I mean start. That would be a disaster for the US. It would be a like putting a match to all the oil in the region. It would blow up in our face."

"What do we do? We have to come back with a plan in two weeks. In two weeks, he could have raped both Monika and Brooke."

"We've planned for this. It was unlikely someone so overt should be taken seriously. There was a slight chance he could offer us something, but very slight. We can't let him go on. We have to take him out."

"Take him out? When? Where? How?"

"This bar is in a rough part of town, and we chose it for a reason. There are guys who come into this bar who'd kill for a hundred bucks. For all intents and purposes, Ahmad has committed suicide already. He flashed a lot of money, and he pissed off the waitress by hitting on her. She's the sister and the girlfriend of two of the roughest guys in the neighborhood. But primarily because of the money, when he leaves here, he'll be robbed. During the robbery, he will offer resistance and be killed."

"How did you set this up with them?"

Allen smiled. "It's not them. It's us. They're in the clear, across town playing in a Police Benevolent baseball game for underprivileged children. If the police get involved—and that's a big if—the bartender will say there were strangers in the bar who saw the money the A-rab flashed and followed him out."

Chapter 44

Ahmad returned from the bar when Allen motioned to him. He must have tried to hit on the barmaid again. Clearly, from the look she was giving him, his advances were unwelcome. Settling into the booth, he said, "American whore! Called me a pig. Can you imagine that? A pig? A pig is unclean. Infidel slut! When I am famous, she will beg to fuck me. The same with your woman, Jonathan. You will not be able to keep her from me."

Allen remained calm, his voice soothing, his hand locked on my forearm. He was talking, but I hardly heard him. All of my attention focused on Ahmad, wanting to kill him. Every muscle in my body doing isometrics. My toes tried to grasp the floor through my shoes. Each finger was gripping the edge of the bench seat I sat on, trying to lift me and the bench. Every muscle in my jaw ached from clenching.

Allen chose his words carefully. "Jonathan and I have discussed the importance of the mission, and he understands. But I must ask that you respect his request to stay away from his women because it is critical to the mission that you and Jonathan get along. When we visit your country, we will respect your laws and customs. However, you must do the same in our country. I understand how your culture considers women, but our culture is different. I'm not asking you to be like us, but merely asking that you keep your disdain for women to yourself. Your ability to work with Jonathan is essential. This one request is all I have. Okay?"

Ahmad looked from Allen to me. It was difficult to determine which of us got the icier stare. Probably me. He was pissed I wouldn't share my women with him, and he considered me a coward for not confronting him myself. Extending his hand, he said, "For the mission, I will agree." Neither side of the handshake had any sincerity, unlike the contempt we felt for each other. As he broke the handshake, he said, "When will we get back together to discuss the mission?"

"Jonathan will contact you. Two weeks from tonight is a good target. It could be sooner. Would sooner be okay?"

"Sooner would be better."

With that agreed, Allen, and I got up to leave. Ahmad stayed to finish his beer and probably make another try at the barmaid. As we walked to the exit, we saw him moving toward the bar. The man was evil. We might have to stand in line for our chance at him.

Outside, the streetlights made a feeble attempt to chase away the dark, dark made more oppressive by the heat and my mood. They cast a dim, unnatural yellow light on the street. In this part of town, a lot of business was conducted at night. Lights were a deterrent to good business. The people who were out tended to stay in the shadows.

"Which way?" I asked.

"We'll go across the street and wait. There are people to the left and right. No matter which way he goes, we've got him." As we walked across the street, I looked to the left and right and saw no one I could identify as a friend.

"I don't see anyone," I said.

"Good. If you don't see them, he won't either. No more talking." Allen had a seriousness to him I hadn't seen before. I guessed this was his "wet" business mode.

The entrance of a religious store provided shadows to hide us and a view of the bar. Ironic! A couple of Christians hiding in wait for a Muslim at the entrance to a religious store. Allen picked up on my thoughts from the smile on my face. He whispered, "More ironic if this were a Jewish deli, but you don't find many in this part of town." He had an earbud now, like the ones the Secret Service use, and talked into his hand. "We're in place across the street. I'll let you know when he's on the move."

The night activities on the West Side of Manhattan were unlike those on the East Side. In fact, they were unlike anything I'd ever seen. These were the streets described by Damon Runyon. The neighborhood and the people had inspired *West Side Story*. These were hardworking, hard-drinking, hard-living people. The hard lives showed on their faces and their stooped bodies, bodies worn down by the hard labor of the docks or digging the tunnels. They didn't seem to care. For the most part, they seemed happy. Strangely, it was more like a small town than the middle of Manhattan. Small kids walked the night streets as much at ease as if they were in a small town in Iowa. Everyone on the street knew someone, with greetings being exchanged.

As we waited, Allen spoke in a low, calm voice. "We got some stuff on Ahmad I didn't share with you. How much do you know about Iran?" I answered with a shrug. He continued. "That whole fucking area is a powder keg that's going to blow up someday. There are a few Christians, but they'll leave soon, as will the Jews who recently emigrated to work in the booming economy. The Iranis are an intolerant people, not just to Jews and Christians, but among themselves, within the Muslim faith. There are Sunnis and Shia, and they hate each other. Some big religious split that took place centuries ago. Had to do with who would lead the faith after Mohammed died. Now it's a difference in laws and the interpretation of his teachings. Anyway, the Sunnis persecute the Shia like you wouldn't believe. I'd rather be a black man in Alabama in 1950 than a Shia in Iran. Some similarity there, now that I think about it. The Shia are the majority in Iran, like black men in many parts of Alabama in the fifties, yet they don't have the power.

"Ahmad is a Shia and wants to use us to fight back. All that shit he said about the ayatollah and the shah and the people in the middle—you can shove up his ass. As far as he's concerned, there is no middle, just his persecuted majority. He wants to use us and our dollars and revolution to make the Shia the force in power. And by force in power, he wants to turn things around and do some righteous cleansing of the Sunnis. Supporting a religious zealot isn't our game. He's got to go—for our interests, for Iran, for the region, and probably for the world. He's one crazy fucker."

The door to the bar opened and ended the discussion. Against the light from inside, it was impossible to tell who had emerged, just a black shadow.

The door closed, and the figure stepped out into the light of the beer advertising signs from the bar. No mistake; it was Ahmad. He turned to his left. Two blocks of a tough neighborhood were between him and Times Square, but he didn't make it that far. He didn't even get to the next corner. One minute he was walking on the street, and the next minute, he was gone. Allen spoke into his wrist and nudged me to follow.

We crossed the street. Halfway to the corner, Allen turned into an opening between two buildings. Where I grew up, we called them gangways. In New York, they're called garbage ways, where people can roll trash from the back of a building to the street rather than drag it through the building. One garbage way served several buildings. The space was dark, with none of the minimal light from Forty-Sixth Street penetrating. In the absence of light, smell and sound dominated the senses in this garbage highway. The unmistakable odor of urine overpowered the lingering smells of garbage. The air conditioner high on the wall emitted a whirr punctuated by the ting of an unbalanced or damaged fan blade striking the casing. The same air conditioner sucking the moisture out of the indoor air and drip, drip, dripping water to the accumulating puddle below it. Music from where? It seemed to be all around us, bouncing off walls.

As I followed Allen, my eyes adjusted to the darkness. A single, dim bare bulb shielded in a wire cage cast more dark than light into the back of the garbage way where we stopped in front of two men holding Ahmad, his hands behind his back and something stuffed in his mouth. Eyes wide with fear, he was inhaling huge breaths through his nose. When he saw me, he relaxed a bit.

I knew what I had to do. Nothing was said. Ahmad tried to say something, maybe begging me to do something. My left hand went to the gag in his mouth, stopping before touching it. His eyes darted back and forth between my left hand and my eyes. My thumb sought and found the soft flesh under his chin surrounded by the crescent-shaped boney process anchoring his lower teeth. The medical part of my mind raced to name the bone and tissue my thumb was touching. I erased that thought process. This wasn't medicine; this was justice.

My other hand came out of my pocket, the Beretta comfortable in my hand hanging at my side, the side away from Allen. That same voice I had heard earlier in Bryant Park came out of my mouth. "Ahmad. You know I am studying to be a doctor." This calmed him. His eyes relaxed. "I think you have a serious brain infection." I flipped off the safety as I brought the Beretta up to his chin, replacing my left thumb with the barrel. As the gun came up, his eyes registered a question, and then the fear returned, black and menacing, iridescence reflecting from the dim yellow security bulb over my shoulder. They were the devil's eyes, and I was looking directly into his black soul. Did he know what was coming? Did he read it in my eyes? Before he could blink again, I pressed the Beretta tight against his skin and pulled the trigger.

I pictured the bullet entering the soft spot under his chin, below and at the open end of the U-shaped bone holding his lower teeth, going up through his tongue and into the palate at the roof of his mouth. There, the soft bones shattered and pushed ahead and to the sides by the .25-caliber wadcutter bullet. The force shattered the teeth to the sides of the wound, driving them up and back. His head went back after the first shot, and I had to lean forward to keep tight contact for the second shot, which found the same path, now an almost empty space.

The bullets and bone fragments found little resistance in the soft tissue of the brain where evil had lived seconds before. The force was so great inside his skull that his right ear blew out, dripping blood and blended brain. The dead man I had known as Ahmad went limp but stayed on his feet, still held by the two men at his side.

Chapter 45

※　※　※

"Jesus K. Christ! What the fuck was that?" Allen grabbed the gun, which I yielded without a struggle.

"Ahmad had an illness, probably a brain infection. I gave him a shot." Again, that same voice was speaking, calm, clinical, just like reporting on a case at morning rounds with the chief resident.

Allen handed the Beretta to one of his men and told him to get rid of the body. A door opened behind us, and several other men came out of the darkness and helped drag Ahmad's lifeless body farther into the dark. As they dragged him away, I noted how little blood there was, just a little trickle from the right ear and a dark spot growing at his chin. Why was only one ear bleeding? Allen intruded on my thoughts. "Jonathan, we had it under control. Why did you do that?"

"I had to. That motherfucker and everything he stood for was pure evil. In the bar, you said he'd be taken care of tonight. I wanted to be part of the team." My normal voice had returned.

"Jonathan, you are part of the team, but we never had any plans for you to be involved in anything like this. More of a behind-the-scenes type guy. That was a professional hit. No noise, no blood. Where did that come from?" Even in the dark, I sensed his eyes wide, burning a hole in me. Grabbing my arm, he turned me toward the street, back into the half-light of Forty-Sixth Street.

"When I was a kid, my uncle and father taught me to shoot. When I got older, my uncle used to tell me things, secret agent or gangster-like stuff. Only, he wasn't either. Once I asked about silencers. He told me you don't need a silencer if you hold a pistol to someone's body real tight. It blocked the gases and acted like a silencer and kept the blood spatter down to a minimum. Looks like he was right."

Now, walking east toward Times Square, Allen asked, "What about that bit about being a doctor and the brain infection?"

"Did you hear that? I didn't know if I was talking or just thinking it."

"Yeah, I heard it. What did you mean?"

"Honestly, I don't know. None of that was planned or rehearsed. When I saw him at the end of the alleyway, something took over. Eliminating Ahmad was just something I had to do. I saw his evil as an infectious disease or cancer on humanity. If not stopped, it would spread and consume the entire organism. The voice—man, my voice, that was weird."

"That voice scared me. The whole thing was scary. Promise me you won't do anything like that again. So many things could have gone wrong. Jonathan, you can't be a cowboy. Promise! There's so much to do together, and I need to have confidence in you."

"Cross my heart," I said, hesitating and not finishing the childhood promise.

At the next intersection, we turned south. Allen continued. "There's another aspect of this you have to understand. That hit was personal with Ahmad. I'm not saying I don't understand what drove you, but in this business, you can't make it personal. Making it personal clouds your judgment. In everything we do, clear thinking is one of our best tools. You must control your emotions." We reached Forty-Fourth Street and turned left into the heart of the theater district. There were few people around, with most of Broadway dark on Sunday night.

"Intellectually, I understand, but it's difficult to think emotion doesn't creep in for everyone. Training as a physician instills the same mental discipline. Stay remote. Think analytically. Don't let emotions sneak in. But everyone knows emotions creep in. When I'm in the clinic, I try as hard as I can to save a child or a young mother or father with children all the time. But I also realize I'll have to steel myself mentally to save a rapist or a cop killer. For me, maybe it's a zero-sum game. What I mean is because I give more in some cases, there's less to give to others. As a physician, I'm not supposed to think that way, but I do, and it doesn't bother me. The same is true in what we do here. Let me ask you to be honest with me for a minute."

"Okay."

"Ahmad was going to be eliminated tonight. You said as much, and if you didn't, I sensed it. True?"

"Yes."

Stopping, I turned to look at Allen, wanting to see his eyes when he answered. "Ahmad was a piece of garbage, mentally disturbed. Did you enjoy— no, let me change that word. Did you get any sense of personal satisfaction knowing he was dead?"

Allen understood what I was doing. "Yes, I felt satisfied a difficult mission with a lot of uncertainties had come to an end." My eyes stayed on him. He knew what I wanted. "Yes, there was a degree of satisfaction that we had taken out this particular piece of garbage."

The noise of New York surrounded us as we walked in silence, a cocoon of muted individual thoughts isolating us from the city noises. I broke the silence. "Is this going to cause problems with Anderson?" While I hadn't seen Anderson since the meeting in the Pentagon, he was a presence whenever Allen and I met. I wondered what had happened to him. Had he moved on after recruiting me? Was he aware of what was happening?

"That's a strange question. Why would it occur to you?"

"Don't know. As I thought about our meeting tonight with Ahmad, Anderson crept into my thoughts. Oh, I've thought of him before, but as I prepared for tonight, holstering the Beretta, I knew I might use it. At that point, the only consequence I considered was what impact it would have on you or him."

Allen's steely eyes softened as I spoke. "Let's get a drink. We could both do with one, and a bit of a talk."

He led me east on Forty-Fifth to Frankie and Johnnie's, an upscale steak-house and bar catering to the theater crowd for over fifty years. A hostess led us to a booth in the bar. Sunday night was quiet, mostly locals with a few matinee goers still lingering over a late dinner. Allen ordered an Amstel for me and a Bushmills on the rocks for himself. There was no talk until the drinks arrived.

He stared at me over his Bushmills with the eyes of a predator—not animal but human, like a pool hustler taking aim on a gimme eight ball. He moved the glass to his mouth, savoring the essence of the Irish before taking a sip, rolling the amber liquid across his lips before taking it into his mouth. "Mr. Anderson has taken a special interest in you."

Now it was my turn to be surprised, and I showed it.

"When I report what happened tonight, he'll be upset with me."

"Sorry."

"Before you apologize, let me finish. He'll be disappointed I didn't see it coming. Ahmad and I probably realized you were going to shoot him at the same time. Once Anderson grasps that, he'll smile. This is one time I wish I reported in person. He never smiles, but he'll smile because your action tonight will confirm his belief in you. If you could take me by surprise, he'll know you're everything he thought you could be."

My surprise level increased a notch.

"I report to him each week on your progress and activities and my plans for you. He's had a special interest in you from the beginning." The Bushmills still at his mouth, he talked over the top of the glass. I don't know whether it was a way to avoid anyone reading his lips or if he enjoyed smelling the whiskey. Maybe both.

"Why?"

"I don't know. It started the first time I put your file in front of him. He studied it for a long time. He didn't ask any questions, just absorbed every word. I looked at it afterward to see if I could see what he saw, but nothing jumped out. He has an uncanny sense about people. It's almost supernatural. Very spooky."

"Did he recruit you?"

"Yes. I thought I was special, and in his eyes, I guess I was. I studied your file with that in mind, looking for similarities between us."

"And?"

"Nothing I could see. So I still don't know how his mind works. He can pick out people like us, who have high moral standards but are able to kill without hesitation."

I thought back to our only meeting and brought the memory of Anderson up. Unassuming was an understatement. If I met him on the street, I'd look around for the handful of young Mormon missionaries he was managing. "What about him? Can he kill without hesitation?" I didn't know if this question was off limits, but I had to ask it.

Allen stayed silent for a full minute. Then he spoke in a low, measured tone. "I'm going to tell you what I know about Anderson. I've been authorized to use my discretion on this, and now is the time." Settling in, I leaned closer to him. "Anderson is not his real name. Seldom do we know the names of those above us, just those we manage." He neither offered me his real name nor allowed time for me to ask. "Anderson entered the seminary at about age seventeen, studying to be a priest."

"No shit!" That knocked me for a loop. I grabbed the Amstel and took a long pull, wishing now that I had something stronger.

"Yes shit! Specifically, he studied to be a Jesuit. As a teenager, he attended a Jesuit high school and fell under their spell. The founder of the order, St. Ignatius of Loyola, a former soldier, made a huge impression on him. He studied St. Ignatius and the order. In particular, he fixated on a part of the initial charter that said priests become "soldiers of Christ"—emphasis on the soldier part.

"After entering the seminary, as he progressed through his studies, he argued with his teachers. He overinterpreted the role St. Ignatius's military background had on the society. He misunderstood the military-like discipline and the 'chain of command' as an indication of militancy. Rather, it was just an attempt to establish order and structure at a time when there was virtually none. He also argued about the role the Jesuit missionaries had in South America and in dealing with the Indians in colonial America. Because the Jesuits were persecuted by the natives in these places, he felt the history of the order purposely downplayed any violence the missionaries may have wrought upon the Indians. They were well educated, a requirement of the Jesuits, and he argued that intelligent men would not constantly turn the other cheek when a kick in the balls might be more effective in getting a heathen's attention."

He paused to play with the ice in his Bushmills, took another sip, and continued. "He didn't graduate from seminary school and never became a priest.

The vows the Jesuits take, poverty, chastity, and obedience, are taken for life, and Anderson took those vows seriously. You can see from his clothes he doesn't spend a lot on himself."

"Except for the shoes and the manicure," I said.

"The shoes were a gift from his mother, and the manicure is something he does himself. He takes pride in his appearance but is not prideful. He has never married, doesn't have a girlfriend, and gives generously to the church and missionary organizations, especially those helping children. When he left the seminary, he enlisted in the marines wanting to be the meanest, best-trained soldier with a mission. But once again, he argued with the marines, just as he had with the Jesuits. He felt the mission was to find the enemy and eliminate the threat. Anderson was in Vietnam in the early years and thought the chain of command was getting in the way. He wanted the brass to give him an objective and then leave him alone. He believed he had a better moral compass than anything anyone else could impose."

There was nothing I could say. I would never have been able to imagine any of this for Anderson. The only thing I would have gotten right was that Anderson wasn't his real name.

"The Company became aware of him when he was in Vietnam. He was effective and took orders well if he agreed with them. They brought him in and gave him his head. They gave him an objective and left him alone. Anderson had incredible success. Over time, they gave him progressively harder and more complicated assignments, and he continued to succeed. They gave him assignments in the gray area. His religious and military backgrounds were never in conflict; in fact, they seemed to work in some strange harmony, always able to identify both the black and the white, eliminating the gray. In his mind, he was able to justify every action he took. Every action was in the name of the good to eliminate the evil."

"Why is he at a desk now? Why isn't he still in the field?"

Allen shook his head. "Just because you saw him sitting behind a desk, that doesn't mean he's assigned to a desk. He still works the field very effectively." He drained his glass and called for the bill, doing a little thing with his hands in the air, his right finger sliding down his upraised left palm. I looked curiously at him. "It's the French way of calling for the bill without shouting. Dragging my finger across my hand is saying, 'add up the bill; I'm ready.' In French, it's called *l'addition*."

"Fuck me! Learn something every day."

"That would be *blaise-moi* in French," he said as the waiter handed him the check. The waiter didn't bat an eye. He either didn't hear, didn't care, or didn't understand.

As we waited for the receipt, I had to wonder about the story Allen had just told me. I knew nothing about his background, as I would expect. The isolation of agents from one another and the need-to-know crap mandated separateness. Yet he had told me about Anderson. Maybe it was just a story with no basis. Create a legend of a boss from a unique background, give him uncanny skills, and tell me I am his handpicked follower. Very effective whether true or not.

We left the restaurant and resumed walking toward the lights and noise of Times Square. I continued where we had left off before our discussion inside. "So, we both took personal satisfaction from this. The difference being the degree. With you, it was a little, for me, a lot. I won't even ask the question. I'll say it as a declarative. If he had threatened someone you loved, you would have taken more than a little satisfaction." Allen didn't react. "So, Michael, we are the same." I felt I had earned the familiarity of using his given name. Anderson had selected both of us, had assigned Allen as my mentor, and we both felt a degree of satisfaction that Ahmad was gone. "I promise, with your help, to be more impersonal in those situations that are not personal. How's that?"

He was looking at me now, agreeing by not disagreeing. "Not more impersonal, Jonathan. Impersonal. One other thing. About your bedside manner. If I ever get sick, do me a favor and get a second opinion before you try to cure me. Don't treat me yourself."

Chapter 46

A t Broadway, we stopped. Allen turned to me. The bright lights bounced
on his sweaty face, which was glistening with moisture in the humid night
and reflecting the colors behind me. A droplet of sweat rolled down his nose,
catching the colors as it fell, stopping at the tip. I was fascinated by this drop,
watching the colors change like a tiny kaleidoscope, waiting for it to drop, not
really listening to what he was saying, focused on the drop until it fell.

"Jonathan, are you okay?"

What could I say? Should I tell him I wasn't paying attention but rather
watching a colored ball of sweat rolling down his nose? "Yeah, I'm fine. You're
sweating."

Frustrated, perhaps with me, perhaps with the events, perhaps both, he
said, "It's hot." The lights of Broadway behind him now caught my attention.
The movie marquees, the storefronts, the neon signs; everything was so alive on
the street. A stark contrast to the dark and death we had left a few blocks away.
"Jonathan, you need to talk to someone about this. You've just undergone a
traumatic experience. I've been through it. It's your first kill. You're running on
adrenaline now, but it'll wear off and you'll come down. That may be difficult."

Focusing on Allen, ignoring the lights, the people, the traffic, the noise,
and the heat, I said, "It may be difficult to understand, but after a year in the
clinic, I'm fine. I've experienced death. I've watched and felt the life of someone

leave their body as I worked on them. I've been through the feeling of guilt that comes with that experience. Could I have done more? Could I have saved that person? I've had the counseling afterward. I know now, as I did those other times in the clinic, I did the right thing. The disease killed Ahmad, not me."

Allen moved in closer, his voice lower, softer. "Jonathan, you put a bullet in his head."

"Michael, I put two bullets in his head. I know what I did. I did what you were going to do. I saved him from being killed by you. Maybe I even saved him several minutes of fear, knowing he was going to die." I reached out and grabbed his forearm, looking into his eyes. "I brought the gun to the meeting knowing I might use it. No, hoping for the chance to use it on him. That piece of garbage threatened to harm those I love. I should have worked out a plan with you, but I was afraid you might say no. It's over, and I'm okay." And I was okay, at peace with myself. Any doubts gone. I could heal. I could save. I could kill—a first kill. I was outside of myself, looking inward. I didn't see a black heart. I saw a rational brain. Allen looked at my hand on his arm. He put his hand on top of mine. "If you need help, I'm only a telephone call away. Anytime, day or night. We'll talk tomorrow unless I hear from you sooner." With that, I watched him until the crowd on Broadway swallowed him.

I stayed a minute, watching the street, the lights, the people, and then I turned and headed south, walking past open shops, cold air rushing out, inviting the sweating crowd in to cool off and spend their money. The adrenaline had worked itself out of my system, and the psychological repair mechanism was replacing it. No matter how much good I believed I had done, some place deep within disagreed and was telling my body its version. I fought the bile rising in my throat. I breathed deeply, swallowing large gulps of air, chasing the acrid taste back down. At Forty-Second Street, I turned east, staying on the north side of the street.

The gang of thugs was in complete control of Bryant Park now. The street might as well have been a fence. To walk on the south side invited danger. The north side offered safety. As I walked, I looked to my right and watched as well as heard them. They were evil.

The New York newspapers documented the violence that occurred on a regular basis in Bryant Park. They described the thugs who took over the park as sociopaths and psychopaths. The police gave them the park at night. To chase them away would mean chasing them to some place where they would terrorize innocents rather than themselves.

Seeing and thinking about them made me think of myself and my actions tonight. Was I a sociopath or a psychopath? I reviewed the clinical signs and symptoms from the DSM II diagnostic criteria in my mind. I was not a loner, had had a good childhood, and had a responsible job—or would have once I finished school. No, I was neither. I had merely done what I had told Allen: protecting those I loved and doing something he intended to do anyway. Allen thought I was defending my girlfriend. To him, that may have seemed trite— killing someone because he might have been threatening a girlfriend. But it was different. The phone call with Monika had changed all that. After she shared the news, her relief at my response flooded over both of us. We laughed, we cried. We talked about the future as only two people in love can. We made plans for the future, for us and for the baby she had just learned we were going to have.

I had done it to protect my family!

ABOUT THE AUTHOR

William J. Kennedy is a retired pharmaceutical executive living in Rehoboth Beach, Delaware. *First Kill* is his first novel. Readers can contact Bill via email – consultkennedy@aol.com.

www.ingramcontent.com/pod-product-compliance
Lightning Source LLC
Chambersburg PA
CBHW070902180626
46817CB00003B/884